League of Her Own

Greenliner Series
Book 2

FAITH O'SHEA

Cover Design by Jaycee DeLorenzo at Sweet 'N Spicy Designs
Formatted by Woven Red Author Services, www.wovenRed.ca

League of Her Own/Sue Campbell writing as Faith O'Shea- 1st edition

Copyright eBook: 978-1-7335712-5-8
Copyright Print: 978-1-7335712-4-1

Acknowledgments

I'd like to thank my editor, Amy from Blue Otter Editing, for her expertise. She has become a valued partner in my writing life and I don't know what I'd do without her.

Jaycee DeLorenzo form Sweet 'N Spicy Designs has done it again. I want to thank her for her patience working with me on my covers.

I'd also like to thank Joan Frantschuk, from Woven Red, who not only formats my work for eBook and print but who has become a valued resource.

And of course, I'd like to say thanks to my family. Jeff, Kait, Juan, Justin, Kathryn, Jaiden, Jakob, Jon-Christopher, Dominic and Liam. They surround me with the kind of love necessary for creating novels that touch the heart.

And to all who read my books, I thank you for taking time out of your life, to journey with me.

CHAPTER ONE

Fiona Barrows sloshed along, trying to keep herself from falling flat on her face. She wasn't wearing the right shoes or the right coat, but she'd left Hoover too long without a break and she hadn't dared waste any time getting her out, not even to change. Her shoes were probably already ruined anyway. She'd never intended to leave the dog so long, but she'd underestimated the stop-and-go traffic in and out of the city and the interview had lasted much longer than she'd anticipated. In her defense, the sun had been peeking through the clouds when she left early this morning, unusual for January, and as she sat answering those hypothetical questions potential employers always seemed to ask about situations she'd never faced before, she'd given no thought to what was going on outside the ivy-covered walls. When she stepped outside the building, she'd gasped as the pelting rain assaulted her face. The meteorologists had gotten it wrong again. She was still bone-cold when she got back to the house but the Weimaraner was dancing around in desperate need of a walk. She'd hoped the dog would be content with a short one down the curling driveway, only to be disappointed.

The weather hadn't improved and now, even her brain was soggy.

She shivered, as the raw wind just beneath the surface of the sleet reared its head, wanting the comfort of warm and dry. She snapped at the leash, commanding a change of direction for home. Whether Hoover sensed her distress or had gotten her fill of wet and cold, she did as instructed, but not two-feet later, found just the right spot to squat and got down to business. Fiona had forgotten all about Izabella's warning that she take a poop bag and paper towels whenever they went out, and now she was stuck. After looking around guiltily, knowing she was going to leave the steaming pile right where it was, she slunk down the street, rounded the corner and headed up the long driveway just as a Maserati came whizzing by, splashing her in the process. She sucked in her breath as the cold spray covered in in grime, her face now dripping remnants of the puddle that had to be six inches deep.

She looked up and yelled, "Asshole," but it fell on deaf ears, the driver no longer in sight.

She swiped at her eyes, drew a hand down over her cheeks, inwardly seething.

She swore under her breath when she saw the offending vehicle sitting in front of the garage.

Who the hell had come calling? A friend of Reid's? Izabella's? Whoever it was, he obviously didn't know they were not in residence.

Halfway up the winding drive, she noticed the man get out of his car, and race to the side door, phone to his ear. There was a moment when she felt triumphant. He'd be standing outside until she got there and would have to be almost as wet as she was. But when the door opened and he slipped in, a shiver of fear raced through her.

Who was he and what did he want?

She approached the door with caution and tried the knob. It swung open easily and she stepped inside. And didn't move.

"Hello. Who's here?"

Her voice cracked, and her nerves quivered as she strained to keep Hoover from advancing.

Seconds later, a man came from the kitchen, a towel in his hand that he was rubbing against his scalp.

Hoover had started to dance which told her the dog knew the man. When she snapped off the leash, the dog went barreling over and was caught in an affectionate hug. Large manicured hands stroked the animal, and he allowed for some kisses.

When he looked up at her, her heart slammed against her chest. The man was gorgeous. Scruffy dark hair, black eyes, and a straight nose, and those lips…held a mocking smile.

"And who are you? One of Hoover's friends? Do you know you are dripping all over the floor?"

He had an accent which only made him even more stunning.

She was fumbling, her brain singed from heat, her tongue tied in knots.

He chuckled at her ineptitude.

"Have you forgotten your name?"

"Yes. No. Izabella and Reid hired me to house-sit and walk Hoover while they're away. My name is Fiona."

"Ah, the dog walker. I think I'll call you Fifi. It suits you. How did you get so wet?"

Irritation at his arrogance spiked.

"Some asshole went flying around the corner and—"

"Ah. That would be me, is that correct?"

She gave him a steely glare. When he chuckled, her eyes narrowed and her irritation with him went up a notch.

"Izabella didn't mention anything about a houseguest."

"That's because she didn't know I was coming. I told her I was going to stick around in New York for a couple more weeks, say my goodbyes, wait until she got back so she could help me find a rental. But when the coach called summoning me here for some practice, I hopped into the car as soon as I'd packed my most essential items and drove southeast. Being early will give me a chance to get to know the city."

He was standing now in all his hunky gorgeousness. She tilted her head to take another look, one minus the lust that had taken possession of her body. There was something familiar about him and it hit her.

"Are you her brother?"

"I am. Enrique Paolo Goulart dos Santos. As of a week ago, a Greenliner. Now that we've been formally introduced, why don't you get out of those wet things. I assume you have dry ones if you're staying here. Then you can start dinner. I'm famished."

Her jaw dropped. Was he kidding? He might look good, but the term *asshole* came to mind again.

"I wasn't hired to be your maid, cook or bottle washer. I'll let Izabella know you're here and then go home. The house doesn't need two sitters."

"*Foi mal.* Sorry. My bad. I just figured you'd be eating yourself and you could cook for two."

"I don't cook. Never learned, never will."

That wasn't exactly true but let him think it was her own decision not to excel at that art rather than tell him how abysmal she was in that part of the house.

"How will you find a husband?"

Who was this guy? Had he time traveled forward from the nineteenth century?

"Not looking for one of those. Don't need one, don't want one."

That wasn't exactly true, but she was putting it off into the unseeable future. She had too many other things to settle first.

He'd crossed his arms over his chest and looked down at her smugly.

"If this is your life, you might rethink that. A man could support you and then you won't have to walk dogs for a living."

She all but stuttered out, "That's what I mean. Without one, I can do what the hell I please."

And with that she waddled across the mudroom with as much dignity as she could muster, stopping only to take off the shoes that were squishing, before heading up the stairs. Her bedroom was the last one down the hall and she went directly into the attached bathroom. And stopped dead in her tracks.

She was a mess. Her curly hair was a mop on her head, her eye make-up was now a liquid trail down her cheek, and her clothes were wrinkled and damp. She didn't own many suits and she wasn't sure this one could be salvaged, the wool now smelling like wet dog.

The day had turned out less than promising, and now she had to contend with the man downstairs.

After stripping down, dropping everything in a heap on the floor, she turned on the shower and stepped in. The hot water felt good, her body still bone-chilled from the walk and the drenching.

She lathered her hair and rinsed it, scrubbed herself clean of grime and grit, and felt almost human once she was dressed in her jeans and sweater. It was her hair that would take time to put in some semblance of order. She yanked and pulled, working at the knots but the tight curls refused to behave. She sighed, put the brush down, and gave up the fight. She'd never be one of those beautiful people who caused heads to turn. She'd been given brains instead of looks and had been satisfied with that most of her life. Today she almost wished she'd been in a different line.

She reached for her coat. It was soaked through and she quickly lifted it from the bed where she'd thrown it, rifling through the pocket for her phone. Once it was in her hand, she looked around for a place to hang the sopping wet garment so it would dry and ended up hanging it from the closet door frame.

Then she plopped down on the bed, holding her cell.

She'd wanted this job, happy to be making some spending cash while she went through the interview process. Every job she'd applied for had been a long shot. There weren't too many out there that sought her qualifications and there were dozens of applicants for every one of them.

Today's didn't go as well as she'd hoped. Even with all her credentials, she didn't have the experience the people in charge were looking for and it undermined her chances of being hired.

Maybe the next one… she shook that thought off, not wanting her stomach to tangle itself up again. She hit the contact button. It took three rings before someone picked up.

"Hello, Fiona. How are you doing? Settled yet?"

Izabella's voice sounded relaxed and happy.

"I have but I'm not sure you'll want me to stay now that your brother is here."

The voice shifted in tone and mood.

"Rique is there?"

"Yes. He was here when I got back from walking Hoover."

"This is not good. He told me he was waiting to move until I got back, when he called about the trade. He is…" She paused as if not wanting to throw him under the bus, but she managed that anyway when she said, "You must stay. He is a slob and my house will never be the same if someone doesn't rein him in. I will double the hourly charge if you agree."

Fiona wasn't sure she could rein him in. Wasn't sure she even wanted to try. It wasn't her usual challenge.

"I don't know, Izabella. He's kind of taken over."

"Of course he has. My brother has been pampered and spoiled since the day he was born. I love him to death but…he acts as if everything should be handed to him on a silver platter."

Fiona nodded in agreement and said, "He wanted me to make him supper."

"Oh, *meu Deus.* I will call him, tell him he's on his own. I will also remind him that he is a guest and you are the host. Please, Fiona. I must count on you being so far away."

Izabella, her husband, Reid, the pitching ace for the Boston Greenliners, and their two children Melina and Alexander, were taking two-weeks of vacation in Turks and Caicos before the start of spring training. Reid would be in Florida until the season officially started and they'd wanted time as a family before he left.

Because she liked them so much, she was willing to give it a try.

"I'll stay for a few days, see how it goes. But I can't promise he won't drive me out before you get back."

He was not only nauseatingly arrogant, but he was so hot she was afraid of getting scorched.

"Thank you. I appreciate it. Let me call him now and talk to him, let him know why you're there and what you won't be expected to do. Check back with me tomorrow, will you?"

"I will. I'm sorry. I have a feeling you're not going to enjoy your stay with this up in the air."

"He is the reason for that, not you. He does what he pleases no matter who it inconveniences. I should be the one sorry. You're the one saddled with him."

Saddled meant horse, meant ride, which lead her mind and body to sex.

She almost laughed out loud. Like he'd ever find her attractive enough to bed. He'd have his pick of all the beauties who clamored for his affection and she had a feeling they numbered into the hundreds.

"I will take care of things here."

"And I will take care of him."

"Talk to you tomorrow."

And with that the conversation ended.

She looked around, not knowing where to put herself. She didn't have the run of the place anymore, not as long as he was downstairs. She paced the room, unable to light.

CHAPTER TWO

Enrique answered his cell on the fourth ring, just before the call went to voice mail, engrossed in the video he was watching.

"*Boa tarde, meu doce irmã.*"

"Don't sweet sister me. What are you doing there?"

He paused the video of himself mid-stride and sat back in the corner of the cushioned couch. There was a smile in his voice when he said, "Izabella, is that any way to speak to your brother?"

"What made you think you could just move into my house, without even asking?"

"What could I do? I got a call asking if I wanted to come out and begin training. I didn't really think it was a courtesy call but an official summons. As you must know, I've been somewhat lax all last season."

"Too many parties?"

"Too many mornings that found me hung over."

It had only gotten worse since his last game as a Mets.

He'd stuck around to watch the Greenies in their quest for a World Series ring, had a ring side seat, along with the rest of his family, to watch them lose four games to three before going home to Brazil for a couple of months. He'd enjoyed every minute of it. The women knew their place there and knew how to make a man smile. He was going back for a week before spring training to scout out the territory for something permanent. Since the trade that sent him to Boston, he'd begun to think it was time for him to settle down.

"Reid says he went out on a limb for you and he's going to kick your butt if you don't give it your all."

"That was one of the downsides about the trade, but the Greenies have a real chance to go all the way this year and I want to contribute to that."

After the disappointing loss, management had gone out and filled in some of the missing pieces and he was one of them. There wasn't a better shortstop out there, if he did say so himself.

"You have to take this seriously if that's your intention."

"I am here to train. Doesn't that tell you something?"

"It tells me that's where the wind is blowing right now. Who knows where it will shift to tomorrow?"

"You hurt my feelings."

"Good. Maybe you'll behave."

"Where did you find Fifi?"

"Fifi? You mean Fiona? You're not calling her Fifi, are you?"

There was panic tucked neatly in the question. He evaded it with the truth.

"The name suits."

"Rique, please don't."

He could hear agitation in her voice, but he wasn't going to abide by her wishes so he skipped the part where he was supposed to promise he wouldn't.

"Where did you find her?"

"She's Jim's niece. I've known her for a couple of years and when he told me she could use the job, I asked. She accepted. She's responsible, mature, and loves animals. I didn't want to board Hoover, and she said she'd be happy to stay at the house to dog watch."

Jim was Reid's mother Melinda's, husband. They'd gotten married last year after reconnecting while Leeni had been re-admitted to the hospital with a cancer diagnosis. Those had been some dark days, but the little girl had gone into remission and was doing well. He smiled when he thought of his niece. She was a crackerjack, just like her father.

Now, Fifi?

"She looks like a poodle."

Her hair had the same kind of tight, springy curls.

"Rique."

He laughed at his sister's indignation. "I'll behave. I promise."

"She's not there to do your bidding. You handle your own meals and laundry and stay out of her way."

"But if she offers?"

"She won't. She doesn't suffer fools kindly and will tell you right where you can shove it. One of the reasons I like her."

"You've become too American. How does Reid stand it?"

"I don't know. You'll have to ask him yourself someday. I have to go. But I will fly home if you get out of hand, and then you'll have to live with the guilt of cutting my vacation short."

"*Querida*, you know I wouldn't want to do that. You're one of my favorite sisters."

"I bet you have three."

"Felicia and Leia would be treating me much nicer than you are."

"You're not living in their house." There was a pause before she asked, "I don't suppose you'd call Jaco, see if you can stay with him?"

"No. I like it here."

Not only because his agent/lawyer was in town, and he had an appointment with Keith on Friday, which was just a couple of days away, but because he thought it might be fun getting under Fifi's skin.

Rique went back to the video as soon as Izabella ended the call. The game was one of his last as a Mets, when he'd gone for a steal at second and was thrown out by a mile. He still didn't understand what had given his intention away. He'd stolen dozens of bases a year, at least he had his first couple of years with the franchise. Last year had been a disappointment, he'd been a disappointment, but the trade had surprised him. Management didn't trade their best prospects and he'd been considered a coup. He'd partied, sure, but what young, single ballplayer didn't? Now that he was on his brother-in-law's team, he wouldn't be able to get away with much. Reid was nothing if not intense. At least on the pitcher's mound. He was one of the reasons the Greenies had made it as far as they had last year, and he wouldn't tolerate marginal effort.

He stood, flicked off the set. He was hungry but according to Izabella, he was on his own. He picked up his phone and Googled Yelp to see what food places delivered. It was too nasty to go back out and pick something up. He'd checked the refrigerator earlier and it was empty. He would have thought Izabella would have left something for her live-in guest or Fifi would have stocked up for her stay here. She mustn't have been kidding when she said she didn't cook.

He sighed heavily, his thumb scrolling his options, not quite believing it had come to this.

All the women in his family were brilliant in the kitchen. His mother Livia had made sure her daughters learned all the culinary skills needed to provide sustenance for the soul. He'd tasted heaven every time he sat down at her table. He wished she were here, but the family had returned to Brazil after spending the holidays with Reid and Izabella. They wouldn't move back to their house in the Hamptons until the baseball season started and then they'd stay until the fall. His father had been a soccer freak, but he took Rique's decision to play a different sport with as much grace as he could muster. He'd known nothing about the game back then, but he'd become one of the most knowledgeable, crunching stats as well as he crunched numbers in finance. He'd attended most of his home games and sat him down at the end of last year, pointing out all his weaknesses, and there were more than he'd realized.

Rique needed this fresh start. By donning a Greenie uniform, he could get back to the basics, re-tool his trade so he was in the winning column again. He needed to settle down, on and off the field. By twenty-five, his father had been living with Julianna a couple of years, had Jaco and Izabella, and even though the relationship had ended in disaster, he'd taken his responsibilities seriously. Julianna's revenge for his leaving was to take her kids and disappear. Paolo was only able to re-connect with his siblings at her passing. Today they were one big happy family. His father and mother had never allowed them to qualify their status. *There are no halves and have nots.*

And if he wanted to be honest, he got along with Izabella better than he did Felicia and Leia. She understood the mechanics of his game, worked at a trade that she excelled in, and could talk to him about anything. He respected what she'd been through, and how she handled it all with grace and grit. When she'd married Reid four years ago, the family still wasn't sure he'd been tamed, but she'd done that, too, with merely her smile and her heart.

He scrolled down the list of suggestions on Yelp and, finally finding what he was looking for, called and ordered. Told it would take thirty minutes to be delivered, he licked his lips in anticipation. He wasn't really in the mood for a fast food take on steak tips, but it was meat and it would have to suffice. He'd have to figure out a better plan for tomorrow night and every night thereafter. With no one around to provide his meals, he would have to improvise. Maybe he'd head back to Brazil earlier than he'd planned.

His sister's words came back to him.

It tells me that's where the wind is blowing right now. Who knows where it will shift to tomorrow?

Was he that predictable? If things weren't working to his advantage, he walked away?

He'd come to Boston to train, not eat, and he had to re-focus his efforts in that direction.

Feeling itchy and bored, he sank down on the couch, dropped his head back and closed his eyes.

He was meeting the infield coach at ten a.m. tomorrow. Leo had told him he was setting up a regimen for strength training, that he could begin immediately, and as soon as a couple of other players showed up there'd be fielding practices. There'd be drills, those endlessly repeated exercises that were supposed to perfect skill levels. There'd be batting practice and sprints. He groaned thinking about it, but Leo had said something about needing to refine his muscle memory. "You've forgotten how to react automatically to routine ground balls. You take too much time getting a grip, and you double clutched more than a couple of times."

In other words, he'd gotten sloppy.

When he'd first come on the baseball scene, he'd been considered one of the premier prospects. He had a ton of range, a strong arm, double-play depth, a quick pivot and release. He was cocky at the plate because he hit with power, and once on the base pads, he could outrun any throw. Consensus was, a team had to be strong up the middle with a good catcher, second baseman, shortstop, and center fielder, but the position that took them into pennant territory was his. Last year the team had come in a dismal fourth.

When he'd been called into the front office, told about the trade, he'd been stunned. The owner had given him a lot of nonsense about his lack of discipline, something that he said couldn't be taught. They'd seen no improvement after the several sit-down's they'd had with him over the season, and they wanted someone with a zest for winning. They were convinced he didn't have it.

When he'd asked where they were sending him, he should have felt shame, but instead he'd been psyched with their answer.

He'd be part of a great team, near family, with better support.

At least he hoped he'd have it. Over the holidays, he'd been scolded at dinner, and not only by his father. Reid had asked what had happened to him last season. When he had no answer, his brother-in-law pointed out that he played harder than he worked. Izabella had agreed and gone one further. He'd become lazy.

He'd gotten pissed and gone back to New York, leaving their opinions behind as well.

While there, each night spent out with a different woman, he began to see a pattern and unwillingly concluded that they might be right.

It's when he'd set his mind to a permanent solution: marriage. No more squandering his time on partying, no more wasting his energy on meaningless activities. He was here to win.

Which meant Brazil would have to wait.

When the doorbell rang, he walked briskly over to the door, exchanged money for the meal, and brought it into the kitchen. The sun was already low in the sky, and darkness was enveloping the room. Thinking it might be better not to see what he was eating, he left the lights off and dug in.

It wasn't half bad. More importantly, it was satisfying his hunger.

Just as he took the last bite, the lights came on.

He squinted up at Fifi, who was standing in the doorway, a look of disbelief on her face.

"You ordered in?"

"Yeah, I was hungry, and you refused to cook."

"And you didn't think to ask if I wanted something?"

He wiped his mouth and gave her a tolerant glance.

"My sister made it perfectly clear I'm on my own which means you are as well."

"Gawd, how can you be so…so…insufferable?"

He studied her stance. Her arms were akimbo, a ruby ring clearly visible on her finger. Her nails were clipped and bare of polish. His gaze was drawn to her eyes. They were a soft gray-blue that pulled you in. She had an oval face, a high forehead, and her hair was in disarray but framed it perfectly. Her nose might be a bit too small to be called classic, but her lips had a pink tinge that was alluring. She couldn't be more than five foot three… about a hundred and five, ten pounds, but she carried it well. There was a strange tingle that slid up his spine. He didn't understand it and it made him more than uncomfortable.

He scrambled away from the island and made a beeline back to the family room, calling out, "Throw that mess away for me, will you?"

He missed the wide eyes and fisted hands and her reluctant move to do his bidding.

Fiona snapped the drawer closed as soon as she'd dumped the plate, still fuming. He was beyond self-absorbed, and those kinds of people always made her irritable. She often wondered if it was a trait handed down, or something hidden in the person's cellular memory that could be edited out.

There were a lot of characteristics that she thought worth editing–stupidity, ignorance, selfish disregard of others, making a more perfect world. There were lines that shouldn't be crossed in genetic manipulation, and maybe that was one of them. Better to make changes through the biomedical research of human disease, on things like cancer, ALS, and arthritis. That kind of breakthrough would help kids like Leeni, who was a more worthwhile cause than the asshole in the other room.

Her stomach growled as she groused. After checking the refrigerator, confirming that she'd neglected to pick up something to heat up for dinner, again, she sighed before she closed it.

She'd have to go the same route as Enrique and order in. Tomorrow, she promised herself, she'd get to the local specialty market. They sold pre-packaged foods that she could zap in the microwave, calzones, pasta dishes, soups, and shepherd's pie. Her mother had done the same, too busy with more intellectual pursuits. Clare Barrows experimented in a lab rather than with an oven. No one in the family had known any different until they got older, and even then, it didn't make a difference. Fiona's sister, Siobhan, had married a man who loved to cook. She'd just have to follow suit.

As she was ordering, a head peeked in through the doorway. "What are you doing?"

As if not hearing him, she continued with her order: carnitas a la Roca, salteñas du carne, queso a la Huancaina com camarones. She figured she might as well order enough for a couple of days just in case she never made it to Butcher's Block as planned.

When she swiped off, he was standing not two feet away. The arrogance was momentarily gone, his expression hopeful.

"Did you order for me as well?"

Exasperation spilled out in a fiery sigh.

"No. Why should I? You completely forgot about me."

"But carnitas? Salteña? I didn't know there were places like that that delivered."

She didn't really know what they were but the descriptions on the menu sounded appetizing, and it gave her the added pleasure of a little payback.

"So?"

His eyes held an inscrutable glint. "That is more to my liking than what I ate."

"That's your problem, not mine."

He was becoming almost conciliatory. "If I pay, will you share?"

She hesitated, thought about it, and then said, "I got enough to last me a couple of days. If you eat some of it, then I'm back to square one."

"If I say I will provide dinner tomorrow as well?"

"Then what do I pick at during the day?"

He rose to his full height, which wasn't as tall as she'd originally thought. He was still able to look down his nose at her.

"You do not pick at this kind of food. You savor it."

"Whatever. I *pick*, you savor. To each their own."

"*Meu Deus.* Do you have no refinement? What is wrong with your… good sense?"

"Not a thing. I eat to live, not live to eat."

"Food can be one of the most pleasurable sensory delights. Do you not find pleasure in things?"

She did but he wouldn't understand in what. They had a stare-off contest until the doorbell rang.

He went racing to the door, not giving her a chance to argue and made the money-for-food exchange.

His smile was wide as he inhaled the aroma. He settled himself down, unpacked the offering and began to dig in. Then stopped.

He looked back up sheepishly, his hands in the air in surrender.

"*Eu sinto muito*. I'm sorry. You get first choice."

She was getting a plate out of the cabinet and a fork out of the drawer, the scent making her mouth water.

"And here I thought you were forgetting about me again, you know, the one who made this possible."

"I am used to—"

"Having your way?"

His silence told her that was exactly what he was used to. She took a seat opposite him, scooped up a bit out of each container and transferred it to her dish.

"What is this?"

"Empanada. With beef. One thing you should know about Brazilians. We are carnivores at heart."

"This is Peruvian, I believe. Are the cuisines the same?"

"Close enough to be siblings."

He had impeccable manners, never spoke until he'd swallowed, used his napkin, had one hand in his lap, and ate with slow and measured mouthfuls. She was trying hard to keep from wolfing it all down. It was good and she was hungry, but he already thought she was a dog, if his nickname for her was any indication, and she didn't want to eat like one.

In order to slow herself down, she asked, "Why are you here?"

The smile he gifted her with was dazzling.

"I'm a Greenliner now, and if I am to help them win, I must get better. I'm here to train with the coach."

"Are you happy about it?"

His smile slipped. "It stings to be discarded but I'll get over it. Contributing to a Mets routing will be my revenge."

"All I know about baseball is that it's a team sport that's played with bats and balls. What do you do? Catch or hit?"

She'd taken a small forkful of the carnitas and…to her surprise, was savoring it, her eyes closed to more fully appreciate the flavor.

"It is not such a simple game. There is much complexity involved. But if I broke it down to its essence, you could say I do a bit of both. You've never seen a game? Not with your uncle?"

Her eyes opened and she began savoring the sensory delight that was Enrique.

When he asked again, "Your uncle? Jim? You've never watched a game with him?", she gave him a toss of her head. "I've been kind of busy over the last few years."

Not that she would have even if she had the time. It would be a waste of an afternoon.

"It is like Jell-O, no? There's always room."

She made a face at him. "Never liked the texture or the way it wiggled in my mouth."

"I am beginning to think you missed out on a lot of life."

She had. Her education had taken all the minutes in all the days of her life so far.

"Like I said. Been busy."

She didn't want him asking what had consumed her, but she needn't have worried. She was learning he had a one-track mind and the conversation always reverted back to him.

"I will get you a ticket to our first game, yes? Then you can see for yourself what is involved."

She waved her hand in front of her and asked, "Does anything on this face suggest a desire to see you play?"

He sat back with a thud.

"It's America's pastime. There's even a song about it. You must know it." He began to sing a few bars before she cut him off.

"I know the song. Even the lyrics suggest one time is enough."

"Once is just a sampling. The more one knows, the more addictive it becomes."

"Yeah? Like what?"

"There's understanding the context, how weather conditions can affect the outcome, the slang, knowing the players and the history, and a team's strategy."

"What if I don't care?"

"Are you averse to learning new things?"

She almost laughed. Her entire life had been dedicated to her curiosity and a driving need to find the answers she sought.

"Only some things."

He was pointing his fork at her and said matter-of-factly, "I am very good. You would not be bored."

She shot him a cool look. "Such confidence. Tell me again why you were traded. I would think such a good player would be wrapped in gold and treasured."

His eyes dipped to the last morsel on his plate, which he ate before answering.

"They are fools and I will prove it to them."

"And how will you do that? Isn't the skill innate?"

"I have the skill...what I need is more..."

When he trailed off, she supplied, "More humility?"

"Humility doesn't win games."

"What does?"

She studied his face, the contours, the coloring, the intensity of his eyes, and then she glimpsed a shadow there. Was it uncertainty?

"Discipline. Hard work. A driving need to be the best."

"Well, if you think you already have the latter covered, what's the problem?"

He glanced up and stared.

"Ah, the discipline. That one's going to take work."

"I have turned a new leaf. I am settling down, putting my nose to the grindstone…"

"You do know your idioms."

"Is that like idiot?"

"No." She looked up and smiled. "But if the shoe fits, you might as well wear it."

"Shoe?"

"Another idiom that seemed to work well here."

She rose from her stool and collected their plates, rinsed them, and put them in the dishwasher.

He had risen and thrown away the trash.

"Good job. I thought that was beneath you."

"When I marry, the woman will do all these tasks. I will supply the money; she will make me a home."

"Is this how all Brazilians think? Or only the male population?"

She leaned against the counter, her arms crossed over her chest.

"It is how we are raised."

"Glad I opted for the good old USA. We're raised to think differently. You'll have to go to Brazil to capture one of these fragile butterflies."

"That is what I have planned. Before the season begins, I will have found someone I can marry and bring here."

"That simple, is it?"

"I am loved in my hometown. It should be easy enough to find who I am looking for."

"What about love? Can you fall in love with just anyone?"

"I will know it when I see it."

"I think it has more to do with heart than eyes. Unless you're looking for some eye candy."

"I know exactly what I want. Beauty will be part of it. How can it not?"

"Right. How could you possibly settle for anyone less gorgeous than yourself?"

He arched an eye. "You think me gorgeous?"

She had to back track fast. If he thought that she thought that…he'd be even more intolerable than he already was.

"Not personally, but you seem to have the dark and handsome down that women drool over."

"But you are not one of them?"

"Gawd, no. If I get married, the man will have to have a lot more to him than just looks."

"I have more than that."

"Yeah, what?"

"I have talent."

"But no discipline, so what good does that do you?"

He looked up at her from underneath his long black lashes and asked, "What is it you would look for?"

"Intelligence, humility, and a kind heart. Oh, and a sense of humor."

It was one of the things that her father had that made marriage to a scientist enduring.

"I can be humorous."

"I know, I chuckle at you all the time, but you can't laugh at yourself. Cocky doesn't allow for it."

"Why would I laugh at myself?"

"Because it proves you know you're human and have faults."

Like the rest of us.

She moved away from the counter, and as she walked by him, he was watching her intently. It made her queasy. She was certainly not one of the beautiful people, and she could only think his attention was on all her deficiencies.

CHAPTER THREE

Enrique watched her go, feeling discomfited. She made him feel inadequate in some way. Mocked his confidence, made him laughable.

Not that it mattered. She was in the minority. Most women he met fell all over him. He could provide references on his ability to satisfy, and his bank account would provide evidence of his ability to take care of the woman he married.

What else was there to it?

He wandered into the family room, grabbed the remote, and surfed for something to watch. Being alone wasn't natural for him. He liked being in the thick of things, with people and conversation, a hotshot in a room of the ordinary. If he was serious about building discipline, he had to make a start, and tonight was it. He was staying no matter how badly he wanted to go out, have some fun. He scrolled until he found the MLB station. They were recapping the trades that had been happening around the league. He wasn't the only one to be picked up by the Greenies. There was a new catcher on board, a guy named Verducci, who'd bounced around the league over the last few years. He was one of the best, according to some of the well-known pitchers out there, but he couldn't hit the ball to save his life. With a dismal .157 batting average, no one was willing to keep him on. The thing was, he probably saved more runs with how he called the game than others with a higher average. A third baseman had migrated from Cuba a few months ago and had been picked up immediately by the Greenies. Mateo Alvarez would permanently fill the position occupied by utility players last year. It had been the first order of business for the front office, and Reid had told him the guy had unbelievable stats and would add a lot to the infield. There was a new left fielder, a guy who'd been in the Greenliners' farm system since college and had been called up for tryouts. The one who'd played last season had torn up his knee skiing just before the holidays and would be out for the duration.

He sat up and turned up the volume when the announcer said, "The Greenliners have just picked up the contract of Milo Buzzley. Once a standout closer, Buzz has had his share of troubles over the last year. After a stint in rehab, he says he's ready to put all his energies where they need to be. Out on the mound."

They had a picture of the guy on screen. He'd guess his age at thirty tops, not that old for a pitcher. He had molasses-colored hair that was short and spiked, a close-cropped beard, more refined than the ones ballplayers seemed to be growing lately. His eyes looked shadowed, as if he was haunted by something in the distance. A broken future? If it was, it didn't bode well for the team. He'd be striving for discipline as well, the need to stay away from the bottle a dire one.

Rique wondered if Reid had heard.

After pulling his phone out of his back pocket, he texted his brother-in-law.

Did you hear?

Hear what?

We have a new closer. Buzzley.

Are you sure?

I just saw the clip. What do you think?

I won't know until I talk to him.

The Larsens must have signed off on it.

Will Larsen and his wife, Nancy, owned the team and were lifelong residents of Boston. They'd made their money in footwear, their sneakers being the hottest thing on the market today. They'd only added to their fortune with the purchase of the Greenliners a decade ago. They'd just promoted Jordan Krasnick, to president and CEO. He'd been with the Larsens since they'd purchased the team, making himself invaluable on the way up the ladder.

Krasnick, DeLorenzo, and Farina must have as well.

Dan DeLorenzo was the man in charge of Baseball Operations and Jethro Farina was manager.

Are you going to reach out?

When I get back. Where are you?

In your family room.

That's a nice surprise. Are you going to stay there?

For tonight. Tomorrow I'm meeting with Leo.

Good. Maybe he can whip you into shape.

I thought that was your job.

You're going to take both of us.

Are you going to tackle Buzzley as well?

He's not family. I'll leave him to Mulligan.

Lucky him.

Go away. I'm busy.

See you soon.

Rique sat there thinking, his head resting on the back of the couch. The team had taken on as many new players as they had old. Would the new dynamics work to their benefit? A winning team was a well-oiled machine, and every working piece had to do the job intended. If any one thing was out of alignment, it affected the whole. He'd known teams who lacked talent but had such a magical chemistry they won in spite, of it. His prior team had the talent on paper but couldn't put it together well enough to climb out of fourth. He'd played a part in that.

He shook his head. Thinking was not his thing and the silence was driving him mad. Even Hoover had disappeared. Taking his courage in hand, he climbed the stairs and walked down to the end of the hall. And knocked on the closed door.

"What?"

He'd expected snide and he got it.

"I'm bored."

He heard an undisguised snort of derision. "And I'm supposed to entertain you?"

He paused before asking, "Do you play cards?"

"Sometimes."

He was leaning against the door frame, his arms over his chest.

"Do you want to play with me?"

"What are you, six?"

The chortle hurt his pride.

"Add twenty and you're on target."

He heard Hoover whine, as if she wanted her freedom, and then footsteps.

When Fifi opened the door, she had a book in her hand, her finger marking her place. He nodded toward it. "Is that what you do for fun?"

"No, it's what I do when I have downtime."

He'd tilted his head to see what the title was, curious as to the genre, but she'd brought it up to her chest, back side facing out, preventing it. He straightened and his eyes met hers.

"You don't mind being alone?"

"Not in the least."

He was feeling it again. Inadequate.

"Never mind, then. I'll find something else to do."

She brushed her hair off her face, as her eyes pierced through him.

"Why don't you let Hoover out. I'll finish the chapter and come down."

He heard her mumble under her breath, "I thought I was house-sitting, not babysitting," but before he could say anything to refute it, she'd closed the door.

Once Hoover was back inside, snow-covered from brushing herself under one of the shrubs, he went into Reid's man cave and riffled through drawers until he found some playing cards. He took the carousel of chips as well, just in case. If he was any judge of character, Fifi would know the rules for Fish and little else. Well, maybe Old Maid.

He was shuffling a new deck when she came into the dining room, where he'd set up shop. He nodded to the bag on the table.

"Look what I found. Cheese curls."

"And you're going to eat them, getting orange crap all over everything."

He was offended by her lack of finesse. In his defense, he said, "There wasn't any other kind of snack in the kitchen and I thought you might like to *pick* at something."

"I only pick when I'm hungry and after eating all that food at dinner, I'm not."

He was beginning to think prickly was a part of her nature.

"Okay, no cheese curls."

He began to shuffle, showing off a little, fanning the cards. "What's your game?"

As she reached over to the chips, took a stack, and began to parcel them out between them, she said without blinking, "Seven-card stud."

The cards went flying with that pronouncement and he looked at her with wide eyed astonishment. There was no way to impress someone who kept you so off-balance.

She looked at him with what could have been distaste. "What? I thought poker was your game when I saw the chips. Don't you know how to play?"

He nodded although he was more a Hold 'Em kind of guy. Bluffing was more in his skill set than drawing the best cards. He was casting glances at her as he gathered the cards up from the floor and the table, and when he had them all, he sat back down and straightened the deck.

"How about Texas Hold 'Em? It'll be more interesting with just two of us."

"I hate to admit it, but you're probably right. Come on, cut the deck."

He placed it flat on the table, and she paused and then knocked on the top, saying "There's no way you could have fixed the deck after that."

"What's our ante?"

He glanced down to see that she'd chosen the twenty five and fifty dollar chips from the carousel. High stakes for a friendly game. It was a good thing it wasn't real money, although she couldn't compete with him in that category.

"Twenty-five?"

She tossed the chip in the center of the table.

He did the same and then dealt them two hole cards, the only ones that would be hidden from each other.

He watched as she squeezed the down-facing cards up, so suspiciously, that he almost laughed. She didn't trust him not to try and sneak a peek.

"I don't cheat, don't need to."

"Your cocky's coming out. Here's another idiom for you. Pride comes before a fall. I take it I go first seeing that we don't have a button or blinds."

That she knew about them should have told him something, but it had gone completely over his head. He nodded as he lifted his two cards. A seven and a nine, which gave him nothing, but he wasn't folding this early. He matched her bet and called.

Her face was blank, wearing what people called a poker face. He wasn't going to pick up any clues from her.

She was fiddling with her chips like a pro when he dealt the flop. The first three community cards that they would use to build their best five-card hand were an ace, a ten and a three.

Still nothing, but when she bet fifty dollars, he matched her again and called. Was she bluffing?

Another glance at her face, another blank stare. Did she have something to go with the ace?

Maldição. Damn it. She was giving nothing away.

He flipped over the next card. It was a jack. Before he could process that he had a seven, nine, ten, and jack, which could result in a straight if the last card went his way, she bet a hundred. The chips toppled onto the stack. He looked up, and she gave him a sly smile. Was she pulling his chain, or did she have the kind of hand that warranted that high a bet?

He slowly fingered the chips needed to match it, threw them onto the pile, and raised her a hundred. He wanted to see where she was going to go now.

"I'll see that and raise you another hundred."

He arched his eyebrow, took her in. "I call."

"You folding?"

"Not yet."

"Let's see what the river holds for us."

He turned over the last card and placed it down beside the other four. Another ace.

It gave them both a pair of aces, but other than that he had nothing to go with it.

When she bet another hundred, he matched and called. He wanted to see whether she was bluffing or not, and the only way to see her hand was to finish it.

When she laid down her hand, his eyes widened. She had a full house, three aces and two jacks.

He didn't bother showing her the piss poor hand he held. It would only prove his stupidity for staying in.

She leaned out of her chair and pulled the chips to her, all but crowing.

She knew how to play, that was obvious. "I believe the question now is, are you always so lucky?"

This wasn't a game of strategy, not with just wo of them. You either got a winning hand or you didn't.

"In cards? Yes. But you're lucky in love, aren't you? I'm sure you'd prefer that to this."

He was mesmerized by the way she handled the deck, shuffling like she worked the tables in Vegas.

"Are you saying you're not lucky in love?"

"Haven't really given a lot to find out."

He cut the deck when she tabled it and she began to deal.

"You've been busy?"

She looked up at him, her eyes intense in their scrutiny.

"You *were* listening."

After an hour of losing almost every hand, he got up and raided Reid's liquor cabinet. He poured himself a finger of scotch, and downed it in one gulp.

Her voice held an edge. "Are you ignoring me again?" She snapped her fingers and added, "Or have I become invisible?"

He flashed his eyes in her direction and she was tilting her head at him, her hair a fiery flame of curls around her face. She almost looked pretty.

"You're looking at me as if I've lost my mind. You obviously have never watched *Soap*."

He was beginning to think he'd lost his. She was causing more of a stir in his bloodstream than was warranted.

"What? Wash soap?"

She snorted. "Right, like I sit and watch a bar of soap for entertainment. It's a TV show. There was a character who thought he became invisible when he snapped his fingers."

"And you watched this?"

"Yeah, the reruns. With my father and sister. It was pretty funny. Their family was almost as dysfunctional as mine."

"What did he do to become visible?"

She snapped again.

With tongue in cheek, he said, "There you are. I wondered where you'd gone."

She burst out laughing, and after he'd poured and handed her a drink, she downed it in one swallow.

She was certainly not what she seemed.

"Rather than walking dogs, you should do this for a living. You'd make better money if you're luck held out."

Her smile lit up her face. "Nope. I only do it for fun."

When he'd asked what she did for enjoyment, she might have told him this was one of those things. He would have been better prepared for the trouncing.

"Where did you learn? In school?"

"No. School wasn't about having fun. It was another one of the ways my father, sister, and I passed the time waiting for my mother to return home from the lab."

"What does your father do?"

"He's a mathematician for the Department of Defense. My father, Patrick Barrows, crunches numbers by day, but one night a week, he plays cards with a bunch of his friends at one of the few remaining men's clubs in the area. He has such an affinity for it, he could have been a hustler. I learned early that if I was going to hold my own against him, I had to keep my face as neutral as I could and learn how to finesse a bluff. I got better at it as I got older, but I never would have thought to use the skill in college. I didn't have the time for that kind of nonsense."

"Was your sister this good?"

"She's a mathematician, too, so yeah."

"Department of Defense?"

"No. High school math teacher."

"Remind me never to play with any of you. I think I won maybe two hands all night."

"Does this mean you're quitting?"

"I'm all out of chips."

"That's the thing about fake money. I can split my earnings and share, or you can just take more and start again."

"Would another hand improve my chances?"

"Doubt it, but who knows. Anything is possible."

"Now it's your cocky that seems to be surfacing."

"There aren't many areas where I can beat you. I have to admit, it feels good."

He took his seat, began to stack the chips before sliding them into the circular holes.

"I don't like losing."

Now that they weren't playing cards, she ripped open the bag of cheese curls and popped a couple in her mouth.

"Does anyone?"

"Probably not."

"How did you handle it as a team last year?"

His eyes shot up. "I thought you didn't watch baseball."

"I don't but if you live in this town, you know that nightly news means sports. If there was an explosion somewhere in the city and the Greenies, Red Sox, Celtics, blah, blah, blah, the list is endless, are playing, that's the breaking story."

"It's an athlete's dream city."

"If you say so. I, for one, would prefer to hear what's going on in the world that might impact my life."

He'd taken the bag away and was eating his own fistful of the orange curls.

"Baseball is like life."

She snorted. "And how do you figure that?"

"It's where you end up that counts, it's based on statistics but filled with anomalies, and it's better to be on a team than alone. You can accomplish more."

"Life isn't based on statistics."

"Sure it is. You can take any person, see where they come from, how they use their talents, who they hang around with, and statistically estimate where they'll end up. It's the anomalies that can change the trajectory of his or her life."

She didn't respond, just ate another handful of the curls and finished the water she'd brought in with her.

He leaned forward, wanting her to understand his passion. Wanting, for some reason, for her to share in it, too.

"It's a game based on mechanics, science, gravity, velocity, experiencing what the body can do in a number of ways. When I get a ball hit toward me, I might have to stretch to my right, pivot, and throw, making sure the ball is on target with the first baseman's glove. You also have to read the ball correctly. How fast is it moving? Where do I have to be to prevent it from making it into the outfield? Will it bounce away from me, and if it does, which direction will it bounce in and can I get there in time? If I'm on first and want to steal second, what is the exact moment I should begin my run?"

"Will your stats tell me how well you do all of that?"

He slumped back.

"Not my most recent. No."

"You've concluded that you need to get married to change that. It's not something that a little discipline would correct?"

"When men get married, they can take their mind off conquests. They have somewhere to go at the end of a hard day, to a home-cooked meal and a woman in their bed every night."

"You need your hunger to be satisfied. Is that it?"

"I guess, in a way. That is true."

"And hunger for a game well played isn't enough?"

He met here eyes. Her curiosity seemed genuine, so he didn't know why he felt she was mocking him.

"After Reid married my sister, his life improved. So did his game."

"It had nothing to do with Izabella?"

"Yes, everything to do with her."

"Then it wasn't the marriage. It was the woman."

She rose from her chair, rolled the top of the cheese curl bag closed, and turned toward the kitchen to put it away. When she reached the doorway, she glanced back and added, "I'm not sure you can find that in any search. I think it finds you."

Her last words lingered in his mind long after she'd made her exit.

He went to his room as soon as he'd returned the playing cards and chips to their proper place.

After stripping down to his boxers, he lay on the bed, his arms under his head.

Fifi was wrong.

It was marriage that did it. Look at his father. He'd spent years with Izabella's mother but never married. It was only when he found Livia that he pledged himself. It was the sanctity of the vows that made them one, and the family that followed.

He had a family with Julianna. It wasn't enough to hold him.

He always thought one woman was the same as the next. It was true that they needed to meet a

certain criteria in looks, manners, upbringing, and domestic skills but what else did he need?

He had friends, he had money, he had fame.

CHAPTER FOUR

Fiona was back in the bedroom chair reading, as if she'd never been interrupted, hadn't spent several hours playing cards with an oversized juvenile, or been disillusioned by his attitude toward women. He made it sound as if one woman was the same as the next. Could he be that clueless or that shallow? Or even worse, could he really mean it? Or maybe the women he chose to date were interchangeable, so much the same that he couldn't tell the difference.

She tried to imagine what his regular date would look like.

Long dark hair that was straight naturally, dark eyes, an alluring figure, a gentile voice, and good manners. She'd probably have to like baseball, at least enough to go to his games without feeling tortured. Could she dance? Yes, that would be important. Rique was a sleek animal and she had a feeling he excelled at it. She remembered seeing snatches of the wedding video from the Izabella and Reid's wedding. He was moving sensually across the floor with a woman who fit her imagined version perfectly. He'd looked roguish in his tux, and she'd spent more than an extra minute admiring his form.

Fine, the woman would be stunning, but would she have an original thought in her head or would all she need to win him over, be an adoring smile and lush body?

She snapped the book closed.

Men were strange creatures. It's why she stayed away from them. Not that she'd been on a lot of dates or held some secret aversion to the male sex. There'd been one boyfriend in high school, a couple in college and beyond, but nothing that lasted more than a few months. She'd been too busy or too bright or too consumed with her schooling and post-graduate work to waste time feeding the male ego. And from what she'd seen they needed it spoon fed.

One guy had dropped her after she scored higher than he did on one of the projects they'd been assigned. Another had dumped her for a cheerleader. None of them had touched her heart, so it hadn't been any big deal. She was a solitary creature by nature, didn't need socialization the way others did. When she was in the lab, she forgot about the rest of the world. It's where her passion lay, and she didn't have much left for anything or anyone else.

Her mother wasn't a great role model on the family front. Clare had made only a sliver of room in her life for a husband and kids. Most of her time was spent in her lab, which she called her home. It was decorated more in line with Clare's taste than their real one was. Her mother was consumed with the earth and the exterior world, an expert in her chosen field, a tenured professor of geological studies at Penn State, who'd written books deemed brilliant by her peers. Fiona had spent a lot of her time in that lab while she was growing up and could have easily followed in Clare's impressive footsteps, but she tired of the earthquakes and sediments, and the stifling procedures and protocols her mother used. She'd certainly inherited the right chromosomes, the right genetic code for the sciences, and strove for the same kind of excellence, but she'd been attracted to the opposite end of the science spectrum. She'd studied the human body and all the amazing, nitty-gritty details of how it worked. It was a magnificent organism, with a complexity that constantly staggered her imagination. Discoveries were being made every day, and she loved playing the part of investigator as new mysteries emerged.

Her mother wasn't sure she had the aptitude for it, had taken a wait-and-see attitude about her talents. It had taken more than an undergrad degree for Fiona to establish herself as a scientist in Clare's eyes. It had taken her dissertation to prove she could think for herself, not performing experiments around a well-versed subject but developing a thesis of her own. It had been a terrifying time and she'd almost quit before she was finished, the ten-hour days, seven days a week, wearing her down. Not wanting to make that call to her mother had forced her to stay the course. It hadn't helped that she decided to forego the suggested year or two off between course loads but dove right into her doctorate program. She was afraid the sabbatical would become a permanent ending to her studies, that working in the real world of research might keep her too busy, too involved to go back to the grind of proving some specialized point to a panel of judges. Unfortunately, it was a requirement if her end goal was her own lab. She'd investigated her options, spent time in various labs, chatted with other students and when accepted to the program of choice, found an advisor whose personality meshed with hers. Researching, testing samples, lecturing, assisting, and writing lab reports had eaten away all the hours in the days, months, and five years it had taken her to complete the program. She'd been judged in glowing terms on her thesis and had been awarded her PhD this past November. It might all be for naught. Her age might be a disqualifier. Employers were looking for experience, something she had in short supply.

Now that she was through, would she make time for other things? Or would she be like her mother, and install herself behind the walls of some lab? She honestly couldn't remember how she'd filled her days before her devotion to science had consumed her. Was there ever a time it hadn't? She'd always been intrigued by how systems worked, the rules and patterns that governed them. It meant there was always a research project on her desk, whether it was some school project or something of personal interest. She'd gone through a stage where all she did was build a house of cards to see how high she could make it. In another, she'd taken up a variety of instruments to study the way they sounded, and why. They were all solitary pursuits, taken up to pass the time, waiting for her mother to come home, waiting to form a friendship, waiting to finish school, waiting to get her degree, waiting to be offered a job. Soon she'd have everything she'd worked for and she needed to try for some balance, more connections and interactions.

Enrique was in the hunt for a mate.

Would she ever look for a man to fill the nights or would she be satisfied with her test tubes, microscopes, and computer printouts?

There'd be no need to navigate the globe like her mother had. No need to explore fault lines or earthquake epi-centers, which was how they'd spent part of every summer. She might be well traveled, but she'd never seen the glittering lights of the major cities. Her mother's work took them to remote places where she'd probed the earth's surface. Today Clare was investigating the results of fracking, a landmine of opinions already under foot, but if she had to wager who'd win, it would be Clare hands down. Her mother had a way with words that made complicated material, understandable. When she presented a paper, it would be clear and concise and the least knowledgeable among her listeners would walk away with a depth of understanding they hadn't gone in with.

She wanted no part of that, but it came with the territory. She'd have to give presentations and fight for grants and funding if she wanted to hold her own in the world of academia. Her lab would provide the environment she needed to gain insight into fighting disease.

Now if she could just find one that wanted her...

Her next important interview wasn't until a week from Friday out in the western part of the state. She'd have to bide her time, keep her nervous agitation to herself and keep calm and carry on. What was going to make that more difficult than she'd originally thought was the man-child down the hall. She was beginning to be comfortable with him. It helped that she felt somewhat superior. He thought she was a dog walker by profession. That was laughable but she liked him thinking she was beneath him. He wasn't trying to one-up her.

She still couldn't get his looks out of her mind. He was such a tempting morsel of male flesh.

She'd glanced up at him from time to time while they were playing cards, when he was deep in concentration. He looked a lot like Izabella, and she determined that they'd gotten a lot of the same genetic material from their father. He had to be the source of their common attributes. They were prime examples of the law of segregation, where offspring have the same chance of inheriting a particular allele, an alternative form of gene, from a parent. She didn't even have to meet their father to know he was a handsome man, with dark hair and eyes and a Galican skin tone that tanned well. That two of his offspring carried his most dominant genes wasn't out of the realm of possibility. The random separation of chromosomes meant traits were passed on independently, and each child had the same chance of inheriting them as another. It was often compared to the flip of a coin. Their eyes were their mothers' contribution, but they gave her too little to go on to gain a clear picture of what they looked like. Clare had passed on her nose to both daughters,

Patrick his eyes and there was a recessive gene going back a couple of generations that gave her her hair. No one could have predicted that.

When her phone rang, she reached over to grab it off the nightstand.

Speak of the devil.

It was her mother. Even though it was after midnight, Clare knew she'd be awake. Their calls always took place between the hours of eleven p.m. and one a.m. Her mother was out of the lab and on her way home. Not liking the thirty-minute drive home in silence, she'd use the time to catch up with one of her daughters. It was apparently her turn.

Without even a greeting, Clare got right to it.

"How did it go?"

"Not as well as I would have liked."

She pressed her lips together and braced for the repercussions of the truth.

"Why? What question caught you off guard?"

She was prepared for that question. It was always the first, *why* being the scientific basis for all things.

"The one about being too young for this kind of plum assignment."

"Bullocks. You're more qualified than people ten years older than you are. And your dissertation speaks volumes."

Fiona pulled her legs up under her and rested her head against the back, letting her eyes flutter shut.

"Wish you were the one interviewing me for the position."

There was a clicking sound that told her Clare was thinking. No matter how many times she'd been told about the irritating trait, she couldn't seem to stop it.

"Just pretend I am. Just remind them that youth brings energy and a fresh perspective. And anyone who can finish the PhD process by twenty-five deserves kudos, not deprecation."

It was her mother's doing that put her in this quandary.

"Sometimes I think you did me a disservice with the double promoting thing."

She'd been too smart for her own good sometimes.

"I should have done the same thing with Siobhan, but I didn't know any better first time around. You were challenged rather than bored."

Challenged in so many ways, Mom.

Two years younger than anyone in class when she got to high school. There was a mile of developmental distance at that age. It's when solitary became her way of life. And college at sixteen meant lots of nights left back at the dorm.

"I was that, Mom. When are you back in session?"

There was a pause as if her mother wasn't sure she wanted to stray from the subject of interviews, but she answered the question asked. "The twenty-sixth."

"Anyone come back early to work with you?"

"Caitlin. I've hired her to be my TA and she wanted to get a jump on it."

She'd heard all about Caitlin Persaud. Brilliant, dedicated, committed. Just the way her mother liked her students. And her daughters.

She'd been tough on both, but from where Fiona was standing it hadn't been a bad thing. She might never have realized her dream if Clare had been less demanding in her expectations.

"At least you're not working alone."

Her mother liked having lots of people around her. Fiona still wasn't sure if it was for the attention or the company. Clare was used to being in the spotlight, and her awards and prestigious position lent themselves to her acquisition of scientific celebrity. Her mother bloomed with an audience, wilted in solitude.

"You could come home and work with me for the week."

Fiona could think of nothing she'd like less.

"Remember I told you I'm house-sitting. I can't leave until Izabella and Reid get back."

She was glad she had an excuse. She didn't ever want to work for Clare again. It wasn't that she didn't share a love of the planet; she just didn't enjoy laboring over the kind of analysis that geology required. The curiosity wasn't there, and her mother always picked up on it. What always came next was a lecture on the benefits of varied research procedures and a soliloquy on discipline.

There will be many times you won't like the detail of some experiment, but you will need to complete it.

There was always a judgement, a discourse, a demand for respect and acceptance.

When she'd left home to attend Boston University and begun to forge her own path, she'd left behind her mother's intrusiveness. Siobhan had left as well, settling in Maine with her husband and the kids, when they came along. They both loved their mother but didn't like being barraged with her strong opinions on how they should live their lives, or what they could do to improve themselves.

"I don't know why you agreed to that, Fiona. You've worked hard for what you've achieved, and it seems a waste of your intelligence to be dog walking."

Condemnation in Clare form.

"This is a nice diversion after all the long nights of study and analysis. The house is huge, and Hoover gets me out exercising a couple of times a day. It is infinitely better than sitting around in my condo waiting for something to happen."

She knew the minute that was out of her mouth it had been a mistake. Her mother proved her point.

"You need to be more aggressive in your search. You need to expand your horizons. Don't just settle for Massachusetts."

"This is where the best labs are, and I would think that's where you'd want me."

"Don't be ridiculous. They have experimental labs all over the country. The University of California is one of them. Have you applied there?"

Fiona didn't want to live in California. She loved New England and hoped she could find a permanent home here.

"I haven't. Yet. If things don't go according to my plan, I'll have no choice but to apply in other cities."

"I can write up a list that would serve you well. The newer facilities might not be averse to hiring someone right out of a doctoral program."

"Mom. I can take care of this myself. Honest. I've got it."

Clare blew out a disparaging breath.

"Fine. I'll let you have some time with this, but I'm still going to talk to some of my peers and get some recommendations."

"I had no doubt."

"I'll call next Friday, see how the interview went. Until then, I love you."

"I love you, too. Talk to you Friday."

When she swiped off, she breathed a sigh of exhaustion. Dealing with her mother was like managing a tsunami, or earthquake. It could be a devastating experience.

Clare didn't seem to understand that she undercut her confidence when she tried to take control. Not that Fiona often let her. She'd apply where she wanted, live where she wanted, but the battles always left her feeling vulnerable. She'd had the same fight back in college when she applied for a job at one of the hospitals in the city. Hospitals were where germs lived and breathed, where viruses were studied, where healing took place. It was her domain and she learned a lot just walking the halls, talking to the patients, doctors, and nurses. She studied families, resemblances, quirks, family genetics by reading patient medical records. Was the person hospitalized because of a hereditary deficiency in heart, blood, organs? Would the children follow the same cellular route? She was still asking those same questions, only now she had some of the answers which was due in part to the forensic biologist who'd become her first mentor. She was introduced to Dr. Tara Robbins by one of the nurses and it was her lab where Fiona had worked during her last year of undergrad study. It was a busy, noisy place and it took her time to get used to the bustling bodies who were trying to pinpoint the genetic fingerprints of the hospital population. Once Robbins understood her discomfort in throngs, she set her to work in an isolated corner, where Fiona used her inherited math skills to fulfill the critical piece of forecasting. She left only when her post-doctoral work took her to a different lab, where she worked on quantitative genetics, another subdivision of the field. There she examined and estimated how much of a variation existed between nature, or environment, and a person's genetic code.

She plugged the phone into her charger and left it on the nightstand. She didn't usually sleep with it so close, needing to turn off the outside world periodically, but she wasn't going to venture into other parts of the house tonight. She did not want to bump into Enrique. Her freedom had been curtailed by his arrival and she could only hope he'd spend most of his days at the ballpark.

CHAPTER FIVE

Enrique awoke to the dog barking. Did she need to go out? Where was Fifi? Had she been negligent in her assigned tasks? He flung the covers off and grabbed his pants. Once decent, he ambled out to the hall and looked down the stairs. The barking had stopped but he could now hear a quiet voice talking to Hoover, as if she were human.

He made his way into the kitchen, where there were steaming cups of coffee in take-out cups, a box of pastries, open on the counter, Fifi eating one of them. She looked showered and dressed for the day and he knew from the bounty on the table she'd already been out. Hoover sat at attention, her gaze on every bite taken.

When human eyes looked up at him, there was a crinkle around them.

"I, unlike you, bought enough for all. I'm not even sure you drink coffee, but I took a chance that you did."

He rubbed his eyes, trying to get the picture of her sitting there out of his erogenous zone. It made no sense. She certainly didn't belong there.

"I do although it is not usually strong enough for me. We have much bolder things in Brazil."

She tilted her head, smacked her lips after the bite of the lemon square, and asked, "If Brazil is so cosmopolitan and exceptional in all ways, what are you doing here?"

"Baseball, of course."

He'd walked over and claimed a cup, took a sip before examining the offerings in the box.

Her voice was tinged with curiosity. "You couldn't play there?"

He was hovering over the box. "I could, but the best are here."

She licked her white-powdered lips, and his heart skipped a beat. He immediately began to inspect the offerings, trying to get his mind off the pink tip of her tongue. It was harder than he'd thought, but he was given a reprieve when she continued her line of questioning.

"Why did you take up baseball? I would think soccer would be the game of choice in your country."

He lifted a blueberry scone out of the box and took a bite. "I like more of a thinking man's game rather than a physical one."

Izabella had accused him of being too lazy to exert himself to that extent. She didn't understand he wanted a more cerebral endeavor, even accused him of being too lazy to play baseball well. Was it a repeating pattern?

"That's an interesting take. Excuse me if I disagree."

He threaded his hand through his hair and then met her eyes.

"About the why?"

"About your wanting to use brain rather than brawn"

He washed the deprecation down with another bite of the flavorful scone.

"Soccer is an aggressive sport. I prefer finesse."

"I can almost believe that. But then again, it could be you don't like to sweat."

She'd obviously never been to a game in late July when the humidity turned every ball player into a wet dish-rag.

"Do you think I have no brain? Or I don't want to use it?"

"I'm sure there are some working neurons, although your take on marriage has me doubting the strength of the connections."

"And you? You walk dogs for a living. Not sure that flexes your brain muscles."

The scone was good and as soon as he finished it, he chose another.

"I find things to do that exercise it just fine."

"Like what?"

"Crossword puzzles, Sudoku, I read books. And I've probably done more in the last few hours than you'll do all day."

Hours? It was only a little past eight a.m.

"What time did you get up?"

"Just before five. I showered, dressed, checked email, and scoured Indeed for a job I might have missed, went into town for sustenance. And now that I'm finished here, I have to walk Hoover."

She got up from the stool, threw her napkin and cup into the garbage and went to retrieve her coat from the closet. He watched as she added layer upon layer, sweater, scarf, heavy down jacket, hat, and mittens.

"I don't think it's reached ten degrees yet. I'm hoping she'll settle for a short one this morning."

Bending over, going nose to snout, she said, "We can make it up this afternoon, can't we, girl?"

The short stub of a tail was wagging back and forth in excitement as Fifi snapped the leash onto the collar.

"Be a good boy and throw away your refuse, would you?"

He narrowed his eyes at her. What did she think? He was a slob?

"Don't worry. I will. How long will you be?"

"I'd love to say five minutes, but based on prior walks, it will be more like thirty or forty."

"I've got to be at the field by ten. I might be gone by the time you get back."

"That's fine. I can handle being alone. In fact, it might be a nice change."

And with that, she was out the door. He got up to peek out the window at her. She was being led down the sidewalk, the leash pulling her instead of her pulling the leash. He'd bet Hoover weighed almost as much as she did.

Once she'd disappeared around a curve in the drive-way, he walked back through the kitchen and toward the stairs before remembering. He backtracked and cleaned up the counter, not wanting to give her anything to complain about.

He'd been surprised she knew so little about baseball. He hadn't met many people living in the United States who didn't know something. It was the number one pastime, with two leagues, the American and National, and thirty teams. There weren't many people who didn't have a favorite. It was totally different in Brazil, although it had opened up in the last ten or fifteen years, with a fairly new national training center that catered to fourteen-through-seventeen-year-olds. It had been too late for him, and if it hadn't been for Tio Yan, his mother's brother, he might never have picked up a bat or a glove. He'd been heavily into soccer but had been playing racquet ball one day when his uncle had noticed how well he hit the ball. He was the one who suggested he give baseball a try. The first day at the park, fielding hits and taking turns in the batter's box, he fell in love with the game. His father was deeply disappointed and hadn't talked to Yan for weeks after the introduction, but he finally relented and found a team that was looking for new players, signing Enrique up and getting him back and forth to practice. He was lucky they'd lived where they did. The city was academic in nature and students from all the universities were enthralled with the sport. Soccer had deep pools of talent and there was little chance of being good enough to play. Baseball was a completely different story and that it was more cerebral, made it even more enticing. Introduced to society by the Japanese immigrants, baseball in Brazil was a mix of cultures, with Latin and American flavors thrown in. He had to relearn many aspects of the game once he got to America. After transferring to the University of Michigan his third year of college, he was acclimated to a new way of playing and was approached by the Mets before the end of the spring semester. He dropped out to join the farm team, against his parents' wishes but all he wanted was to play ball. And to play for one of the premier teams in the league was too good to pass up. He did well in double A and moved up and down between the minors and majors as they needed him. His first year in the majors was exceptional. He played behind one of the best at the position, gaining experience during his off days, and was able to rack up a .357 batting average and handle shortstop like he was made for it. What he didn't like was sitting on the bench and it showed. He lost the attitude that had gotten him there, and his stats fell. Whether the front office thought him a lost cause and had given up or wanted him to get more playing time, he wasn't sure, but he was glad he'd been traded to Boston. He'd be out on the field every game and he a chance to regain his footing. He'd become the face of Brazilian baseball, a player who'd made it to the big leagues. He hadn't only let down his team, but his countrymen as well. He had to admit Izabella was right. He'd gotten lazy.

It was time to gear himself back up. He had goals, and he was going to make sure he achieved all of them.

He arrived at Harborside Field fifteen minutes early, wanting to prove his commitment. Farina was in his office and asked him in as he was passing by. They'd spoken by phone right after the trade was announced but hadn't had a chance to sit and talk yet. About the expectations.

Farina would have them. Especially after last year's race toward the pennant. He'd been close enough to taste it. It had to leave a man hungry.

Enrique took a tentative step inside and faced the grizzled old-timer. From what he knew, Farina was just shy of sixty. He had a horseshoe ring of white hair, deep-sunken eyes and wrinkles from squinting at the sun-drenched field. The man was a peanut-eating machine during a game, smoked over a pack of cigarettes a day. Chewing gum replaced both in his office but he must have tucked it inside his cheek like snuff because his words were clear, not garbled.

"I'm glad to see you here. I hope it means what I think it means."

"It does. You will get one hundred per cent out of me. That I can promise."

Farina leaned back in his chair, his hands fisted over his chest.

"Upper management thought if you had regular playing time, you'd spend more of yourself out on the field. I wasn't so sure, but I'm willing to give it a wait-and-see attitude before I make any judgements."

He didn't like hearing that the manager wasn't a fan, that if this had been left up to him, he might be in some other city, playing for some other team.

After retrieving the gum from his mouth with pinched fingers, Farina dropped it in the waste basket, unwrapped another piece, and held it.

"I talked to Reid before the trade was made. He thinks you've got potential. We all think you have potential, but that doesn't mean dick if you're not willing to live up to it."

"I agree."

What else could he do? The number of people who had given him the same speech was adding up. He had a problem and he needed to face it head on.

"Good. Leo's waiting. I want to hear some good things from him. Don't let us down."

Farina popped the gum into his mouth and started softening it up.

Enrique rose, adjusted his sweats, tucked in his tee shirt, and turned to leave.

"Oh, and dos Santos. Get rid of the New York merchandise. You're a Greenie now. Look like it."

Enrique glanced down at the team name emblazoned across his chest.

Meu Deus. Brilliant move.

He'd just pulled a shirt out of his bag and put it on without paying too much attention. That had to change as well.

"Yes, sir."

He made his way through the tunnel down to the locker room. The polished concrete shone underfoot. The walls were freshly painted, no longer peeling and layered in grime. He'd been given a tour of the stadium during the Greenies' run for the World Series. He'd come into town along with his parents to watch a couple of the home games and Reid had shown them around the modern facility. It was brand-spanking new, finished just ahead of last year's season day opener and there were some who argued it was one of the reasons the team had played into October. Gone were the dilapidated buildings, the uncomfortable seats, and all the remnants that reminded fans of an outdated Fenway Park. Bogs had been built around the same time as the one on Lansdowne Street, designed by the same architect, the big green wall a signature for both. Where Fenway had been revamped and updated, Bogs Field had been left to deteriorate, until it was finally abandoned to the college that sat adjacent. It had been demolished in favor of dorms as soon as Harborside Field was ready to house the old team. Its signature landmark now was the Boston Harbor, a backdrop that provided a variant wind speed and direction that had been absent at Bogs. On certain days, it could carry a ball, not only out of the park but out into the depths of the waterway. There might be no history here, but it didn't matter to Greenie fans. What they cared about was winning and the team was ready, willing, and able to do that for them.

Today, the underground space was eerily quiet. Within a couple of months, the place would be a buzz of activity. He could almost smell the aromas that would permeate the tunnel once it was open to the public, things like hot dogs, pizza, greasy French fires. They had gourmet selections, but he always went for the standard fare which was reminiscent of his younger days. It sparked something primal, and he quickened his footsteps, wanting to get down to business.

He stood at the threshold of the locker room, scanning the space, wanting to fit in, wanting to contribute.

Today, the green cubbies were empty, no names assigned, no uniforms hung from the hooks with care, no equipment littering the space. By the beginning of April, the room would be jam-packed with his teammates dressing or undressing, smiling or scowling depending on whether they'd won or not. A TV screen was attached to one of the walls where the manager or coaches would show videos of missed plays and missed opportunities.

He rubbed his hands together in anticipation. He couldn't wait to get back out there.

"Right on time."

Leo had come up on him, a cap in his hands. He had a full head of hair, graying along the edges, and Rique wondered if it was a coach's curse to age before his time.

Scowling, he said, "Strip that shirt off now. I'm sure I can scrounge up something less fucking ugly."

Enrique did as told, and within a couple seconds, a ball of cloth hit him in the chest and he grabbed it.

"Glad to see your reflexes work."

After scrambling into it, Enrique tucked it in.

"We need to talk about a number for you. Have a preference?"

It was the first thing he'd checked out as soon as the trade was a done deal. Some players were fanatical about what number they wore. Him not so much. He was willing to take anything between zero and ten. When he saw the number, he'd worn while he was at Michigan was available, he looked no further. It had served him well.

"Has anyone taken two?"

"Nope. You're the first newbie who's arrived, and around here it's first come, first served. Have anything to do with the Mets' shortstop?"

"Not really, although it's another reason it works for me."

"He's your competition?"

They might not play against each other often, but he'd be the benchmark for success, and Rique' would be comparing their stats all season.

"He is."

Rique dumped his gym bag on the floor by one of the benches, dug out his sneakers, and toed off his Vans.

Leo was standing, watching him, his arms folded across his chest. "I have to admit, there were some here who weren't exactly thrilled with this trade. Do I need to tell you why?"

Rique finished tying the athletic shoes and stood so he could face the coach.

"I've been getting my fill of opinions. I have to admit some of them are reasonable."

Leo nodded. He seemed satisfied that he didn't need to go into details.

"The position you'll be playing is the most important one out there and you'll be playing for one of two Boston teams, whose history goes back close to a hundred years. We were here not long after the Red Sox and although we might have fewer fans, the ones we have are rabid."

Enrique knew that, had seen it for himself when they played a game at Bogs Field before Harborside was finished and when he was a spectator during the championship game.

"We might be willing to have some patience, but the fans won't be. You're going to be under pressure to perform. Are you ready for that?"

He was getting pumped thinking about it, the adrenaline rush making him almost giddy.

"I do my best work under pressure."

"I think you might be right. I've watched some of your clips, and you have it. But we're not going to allow you to turn it off and on at will. We're looking for consistency whether you're on the field or not. Got it?"

He nodded. There was nothing to say to that.

"Matteo is going to be here tomorrow, Seb the day after. You'll be training together for the next two weeks. Then you'll have a week off before it's on to Sanford. Today it's you and me. Let's see what you can do."

For four hours, they worked indoors, the snow on the field preventing them from performing drills outside. Weights, squats, bike, treadmill, push-ups, medicine ball slams, all meant to strengthen his core, and they took time in between to rest and regen.

He was one big sweat ball, throbbed like a toothache when he was finished, but he felt good for the first time in months.

Leo threw a towel at him and he used it to wipe the salty moisture off his neck.

"I'll be pushing you like this from here on in. I want to see what you're made of.

There's an indoor facility we'll be using for field practice and batting, and I'll make sure to keep you injury free until the season begins. I expect you to get eight hours of sleep, drink lots of water and if it's possible, put away the booze for now. Eating healthy wouldn't hurt, either. Why don't you shower and get out of here? Same time and place tomorrow."

"See you then."

Enrique pulled the towel off his neck and wiped his face again as he ambled toward the shower room, thinking about last night and the tumbler of scotch he'd thrown back. And the woman who had beat him at cards talked about discipline. If she stuck around, he might be able to do as instructed. She was interesting and kept him entertained. He didn't even mind that she was laughing at him most of the time. She'd been on the edges of his mind through the workout, her look of disdain a great motivator.

He'd been given the same advice last year, but he hadn't listened, too pissed that he saw very little playing time, although he didn't really expect them to take out the all-star and put him in any more than necessary. He hadn't thought it would grate on his nerves the way it had but he liked action, not sitting. He'd gotten bored but now...he'd have no excuse not to live up to the expectations. He'd been handed the ball and glove, and they were going to get the best performance out of him that they deserved. That the fans deserved.

He had a feeling that Fifi might help make the difference. Until he settled down.

His attitude could only improve once he got married. Spending eight hours in bed wouldn't be a hardship. It was the choosing that kept him busy, kept him out until all hours of the morning, one drink leading to the next. With one giant step, he could erase all his bad habits. He'd be gearing up to get the job done. He'd thought he'd have a week for his search, but it looked like he'd only have a couple of free days before flying to Florida for spring training. He wanted to be there early, start working out in the good weather, fielding, batting, and getting to know his teammates. He had a good feeling about his plan. It was going to work. He could put his adolescence behind him and get down to the business at hand.

As he was driving back to Izabella's, he wondered if Fifi would be there. He'd promised he'd supply the dinner tonight, and although it was too early to pick something up, he'd worked up an appetite. With nothing in the refrigerator to satisfy, he decided to stop at the store on the way back and pick up a few things to hold him over.

CHAPTER SIX

As soon as Fiona got home from the unexpected interview, she let Hoover out and changed. It had gone better than her last one had, but it wasn't her dream job. It was in genetic-based research, cancer related but for a pharmaceutical company. She was not a fan of the big pharma industry but if it was all that was left to her, lack of experience not a deal breaker, she might have to settle. Or look elsewhere. If the job had been part of pharmacogenomics, she might have weakened. Then she would have worked at analyzing the human genome and how heredity impacts a patient's reaction to certain drugs. One of the biggest causes of death came from adverse reactions to prescribed medication. If scientists could determine a simple test to detect the DNA idiosyncrasies, the wrong drugs might well be avoided. She'd yet to meet a pharma company willing to go that route. Why would they? Millions of dollars might be at risk. They might be averse to it, but a new brand of personalized care was being pursued by doctors, one that required a complete genetic mockup. It gave the physician all the information needed to identify which pill fit the unique blueprint of an individual patient for the best results and the fewest side effects. That hot issue could sway her to shift her long-term goal, which for now still targeted proteomics. She firmly believed that the study of proteins could end up uncovering more about genes…than genes could. It hadn't made a big splash in the field of science as of yet, which was one of the reasons she'd chosen it for her thesis. The complexities of the subject matter were making it slower going than in the fields of stem cell research or the genetics of infectious disease. In her more sensible moments, she knew that no reputable lab would hire her on as lead, not at her age. She might have to do the assistant thing, like she had during her doctoral work. There were a lot more jobs like that around, but she'd put off applying for them. Shoot for the top was what her mother always told her, and that advice had become cellular.

She was just about to get out the cheese curls for something to pick at, the guest in the house inhaling the last of the food ordered last night, when she heard the back door open and heavy footsteps.

She turned to see Enrique carrying several large bags of groceries from Whole Foods. She jumped into action and took one from his sagging arms and hefted it on the counter.

"Did you buy out the store?"

He gently released his load and stepped back.

"I remember my mother telling me to never go shopping when hungry. I may have done a lot of impulse buying."

She could nag him about discipline, but he was right, or rather his mother was. She'd made that mistake herself many a time and ended up throwing away some of her more ridiculous purchases.

"Help me put it away? I have no idea where some of this should go."

After diving into one of the bags, she pulled out containers of tuna salad, chicken salad, cold cuts, potato salad, two containers of sushi, a pre-packaged meal of lasagna, and a couple of chipotle beef quesadillas. She knew there was plenty of room in the refrigerator, so she began to stack them on the empty shelves according to size.

She glanced over to see Enrique withdraw some apples, grapes, asparagus, broccoli, plantains, mangoes, a variety of cheeses and crackers and place them on the counter.

"What were you thinking? You have to cook some of this stuff."

"I am well aware of that. Did you ever consider for a minute that I can cook?"

She was startled by the simple question. "No, actually. Not once."

He laughed at her and it made her insides quiver. He had a good laugh, almost musical.

"Well, I can. I even enjoy it from time to time but don't tell anyone. It's one of my deep, dark secrets."

She gulped. She didn't want to know his secrets. It was too intimate. Needing to feel a little more in control, she scoffed, "Not manly enough for your reputation?"

"Some of the best chefs in the world are men, so that's not it. There's something about a person taking the time to create a meal for you that satisfies more than hunger."

She could picture it. Some beautiful brunette, apron on, high heels, candlelight, serving him some exotic meal. Her leaning in as she placed the plate in front of him, him enticing her with warm, sensual eyes.

She tried to weigh down her response with sarcasm.

"You like being pampered."

His expression stilled and he became serious.

"I like someone doing something nice for me. I reciprocate in other ways."

"And what ways would those be?"

There was a sensual glint in his dark, penetrating eyes.

"I satisfy in more physical areas."

She bet he did. The coil of hunger tightened but it wasn't in her stomach. It was lower.

"It's not a two-way street?"

He straightened, a momentary look of discomfort crossing his face. "I get what I need out of it."

"I bet you do."

His eyes narrowed suspiciously, and he took a step closer. She took a giant step back. He was far too close for comfort and his eyes had a devilish gleam in them.

"Afraid of me? Or the topic?"

Suddenly, her pulse was erratic, her breathing more labored than she wanted. As her heartbeat quickened, she retorted tartly, "Neither. You told me you're ready to settle down, so this would just be…a diversion for you."

His voice dropped an octave. "I am not thinking about seducing you, Fifi."

She could feel her cheeks burn in embarrassment. What had she been thinking? Of course, he wouldn't try to seduce her. She was so not his type.

"Good. I have an aversion to being sweet-talked into bed."

"I wouldn't have to say a word. All I would need to do is this."

With one step, he was in her space, his hand on her neck, and he was drawing her face to his. All she could do was stare at his lips, wondering what they would taste like, feel like pressed to hers. She was frozen in place, her brain screaming at her to move away, but there was another part of her that ignored the wise warning.

She was almost relieved when he stepped back. Almost. The curiosity about those lips had gone unanswered and she felt a rush of disappointment.

He'd gone back to emptying the bags, as if what had happened was no big deal. Had it been a game to him? Like a cat with a mouse?

If so, he was more than the asshole she'd originally thought.

Not wanting to make it seem she'd been affected by his nearness, she began collecting the food on the counter and going through cabinets to see where things should go. The silence hung heavily as she tried to regain her equilibrium. He threw it off again when he said, "Maybe instead of ordering in, I'll cook for us tonight."

His voice was smooth, without guile. "How would Brazilian stroganoff sound?"

Her mouth watered. That was happening a lot around him. If not for the food, then for…

Her voice cracked when she said, "Good."

She was standing with her back to the wall of cabinets, as if she were protecting them from an intruder. He glanced over at her, his smile lightening up his face.

"I think it might be satisfying to be the one to create the dish. What time do you usually eat?"

"When I get around to it." Her voice sounded so breathy, she didn't recognize it as her own.

He patted a bulky brown package. "I have to marinate the beef for an hour or more so why don't we say six?"

"Okay."

He opened the fridge, put away some of the food that had come out of his sack, and took out some of the things she'd put in. He began to cut up some of the cheese and put the squares on a plate. Adding some crackers and a bunch of grapes, he said, "I worked up quite an appetite this afternoon. I think I'll just pick until dinner."

Hoover jumped up, put her paws on the counter and was ready to swipe some of the appetizers. She caught her just in time and yanked her down as Enrique lifted the plate high into the air.

"That was close."

"I'll take her for a walk, let you finish up."

"I'm actually just getting started."

Before putting on her coat and all the layers that went on underneath, she snatched a piece of cheese and a couple of grapes and popped them into her mouth.

"This could take a while."

Not only because of Hoover's love of the outdoors, but her own need to escape the confines of the kitchen. It had gotten much smaller than it was this morning.

It was still cold out, but the sun was shining high in the sky. She raised her face to feel the warm rays on her skin, but she wasn't able to enjoy it for long. Hoover was straining, letting her know there was another dog across the street, the wagging tail signaling a hello. Didn't matter if it was animal or human, Hoover was the more social of the two.

Fiona snapped her leash, commanding, "Leave it," and Hoover fell into step beside her. They walked companionably toward the center of town, stopping every few dozen feet to satisfy her furry friend's olfactory obsession. She'd come to enjoy her time with Hoover. Walking was a great way to recharge her energy and she'd needed this. After this morning's interview, she'd been taken for a tour of the facility, then to lunch. It was a cafeteria with lots of noise and people jockeying for a place in line. It was a nightmare. She preferred small groups but couldn't have declined the invite, so she'd sat through it, her focus more on eating than on conversation. She performed best with only mild sensory stimuli, and she was sure she'd blown that last part of the interview by being so scattered. Enrique only added to it. Her body thrummed with a jagged vibration whenever he was around, and it made her jumpy and restless.

When she returned to the house close to an hour later, she felt better, her mind clearer. After she unsnapped the leash, Hoover made a mad dash to see what was going on in the kitchen. Fiona shed her clothing one layer at a time, hanging her coat in the closet and trailing behind.

Enrique had his back to her and looked to be washing something in the sink. The room was no worse for wear, the only thing out of place, a platter of cut-up mushrooms and onions.

"How's it going?"

She was rubbing her hands together, trying to get some blood circulating again. Even with mittens on, her hands had lost feeling.

His head swiveled in her direction, and he was wearing that million-dollar grin.

"Well. The meat is marinating, the vegetables are ready, and I have cleaned every utensil used. I don't want you to have anything to use against me. How was your walk?"

"Invigorating."

Hoover, after examining every square inch of the room for some morsel that might have fallen to the floor, plopped down on the hardwood floors and emitted a sigh of longing.

Wanting to forget about the interview and the fact that she had no job, no definitive future, she asked about his. "How did your training go?"

"Very well. I am impressed with Leo's methods. He's the infield coach, and I'll be working with him over the next two weeks. There will be two others joining me. Matteo Alvarez, he's from Cuba and will play third base, and Sebastian Layden, who's been with their farm system, will be in left field."

"What's a farm system?"

She'd taken a stool at the island and was suddenly interested in knowing about the game. She might find it hard keeping up in groups, but she loved to talk one-on-one. Especially with him.

He leaned against the counter and explained, "It's where young players get experience. Every team has a triple A team and double A team among others, and those drafted work their way up until the hit the big show."

She assumed the big show was slang for the big leagues.

"Sort of a metaphor for home grown. That's cute. Where did you farm?"

He chuckled. "I played with the Gulf Coast League my first year. Then out of Trenton."

He rose and got a big pot out of one of the drawers, placed it on a burner and poured some oil into it. He squashed and peeled some garlic before adding it, then picked up a thing-a-ma-jig to scrape along the bottom. After opening a container, he lifted out chucks of beef and placed them in as well. He readjusted the heat and stood over the pot and watched the sizzle.

"Did you play much while you were in New York?"

"No. They have an all-star shortstop. I spent most of my time on the bench as back-up and pinch hitter. I filled in for him and the second baseman when they needed a day off."

"I bet you didn't like that, being the best and all."

"Even I have to admit, the guy is better. But only to a few."

"Another one of those deep, dark secrets?"

"As a matter of fact, yes. I am sharing many with you."

He glanced up from his pot and his eyes were questioning, as if he didn't understand that himself.

She shrugged in response. "I have that way about me."

Not exactly invisible, but insufficient enough that she offered no threat. Women in science had to do incredible, mind-provoking things to be noticed, and even then, they stood outside the circle of acceptance.

He was looking at some point in the distance and then began talking as if to himself. Her invisibility cloak was doing its job.

"I got inside my head, but not in a good way. I figured I'd never get the starting position, so I started slacking off. Then when I'd get into a game, I'd screw up. It didn't endear me to my teammates."

She didn't know whether he expected a response, but she gave him one just to prove she was here.

"I guess I can understand that. It sucks when you have what it takes but something holds you back."

She didn't have to guess. She knew but she wasn't ready to share her own deep, dark secrets with him quite yet.

His eyes found hers, as if remembering he wasn't alone, and he shrugged, admitting, "I'm what's holding me back."

He went back to his task without another word. Added the mushrooms and onions to the pan and stirred. The scent began to permeate the room. She inhaled, teasing her stomach. He brought her back from the sensory experience, his expression somber.

"I let my thinking affect my attitude. Someone once said that your success doesn't come from your talent, it comes from what's in your head. The game's ninety per cent mental. That's what I meant when I said baseball was a more cerebral game. In soccer, you run, chase, steal the ball, run some more. There's strategy but you don't need the attention to detail that you do in baseball. You don't have the seconds to think between pitches or a throw that should be automatic."

"What are you thinking now?"

"That I have a chance at starting at a position I am good at, for a team that came close to winning the World Series last year. I'm in a good head space and I intend to stay there."

"New leaf?"

"New attitude."

"It's easy to have that now, isn't it?"

She'd have a new lease on life if she could get a job. It would make her feel useful, and it would signify her last eight years hadn't been a waste of time. Was she going into her interviews with a preconceived notion she wouldn't be hired? If she was, the members of the hiring committee would pick up on it… She'd have to go over a mental checklist, see where her answers were deficient in confidence.

"It would be if there wasn't a lot of…uncertainty attached to it." He looked up, met here eyes. "What if I can't get back to where I was?"

Interesting question. She asked herself the same one daily and suggested to him what she'd been telling herself.

"Then I guess you'll have to work harder."

"That's why I'm here early. I wanted to get a jump start on it. Figure out what the expectations are. If there's a lot of pressure on me to win, I might… not—"

"I thought you said it was a team sport. There's no *I* in team, is there?"

He laughed then, lessening the tension he'd been radiating.

"There isn't, no."

"Any expectation for you to carry the team would be your own. That leaves an *I*, with nowhere to fit."

"I like that. You have a way with words that hit the bull's eye. Can I hire you to be my mental coach? Then you won't have to walk dogs in the cold for a living."

It was on the tip of her tongue to tell him the truth, but she bit it off. There was no reason for him to know. Soon, she'd be gone and so would he, never to meet again. And it was almost fun keeping him in the dark. People looked at her differently once they knew she was smart. He thought she was a bit loopy with a slightly off-the-grid kind of job and she was enjoying it.

CHAPTER SEVEN

After Enrique had dished out the meal, he took a seat across from Fifi at the kitchen table, quite pleased with the way it had come out. He felt a sense of pride in a job well done, and that he'd created it from the ingredients he'd purchased himself made it even more satisfying. He just hoped she liked it. He'd never done this before, cooked for someone other than himself, and he was surprised how much he'd enjoyed it.

He held his breath as she took her first mouthful.

When she licked her lips and smiled, he let it out.

"It's very good. Is it a family recipe?"

"Yes. My mother gave me the recipe when I moved away from home. I have a box of family favorites packed away somewhere, although I haven't used them all yet."

Fiona ripped off a piece of roll he'd heated for dipping, soaked it and popped it in her mouth. This cultural delicacy didn't have noodles, so he'd supplemented the staple with another kind of carb.

"What does she look like?"

He flashed his eyes up at her. The question had come out of nowhere. "You want to know what my mother looks like?"

"Yes. I see the similarities in you and Izabella, so I know you get those traits from your father, the common denominator. What did you inherit from your mother? Paint a picture."

He tilted his head in concentration, summoning up an image of Livia.

"She has auburn hair, a light complexion, deep amber eyes—"

"The shape?"

He pinched his lips together. "Mm. I've never thought about it before. Give me some examples."

"Almond, wide-set, sunken, puppy-dog, round—"

"Yes, round."

"Like yours."

"Yes, although I think mine would be like hers not the other way around."

She rolled her eyes at him. "You're right. What else?"

"Hands and feet. She has a lower arch than my father and she has longer fingers. My father's are on the stubby side. Why the interest in my genetics?"

She hesitated for the briefest of moments before stating, "Just curious is all."

He rose half way out of his seat and extracted his wallet from his back pocket, pulled out a worn photo from one of the compartments. "Here, not that you see her very clearly. It's too small to get the full affect."

It was a picture of the whole family, Jaco and Izabella included, on one of their visits to Brazil. Paolo had hired a photographer and they'd sat together. From looking at it, you couldn't tell it was a blended family.

Instead of the smile he'd thought he'd see on her face, there was more an expression of analysis, as if she was measuring something quantitative. She proved it when she said, "She's on the small side, as is your father." The smile came when she looked up and joked, "Probably why you didn't get the tall part of the threesome that wins hearts."

She had skipped that when she'd described his appeal to women, mentioning only dark and handsome.

Almost indignantly, he scoffed, "I'm not that short."

"You don't have to get defensive. It's not a criticism. Just a fact. You're not what most refer to as tall. You're what five ten, five eleven?"

"Somewhere between there."

"You're dad the same?"

"Yes. I always thought I got the best of both. You're telling me I have a deficiency."

She chuckled. "I'm not telling you anything of the sort."

He knew he was sounding childish, but he couldn't seem to control his next question, as if to prove she had one, too. "Who'd you get your hair from?"

She never flinched, and with deprecating humor, she said, "The mailman?"

"For real?"

She rolled her eyes and shook her head. "No, not for real. I'm the only one in my immediate family who has curly hair. I'd have to go back a couple of generations to find that unruly gene. Are you implying it's a *deficiency*? I've got more than one and I've learned to live with them."

"I shouldn't have asked. It was doing exactly what you've accused. It was mean."

"And calling me Fifi?"

He certainly wasn't going to tell her it was what had popped into his head when she told him her name. Maybe it was the dog-walking thing, maybe it was her hair that reminded him of his family's poodle, maybe it just suited her. It wasn't the nicest name he'd called a woman, but she was stuck with it now.

"Your name is Fiona; some might call you Fi. I've doubled it."

She'd pushed the bowl away. It was wiped clean of sauce which made his chest swell with pride. It was gone in a flash when she cut him a sharp look.

"No one calls me Fi."

Frustration spilled out along with another revelation.

"Okay, to be honest, I remember faces, but I have a terrible memory for names. It helped me remember yours."

"Mnemonic association. Interesting. I hope your future wife has a name you can play with. It will make it easier to cry out her name…at the right time."

"I will know her name when the time comes."

"I'd refrain from giving her a dog's name. It might hamper any attempt at getting her to agree to marry you."

"I didn't give you a dog's name."

She picked up her phone and her thumbs began to type. Then she waited. Then scrolled.

What was she doing?

"Okay, mea culpa. Fifi's not even in the top fifty names."

"You just Googled that?"

"I was curious, so yeah."

"Curiosity killed the cat."

"But wasn't it an answer that brought her back?"

"Perhaps. It could also be that that particular cat had nine lives and hadn't used them all up yet."

He noticed a smile slip out before she got up and began to clear the table. "The meal was delicious, and I thank you for sharing it."

"That was the deal, was it not?"

"It was but you went over and above. You also bought lots of things to pick on. I'll be in seventh heaven tomorrow."

"No plans?"

"Not really. I…I've decided to look at this as a break. I've worked non-stop since high school and I'm beginning to think I deserve one."

"Walking dogs?"

"That…among other things."

His phone rang and he swiped to answer, leaving the room as soon as he heard the voice.

"*Oi, meu amor.*"

Giovanna was one of the women who'd struck his fancy last trip home. Long honey-colored hair, exotic eyes which always attracted him. She was a bit taller than he was, but he didn't think that would be a problem. The thing that was hanging him up was her lack of curiosity about the world. He was afraid life could get boring with someone less intelligent than he was, someone who yessed him to death.

"When are you coming back Enrique? I am missing you."

Her accent was thick, but she was making the attempt to speak in English, something he required of all the women he was considering a match. If they were going to live in Boston, she'd have to be able to communicate with his friends.

"I've got a couple of weeks here, then a few days there before the season officially begins. It won't be long now."

"You can't come sooner?"

He was sure she'd meant to coo but it had come out as a whine. It was turning him off.

"I can't. I have an obligation to the team. That will come before everything and everyone."

"You will put me last? For a game?"

"Not last, Vanni, but during the season my focus must be on my job."

"I will be bored while you are away, no?"

Probably. Without anything to occupy her mind…

He'd been wrong in thinking she would fit the mold. He mentally crossed her off the list.

"I think it best you stay in Brazil. Your playmates are there."

"Let me know when you get in. Maybe I can convince you otherwise."

"Probably not a good idea. Goodbye."

He swiped off, studied his phone.

What had seemed a sure thing had crumbled to dust. Fortunately, there were several other women he could woo who weren't so self-absorbed.

He was pulled back when he heard the slider opening to the back yard. Fifi must be taking Hoover out, and he backtracked into the kitchen, the spotlights casting a glow across the snow-covered lawn. Woman and dog were chasing each other, slip-sliding on the crusted ice. When Fifi fell on her rear, she laughed, and he felt a smile of pure masculine pleasure spread across his face.

After grabbing his coat, he joined them, Hoover racing over to butt against his side in a happy dance.

It threw him off-balance, and he found himself sitting on the hard, cold ground after losing his footing.

A laugh erupted, his self-deprecation surprising him.

"It's a bit slippery out here."

He did his best to get up, but his shoes had no traction. Fifi had come out prepared, her boots better able to handle the ice and imitating a penguin, she walked over to where he sat and extended a hand.

By the time she helped him to his feet, Hoover was ready for another romp around the yard. Fiona found a stick that was half-buried in the snow and threw it, Hoover immediately setting off to retrieve it. The dog brought it back but was unwilling to let it go so the game could continue. Fiona tussled with her for it, but she wasn't willing to let her fingers get too close to the teeth that gripped it. She raised her arms in the air and said, "Fine, be like that."

She jumped back when Hoover was hit with a flying snowball, wet slush exploding all over her coat. The canine yelped, dropped the stick and went charging after him as if she knew he'd thrown it. He could hear FiFi's laughter as Hoover chased him in circles until the dog took him down, her paws resting on his chest as if proving she was winner of their game.

He rubbed her head, she licked his face, then trotted off to pee. Once she was done, she returned to the door and barked, wanting in. Fifi ran over, gave her some loving before sliding the door open and bounded in after her. He carefully trailed behind.

Her cheeks were pink from the cold, her smile infectious.

"I have got to get a dog when I finally have a bigger place."

He shrugged out of his coat and was ready to dump it on the stair rail but stopped just in time. He took hers, and while he was hanging them side by side, he asked, "Where do you live?"

"A four-room condo in the next town over."

"Rent, own?"

"Rent. I don't know where I'll end up, so I don't want to buy until I do."

He scratched at his temple, trying to understand.

"You would relocate for walking dogs?"

A small frown appeared on her face, her expression one of uneasiness. Then it was gone, and she said, matter-of-factly, "You relocated."

"I'm making a bit more money than you are. I go where they pay me."

"And you would have gone to…" She looked up and met his eyes. "Who's the worst team in the league?"

He didn't even have to think about it. "Cincinnati."

"You would have gone there?"

"I have no choice at this point in my career. I'll need to play a few more years before I get the right to decline a trade."

"That's kind of like slavery, isn't it?"

She was glad her days of slave labor were behind her. That was one of the downsides to being a doctoral student. Very little pay for lots of hours.

"It's the way it's done."

"I'm not sure I'd like it."

"I got lucky, so I can't complain. What do you want to do tonight?"

Taking a slight step back she asked, "What do you mean?"

"I've been told I have to live clean and healthy, which means I can't go out. I'm hoping you'll take pity on me…again…and help me find something to do."

She seemed to relax at that, and a smile tugged at the corners of her mouth.

"It's a good thing I did a summer as camp counselor, although I think arts and crafts is all that's left. We've already tried to run around outside, and we can't swim or canoe."

"There's a theater in the basement."

She narrowed her eyes at him as if he had an ulterior motive.

"Is there? I haven't been down there."

"Reid had it built after they moved in. One night when I was here last year, we binged on the Fast and Furious series."

He grabbed her hand and tugged her along behind him. He flipped on the switch and made his way down the carpeted stairs to find another living space, a hallway and a room off to the side that held cinema-type seats and a professional screen. When Reid did something, he usually went overboard.

He'd felt some resistance as they entered the darkened space and asked, belatedly, "You do like movies, don't you?"

"Not without some candy."

"Your favorite?"

"Twizzlers."

"Mine's Mounds. Let's investigate, see if they keep a stash."

He opened and shut cabinet after cabinet, to no avail. Throwing up his hands, he exclaimed, "How can they not have anything munchable down here?"

She was examining every inch of the room as if she'd never seen one of these before. Almost absent mindedly, she reminded, "We still have the cheese curls."

She was right. He'd also picked up some chips, pretzels along with the cheese and crackers.

"You go through the movies and find one you like while I scrounge around upstairs."

He raced up the stairs, and as he assembled a platter of finger foods they could pick at, he realized he was enjoying this. He'd never been on this side of things, most women falling all over themselves to satisfy him in every way. Instead of wondering what would be presented, he was making those choices and he wanted them to include what he thought Fifi would like. She didn't seem to have the kind of sweet tooth he did, so it probably wouldn't matter that there'd be no candy. His sister Leia was a picker. She opted for salty. Where he might eat half a cassava cake, she'd eat a bag of chips. When he had stuffed as much on the platter as he could, he opened the refrigerator, hesitating only a minute before grabbing two beers. One Heineken couldn't hurt him, could it? He made a promise to himself to switch to water later. He shoved the beers into his pockets and carried everything carefully down the stairs. Hoover was bumping his butt the entire way, in the hopes a morsel would fall into her waiting mouth.

She was sorely disappointed. Even more so when he told her to go lie down.

As he proudly set the feast down between two seats, he noticed several movies Fifi had picked out as possible screenings. A couple were science related, one was about dogs being trained as seeing-eye companions, and the last sounded lame.

"These are your choices?"

"They're sitting there, aren't they? Do you know they have dozens of them?"

And you picked these?

He gave her a quizzical look. There *were* dozens to choose from. He tended to like action or sports related. Even the new Marvel movies would have been preferable. She obviously had no taste in movies.

"It's become a family thing. Probably why they have *Pick of the Litter*. We probably should have discussed what kind of movies we liked before we got down here."

Or at least what genres he could do without.

"I used to like movies. I haven't been to one in years. This might be fun."

He looked down at the cover again and doubted it.

CHAPTER EIGHT

Enrique didn't look impressed with her choice, not that she could blame him. She'd almost chosen something else after reading the description, but these two actors had starred in a film she'd watched as a kid, one she'd enjoyed. They hadn't been together on screen in almost ten years and it proved too much of a curiosity for her to put it aside.

As soon as he'd set up the video, he sat down beside her. The screen flashed with the intro credits and she settled in to watch the story unfold. It only took a couple of minutes for her to know she'd made a very bad choice and that the movie was going to be a dismal failure. She munched on a piece of cheese, already bored with the dialogue, a ping-pong game of verbal banter, every line falling flat. She had one word for both the characters: insufferable.

She turned to look at Enrique's profile, trying to gauge his expression. His face was scrunched up as if he was being tortured and she almost laughed.

"We can shut it off."

"We might as well give it a chance."

When the banter moved in location, it transitioned from bad to worse. There was no point to the endless harangue of their useless lives. Needing more stimulation than the scene provided, and prompted by the title of the movie, she asked, "Would you ever have a destination wedding?"

He'd been munching crackers, the sound of the crunch carrying over to where she sat. It held more entertainment than what was on the screen.

"If I am married in Brazil, it will be one for those who live here."

She slid to the side of the chair so she could talk face-to-face.

"That's true. How many will have to travel?"

He pulled his leg under him and seemed more comfortable with this dialogue than the endless stream of nothingness that was coming over the speakers.

"Izabella, Reid, Leeni and Alex. Jaco and Terry. Keith and Sofia, with their kids…"

"Who's Keith and Sofia?"

"Keith's my agent and attorney. Sofia is his wife. Izabella introduced me when I was offered my first contract. He's one of Reid's best friends."

He must have thought he'd satisfied her curiosity because he'd stopped there.

"Okay, go on."

"Probably Melinda and Bill."

She was surprised when they were added to his list.

"You know them that well?"

"They're at most of the celebrations, holidays, birthdays, so well enough to consider them family. And of course, some of my teammates, past and present."

"It sounds like there'll be lots of people."

"More than likely. My family is quite extensive."

There was a lull and she put her attention back on the movie, hoping there'd be a bump in activity, excitement, something…

He'd finished his beer and got up. "I'm going to grab a water. Want one?"

She nodded. Her beer was empty but more from needing something to occupy her mind than taste. "Pause it if you want before you go."

"No…I'm not sure I'll miss much in the next five minutes."

She gave him a weak smile and watched him leave. The plot was one dimensional and the two characters weren't very stimulating. Neither was their conversation. She should have chosen *Wonder Woman*, like she wanted to but thought it too female driven. In his absence, she had no alternative but to put her attention back on the screen. The only thing it gave her was another topic of conversation. When he finally got back, glad for the diversion that was him, she asked, "How did your parents meet?"

He slunk down in his seat, his legs out in front of him, his hands holding on to the bottle. Her chair was raised in recliner fashion.

"At a function. Papi was the president of a bank in São Paulo and Mama was one of the vice president's secretary. He was still with Julianna, Izabella's mother, but left her soon after. They tell me it was love at first sight."

That was a fairy tale if ever there was one.

"Do you believe in that?"

His full mouth set in a grim line. "I don't know. I have never felt that kind of…instant connection to a woman. I can't doubt them, though, because they are still very much in love close to thirty years later." His brows lifted and he drew back to study her face. After a moment's pause, he asked, "How about yours? How'd they meet?"

She frowned thoughtfully. "In college. Math class sophomore year. It wasn't love at first sight, at least they never talked about it like that. They're both logical and analytical so affection was at a premium in our house. I can't see them madly in love with anything except their work."

"That's kind of sad."

She felt wounded by the truth but shrugged it off. "It worked for them. They've been married almost as long as yours."

The conversation was going strong now that they'd pretty much given up on the movie. It had become background noise, the kind that didn't annoy.

"How many times in your life have you been in love?"

He smiled. "I think I can answer better to how many times I thought I was in love. The first time I was all of five, in love with the little girl down the street who could beat me at foot races during recess. For some reason, I like a challenge. I went to her house every afternoon to play for a couple of months, and then one day when I got there, she was entertaining one of my friends. I was devastated."

She returned his laughter and asked, "How long did it take you to get over the heartbreak?"

He flashed her a sexy, wicked smile. "Maybe three days. Then it was the little girl with the curls who caught my eye."

She chuckled mockingly. "Did you call her Fifi?"

"Of course not. It would have hurt her feelings."

"You had them then. When you were five. Feelings."

"You have pierced me to the core."

She doubted that given the smirk on his face. Wanting to wipe it off, she said, "Maybe I'll start calling you Bailey. It's the number one dog's name for males, you know."

He looked affronted. "Do I look like a Bailey?"

She had to laugh. He certainly didn't. Bailey would be a gentle golden retriever, funny and playful. That wasn't Enrique. He smoldered. "I guess not."

She didn't dare ask him if she looked like a Fifi. She was afraid of his answer.

He'd taken a sip of his water before asking, "How about you? Any tales of romance?"

"Same age, or thereabouts. There were three boys who lived down the street who I used to catch frogs with some afternoons. I swooned on sight."

His eyes widened. "For all three?"

She shook her head. "For the frogs."

"Did you kiss one?"

"Ugh. No prince is worth that."

Before she knew what he was doing, he leaned over and placed a quick kiss on her lips. His clean, spicy scent invaded her nostrils and it would have weakened her knees if she'd been standing.

"Someday you might find one that is."

His voice had gone low, and it vibrated through her.

Not wanting him to know how the feather-like kiss affected her, she forced a laugh and said,

"I think I'll stick to frogs."

They were safer than this kind of man. He was way out of her league in every way. If she gave in to the attraction, she'd be left with not only a broken heart or bruised ego, but another reason to stay away from romance.

His expression shifted slightly. His eyes had narrowed, his lips slightly open as if he was ready to say something of great import. She waited patiently but he added nothing.

"What?"

He shook his hair off his face and leaned his head against the back of the chair, refocusing his attention on the movie.

He hadn't expected the jolt from her lips. It was like an electric spark had gone off as soon as he touched her. He was going for playful, to counter what she'd said about frogs and princes, but it had shaken him to the core. Amusement evaporated as soon as she said she'd stick with the amphibious. She'd obviously not felt the same mule-kick to the gut.

He didn't understand it. She was not his type in any way. Not in looks, not in temperament, not in the social graces. She liked being alone; he loved to party, she was a small-town girl; he was cosmopolitan, she didn't know the rules to his game; he was addicted to it.

He glanced over, still trying to decipher the explosiveness that had resulted from such light pressure. What would it feel like to go full tongue? The obsessive need to find out had him squirming in his chair.

He tried to discipline his mind and body, push thoughts of Fifi away. His brain was not cooperating even as he forced himself to listen to the inane dialogue of the movie still playing. He sat up when one of the characters said that love had nothing to do with like. Was that true? How could you love someone if you didn't like them? He liked scores of women but felt no particular passion for them and yet the ones he chose to bed, he usually didn't like at all. Was it possible to have both? Was that what he'd be looking for in a wife?

He seemed unsure of his mission now. Having grown up in a family where love was a constant, where everyone got along, he knew he couldn't settle for less.

"Rique? Are you okay?"

He flashed his eyes at her and there was a look of concern.

"Why do you ask that? I'm fine."

"You can't seem to sit still, and you've gone pale."

He couldn't seem to take his eyes off her lips or tamp down the need to feel them again.

"Do your parents like each other?"

She glanced at the screen, then back at him. Did she know why he was asking?

"I guess so. In some weird way. My mother is a serious scientist, puts most of her energies into her work, and she might be a tad too intense for a lot of people, but my father's her equal, with the unqualified ability to make her laugh. I think that's what's kept them together all these years."

"If your mother could be with anyone, who would she choose?"

"Are you asking if she'd pick my father? I'm not sure. I know she'd like to meet Charles Darwin, Leonardo da Vinci and Florence Bascom but seeing that they're all dead, and she's met most of the world-renowned, living geologists, maybe she would."

"My father would choose my mother every time. Is that a rare thing?"

"It might be rare, but I think it would be valuable in a marriage. Are you beginning to realize finding that wife of yours will involve more than you thought?"

He was. He hadn't thought along these lines before, even though Izabella had told him as much when he'd broached the subject with her. What he'd counted on were the number of women who'd been attracted to him, the number of women he'd wanted. But he had to look at it in a different context now. Could he want someone for more than a night? For a lifetime? Could he base a marriage purely on lust?

He blurted out, "I would need to like her."

Otherwise he wouldn't want to go home. Not until bedtime. Those hours in between could only spell trouble.

She issued a deep, slightly aggravated sigh. "Are you saying that's more important than love?"

He let loose a breath that was half frustration at the thought, and half disbelief that it might be true. "Perhaps it is."

He was going to have to reorganize his list. It would have to include some of those women he liked. If there was no passion, he'd just learn to live without it. His heart ached at the thought. Was he willing to make such a sacrifice?

"Why don't you just wait to find the right combination?"

He felt the intimate probe of her eyes. the dove gray muted but direct.

With as much determination as he could muster, he said, "It is time for me to settle down."

She took a sip of her water and said off handedly, with just a hint of sarcasm, "I didn't realize men had the same ticking biological clock as women."

Irritation flared. She was making fun of him. "We don't. Not for children. I need a wife so I can stop my wild ways."

When she placed her hand on his arm, he felt an unexpected tingle.

"Rique, you don't need a wife for that, you need discipline."

"A wife will provide the incentive for it."

"If you can't fund that on your own, you'll always be dependent on someone else."

She stood, picked up the empty platter and turned to go. "This movie sucks, and I'm tired. I'll see you in the morning."

He listened to her footsteps receding and then slouched back.

She was right. On two fronts. The movie had sucked. And he needed to control his own impulses. If he didn't achieve his goals, it wouldn't be because of some unknown person he thought essential to his life, it would be because of some flaw in him. Something he didn't want to admit, but… What did Fifi say? If the shoe fit…

He'd have the next two weeks to work on his discipline. That would be his focus, to attend to the tasks at hand, a hundred percent. He'd confine himself to that one thought. He was the master of his mind, wasn't he? He'd get rid of all distractions, put all his energies into practice, wouldn't allow himself those few seconds of idleness that took him off his game. No drinking, no women, eight hours of sleep, good food. He had the talent to be great, but so did a lot of other players. It's how they got to the big leagues. He needed a mental toolbox, with a different variety of attitudes than he'd been packing. Laziness was out. So was wishing he'd do well here. Action was in along with concentration and a dedication to detail.

Marriage wasn't being ruled out even though he was prepared to attend to his baseball career, with single-minded focus. He hadn't told Fifi the whole truth about settling down. He wanted that not only to help him become a better player, but also for himself. He'd seen what love could offer, first through his mother and father, the way their faces would light up as soon as they saw each other. He'd seen what love had done for Izabella and Reid, and what it had given his sister Leia, who'd just gotten engaged. Being in love had changed them. No longer facing the world alone, they were two people working as one, with common goals and dreams. He envied their silent communication, the shared looks, the simple touch that brought a smile to their faces. They had found *the* person who made them feel special, who was interesting and exciting, who moved the right way, spoke in the most perfect voice, and who physically pleasured them. He was tired of meeting new women, weary of their expectations and assumptions of who he was, disillusioned by his own. He was looking for meaningful, wanted to explore the depths of a potential partner, and wouldn't settle for less than an authentic relationship. Desperate for the headiness of being in love, he hadn't taken some important things into account. The woman, for example. His list would have to go. He knew everyone on it, and he could find fault with every one of them. He'd been fooling himself thinking there was one of them he could share his life with. He'd gone out with enough beauties to fill a stadium. He'd been drawn by the externals, turned on by the way they looked. Had he ignored all the rest? The ones who didn't fit his version of attractive? Did she really need to have long, dark hair? Be a classic beauty? Like the social scene and be better at useless chatter than a homebody who had intellectual depth? He was creating a new image of who might suit, but she was so outside his comfort zone he wasn't sure he'd be able to find her in just one day. Or one trip home.

It was a distraction he needed to put away. At least for now. His trip to Brazil was two weeks away. Only then would he give himself over to finding the woman of his dreams.

After he shut the theater down, switched off the lights, he walked slowly to his room, where he hoped to get a start on those eight hours of sleep.

CHAPTER NINE

Fiona had made toast for herself and was absentmindedly sharing a piece with Hoover. She'd gotten up early again, the need for sleep not as dire as other more physical ones. Her mind seemed more intent on reliving the kiss than getting some rest. She could still feel it, and the memory was altering her metabolism. The chemical processes that served as life maintenance had become combustible and it was doing a number on her.

A flare of anger swept through her.

He had some nerve playing that kind of game with her. And she was sure that's all it was. How could it be anything different? He was planning a trip to Brazil to find a bride, so why was he messing with her head that way?

The only reason your head's messed is because you're attracted to him. You and about a hundred other women.

Her head had been messed as soon as she'd seen him standing in the kitchen, for fuck's sake. Even after being drenched by his careless driving, she wanted to do several really stupid things, like run her fingers through his hair, kiss those kissable lips, undress that toned body. She'd never had that kind of seismic reaction to anyone before, but as soon as he called her Fifi, she'd disassembled, and gotten a grip on her emotions. He'd told her exactly what he thought of her, but it hadn't stopped her from wanting what she couldn't have. He wasn't it. If she ever fell for someone, there'd need to be a correlation in genetic markers between them in such things as appearance, height, and IQ. It was a risky proposition to try and catch the best-looking guy around, at least for her. She'd be better off going for someone who matched her in height or intelligence. She had to stop panting like a puppy dog around him. She'd be confirming the name Fifi fit.

It wasn't like she hadn't tried. She'd done her damn best to avoid him but even retreating to her bedroom hadn't worked. He'd come knocking, like she was a friendly stray dog whom he could play with for a time.

At the mention of cards, she'd perked up and had gone running like he'd thrown her a stick. She wasn't competitive by nature, but his arrogance had clicked a switch, and with her usual good luck and deadpan expression, she'd trounced him badly. He'd handled it better than she'd expected, and she'd gotten a glimpse of his humility. Who knew he had it in him? He hadn't been as put off with her skill at as she'd thought. In her experience men didn't like losing to a woman, tended to shy away from anyone of the opposite sex who was equal to them in intelligence or more successful in any way. The kicker was, she'd actually enjoyed his company.

If he'd only stopped there, she might have survived the longing. But no, he had to throw her another bone. Two if she were counting. Dinner and a movie. It was almost laughable.

It would have been bearable if the movie hadn't sucked. Because it had, they'd engaged in conversation. She'd been holding her own, and then he fucking kissed her.

The chemistry in her brain had gone haywire, her hormones went to peak alert, and her heart had hammered as if she'd run several miles. Uphill.

What was she supposed to do with that?

Nothing. Not a god-damned thing.

She couldn't let her girly parts have any say in it, otherwise…

Hoover alerted her to his footsteps, and she quickly got up from the stool so her back would be to him when he entered the room. She couldn't afford to be sidetracked by his looks.

"Good morning, Fifi. I see you're up early."

His voice had that soft, buttered appeal that would have gone well with her toast. Wanting to shut down any feelings that might be developing for him, she said irreverently, "Not for me."

"It is for me and I have to admit, I feel great. This eight-hours-a-night thing might be just what I needed."

It seemed he wasn't going to let her surly mood affect his, so she took another bite.

"Makes sense with all the hard work you'll be doing today, you know, things like running."

"It expends a lot of energy."

He sounded insulted, which was what she was going for.

She twirled around to face him, and her guts did the jig she'd hoped to avoid.

He was in sweats, a long-sleeved tee and bare feet. How could anyone look so frigging good after just getting up?

She gulped back a moan.

"You play a game for a living. It's probably one of the reasons you can't seem to grow up."

His hands went to his hips. His face turned into a scowl.

"Did you get up on the wrong side of the bed this morning? Or is this your usual morning mood?"

"I…"

She dipped her eyes to the floor. She had to own her dismay with the living arrangements not shove it back at him. He was here for the duration and she had to deal with it.

"Not my usual. I'll make myself scarce until my mood improves."

As she went to walk past him, he reached out and took hold of her wrist. "Did I offend you in some way?"

She could have suggested his choice of a name for her might have offensive implications, but the tingles that were shooting up her arm didn't help her infected brain. She had to look at him as if he were a virus, attaching to her as host. There were a lot of different ways she could reject it if her immune system was working properly. The problem was, it wasn't.

Not in full command of her senses with him standing so close, she blurted out, "Don't kiss me again and all will be well. You're not a frog or a prince and I can do without your mouth on mine."

He dropped her arm and stepped back.

"I meant no harm."

"I'm sure you didn't. It's just another game you play."

"I wasn't doing anything of the sort."

"No? There is tactile acuity to the lips and a disproportionate number of neurons that are stimulated in the brain when they touch any part of the body. You kiss when you want to maximize intimacy. That was not your goal so it must have been a game, or more plausibly your ego."

He was looking at her as if she'd just spoken Martian. She'd gone and done it. Made this more a science lecture than a simple meeting of lips. If there hadn't been such a sensory overload, she might have been able to leave it at that.

"I'm going out. Hoover should be good for the next couple of hours and I'll be back by then. Have a nice day."

He didn't say a word while she got her coat on, just stood gawking at her, which made her move a little faster to be gone.

As she streaked out of the house, and into the garage, she thought, *Well, that should cure him of any further curiosity as far as lips and kissing are concerned.*

As soon as she started her car, with the garage door rumbling up, she dropped her head on the wheel, wanting to cry. She'd just made a complete fool of herself. If she could turn back the clock, turn down the offer to house-sit, spend her time hunting down a job, she'd do it. She felt miserable, not only because she'd gone off on him for being male, something he couldn't help, but because she was enamored of all that maleness.

After pulling herself together, needing to leave the shameful exhibition of scientific proficiency and infantile behavior behind, she reversed out of the driveway. Without a destination in mind, she drove aimlessly, or so she thought. When she arrived at her alma mater, it didn't come as a surprise. She'd been on automatic pilot over the last five years and all she had to do was point her car in the right direction and it would take over. It was her home, comfortable and familiar. It was where she could think deep thoughts, expound on scientific theory, and not be found wanting. Her thesis advisor, Terry had not only been her mentor but like a mother, one who truly cared about her failures and successes. Clare only wanted to hear only about the wins.

She climbed down the marble steps to the basement, letting the confines of her life here surround and protect her. She knocked on the door to Terry's office and heard, "Come in."

When her advisor looked up to see her standing there, she got up and came from behind the desk for a hug.

"Well, if it isn't my favorite doctoral student. Come, sit. Tell me what you're doing."

Feeling forlorn, she admitted, "Dog walking and house-sitting."

Terry's forehead creased with her frown. "You've been out on interviews though, haven't you?"

"Two so far. One next Friday. Not a lot in between. I'm concluding that I'll have to assist rather than lead. No one is willing to give me a chance."

Terry motioned her to sit and then took her place behind her desk. Her expression was one of concern. "It's only been a couple of months since you were awarded your doctorate. Your thesis hasn't even been published yet. The offers will come, Fiona. You've got too fine a mind for them not to."

"It's just such promising research and I want to pick up where I left off. I'm not good with idle."

Once you'd walked that path, spent hours in the lab working on the complexities of genetics, it became your life. Without the lab, she had no identity. She knew that establishing oneself as a scientist took time, especially if you were a woman, but what she knew in her head didn't translate well to her heart. Or ego.

Terry leaned forward and said, "I could use another set of hands here if you're willing to lend them."

Fiona wanted to leap at the chance, but that would be like waving a white flag, surrendering to her doubts. It would also mean abandoning Izabella, something she wouldn't do.

"I can't accept anything until the family I'm sitting for comes back. I know me. Once I step foot in the lab, I'll forget all about my furry friend."

Terry tugged at her bottom lip. "I also might know someone to talk to about your situation. You wouldn't be working at a university but a biotechnology company. They're doing a lot of outside-the-box research and you might be a nice addition to the team."

"Sure. I'm beginning to think I should take anything I can get right now. My mother's suggested I look in other parts of the country."

Terry sat back, her arms resting on the arms of her chair, her hands steepled under her chin.

"This does not sound like the woman I met with just a few months ago at her exit interview. She was confident about her future, excited about the prospect of running a lab. What's happened?"

Fiona shook her head. "I'm feeling a bit vulnerable right now. The interview I had at Harvard didn't go well. Maybe I'm overshooting my talent."

"I know that's not the case. You've got exactly what it takes to succeed. It's your ambition and single-minded focus that concern me."

"What? Why?"

"You need more balance in your life, Fiona. How often did you take a night away, to play, grab a bite with friends, go on a date?"

"Never found anyone I wanted to get to know."

Mumbling under her breath she said, "Until now."

Terry sat up, looking intrigued. "Well, well. Sounds promising. Who is he?"

She shook her head, rubbed her hands over her face. "There's a guy staying at the house, the brother of the woman I'm house-sitting for. He's…getting under my skin."

If she was working, she'd be able to put him out of her mind.

Terry arched her eyebrow and asked, "How?"

"He's a ballplayer, one of those beautiful people you want to hate."

"But you don't."

She snorted, "Not enough."

Instead of commiserating as expected, Terry asked, "Does he play for the Sox or the Greenies?"

She stilled. Her former professor was waiting patiently for her answer, so she stuttered out, "He's just been traded by New York to the Greenliners."

Terry's jaw dropped open in surprise. "Enrique dos Santos?"

Fiona's eyes widened. "You know him?"

"I know of him. He's the real deal although he hasn't had a chance to play the position permanently over the last couple of years. And he'd get under anyone's skin."

"And you know this how?"

"I must have mentioned that my husband's a real baseball freak. Sox his first love, Greenies come in a close second. He gets to watch two games a night if so inclined. I've watched here and there just to see the guys move. *He's* poetry in motion."

She was sure Terry must have mentioned the thing about baseball, but it wouldn't have stuck in her memory, her mind too filled with proteomics. They talked about a lot of things over the years over coffee, fast-food lunches and apple-crunching dinners, unless Arnie, her husband, dropped off some take-out for his lab-rat recluse of a wife. Fiona liked him. He always got enough for them to share. Did baseball fill his nights as he waited for Terry to get home?

"I guess I forgot." She'd also forgotten something else. "What does Rique play?"

Terry fell back against her chair, a knowing smile on her face.

"Shortstop. It's a key position and the fielder has to contort his body to scoop, swivel, and throw. It's like a ballet dance with muscles rippling. Excuse me if I start to drool."

Fiona felt something funny in her chest, wasn't sure it was a laugh bubbling up, trying to escape or a lump that had developed. What she'd diagnosed was a burgeoning need to see him in action…or was the better word obsessive?

"Is that the only thing you like about the game? Watching the men scoop, swivel, and throw?"

Terry was not shy about her discussing things Fiona thought should remain private, so it wouldn't surprise her if it was the only redeeming quality about the game.

"I enjoy it at times, been to my share of games over the years. Some days you have to get out of the lab and it's a nice diversion. My husband sat on the edge of his seat last year, watching his two favorite teams battle it out to see who came out on top. With the new additions, the Greenies might just go all the way this season. Either way it goes, Arnie can't lose."

"Rique wasn't supposed to get here this early but he's come in to train with the coach."

"Good. I'll pass on that tidbit to Arnie. He'll be psyched to hear it." She rocked back and forth in her chair, began to chew on her pen. It was her thinking mode.

"Is your reaction to him physical, mental or emotional? Are you feeling less than or…too much?"

Fiona flashed her eyes up. "None of the above."

"I don't believe you. I've never seen you thrown off by someone before. You take everyone in stride. You're attracted to him."

She wanted to deny it but couldn't get the lie out. Instead she muttered, "Who wouldn't be?"

"And you don't think you'd have a chance with him?"

She shook her head. Vigorously. "I don't want a chance with him. I also don't want to feel this kind of attraction."

Terry winked and wriggled her eyebrow. "Lust can be a beautiful thing."

"I wouldn't know about that. This is my first interaction with it."

Terry leaned forward and said conspiratorially, "Rip his clothes off, have your way, and then forget him."

Fiona had a feeling the first two might be doable if she was a different kind of woman, but the third, after accomplishing one and two? She wasn't sure.

"I might want to wait until the night before I leave to do that. It would be even more embarrassing to have to live with him after doing something so bold."

She'd never have the nerve, but it might be fun to fantasize… The shiver told her she was wrong. It would be dangerous.

Terry seemed to be chewing on her predicament, along with the pen, before asking, "Can you move back home?"

"I promised Izabella I'd stay. She says he needs someone to keep him in check."

"And you're that someone. Interesting."

"He's working on discipline which means he's staying at the house nights. Expects me to entertain him."

"Even more interesting. I can provide some guidance on how if you want." The wink that followed was conspiratorial.

Fiona rolled her eyes. "Thanks, but no thanks."

"I'm going to play the advisor card, which allows me to offer a personal opinion on your... unwillingness to experiment."

"This is one experiment that defies logic. And if I remember correctly you told me once, if the brain is distracted you risk safety. And he can be very distracting."

"When will you ever have this chance again? Bedding someone like dos Santos isn't something you pass up…" Terry looked up as she smiled, "… if you're single that is."

"Bedding a ballplayer has never been on my to-do list and I'm not sure I want it as an add-on."

"Fiona, live a little. Mix it up. You might find an endless number of possibilities."

When Terry read the stony look on her face she shrugged and said, "Suit yourself. I'm not sure I could be so blasé about it."

"That would mean I was used to jumping into bed with strangers and it was no big deal anymore. That is not the case."

"I wasn't speaking about you."

Too much information. If people thought scientists were conservative and stuffy, they hadn't met Terry. She was a child of the sixties even though she was born ten years too late.

"You think you can get me tickets for opening day? It might earn me a night of gratitude if you could."

"I can ask."

"Thanks. I'd appreciate it. Now, do you want to visit the lab? See what we've been up to since you took your test tubes and went home?"

"I'd love to."

She felt the thrill that always came with the word *lab.* It almost drowned out the other thrill that was becoming a persistent ache. She glanced over to Terry, who was walking companionably beside her, and wondered if she could do as suggested. The ache began to throb.

As soon as Fiona walked into the bustling lab, all her insecurities fell away, along with the physical thrum that came with thoughts of Rique. Cubicles, each with its own computer, had stacks of lab notebooks and the reams of paper it took to record test results that came from the quantitative and reliable methodologies used. It held the kind of fascination she needed to flourish, a work environment that was ever-changing, unpredictable, and full of surprises, understandable considering their subjects, the human being. Terry was a clinical geneticist, whose job it was to interpret and communicate the results of DNA samples in order to verify or refute a suspected genetic disorder. The lab rats working here were a mixture of students, scientists, and support staff, who spent time developing new procedures of extracting information from the human genome. Terry taught classes, which she said was the brightest part of her day, working with a new generation of scientists who were as enthusiastic as she'd been at the beginning of her career. Her worst was diagnosing an infant's incurable disease. It was what made her work harder, smarter, to eradicate those emotional moments of anger and frustration. She was the person Fiona would emulate when she had a lab of her own.

Two of the lab rats welcomed her with wide smiles. Kim Foster and Lucy Henson were still struggling through the last year of their doctoral program, assisting in Terry's clinical trials and diagnosis while trying to complete their own research.

Kim asked, "Do you have good news for us?"

She was asking in her own interminable way if she'd found a job yet.

"Not yet, but soon."

Hopefully.

"You'd better. I need motivation to keep going. I'm in the writing phase and it's slow going. I have a way with testing samples, but not with words and explanations."

Terry reminded, "Mind on what you're doing, please. The last group of test samples were done incorrectly. We have enough to do around here. We don't need to duplicate efforts."

She could see Kim's cheeks pinken. She had the kind of complexion that showed the slightest bit of embarrassment.

"Yes, ma'am."

Erin Lambert came running in, her white lab coat flapping, as she searched for the other arm that was dangling behind her.

"I'm sorry I'm late. I picked up the buccal smear on my way in. I'll get working on it now."

Terry shared, "New patient. Six-month-old. We told the parents we'd rush it."

Fiona nodded in understanding. Erin would be looking for changes in the child's DNA that would lead to a diagnosis. That was the one thing she wouldn't miss about being here. All those times they'd come to the unbearable conclusion that the genes had gone haywire and were about to short-circuit a lifespan. She preferred her own specialty where she dealt with gene mutation in general and didn't have to decode life from death in an individual.

"I'll let you get back to work."

Terry glanced up from the computer printout of test samples she was reviewing and said, "Keep me in the loop. If I come up with an alternative, I'll call. And rethink that stance you've taken on a certain baseball player. I want quantitative and measurable stats if you move forward with it."

She winked before she shifted back to her analysis.

CHAPTER TEN

Enrique was still stinging from Fiona's verbal assault as he walked through the underground tunnel at Harborside. How the hell did she know those facts? The ones about kissing. Neurons, tactile acuity, maximizing intimacy. It sounded like a hypothesis, a scientific supposition about mouths and nerve endings. What it suggested was that the brain had a lot more to do with the sensations of mouth-to-mouth contact than the other body parts he'd relied on in the past.

And of course, now that she'd told him not to kiss her again, there was a driving need to do just that. But the next time, and there would be a next time, he'd have to draw it out, feel those nerve endings, that brain-to-brain exchange. He barked out a laugh. Like he'd be able to concentrate on his brain cells when she was wreaking havoc on other cells that were far more assertive.

"What's so funny?"

Rique looked up to see Leo leaning against the door frame of his office as if waiting for him to show up. He glanced at his watch and released a sigh of relief. He wasn't late.

"Come in. There's someone here I think you know."

Leo stepped back and let him enter first. Sitting in a chair was a round-faced, dark complexioned, dark-haired man, mid-twenties, with a baseball physique. He wore a baseball hat with the Alfareros logo, the top of a bat that contained a ball with stitches within its lines. It was the Cuban team Alvarez played for. He smirked. It looked like there was another player who was unwilling to leave behind some of his personal belongings. He wondered if Leo was going to say anything. When he jerked his thumb in the direction of the hat, all the coach did was smile. Mattie whipped it off his head, ran his hand through his thick hair and smiled weakly before getting up and giving him a hug.

Rique slapped him on the back and said, "Good to see you again. Happy to finally be here?"

"I am."

Mateo had stayed with Rique's family in Brazil while waiting for his visa to be approved. He'd emigrated to Mexico, met up with the Greenliners director of player development, who introduced him to Keith. One thing had led to another and he'd ended up at the dos Santos villa in Rio. They'd gotten to know each other fairly well while he was there, partied some nights, but the guy didn't seem to date much. He often wondered if he'd left a woman behind and hadn't gotten over her yet, even though he'd denied it when asked.

"When did you get here?"

"Late yesterday."

Rique thought it a shame that Mateo had defected a few months before an agreement had been reached between the Baseball Federation in Cuba and the MLB League that allowed Cuban players to retain an agent and sign with an American team. He knew there were certain requirements that came with eligibility, but he was sure Mateo fulfilled them. Up until just last month, any Cuban who wanted to escape their homeland, play in the States, and pursue a U.S. contract, had to be smuggled in, usually by unscrupulous agencies. Over drinks, Mateo had shared some horror stories about other Cubans who currently played in the big leagues that included ransom, torture, and even death, something akin to human trafficking. He'd said he'd been saved by Divine Providence, arriving in one piece, but didn't elaborate any more than that.

"Where you staying?"

"At one of the hotels in the area. For now. Keith told me Alicia is working on something more permanent."

Alicia was the director of player development who'd gotten Mattie here and from what he'd heard, she'd had to move mountains to do it. He hadn't been introduced yet, but he was looking forward to meeting the woman who'd climbed so high on the ladder of a very male-oriented sport

Leo interrupted the reunion. "You can catch up later. Seb had some family thing so he won't be here until tomorrow. He's been with the farm system and knows the culture. With spring training right around the corner, I only have a month to get you guys up to speed."

Rique laughed. "You mean yesterday wasn't business?"

"That's what we call orientation around here."

"Will Mattie go through the same?"

"Doesn't need to. He hit .300, stole fifty-nine bases and had no errors last year. If you could have said the same, I wouldn't have had to put you through your paces."

In a gruff voice, he added, "He might have brought a hat, but he didn't come with an attitude."

Rique's hands went to his hips and he scoffed, "I don't have an attitude."

Leo raised his eyebrows. "Okay, how about the I-don't-have-to-give-it-my-all syndrome."

He wanted to say he didn't have that either but couldn't. Leo picked up his keys, his clipboard and his phone. "Come on, you two, we're going on a field trip."

They left the city by way of team van and traveled fifteen minutes south. Leo small-talked with them during the drive or tried to. He was the only one who did a back-and-forth. Mateo hadn't uttered a word, but then again, he rarely did. Rique had initially thought the guy didn't understand English. Where most everyone in the world learned English as a second language, Cubans not so much. There'd been a lifetime of animosity between the mainland and the island, and it had only been in the last few years that the hostilities had lessened. He'd found out soon enough he understood it extremely well.

Rique glanced over at him from time to time. Mattie's expression suggested he was in deep thought, and he was just about to ask him if he was okay when Leo pulled into the parking lot of the facility. They ambled over and walked in after opening the glass door. A receptionist at the front desk greeted them.

"Good morning, Leo. It's already for you."

"Great, Gretchen. Thanks."

They went down a short passageway to the left and entered a huge open area. The room, if one wanted to call it that, could have been lifted up and replanted anywhere as a real live park. The lights overhead were the only thing unnatural about the place. The bases were laid out ninety feet apart, and a hitting machine stood on the pitcher's mound, the coach standing right beside it, an evil grin on his face. It didn't take long to get the torture underway. There were sliding and double-play drills, parachute runs to exercise twitch muscles, along with neuromuscular training moves that squeezed the quads and worked the hip flection. When they brought the flat paddles out, Rique groaned. They were worn like a glove and designed to force an infielder to catch with two hands. He had to stop the ball with the paddle while simultaneously covering it with his other hand. It stung every time the ball hit it and Leo was giving it all he had. He could feel his hand swelling throughout the drill, and he wasn't sure his glove would fit after the damn exercise. Watching Mattie hustle for every ball hit to him made Rique feel as if he'd been phoning it in. After some soft tosses, they faced the hitting tee. What seemed like a little league fundamental, was used by every team and thought to be one of the most essential tools for batting practice. It was where a good hitter fine-tuned his skills and perfected his art. Rique was often bored by the repetition, and he'd been told by his former coach that if he didn't like practicing his swing, he should get out of the sport. That wasn't going to happen, so he'd just have to suck it up. It was all about discipline.

Mattie was up first. As Rique watched, he became mesmerized. The third baseman not only had power, he had balance and control and his timing was impeccable. He must have stoked six that would have made it out of the park if he'd been standing in the box at Harborside.

When it was Rique's turn, he stepped into the batter's box. He kept his mind sharp and focused on every step of his swing. Mattie gave him pointers after his first few attempts, and he started to feel comfortable in his stance. He began to approach the ball with more confidence, until he was making contact at the meat of the bat, hitting it farther and farther into he outfield.

When he was done, Leo came over and slapped him on the back. "I think we found your hitting buddy. Good work."

He looked over at Mattie whose brow was furrowed. He was all about focus, grit, and determination. Rique could learn a lot from him.

Finally, after several hours of being run ragged, they were set free. Rique all but limped back to the locker room once they returned to their home base. He ached everywhere, and he'd bet there were bruises on his bruises. He couldn't help but notice that Mattie's stride was normal, like he'd just been for a walk in the park.

"You didn't feel any of that?"

"Yes, I felt it. I've had no full-out practice in a long time, and Leo used some tricks that I've never seen before. A paddle should be illegal."

He laughed even though it hurt and groaned, "I think it is."

Mattie chuckled. It was the first time he'd cracked a smile since arriving.

After showering, Rique hung around and waited for his new teammate. When Alvarez finally exited the shower room, a towel wrapped around his waist, Rique asked, "Want to grab a coffee? Catch up?"

"That would be nice. Thank you. I'm not sure about what to do now that I'm here."

It had to suck. Mattie had been surrounded by the dos Santos family for the last several months, and now he was on his own. There was nothing worse than feeling the let down of that. He should know. He'd felt that way his first year at Michigan before he'd made friends, gotten to know the area.

"I'll help you figure it out."

Mattie had begun getting dressed. They'd both known enough to bring a duffel of clean clothes. Who wanted to put on an ugly, sweat-soaked shirt after cleaning up?

"I'd appreciate that. The city is so big."

He could have laughed outright at that. Boston was small compared to LA, Chicago, or New York. Or where he came from.

"You lived in Rio for close to four months. You never felt overwhelmed, did you?"

"I did. When you weren't around, I stuck pretty close to your home. I was afraid of getting lost, or worse. The town I come from wouldn't even make the map here."

"This is downsizing for me. Rio to New York to Boston. I should be feeling cramped."

But he wasn't. He was finally feeling as if he'd found his home.

"I'm staying with Izabella and Reid. They live about twenty miles north. She gave me the name of a real estate agent. If you want, I can have her look around for something for you."

Rique had decided not to use her. Izabella would know better what he needed, so he was going to wait for her to show him around.

Mattie asked, "Alicia is taking care of that, although I'm not sure where I'll end up. Where does Reid live?"

"Andover. It's small, but it has its fair share of athletes as residents. Reid grew up there, but you can live anywhere you want in the area and be happy. Boston's a big sports town, and two of their teams, football and baseball, have a lock on their leagues. Hockey and basketball are competitive." He laughed and added, "They're going through a drought right now. It's been all of four months since their last championship. The fans are waiting for the Patriots to win the Super Bowl and get them out of it."

He shrugged when Mattie gave him a lukewarm smile. He obviously didn't appreciate the joke. He watched his new teammate slip on his street shoes, which wouldn't keep him warm in a foot of snow. He'd have to show him around, give him some advice about how to survive the wintry blasts of cold here.

"Your feet will freeze in those things. You've got to get some boots. It's the first thing my sister told me to get when I moved to Michigan."

"It is good you have family here. As you know, I've wanted to come here for a couple of years but put it off, not only because of the stories of imprisonment but because leaving my mother behind was difficult. It was she who finally convinced me to make the move. If anything were to happen to her, I would be desolate. We are all we have."

"Will you be able to bring her here?"

He paused, as if trying to choose his words carefully.

"There is a lawyer working on it. With our government, one never knows."

There was sadness in his eyes. Was that why he wasn't smiling, even though one of his dreams had come true? There was more than Mattie was letting on, but he'd never been able to ferret out what it was.

"Look, instead of coffee, why don't you come with me. We can pick up dinner and talk. I can drive you back to your hotel later tonight."

Mattie looked up as he hefted the duffel over his shoulder. "I'd like that. I am ready if you are."

They walked through the tunnel toward the parking lot, the snow crunching underfoot, muscles he didn't even know he had screaming at him with every step. He tried to ignore them.

"Once we get to Florida, we'll all be in pretty much the same boat as you are. There'll be some families there, but a lot of wives stay home, their kids in school. And the weather will certainly be more to my liking."

"That's a month away, is it not?"

"Some players go down as soon as the trucks get there. I'm making a quick trip to Brazil as soon as the caravan leaves and will stay only a few days before heading to Sanford."

Rique was walking more slowly than usual, Mattie slipping around, trying to maintain his balance on the icy strip of pavement.

"You don't get snow in Cuba, do you?"

"No. This is my first taste. And it's much colder here than at home. The temperatures don't go less than sixty degrees in January."

Rique chuckled. "Opening day's no picnic. It's still cold into April and opening day's earlier this year than in the past. According to the schedule, it's scheduled for late March. We freeze for at least a month before it gets comfortable."

"I must get used to it."

"Pick up some warmer clothes. And the boots will help."

When they got to the car, Mattie whistled, circling the car and taking in every inch.

"This is what money can buy here."

"This and a whole lot more. You must have gotten a signing bonus."

Rique popped open the trunk, thinking he'd throw in their duffels but all he could muster was a painful toss.

As he looked at the small space provided for a passenger, Mattie said, "Not much room."

For the first time, Rique thought the same and winced as he contorted his bruised body behind the wheel.

"You have to sacrifice something to race like the wind."

After inserting himself into the seat like a letter in an envelope, the third baseman replied, "You really don't know what sacrifice is if you can say that."

Rique gave him a quick glance before revving up the engine. For the first time in a long while, he felt the sting of privilege.

They drove up Route 93 in silence, Mattie taking the time to survey the landscape, until he asked, "Is it always this barren?"

"No. Only in the winter. Every season brings something new. It was the same in New York. You get used to it. Almost. You could have held out for a warmer climate."

"The Greenliners were the first to offer me a deal. Keith was happy with it, although I'm not sure he…what do you call it? Shopped me around. With all fees I had to pay to get my release, I just wanted it done and signed."

"What kind of fees?"

Mattie's face hardened. Rique wasn't sure he was going to answer him. In a voice devoid of emotion, he said simply, "Let's call them travel fees."

Rique glanced over, waiting for him to expand on that, but Mattie had withdrawn into himself. There was pain there, he could feel it. He needed to lighten the topic, so he asked, "How did you find Keith?"

"He was recommended to me by… someone I know."

"He's one of the best."

Mattie's shoulders seemed to lose their tension. "He's been very helpful."

"You do know some people here after all. His office is in Andover. I was supposed to meet with him on Friday, but he had to fly out and meet with a new client in the Midwest. We covered what we needed to by phone while I was driving in."

Mattie was back to staring out of the window. He was rubbing his forehead with his fingers.

"I hope Alicia finds me a place to live where there are people. In the city. It will help me get around and I want commotion. After living in Camaguey… well people walk everywhere. I think I can do that there."

Rique looked over and said with a short bark of a laugh, "I'm trying to avoid commotion. It gets me into trouble." He had to admit, he wasn't minding his self-imposed isolation. He'd never felt better, and now that he'd refocused his energies on baseball, he was all in.

Mattie asked, "What kind of trouble?"

Without thinking, he swiveled his head to look at his passenger and a neck muscle spasmed in protest. As he tried to work it out, he admitted, "As you know, I tended to party a little too much. Like I told someone, I've turned over a new leaf. Shit. I should call Fifi and tell her I'm bringing home a guest."

"Who is this Fifi?"

"The Jacksons have gone for a little R & R before spring training. My sister hired her to house-sit and dog walk. She's been staying at the house since before I got there."

Mattie sounded incredulous. "Her name is Fifi?"

Not having her cell number, Rique thumbed the house's landline and it began to ring.

"Her name is Fiona but—"

Just then her voice came over the blue tooth.

"Hope you're not calling to see if I made dinner."

"You've made it perfectly clear you don't cook. I'm calling to tell you I'm bringing someone home with me."

There was a pause and then a flippant response that he wasn't expecting.

"I'm not leaving so you'll have to bring her to your room and stay there."

He blinked and could hardly believe that hurt as well.

"It's one of my new teammates. I've actually known him for a few months, and we trained together today. He's from Cuba and doesn't know anyone here, so I thought we could hang out."

"Oh. Do you want me to order in?"

Her voice had softened, and he thought it might have held an unspoken apology. That her nose had been out of joint with the thought he was bringing a female home made him feel warm and fuzzy for some reason. He couldn't stop the corners of his mouth from twitching into a smile.

"You might as well. I figure you've got all the delivery services on speed dial."

"Not all yet, but I'm working on it. What does he like?"

"I don't know. Say hello to Mateo Alvarez and then you can ask him."

"Hello Mateo Alvarez. Are you as much of a carnivore as your new friend?"

Mattie mouthed the word *carnivore* with a question in his eyes.

He mouthed back *meat eater.*

"Yes. I like meat."

"Okay, I'll see what I can rustle up. You almost here?"

"We are. Just getting off the exit now."

"It might take longer for the food to get here but I'm on it."

"Thanks."

"See you in a few."

He ended the call, a grin on his face.

"You like this woman?"

Mattie must have read the smile wrong. He was glad to be eating soon. He was ravenous.

"Just met her on Monday. She's...different."

"Different how?"

There was a look of interest on Mattie's face that didn't sit well.

"I get the feeling she's a science geek. One parent's a geologist, the other a mathematician, so it would follow."

"You haven't asked?"

No, he hadn't. There'd been no need to. He knew what she did for a living, although he still couldn't understand why. She had to be smart if her DNA had anything to do with it. You couldn't be dumb coming from that kind of genetic pool. And that scientific exposé on kissing had to come straight out of a geek textbook.

"Knowing where she comes from and what she does, I thought it would make her feel bad if I asked if her parents were disappointed in her."

"What makes you think they'd be disappointed in her?" His expression grew wary. "And why in the world would you put it like that?"

"Because I'm disappointed. She has a brain. She should be using it."

"There are people who don't understand why I am a ballplayer. They say the same thing, consider what I do a game."

"It takes intelligence to do what we do and do it well."

"It does but it takes a certain kind of person to take care of dogs. Patience, kindness, the ability to amuse."

He had to agree with that. She'd been the best entertainment he'd had…ever. She kept him on the edge. He never knew what she was going to do or say. And she constantly surprised him.

She played cards like a pro, knew her science facts, made angels in the snow as Hoover chased around her flapping arms. And she could kiss…

How would you know that? It didn't resemble a kiss in any way. Too light, too innocent, too quick.

What they said about less being more had proven true.

As they pulled into the driveway, there was a blue Beetle Bug in front of the garage door. It suited her and he could see her during the summer, the top down and singing at the top of her lungs. He liked the picture that had formed. He wondered why she'd left it out. She'd gotten dibs on the third stall which was empty. Was she planning on going out later?

Mateo snapped him out of his thoughts.

"Nice house. And they are everywhere. This is nothing like where I come from."

"There's a range. Big mansions, five-room Capes but a good percentage of the residents live well."

"I can see that."

Enrique hobbled out of the car, deciding to leave his bag where it was. He didn't want to walk the extra steps to the trunk. He could grab it when he got back from returning Mateo to his hotel. If his body hadn't atrophied by then.

The side door was unlocked and when he entered the mudroom, he called out, "We're here."

Mattie was taking it in, and when Fifi materialized, he smiled generously.

"Thank you for having me here."

CHAPTER ELEVEN

The new guy walked over to shake Fiona's hand, with an ease Rique lacked. Rique's steps were awkward, more a limp than a gait. She met Mateo's eyes and said, "I wish I could say *mi casa, is your casa* but it isn't mine." She turned her gaze over to Rique and added, "Tough day?"

With his hand on the counter, he stretched out his leg and rubbed his thigh muscles.

"You could say that."

Nodding her head in Mattie's direction, she asked, "Did he get to watch?"

She had that smirk on her face that he'd come to expect.

"No. We were tortured in the same way. He's obviously super-human…or bionic."

"Always puts out a hundred percent, so his anatomy is accustomed to hard work?"

He sniveled. "I'll get there."

"I'm not sure you'll get to the table."

"Once the food gets here, I'll find a way."

"You still have about twenty minutes. Get your wallet ready. I'm not putting out for the spread."

"I didn't expect you to." She heard a couple of his joints creak as he pulled out his wallet and handed it over.

Feeling somewhat sympathetic, and almost pleased that he'd worked himself hard, she asked, "Either of you want a beer?"

When she looked over to see if Mateo wanted what she was offering, he was wearing a lopsided smile as if he was enjoying their banter. He was dark and handsome and had the extra benefit of the tall piece, but he didn't cause the kind of tremors his cohort did.

Rique answered for both. "Sounds good, but only if you're willing to walk over and get it for us."

And it wasn't the new guy's smooth, accented voice that rumbled through her like thunder, it was that one.

The only way she was going to keep the longing at bay was to find the humor in the situation. His situation, not hers. On her way to the refrigerator to get the Heinekens, she said, "Why don't you find a chair to collapse in before you fall flat on your face."

He grunted in response. "Come on, Mattie, we'll eat at the table."

She shook her head. She'd have to set the table and serve, not something she was going to let him forget once their guest was gone.

There is no our. The guest is his. You're not part of a couple entertaining one of Rique's teammates.

With plates and utensils in her hands, she approached the two men, and as she placed the dishes on the table, she asked, "Which part of Cuba are you from? Havana?"

"A small town in Camaguey province. It's on the other side of the island."

"You're a long way from home."

There were a million questions she wanted to ask about his country, but she capped her curiosity, hoping things would come out during conversation.

"I am."

"When did you get here?"

"I flew in yesterday."

She felt her eyebrows quirk.

"You can do that? Just fly out?"

He explained how he'd left a few months ahead of the new standing, which she assumed had helped him navigate the rocky terrain of defection, and where he'd stayed waiting for his visa to be approved.

"You already knew each other then."

"A bit. Rique was rarely there."

He gave her a sheepish look, which lead her to believe he was too busy with his extra-curricula activities to be at home much.

"You fit the parameters set by the agreement?"

"I am twenty-six and have been playing for seven years, but I came too soon for that to matter. I had to go another route."

When he didn't elaborate, she said, "That's a long time to play professionally. You must have been a baby when you started."

"In my country the most treasured gift at Christmas is a ball and bat. My first was made out of a tree limb."

"Like a branch?"

"There is little money there, and few things one can buy if they had it to spend."

"You don't get paid to play?"

"Very little. We are expected to play for the glory of the homeland."

He sounded bitter rather than proud or patriotic.

"No multi-million-dollar contracts??"

"Not even multi-thousand-dollar ones."

Rique sounded as amazed as she was. "Cuban baseball is world renowned and you guys are local heroes. That sucks."

"It does. That is one of the reasons so many leave." He took another sip of beer before asking, "How long have you played?"

"I started when I was twelve."

Fifi looked down her nose at him. "Really? And you look like that after a practice?"

The doorbell cut off any chance for Rique to say something in his defense, and she left him with his mouth open as she went to answer the door, taking his wallet with her. What she found when she flipped it open surprised her. It wasn't the stash of money stuffed into the billfold, it was the picture of his entire family he'd shown her, tucked into a side compartment. It signified something...significant but she didn't dwell on it. She couldn't afford to buff his more positive traits.

After handing over the cash, adding a sizeable tip, she took possession of the bags and carried them over to where the men were sitting.

Rique was sniffing the air but made no move to rip the staples off and dig in.

"What did you get?"

She began to unpack the containers. Mattie helped with the second bag.

"A bunch of stuff. The menu was in Spanish. At least I think it was, so I had to improvise. They had a brief description beneath the specialty, so I ordered anything that suggested it was steak, oxtail, pork chops, or chicken."

Mattie's voice registered surprise. "This is mofongo. It's one of my favorite foods."

"I had no idea what it was, but it is made with plantains, so I figured why not."

Rique's eyes danced with pleasure. "Where did you find this place?"

"It's in Lawrence, where there's a large majority of Hispanics, Latinos, etc. And you being in one of those groups, I can never remember what qualifies as what, I thought it would suit."

There was amusement in his eyes. "I don't speak Spanish so I'm neither. My ancestors come from Portugal."

She made a face back at him. "That's right. Sorry. Didn't mean any offense."

"None taken. This might make Mattie feel more at home."

His teammate had already begun to eat, having taken a bit from every container. "Will they have food like this in Boston?"

"I'm sure they will. Is that where you want to live?"

"Yes. I believe I will assimilate faster. It is more diverse, I would think."

Rique seemed to be enjoying the fare and said to Fiona, without looking up, "You find the best foods."

Her chest began to puff in pride.

"I'm a pro at speed dial, remember."

"I am beginning to think it's a skill to be proud of."

The men were eating with gusto. If they'd worked as hard as it looked from Rique's stilted movements, they'd earned their gluttony.

But she was curious.

"What position will you be playing, Mateo?"

He wiped his mouth with the napkin she'd supplied and said, "Third base."

"That's right. Who played it last year?"

Rique was the one who answered. "No one person. They tried several over the course of the season. I think third base was their number one priority."

"Who else have they bought…traded…acquired?"

She vaguely remembered her Uncle Jim telling her the team was looking for a few good men.

"I told you about Sebastian Layden."

"Yes, he's been raised on your farm."

He sent a smile in her direction before adding, "They brought in a free agent, Rafe Verducci, a catcher who they call Verdi because he's a genius behind the plate, and a new closer, Milo Buzzley. He was dropped by the Brewers late last year."

"How does Verdi represent genius behind the plate?"

"He can compose a perfect game."

Okay, she got that part, Verdi, composer, Italian, but compare him to a catcher? "I thought it was the pitcher who did that."

With what looked like strained patience, Enrique explained, "Catchers are probably the most important members of the defense. They see every aspect of the field, are involved with almost every play and they call the game. It's their job to bring all parts into one whole. They also have to know how to handle the pitchers, know where their strengths and their weaknesses are."

Mateo added, "And they have to have an arm and accurate throw to decrease the odds of someone stealing. There are a couple of catchers I wouldn't dare try to beat."

"What do they steal?"

"Second base."

She shook her head. "Why would they do that?"

"The chances of scoring are better from second than first. All someone would have to do is hit a single to left to get the guy on second home. Runs are important. They win games."

She rolled her eyes. "That much I know."

"We really do need to get you to a game."

"I have a feeling I'd be more confused when I left than when I arrived."

"I have a feeling you're right. It takes years to understand the nuances."

"I'd rather be walking a dog, anyway."

"Why?"

Rique sound almost angry, as if it was beneath her.

"Walks are good for you, and I like being outside, engaged in a mindless activity."

"You like mindless?"

She felt her cheeks heat up.

"At times. It helps quiet the chaos."

"And what chaotic thoughts do you have?"

She blew off some steam in his direction.

"Where's my next meal, my next job going to come from, where am I going to find the money to support myself, pay my rent?"

Will anyone take a risk on me? Or will I have wasted all that time and money, all those long hours in the lab, burning the midnight oil, writing my dissertation.

She looked deep into his eyes, saw pampered, privileged, spoiled. She tried to look past those traits to see the kindness that prompted him to befriend Mateo, the winces that told her he'd given it all he had today. It didn't work.

"I don't think you'd know anything about those kinds of thoughts."

More quietly he said, "Walking dogs will not make you rich."

Duh.

Problem was, the career she'd chosen wouldn't, either, not until she was an established scientific celebrity, like her mother. Not that it mattered. She wasn't in it for the glamor, success, or money.

She glared at him. "Some people don't need to be rich to be happy."

He shook his hair off his face, took the last gulp of his beer, and said, "It certainly doesn't hurt."

His grimace suggested it hurt to move in any way. It shouldn't have made her feel this light and happy.

"Says someone who can't walk right."

"There's a price you have to pay to get what you want."

"I'm finding that out."

She wanted things that seemed beyond her reach and, fuck her, he was becoming one of them.

After they'd finished cleaning up, packing away the leftovers, Rique said, "I think there's a hockey game on. You want to watch or get back?"

"If you don't mind, I will stay a bit longer. I should get familiar with the home team. But you? Do you need to soak?"

"I'm good. I can do that later. It might help me sleep."

Hoover had behaved well while they ate, but now she was whining for some attention.

Fiona had gone to get her coat when Rique said, "You going out?"

"With my friend here."

"Oh, okay. Your car is still outside so I thought—"

"Shit. Thanks for reminding me."

As she shrugged into her coat, he said, "We'll be in the family room."

She freed her hair from beneath the collar, zipped up, and moved to slider. "Enjoy your game."

"Aren't you going to join us?"

She stopped short of her destination and looked back at him. "Nope. I don't only have an aversion to baseball, I have one to all sports."

She slipped outside after Hoover and watched her race around the fenced-in yard, seemingly happy to be free. The sky was clear, and the stars were out and visible. There had to be hundreds of them, all twinkling so very far away. She breathed in the clean air, thinking about Mateo and how far he'd come to do what he loved. Would she have to do the same? Leave home, move to an unfamiliar place where she didn't know anyone? Assimilate into a different culture?

Her specialty was the next big thing in genetics. There had to be someplace on the East Coast where she could set up her lab, some university or hospital willing to fund that kind of research. With the advancement in mass spectrometry technology, the field had been expanding to the point where scientists could now fractionate the complex protein samples for analysis. Because proteins did the heavy lifting in the human body, carried out every command issued by the genes along the DNA spiral, any mutation that occurred, happened at the proteome level. She thought they could be decoded but categorizing them all wouldn't be easy. That's why the research lab was so important. It could take years to gain any ground, but if successful, it would not only enhance scientists' understanding of the relationships between gene, cell, and protein, but it would enable doctors to prescribe the best medication and treatment for an individual system.

She closed her eyes, visualized what she wanted. A room that didn't have to be big, that housed her and a couple of doctoral students, a refrigerator for storing solutions, chemicals, and kits, a deep freezer where she could store cells, tissues, and proteins, an auto-clave for sterilization, an electrophoresis system for profiling her DNA fragments, and a gel documentation system, which she'd use to display those fragments after the profiling run. Okay, maybe the room had to be bigger than small, but she'd be willing to work in a closet if it fit the necessary equipment.

She saw it as clearly as she saw the stars overhead. She just wondered if her dream was also a million miles away.

When she returned to the warmth of the house, she could hear muted voices coming from a room down the hall. It didn't sound like the guys were watching hockey. The announcer was yelling something about the ball being out of there, and the talk in the family room was animated. The two things she knew about hockey: there were skates and pucks involved. Making as little noise as she could she walked to the edge of the room to listen in on the discussion and to take one more look at a bruised and battered athlete. Rique glanced back at the doorway as if he somehow knew she was there and his eyes all but lit up.

"Come here. You've got to see this."

He picked up the remote and rewound the play, making room on the couch for her. Nestled between the two men, she paid close attention as Rique described what she was going to see. It was one of the Greenliner games at the end of last season, when some guy Ovitz, hit a ball four hundred and thirty feet to win the semi-finals game for the team. She watched the first baseman take a couple of swings, balls flying in every direction but forward, and several balls he let go by before slamming it out toward the harbor. Then there was a lot of running by the team in green, and a lot of standing and watching by the team in white.

Rique asserted, "That guy is clutch."

"I thought you were going to watch hockey?"

"We found this when we were surfing and decided to dissect the second Greenie game of the World Series, instead."

"You do realize I have no idea what you just showed me or why it was important."

He met here eyes. He looked disappointed by her lack of enthusiasm.

"It's important because Ovitz is one of the best in the game. He always gets a hit in clutch situations and almost single-handedly got the Greenies to the Series last year. He's learned how to take advantage of the wind coming off the water."

"I thought it was a team sport."

"It is. That's why Mattie and I are watching this. We're part of the team now and intend to make a contribution. Mattie will probably bat third, with Ovitz as clean-up. That one-two punch should be enough to take us all the way."

Her eyes grew wide. *Clean-up? One-two punch?*

Not knowing what to say, not wanting to further prove her ignorance, she asked, "Where will you bat?"

"Mattie's going to work with me. He made a couple of good suggestions during batting practice today that helped. I've got speed but have lost my eye for the ball, so I'm not sure."

"What does speed have to do with it?"

"If I can get on base, and if the men who come after me get a hit, I can round the bases quickly and hopefully score. If I can't get my batting average up, though, I'll be at the bottom.

That makes sense.

Mattie said, "He'll probably lead off. It's the smartest place to put him."

"Because of his speed."

"Yeah."

She suddenly had a burning desire to see him play. Wanted to see him running, pivoting, doing the things Terry had talked about. Sitting next to him wasn't helping, the heat emanating from his body inching hers to boil.

"I'll let you two keep dissecting. I've got to get my car in the garage and then I'll take Hoover with me, but if you get back late, she'll probably nag you to go out one last time."

"No problem but I won't be late. We'll just watch the rest of the game and then I'll take Mattie back. I'm beginning to see the benefits of a good night's sleep and I'll have to soak first."

His eyes met hers, and for a second, she got lost in them.

She doubted she'd get to enjoy those benefits, because her body was coiled and ready to spring.

CHAPTER TWELVE

Rique watched her go, feeling her absence as soon as she was out of sight.

What was it that made him feel different when he was with her? He'd have to put her on the list of women he liked, even though she knew next to nothing about baseball. There'd been a lot of women on the list who didn't like the sport, they just tried to hide the fact because of who he was. Fifi was honest and direct. He always knew where he stood with her and it meant he could trust her. He liked that and was beginning to suspect that it was important in a relationship.

His mind wandered as the game continued, paying only the briefest attention to Mattie's attempt at conversation. When he said, "It's time for me to get back," Rique looked up to find the game over.

Mattie leaned back, his arm resting on the back of the couch, as if he'd changed his mind and decided to stay a while.

"You like her."

Had he been so transparent that Mattie had picked up on his thoughts? After hesitating for a moment, he admitted the truth.

"I do."

"Are you going to do anything about it?"

He chewed on his bottom lip and then shook his head.

"I can't. Wouldn't be fair. I'm heading to Rio to find a wife, so it would be only a temporary diversion." Although he was beginning to feel that diversion would be a road well taken.

Mattie asked, "You want a hometown girl?"

"Yeah."

The why was starting to wriggle itself into consciousness. Why did he think the highest standard for beauty lived there? He'd met many gorgeous women in the States, had bedded his fair share, so what was it that was pulling him back for the most important date of his life? The one at the altar. He had to consider that it was something other than beauty. The women there were more direct, less coy. If they wanted to talk, they would make eye contact. The people were more affectionate, kissed for the fun of it, and touched more. The women there also expected compliments, to be coddled, they handed out endearments like candy, and sarcasm was lost on them, an art the Americans excelled in. Was he merely seeking the familiar?

After finding his way back from his thoughts, he came right out and asked, "Did you leave someone behind?"

Mattie dipped his head, then looked around, making sure not to make eye contact when he said,

"No. I don't date seriously. I put too much energy into baseball to have anything left over for someone else."

He got the impression Mattie was not telling him everything, but he figured he had the right to do so. They still didn't know each other well enough yet to be confidants. His curiosity prompted him to ask, "Do you think you'll marry someone from Cuba when you're ready to settle down?"

Again, he avoided eye contact.

"That would be impossible because I can't go back."

Rique felt mildly curious. He threw his leg over his knee and asked, "What are the women like there?"

Mateo looked over and met his eyes, a downward turn on his lips. "Proud and temperamental. And some a bit free-spirited for my taste."

He joked, "That could be a good thing."

"If that's what you want. I would prefer a woman I could trust."

Rique felt his mouth dip into a frown. He'd prefer that as well. If he was to marry a stranger, would he find out too late that he couldn't? Shaking the doubt off, he asked, "What's it like there?"

"I'll tell you all about it while we drive. I've got to get some sleep if the coaches have another day like today planned."

Rique managed to maneuver himself back into the car, his body finally understanding what he'd done to it. It was in major revolt.

Mattie filled him in on some of the finer points on what life was like in Cuba that he'd skipped while in Brazil. He told him about his mother and the sacrifices she'd made for him, the house he'd lived in that had been passed down through the generations, real estate up until just recently unable to be bought and sold. It was certainly a different way to live, a culture that put the state before the individual.

When Rique pulled into the circular drop-off in front of the hotel, Mattie looked up at it, his hand on the door latch.

"It gets lonely here sometimes. I'm anxious to get to Florida."

"You're welcome to come back to Izabella's with me anytime. I'll be looking for a place as soon as my sister gets back, and then I can invite you to stay until you find a place of your own."

"I'm hoping Alicia finds me something soon. This weekend would be good."

"If you want company, I'm available."

"That is good to know. At least I'll be busy over the next few days. I like that

I'm working out again."

"Do you want me to pick you up tomorrow?"

Rique knew he'd taken a cab to the field this morning.

"I would. Thank you. See you then."

As he drove away, Rique believed he had his first real friend on the team. They were men from different countries, who spoke a different language, but who were looking for the same thing. A World Series ring. He should have spent more time getting to know him while he was staying with his parents. He was a good guy and if today was any indication, they were going to work well together.

The highway was empty, the darkness encompassing, but it lent itself to meditation. He thought about all Mattie had told him. Would the Cuban come to like life here? He had. For as much as he loved his homeland, he didn't want to live there anymore. His family was moving to America, one member at a time. First it was Jaco and Izabella, through no intention of their own, but they had become completely Americanized. He was next, with his move to Trenton. His sister Leia had met her fiancé in New York and was planning on moving there when they married. His parents had bought the house in the Hamptons to be close by. He wouldn't be surprised if they moved there permanently. His father was at retirement age and had done quite well for himself, although he couldn't see his father doing nothing. He could fly back and forth, consult, or get a green card and work here. Izabella and Jaco could bring them all here, being citizens. He was going to look into what it took to become one.

So why are you going to Brazil to look for a wife?

He knew the answer. He knew what he needed in a mate and he wasn't sure he could find her here.

When the image of a woman with dove-gray eyes and springy curls came into focus, he pushed her out. He was glad she was no where to be found when he got back to the house.

Finally alone, the house quiet around him, Rique stood in front of the bathroom mirror. Having discarded his shirt, he touched the bruised and tender skin around his rib cage. He had forgotten how much he hated that flat paddle. How many balls had bounced away from him until he got his rhythm back? And every one of them had bounced off his body as he tried to keep it close.

When he heard the gasp just outside the door, he knew it looked as bad as it felt.

"What the hell happened to you? Did they use you for target practice?"

He made the mistake of glancing over at her. She was dressed in flannel night pants and a tee, a robe thrown carelessly over it. He could see her nipples poking the material, and the tenderness in his muscles got commandeered by the look of her.

He sighed, not only at her concern but at his inability to reach out.

"This is what happens when you have let yourself become lax."

She made a move to step inside, her arm extended as if to touch one of the imprints, then stopped.

"Do you want me to rub ointment on you or something?"

He felt a prickling sensation at the thought of her hands on his chest. Her fingers weren't long, but they were feminine. She wouldn't be able to scrape long nails down his back, because they were short, but they were manicured. His pulse had quickened, and need was beginning to throb.

He shook his head, knowing danger when he saw it.

"I will be fine. These are signs that I am working hard again."

"War wounds?"

He nodded and asked, "What are you doing up?"

He wouldn't have disrobed if he'd known she was prowling around.

"I was hungry, thought I'd grab something to eat. What are you doing in this bathroom? You have an en suite, don't you?"

"I didn't want to climb the stairs just yet."

A smile slipped over her face, but she quickly apologized.

"Sorry. I shouldn't find humor in your suffering."

"After my telling you that I'm the best, and seeing evidence that suggests otherwise, I don't blame you for mocking me."

"I'm not mocking, honest. It looks like you've done what you promised. Although I didn't realize that new leaf you were turning over came in blue and purple."

He could do nothing but chuckle. "Mind if I join your raid? I'm kind of hungry myself."

Not only for food.

"Don't mind at all. I'm hankering for some of that chicken. I didn't eat much of the meat for fear the carnivores around me would cast their sights in my direction if there wasn't enough to satisfy them."

She was right to worry. Appeasing his physical hunger would be easy. It was the sexual craving that was becoming a problem.

When she met his eyes, she skittered away as if she read what was in them. It was desire, pure and simple.

"I'm sure Reid has a balm for bruises. Look in the cabinet, see if you can find something. I'll make our assault on the refrigerator."

She'd already made an assault on his senses, and it took him more than a moment to modify his penile discomfort before he could begin the search. He found a jar and was ready to bypass it thinking it was one of Izabella's moisturizers, but noticed the words muscle pain relief written in scroll across the front. He unscrewed the top and inhaled, then read the ingredients. He'd planned on soaking in the tub to loosen the knots that seemed to have taken refuge in every muscle in his body, but he couldn't pass up the other option of sitting and eating with Fifi, so he'd changed his mind. He slathered the balm all over his arms, chest, and thighs with deep tissue massage. He groaned as he did, believing he could have orgasmed, he was so tightly wound. He stopped just short of that goal and put his shirt back on. He left the jar on the counter, knowing he'd need it again before practice tomorrow.

After taking a breath, he went to find Fifi.

He made his way slowly into the kitchen, where she was sitting, two plates on the table, one empty, one piled high. As he eased himself into a chair, she was sniffing the air just like Hoover might have. "You don't smell bad. Did you find anything?"

He gave her a lop-sided smile. "I did. My sister must have found it on one of her essential oil websites."

He reached for the containers and emptied them one by one onto his plate.

"Thanks for ordering with Mateo in mind."

"No problem although I just guessed at what kinds of food they eat in Cuba."

He looked up into her clear gray eyes. They were soft like a dove, and for once the look was one of approval.

"It doesn't sound as if they eat all that well there. I think anything substantial would have been fine. You didn't need to order Hispanic."

"It was actually advertised as Mediterranean. I'm becoming a fan."

It was similar to what they'd had the other night. She was holding a piece of shredded chicken in her fingers. "He seems nice."

"He's talented. That's what counts."

"Isn't chemistry important as well?"

"Actually, more so in some cases. You'd know the science of that better than I."

He could feel her tense. "What makes you think so?"

He was ready to mention her treatise on kissing but shrugged it off and said instead, "You said your mother's a scientist, your father's a mathematician. Don't those kinds of traits get passed down the same way the color of my hair and eyes did?"

After pausing only for a second, she nodded and said, "Yes."

His fork was poised for another mouthful but before he brought it to his mouth, he said. "Explain it to me."

"It's all in the DNA."

"How does it get parceled out?"

Her eyes had narrowed as if he'd somehow uncovered a deep, dark secret.

"You're implying that I know about this."

"I'm implying you're a scientist, if not by profession, then by osmosis."

He heard her breath tremble out.

"My mother's a geologist, not a geneticist."

"Even I know a little bit about it. What I remember, and correct me if I'm wrong, is that my DNA is made up of all genetic material that goes back as far as…the big inning." He laughed at his own joke. "Some have said that baseball was taken right from the Bible…In the beginning, in the big inning. Get it?"

Her chuckle sounded like a spontaneous response to something stupid.

He rolled his eyes at her. "I take it you like more serious subjects. Back to my DNA. I have fragments of every person on my family tree, from all who came before, through reproduction. I should have a relative who's an athlete, which I do." He looked up to see her mouth slightly ajar and her eyes wide in surprise. Rather than comment, he went on, hoping, for some reason, to impress her with his depth of knowledge on a subject other than baseball. "I should have some of my father's financial skill hiding out somewhere along the double helix, along with my mother's social skills. I think you can even inherit things like curiosity and logical thinking from a parent or grandparent. You know some of my hand-medowns while I know few of yours."

He grinned. "Paint me a picture."

It was as if she were tongue-tied, and he now suspected she was holding out on him.

"I'll start it for you. You don't cook so you don't like puttering around the kitchen. Not very domestic from what I can see. Maybe you'd prefer a lab like your mother or some complex mathematical equation to solve like your father. You have intelligent eyes that seem to probe into the very heart of things and..."

He was going to say she looked like a nerd but thought she might take it wrong, so he kept it to himself.

"And...go on."

She was intrigued.

"The night we played cards, I got the impression you don't let your emotions control you. You can be playful or otherwise you wouldn't have gone outside and made snow angels for Hoover. You're organized, disciplined, and you're real. There's no artifice about you. How am I doing so far?"

She actually couldn't believe how right he'd gotten it, how well he seemed to know her already. And for him to know so much about genetics?

"Where did you learn this fundamental knowledge that you've entertained me with?"

"I took biology in college. It was broad based, but I got a rudimentary understanding of how it all works."

"How many years did you go?"

"For a couple in Brazil before I transferred here to the States. Then I had to choose between academics and baseball. I think it's obvious which way I went."

"Why did you leave when you did? They don't give you time to graduate?"

"They do, yes, but when I was drafted by the Mets in my third year, I dropped out and signed the contract. I wasn't sure there'd be a better deal than the one they offered. Besides, what was the purpose of majoring in sports broadcasting if I wanted to play the game, not call it?"

"You took biology for that?"

"I would have preferred human anatomy. Learning about muscles, bones, and organs would have given me information I could have used, but it was full up by the time I registered. During the first couple of years, they make you take lame things like science, math and literature so I had to pick something else."

Lame?

"You don't consider them important subjects?"

"Sure, for someone like your mother. Not for someone like me. What kind of subjects are available for dog walkers?"

There was a defiant gleam in those dark eyes, as if he wanted her to set him straight. She wasn't going to give in to the curiosity burning there. With a set of her chin, she said, "Kennel 101 and How To Avoid Crazy Drivers 322."

He gave her a soft chuckle as if remembering.

"You didn't do too well in that the day I arrived, am I right?"

"I had actually mastered it, but when you lose your focus, you don't see what's coming."

"Like a pitch or a ground ball. I can relate to that."

She understood the ground ball but, "Why a pitch?"

"The ball is coming at you at close to one hundred miles an hour, and you have to make a decision to hit it or let it go as soon as it leaves the pitcher's hand. If your attention is on something else even for a split second, you're either late with your swing or miss it entirely. Strike one."

A hundred miles an hour?

"Isn't that dangerous?"

"Only when the pitcher's pissed and goes for your head."

Her eyes widened. "They do things like that?"

He laughed outright. "Someday ask my brother-in-law about revenge on the mound. He'll have some good stories for you."

Reid did things like that? She'd always liked him. Now, she wasn't so sure.

"And the referees let them get away with it? I'd say that's intent to harm with a deadly weapon."

"They're called umpires and the pitcher can get tossed out of the game if it's blatantly intentional."

"It's not always intentional?"

"They usually have control of the ball but sometimes they slip up. They're out there to strike you out, not flatten you."

"And you have to stand there and hope for the best?"

"You usually know when a pitcher's pissed, and then you just pay even closer attention to where the ball's headed."

"What would make him that angry?"

"A batter hugging the plate, one of our pitchers losing control and hitting a batter in the previous inning, when one of our guys is hurt with a cleat while sliding, or some other misdemeanor."

"How do you a hug a plate?"

"By leaning too far into the strike zone."

She shook her head. One question answered led to another but he looked tired and she knew he was hurting.

"You should probably get to bed. You've got another round of torture set for tomorrow, don't you?"

"I do and you're right. Thanks for the supplemental meal."

He rose slowly and began to pick up his empty plate.

"I've got this."

He looked at her sheepishly said goodnight and limped off.

CHAPTER THIRTEEN

Fiona once again had morning coffee waiting for Enrique. She would have been up with the birds if they hadn't been finding warmth in places other than the trees, and she'd already gotten most of her chores done by the time he came down. She scrutinized the new gear, the word *Greenliner* running down one of the legs, and one a long-sleeved tee emblazoned with their logo, an old-fashioned trolley car. He seemed better this morning, hobbling less, but he turned up his nose at the pastries. He threw something at her, and she had to lean down to grab it.

"What's this?"

"One of the sweatshirts they had made last season before the playoffs. I picked up a couple of pieces of merchandise yesterday. Going in with my Mets tee shirt didn't go over well. I thought you might like one as a souvenir."

She held it out. Written across the front was the Greenie logo and the words *Bring It.*

He explained, "The Red Sox went with the phrase *Do Damage.* When they won, it changed to *Damage Done.* If the Greenies had won the series, they would have made new ones that read *Brought.* Maybe we can bring it next year."

She mumbled a thanks and put it on. It was a little big, but she didn't mind. It was warm and that's what counted.

"Looks good. First step in becoming a fan. Once I get my shirt, I'll give you one of those, too."

She glanced up to see him staring at her and it softened her resolve to stay in the neutral zone.

He broke eye contact and announced, "I need protein if I'm going to survive the day. Anything left over from our meal last night?"

She brushed the powder from the doughnut off her hands and shook her head. "We pretty much finished that off the second time around."

He opened the refrigerator to peer inside.

"Ha. Leftover stroganoff. I forgot about this."

After heating it up in the microwave and wolfing it down, he dumped his dish in the sink, along with the glass container. He grabbed a water and his coat and all but ran out of the house as if excited to get going, the prospect of pain apparently an appealing one.

He yelled a good-bye as he bolted out the door.

As soon as he did, she called her uncle.

"Hello, pretty miss. What's up?"

"Are you working today?"

"You know I have a three-day weekend."

She also knew he went into work every so often if one of his patients needed him.

"I was wondering if you could spare some time today to give me a baseball-for-dummies instructive."

"You want to learn the game? To what do I owe this miracle?"

He'd been trying to get her to a game since even before he hooked up with Reid's mother, but she'd always turned him down. She wished now she hadn't. Melinda loved the game, used to act as Reid's catcher when he was growing up, and Jim was able to enjoy his passion for the game, in a way he hadn't thought possible.

"I don't like being at a disadvantage on any subject and Izabella's brother is here. He talks, I listen, but no one translates."

"Come over for lunch. I'll make something to eat and then we can get down to business."

"Thanks, Uncle Jim. I just want the basics."

"That will still take hours, my girl."

"You're kidding? There's balls, bats, gloves, and bases."

"And a hell of a lot of intricate details in between, which is right up your alley."

He should know. He'd take care of her and Siobhan when they were younger and he still lived in Pennsylvania, stayed at their house when her mother was obsessed with some new finding and her father's job took him to conferences around the country. He was her mother's brother, another scientist at heart but who'd gone a different route. He was a healer, had given thirty years of his life to nursing in the oncology department at a children's hospital near Philadelphia and then one in Boston. He'd seen his share of death, which made him more sensitive than her parents, more affectionate and openly loving, and she adored him. When he'd moved east, she'd missed him more than she would have her parents, and he was one of the reasons she came to Boston for college.

"I actually figured that out for myself last night when I asked Rique what hugging the plate meant."

"I've got some saved games on TV, which I can pull out if you want a play-by-play."

"Do you have any of Reid throwing at a batter?"

"I might. It only happens when someone disrespects his strike zone."

"This sounds more like two rival gangs than two professional baseball teams."

"It does, doesn't it?"

There was a chuckle in his voice as if it were funny. She could only reply, "I never thought of it as a contact sport."

"It isn't, not like hockey or football, but you can get hurt out there." He changed the subject on a dime by asking, "How are the interviews going?"

"I don't know. The experience I have doesn't seem to mean shit. I've got one more scheduled for next Friday in Amherst. Then I go second tier."

"And second tier is..."

"Other."

"Hold out. You'll get something."

She would if she could afford to. It wasn't only that money was tight. She needed to sink her teeth into a project.

"I will as long as I can."

"If you need a loan—"

"Absolutely not. I'll manage."

"What good is it to have a family if you can't rely on them in times of...scarcity?"

"Are you sure you and my mother came from the same sperm and egg donors?"

"Pretty sure. If not, I wasted a lot of time with you and Siobhan."

"Then I'll have to take your word that you came from the same parents."

"Your mother was always more driven than I was, and she needed to shine. Our parents weren't exactly touchy-feely either."

"That gene should have mutated out."

"I think it did. Siobhan's a great mother."

"She isn't as driven as I am. Does that make me like you know who?"

"Depends. I'd like to think you're going to live a more balanced life. Find a guy, fall madly in love, have kids and close the door to the lab every night."

"I can't even find a job, never mind a husband."

"Hold out for that as well. It's usually worth the wait."

He should know. He was single until he met Melinda. He had lived with someone before that but the way he told it he wasn't very good husband material and the woman broke it off after six or seven years. It's what had prompted his move. He'd been wrong. He was excellent husband material, or maybe he'd just found the right woman for him.

"I don't think I'll have a choice. There's no one pounding down my door."

"When it comes, you'll fall flat, with the proverbial stars circling. We'll talk more when you get here. Say around noon."

"I'll be there."

They only lived a few miles away so it wouldn't take long. To kill time, she puttered around the house, did some wash, and spoke to her sister, who was on her lunch break. It was always good to talk to her and she gave her the pep talk she needed. They were close even though they lived miles apart. She got up there when she could, not wanting to miss many of her niece's and nephew's milestones, and Portland had a nice vibe for relaxation. She'd promised to get out there before spring, although she wasn't sure she'd be able to keep it. It'd be hard asking for time off if someone deemed to hire her. She grabbed her pocket book and keys, giving herself five minutes to go across town. Her uncle had moved in with Melinda before they got married, and she lived in the same town as Reid and his brother

Nolan. They were known as townies, a fourth generation that had roots here.

When she rang the bell, it was Melinda who answered. She was still in a wheelchair, having broken vertebrae in her back in an automobile accident when Reid was just a kid, although she used braces outside the house to get around.

"Welcome, Fiona. It's so good to see you."

Fiona kissed her cheek and dropped her purse on the hall table, the dog beside her excited to be here.

"I hope you don't mind but I brought Hoover with me. I didn't want to leave her alone for the day."

Melinda was giving Hoover a hug, rubbed his ears and got a whimper of happiness in return.

"Of course not. She's my buddy, aren't you, girl?"

Melinda had lived with Izabella during Leeni's recuperation, which meant she'd lived with Hoover as well.

Fiona followed her aunt into the family room, the wheels of her chair sliding across the hardwood floors with ease, the dog's paws scratching the surface. Melinda had only become that designation a few years ago, when she'd married Jim, but she treated her more like family than her real one did. Fiona was always welcome here and had dropped by for many a dinner while she was in school.

There was a fire burning brightly in the grate, spreading its warmth throughout the room. It felt good, but she hoped she didn't fall asleep during the lesson.

Jim hugged her and said. "I've got this all teed up and ready to go. Lunch first or should we take the time later as a break? You might need one."

"I don't want to take up too much of your time with this."

Jim sat in one of the overstuffed chairs and motioned for her to take the other. She stripped her coat off, unwound her scarf, and laid them on the back of the chair and sat.

"This is one of our favorite pastimes and we haven't seen a good game since October. We're both kind of excited about getting back to it."

Melinda had a warm smile on her face when she said, "The trucks will be leaving for Sanford soon. It's a red-letter day in this house."

She'd heard all about the trucks, like a caravan carrying gold.

"What's so precious about the cargo?"

Jim was the one who answered. "Everything you need to run a baseball team is transported, uniforms, spikes and turf shoes, bats, thousands of balls, batting gloves, jackets, helmets, golf clubs, bikes, and lots of other things. More than that, it signifies a new season is about to begin."

He'd pulled out a Greenies baseball cap from his back pocket and handed it to her. "You can't be a fan without one."

"Who said I was a fan?"

He must have noticed what she was still wearing. She hadn't taken it off since Rique had thrown it at her.

"Looks like I'm not the only one pressing the issue. Where'd you get the sweatshirt? Our new shortstop?"

She nodded, knowing Jim was reading something into it that wasn't written.

"If you want to know baseball, you have to pick a team. Only then will you feel the thrill of a win and the agony of defeat."

Melinda, who'd taken a position next to her husband, said, "The first year Reid was here, they had an awful season. It was hard to watch."

"So why do you?"

"For me, it's personal. My son plays. But once you've gotten the bug, it's hard not to."

Jim was leaning toward her and she could feel his enthusiasm. "I've been watching since I was a kid. And when my father would take me to a game, it was the highlight of my year. There's nothing like the smell of peanuts roasting as you walk toward the gates, the cheering of the crowd, the crack of the bat. All clichés but true. Your dad watches occasionally. It's a mathematician's kind of game. Lots of stats involved."

Fiona remembered him watching some nights before bedtime, but he never showed any real emotion, never the kind of animation that Jim was displaying.

"He did. He usually had a book in his hand, so I always thought it was on as background noise."

"Fans come in all shapes, sizes, and intensity."

The way they rooted for their teams showed the great disparity in personalities.

"Who's his team?"

"Phillies, which is another National League team." He chuckled. "We've made some serious wagers over the last few years."

That meant they'd kept in touch. That came as a surprise as well.

"Have you always followed the Greenies?"

"Since moving to Boston."

"Why them?"

What she was really asking was why not the Red Sox, the more popular team.

"Aside from the fact that Reid's played for them since I met Melinda and I love my wife, I'm a purist at heart. I never did like the designated hitter assignment. And there's something about going against the grain, rooting for the small hometown business instead of the big corporate entity."

"Explain about the hitter thing."

"When I was kid, pitchers were part of the hitting rotation, usually batting ninth. Most of them weren't very good. Still aren't. So back in the seventies, the American League changed that by instituting a non-position. The DH is merely a filler in the order for the pitcher, and he's usually one of the aging players who excels at hitting but has outlived his usefulness in the field. Yes, it's prolonged the careers of some of the greats, but if a pitcher's part of the team, he shouldn't get a pass. The National League has held out but there's talk of them finally capitulating. I'll be wearing a black arm band the day that happens."

"What happens when they play each other?"

"Whoever has home team advantage determines the line-up. At Harborside, the pitchers hit, at Fenway, they don't."

"Any other differences?"

"Nope. That's it." He glanced over at Melinda and smiled. "Other than having a son-in-law on the team. It makes it much more personal."

Melinda smiled and added, "Happy wife, happy life."

Jim picked up the remote and gave her an intro into what she'd be watching. "This game is one between the Greenies and Mets, when Enrique was first called up because the star shortstop had gotten hurt. He was with the team for a couple of weeks before being sent down again. Everyone thought he was going to be the next greatest thing since…sliced bread."

"But he wasn't?"

"He disappointed when he got there for good. He was used as a utility player, a pinch hitter, sat on the bench a lot. I think he's best when he plays every day."

"Isn't everyone?"

"No. There are some players who know their role and perform it well. It's what makes a great team great. I'm showing you this game so you can see the difference in his play when we watch something more current."

There was a sliver of unease with her uncle's explanation.

"Why is Rique playing a central role in this lesson?"

"You've come to me for a reason and I believe he's part of it."

She wasn't going to admit anything about *that.*

"I just don't like feeling dumb when he talks to me. I didn't even know there are umpires. I called them referees."

"When we're finished, you'll not only be able to understand what he's talking about, you'll know how he's played. You ready?"

"I guess." She sat back as the saved game began to play. She was anticipating boredom, but as she watched Reid pitch, her uncle explaining what each one was, slider, curve, fast, cut fast, which were his specialties, she began to feel the rhythm, tried to follow the trajectory as it spun toward the plate. When Enrique came to the plate, he gave Reid a small salute and a wicked grin.

Melinda pointed out, "They weren't related yet. Reid was still giving Izabella a hard time, so that wasn't a friendly gesture. It was more of a *Don't fuck-with me-or-mine.*"

Fiona was mesmerized by the swing of the bat, the power behind every stroke. When he got the right pitch, there was a resounding crack, and the ball went sailing over the outfield and left the park. There was another salute as Rique ran the bases, his leg muscles rippling, his strides long and sure.

Her aunt and uncle gave her a play-by -play of every hit into the outfield, every ground ball, and she concentrated most on the man she was living with, his body, just like Terry said, poetry in motion. She watched him dive head-first toward a ball, and somehow spring right back up and hurl an arrow of a throw to first for an out. He made a double play, flipping the ball to second base from a crouched position, shaving seconds off the throw.

He was third in the line-up, which her uncle dissected for her. The best hitters were up first, having more times at bat than those at the bottom.

"Mateo Alvarez was over for dinner last night. He's the new…third baseman, from Cuba. They were talking about him being third up, before the clean-up hitter. What's that?"

"Yeah, we know. He stayed with Izabella's family while he was waiting for his visa to be approved. They liked him. Said he was quiet and serious."

"I just found out that Rique already knew him before yesterday."

"I think that will work to Mateo's advantage. Keith's the one who arranged it and he usually knows what he's doing."

"Keith is?"

"Their agent. Signed both. Reid's best friend since high school."

She mused about that before getting back to her original question. "Why will Mateo be hitting third and what's a clean-up batter?"

"Third batter up is the best hitter, the fourth in line is the one with the most power. He's expected to drive in runs."

"How about the first? Mattie thought it was a good idea to put Rique there."

"He's called the leadoff. His job is to get on base, use his speed to make things happen. Steal second, take an extra base if the next guy hits a single. He needs to be patient, take as many pitches as he can without striking out, let the guys on the bench see what kind of stuff the pitcher has that day. Rique has the speed. I'm not sure about the patience."

She ruminated over that. It would take discipline. Her uncle brought her back by asking, "Time for a break?"

"Yeah. My head's spinning."

"I made tuna fish. That okay?"

"Sounds good."

When they sat down, she took a bite of the sandwiches made with sour dough bread, one of her favorites. They were accompanied by chips, carrot sticks, pickles, and cookies for dessert.

"We can have a question-and-answer session while we eat."

But once Jim got going, it became a tutorial as he filled her in on the draft, the stadiums, the leagues, the schedule.

She'd just crunched into a pickle and was fighting off the effects of garlic and dill and wasn't sure she'd heard him right.

"They play how many games a season?"

"One hundred and sixty-two. Only get a day off here and there and a lot of time is spent traveling across the country, playing more on adrenaline than sleep. They have to take good care of themselves or they burn out fast."

"Football players play once a week, right?"

"Yeah, and the hockey league mandates a few days off after so many games, and a week sometime during the season."

"Doesn't sound like the…The MLB, right?...cares about their members."

"MLB, major league baseball, and it's up to the coaches to take care of them. One of the reasons the Red Sox did well last year is the coach made sure the pitchers didn't lose steam going into the playoffs."

"How about the Greenie coach?"

"He's an old goat. Been around forever. I think they need some new blood there, but I don't make those decisions."

Melinda was wearing a wide smile as she patted her husband's leg. "Your uncle does quite well as a sideline coach, though. Tells Farina what do from the couch."

He harrumphed. "He rarely listens."

As soon as lunch was over, Fiona took Hoover out to pee, then they were back in front of the TV, a game Rique played last year on the screen.

"Mets and Greenliners are in the same division and play each other frequently throughout the season. In this one, the regular shortstop had a day off and dos Santos was substituting for him. You've seen him at his best; now you'll see one of his worst. He was sloppy, with a lack of focus, making three errors, one of which cost the team the game. The shortstop is supposed to lead the infield, should be the best athlete on the team. He has the potential but isn't living up to it."

Reid was pitching again, which was probably why they'd saved the game, and he struck Rique out every time he got up to bat. She noticed a different man standing in what she now knew was called the batter's box. Gone was the power, gone was the intensity. No wide grin, no evil smirk.

Instead it was Reid who'd saluted him after the last strike called, each and every time. Rique didn't seem pissed about it. He looked more resigned. It looked like he'd lost his passion. She thought his poor performance was due more to that than a lack of discipline.

"The difference is obvious. Even I see it. Is that why he was traded?"

"Not sure. It was a crazy move in some camps. The shortstop they have now will be retiring at some point and they've given away the next best thing."

"They gave him away? Do they exchange players, one for another?"

"No, they trade away the contract. I was surprised the Greenies picked his up."

"Why? Didn't they need someone in that position?"

She had no idea who played it last year, hadn't cared in the least.

"Napolitano is one of Farina's favorites but he's getting older and isn't talented enough to be a an all-star, in that position. Nilsson's the one that brought dos Santos in, along with the others. She's done a great job so far anchoring the team with young guys who just might get us that ring."

"And Nilsson is?"

"VP in charge of Player Development."

She considered all of this before asking, "Will Napolitano be let go?"

"No, they'll keep him on the bench as a utility player. It's a demotion but he's still on the team. That has to count for something. Have you gotten your fill yet? I don't have any more of Rique's games, but I have dozens of Reid's."

"I think I'm good. I have a basic understanding of the game, but I have to admit, it's kind of boring. There's a lot of downtime."

"That's because you're under thirty."

"What does that mean?"

"Technology is killing the fan base. Kids today want fast, instant gratification. They don't want to watch every game, every pitch. They watch the first three innings and if there's not enough action, they turn it off and catch the highlights at the end. They're fans but not longstanding ones."

Melinda added, "They might catch the throw that gets the runner heading home out, but they've missed the execution that led up to it."

"They miss the nuances."

"Exactly."

There was a lot to mull over but she wasn't sure why she'd bother. Once she was no longer living with a baseball player, she'd never use it again. She couldn't see herself sitting down to watch the whole game, even though it might be interesting to see if she could pick up those nuances her aunt and uncle had referred to. It had more to do with her love of patterns, how things worked than anything else.

"Come to opening day with us. It isn't for a couple of months, and you might have a job by then, but taking an afternoon to play might do you some good."

"I'd better have a job by then. If not, Mom will have interviews lined up all over the country for me."

"You've gotten good at keeping your boundaries in place."

"Only when I have good reason to. If I'm still unemployed, I won't."

Jim kissed her forehead. "You'll get something. I'm sure of it."

She leashed Hoover, wishing she could be as sure, and set off for Izabella's, her mind still a whirling dervish of facts. Maybe she'd watch another game when she got there, to pass the time. It had more to do with studying the patterns, seeing how things worked, and she suddenly wondered when she'd lost her mind.

CHAPTER FOURTEEN

By late afternoon, Enrique was worn out. Giving it all he had was taking a toll, but there was no way he was going to let his teammates show him up. The addition of Seb to the practice was a boon. The guy was a walking jokester and made the drills less daunting. He'd found humor in most everything, and they'd laughed all the way out of the training facility. Even Mattie, usually so serious, had cracked a few smiles.

The guy was as different from him and Mattie as day was to night. He was tall and blonde with a shaggy cut, blue eyes, and light complexion. He was home-grown, having lived in a small town in eastern Massachusetts, although he'd gone to Louisiana for college. He looked more like a West Coast surfer boy than a professional baseball player. He'd been picked up his last year at Tulane by the Boston team and had been in their farm system since, working his way up to the big leagues. He'd finally made it and he'd told them he wasn't going back. Today he'd proven his worth.

He'd also kept them entertained during the drive back to Harborside, with little tidbits about the team's history and the new park.

"Left field is different now than it used to be, no more nooks and crannies. All I have to worry about now is the plexiglass and the harbor. It would have been tough following in Calipari's footsteps. He was an icon and he covered that wall like he was part of it."

Mac Calipari had worked left field at Bogs for over a decade and had been inducted into the Hall of Fame as soon as he was eligible, not only for his Golden Glove prowess but for his hitting, as well.

Mattie asked, "What's he doing today?"

"He's manager of the triple A team in Pittsfield. Thank God I didn't have to play for him."

Rique narrowed his eyes. "Why? Is he tough?"

Seb scrubbed his face but before he could answer Leo voiced his opinion. "No.

He's done some good things there. He's approachable, communicates well and has a passion for the game that's transferrable."

Rique arched his eyebrow at Seb and the outfielder admitted, "I dated his daughter in high school…and let's just say it didn't end well."

When Leo had barked out, "What the fuck?" Rique thought it had to do with Seb's former relationship with Mac's daughter, but the burst of a siren grabbed his attention.

Red and blue lights were flashing just ahead of them, an ambulance pulling up to the side bay at Harborside. Enrique grabbed the seat in front of him, leaning forward to get a better look at what was going on. Seb and Mattie did the same. Leo brought the car to a screeching stop and scrambled out from the driver's seat, the rest clamoring out after him. After catching up with the EMTs who were rushing into the side entrance, he bellowed, "What the fuck happened?"

The man ignored him as he continued through the tunnel toward the offices. It was his partner who offered, "Possible heart attack."

"Who?"

Leo's tone held an anxious undertone.

She went ahead without answering his question, but when the medical team made a beeline into Farina's office, they all knew.

The female turned and said, "Please remain out here."

Todd Cantrell, the equipment manager, was pacing furiously outside the office. A couple of his assistants were standing off to the side.

Leo barked, "Well?"

Todd stopped, turned to look at Leo, his expression one of stunned surprise. Even though he had his fingers steepled over his nose, Rique could tell his skin was pallid. At Leo's command, he dropped his hands to his sides and explained between short, jerking breaths. "I popped my head in to ask how many sets of golf clubs he wanted to send to Sanford and found him slumped over, unconscious. He was cold to the touch and chalk white. I immediately called for help." He stuttered, "It doesn't look good."

Leo took up the pacing, and all Rique heard was a chant of "Shit, fuck," as he did.

He exchanged glances with Seb and Mattie, the three standing stock still, not knowing what to do or what to say. The smiles had been wiped away and in their place were twitches and blinks.

Was it as serious as Todd thought? Would it impact the upcoming season? What would happen if Farina couldn't come back? He was a crusty authoritarian, an approach that was going out of style in baseball management. He barked rather than talked, and he didn't like his role being usurped by the front office. There'd been talk about replacing him this season, and Reid had been surprised that he'd returned. With only one year left on his contract, he probably wouldn't next year no matter how well they did this season. Organizations were going with younger men, not the grizzled lifers who'd been in command of every aspect of the game and the team.

A few more members of the staff had congregated outside the office. One leaned against the wall. A couple were talking in low voices. There was a kinetic energy that hummed beneath the hush. It didn't take long for them to know the outcome.

When the stretcher was wheeled out of the room, a sheet was covering the manager.

Leo stopped cold, his face as white as a ghost.

"Holy shit." He looked up at the male EMT and asked in a hoarse whisper, "Is he dead?"

The covered body gave the answer, but Rique didn't think anyone standing there thought it was possible and they needed it to be spelled out for them.

"He was already gone when we got here."

They all watched speechless as the gurney was led to the exit.

Leo was scrubbing his face, a look of pure panic covering it. He looked up to see his three players standing mute, shuffling their feet.

"I've got to make some calls. You guys get showered. Everyone else back to work. There's nothing we can do for him now."

Rique thought there might have been tears collecting in Leo's eyes, but he turned away so suddenly he couldn't be sure.

The three players hadn't moved, their eyes still darting at each other, still not believing what had just happened.

It was only when Leo had disappeared from view that the three Greenliners ambled toward the locker room.

It was Seb who asked, "What the hell will they do now? We're so close to spring training. Bringing someone new in will shift the whole program off its axis."

Mattie asked as he stripped off his sweaty tee shirt, "Will they promote Leo? One of the other coaches?"

Seb shrugged his shoulders. "I have no idea."

Rique retrieved his phone from his bag. "I'm calling Reid. See what he thinks."

He wasn't willing to text this kind of news, not that telling him voice to voice would be any easier. Reid liked Farina. He'd cut him some slack when Leeni was in the hospital, when Reid was burning both ends of the candle. They had a mutual admiration for each other, and he knew Reid would take this hard.

When his brother-in-law answered, Rique hesitated, not quite sure how to tell him the news.

"Did you call to practice your heavy breathing?"

It was such a Crackerjacks thing to say. He'd usually laugh, but not this time. He knew what he was about to tell him would cut his legs out from under him and he couldn't find the words.

"No. Sorry. Are you sitting down? I think you should sit down. Is Izabella there?"

"I'm not sitting, and Izabella is in the other room. What the hell's going on?" His voice had taken on an edge. "Is it my mother? Your father?"

He paused and, with a rushed breath, said, "It's Farina. He had a heart attack. He's dead, Reid."

Now it was Reid's turn to breathe heavily into the phone.

"What?"

It was more croak than question.

"We found the ambulance here when we were finished with drills for the day. The EMTs are transferring the body to the morgue and Leo's making the calls now to let management know. What do you think they'll do?"

He could almost see the pitcher, his fingers massaging his forehead, his mind trying to make sense out of the insensible.

"I can't think that far ahead right now. Let me wrap my brain around this first. Okay?"

"Yeah. It's just Seb, Mattie, and I are a bit nervous right now. We thought we knew what we were getting into. Now? Our futures don't look as secure."

"This is so like you. This fucking disaster will affect everyone, not just you. I gotta go. I'll call you back later." There was a semblance of gratitude in his voice when he added, "Thanks for letting me know."

Before he could say anything else, Reid had ended the call.

He stared at the cell before putting it back in his bag.

"He's in shock. He said he'd call me back later."

He should have been more sensitive to Reid's grief. His brother-in-law had a working relationship with the manager, had formed a bond of sorts and had flourished under his guidance. Rique hadn't yet, and even though it was a gut-wrenching experience, he hadn't lost a mentor or a friend. To call Reid asking about the precarious future had been selfish but he was glad he'd made the call. At least the pitcher would have a heads-up and wouldn't be caught blindsided.

There was a heaviness that followed the three players into the shower room. No one spoke, the only sound that of water cascading against the stalls. Rique lathered himself raw, trying to wash away the feeling that he might find himself traded again. He had to keep in mind it was Farina who hadn't wanted to take the risk on him. The front office had ignored his sage advice so maybe…

Was he safe? He hoped so but he'd have to redouble his efforts, practice hard, show the new guy he had what it took to win.

He was the last one out, the others already dressed in street clothes. As he wiped himself off, Seb said, "I think this calls for a stiff drink."

He was on that page, even though he'd promised Leo he'd behave himself. These were extenuating circumstances, though, and he had a feeling Leo would be drinking heavily tonight himself. His job was at risk now, too. Managers always brought in their own staff and Leo might have held his last training session.

Mattie added, "Maybe two."

Just as Rique was tucking his shirt in, Leo walked into the room. He looked like he'd aged ten years.

"Will is contacting Farina's wife, letting her know, and is meeting her at the hospital. The management team will be meeting this weekend to discuss replacing him. And no, I have no idea who's in the mix of possibilities. Jordan will be issuing a statement to the media as soon as he lets everyone in the organization know what's happened. You've got the weekend. I'll be in touch about Monday. I have a feeling everything will be suspended until after the funeral."

Now that Rique had gotten into the swing and sweat of things, he didn't want any down time.

"Can we use the facility on our own?"

"Your job should be safe, dos Santos. It's mine I have to worry about."

Enrique chewed on the inside of his mouth, not knowing what to say to that. "You've set some benchmarks for me. I want to continue to meet them."

"Glad to hear it. You can be one of the best if you give it your all. Any manager they hire will expect you to do that."

"As they should."

"You can't depend on me to get you there. Discipline is a solo act."

Fifi had said something similar. Now it was up to him to clarify just what that meant. He had to set specific goals for himself, not off the field, like finding a wife, but on it. He knew where he wanted to go. Now he had to get to it, despite pain, adversity, and boredom. He'd let these things control him before. Now he had to reject them, grow into the role he expected himself to fill.

Leo looked like he was about to fall over. He stuffed his shaky hands into his pockets and said,

"Why don't you guys get out of here. Go have a drink. You had a front-row seat and I'm sure it had to have thrown you as much as it did me."

Leo shot Rique a look. "Just don't get crazy," and then he walked away, his shoulders slumped, his gait slow.

Seb sighed and issued a "Shit, fuck," of his own. He grabbed his bag and said, "You heard the man. Let's grab a drink. That drained the crap out of me."

It had blindsided every one of them. Rique felt disconnected from reality, as if it had all been a bad dream. Watching that gurney roll out had been hard, and he didn't even know the man all that well. What had it been like for people who knew him, worked with him, laughed with him?

Shit, fuck.

"Come on, let's get out of here. We'll hit the place the team goes after a game. It's not far from here."

It was a cozy pub that served the standard fare of hamburgers, fries, and beer on tap. It was a new hangout, not far from Harborside. Their old haunt was back in the Fens but the one thing that hadn't changed over the last year: the fans were a constant.

Seb followed him over in his own car, and they parked in the back, the lot not yet filled with night-time revelers. After entering, they sat at three vacant stools at the bar and ordered, the TV low in the background.

"Hey, guys. You Greenie newbies or wannabes?"

The stocky bartender was polishing the slate-black counter when he asked.

"Both, I guess. How could you tell?"

"Been serving ball players for over a year now. You all look the same."

Seb looked at both Rique and Mattie, his eyebrow arched.

"We do?"

The guy laughed and admitted, "Not looks per se, but the way you carry yourselves." He pointed the cloth at them, one at a time. "Third base, left field, shortstop. I'm a fan. I shut the TV off at night only after catching up on the latest

Greenie news. Welcome."

Seb introduced them by pointing like the bartender had, "Mattie, Seb, Rique."

"Knew that, too."

Rique thought, *There's something you don't know yet.*

But they didn't enlighten him. When he went to tend to other customers, the three sat quietly, draining their glasses and as they waited for a refill, Seb said, "Have any of you been that close to death before? It was a first for me."

Mattie concurred. "I'm glad I wasn't the one who found the body. You can smell it when death is in the room."

Rique was numb. Change was coming and he needed to be ready for it. He took a long swallow of the dark amber ale, licked his lips, then said, "I still can't believe it. It's going to seem strange not to see his face every morning."

And he'd only been there a week. What would it be like for the men who really knew him, Todd, Reid, Leo?

"I wonder when it's going to hit the news."

They'd gotten the group text on their way over.

"Shouldn't take too long. They'll want to get ahead of it. Now that everyone in the organization knows, it's sure to leak."

No sooner had Rique said that than there was a bulletin, the words *breaking news* flashing across the screen.

A well-known sports reporter, tied to the local station, was standing outside Harborside Field. He was set up in front of the darkened steel and glass structure, a mic in his hand, a grave expression on his face. The water behind him seemed to glisten in the background, chips of ice floating like broken corrugated wafers. Docked boats, lining the lip, could be seen farther down, and sailboats without sails were bobbing in a discontented sea. It reminded Rique of a black-and-white photograph, the exterior barren, the snow-covered streets and the naked trees the right kind of backdrop for the story to come.

Seb asked the bartender, "Can you turn this up?"

The stocky man picked up the remote and did as requested.

The reporter's voice now carried across the room.

"Late this afternoon, EMTs were called to Harborside Field, but by the time they arrived, Jethro Farina, manager for the Boston Greenliners, had succumbed to a heart attack. Farina was a fixture in the clubhouse for the last eight years and helped the team advance to the most recent World Series against one of their rivals, local adversaries from the other side of the city. We will be awaiting word as to who will take over the team with his death, but we will bring you reports as they come to us. This is Nick Murphy, Channel Five News."

Quiet had descended on the patrons in the bar as the news filtered through. Then there was a rush of commentary about the manager, the team, the future. Most of the talk had to do with the replacement. Names they were all familiar with were being bandied about, and any one of them could be the successor. It was anyone's guess at this point.

The bartender gave them an intense stare.

"You knew?"

Seb nodded. "Upper management told everyone before releasing it, so yeah. That's why we're here. Drinking." He lifted his empty glass. "Another round, please."

Before they had time to blink, their glasses were replaced with new ones.

"These are on the house."

Rique said, "Thanks," and then asked, "Did you know him?"

"Not personally. He never came in, but I've heard lots of stories from the players who did. I think they'll miss the old goat. Any inside information about who'll be replacing him?"

Seb took a large swallow before placing his glass back on the countertop.

"Yours would be as good as ours."

He looked at his two companions and asked, "Another?"

Rique was ready to agree and took hold of himself. *Don't get crazy* ambled through his brain.

"I'm out." He looked at Mattie and asked, "You want to come back with me tonight? Being alone will suck."

"If you don't mind, that would be good."

Rique then asked Seb, "How about you? Will you be alone?"

"Only if I choose to be. I'm just not sure it would be fair to go out with someone in this kind of mood. I wouldn't be good company."

"Why don't you come as well. We can commiserate at Reid's."

"Can we eat? I know I shouldn't be, but I'm famished."

Rique had been ignoring his growling stomach, not wanting to admit he was hungry under the circumstances. Now he had an excuse to find food.

"I'll call Fifi, have her order something. It'll be there by the time we get back."

Mateo shook his head. "Her name is Fiona and she has very good taste in food."

Seb was licking his lips. "A home-cooked meal would be great. There's something comforting about that when you've faced death."

Rique snorted. "If that's what you want, you'd better find someone else to provide it. Fifi doesn't cook. She orders in exceptionally well, though."

Seb threw some cash on the bar, covering all of them, before rising and shrugging into his coat.

"The company is really what I need. Where are we headed? You said Reid's?"

"Yeah, I'm staying at his house until I get my own place. It's about twenty-five miles north. You okay to drive?"

"Two beers don't make a dent."

"Then let's go."

When he made the second call in two nights for some food delivery, Fifi was uncommonly civil.

"I heard the news. I'm sorry about your loss."

"It's a team loss. They're bad enough on the field but off is much worse."

He told her about arriving at the field just in time for him to be pronounced dead. She commiserated with him and ended the call saying, "I'll take care of dinner."

"Great. There'll be three of us. Mattie and Seb were with me when it happened.

No one wants to be alone."

"You're paying."

He couldn't help but smile. It was the first since practice.

"I am."

CHAPTER FIFTEEN

Fiona made the call to yet another delivery place. This time she went with her mood, knowing it would definitely satisfy the meat lover in Rique. He'd added another man to the mix, and she'd understood why. She could only imagine what it had been like to see that stretcher pass by, knowing the man lying beneath it had held their futures in their hands. With his death came uncertainty.

She'd already heard the news about Farina from the TV before he called although she didn't know that he'd witnessed the ordeal at the time. She'd been waiting to hear the weather report and was playing tug-of-war with Hoover when the story broke. She remembered her uncle's opinion of the man, that he was one of the dinosaurs, with a bite as ferocious as his roar. Would the front office now have the option of bringing a friendlier, kinder man into the role? Having only been introduced to the game this morning, she had no idea who that might be. She wasn't sure anyone knew. Reid certainly didn't.

Izabella had called soon after the announcement, letting her know that they'd be cutting their vacation short and mentioning her husband was as much in the dark as everyone else concerning a replacement. They were coming back for the wake and funeral, which they assumed would take place sometime that coming week. Once they returned, her services would no longer be needed. She'd be back at her own small condo soon. She scanned the open space, knowing she'd miss all the room to roam. Suddenly her arm itched, from a prickly sensation that felt like a worm crawling under her skin. Though she hated to admit it, she'd also miss the man she'd been house bound with.

He was spoiled and pampered, used to having his own way, but there was also an underlying sweetness about him that made the flaws less annoying. He loved his family, took care of his friends, even the new ones, and was doing his best to change his attitude. At least out here in their shared space. When she got back from her uncle's, restless and kind of bored, she'd peeked into his room, where his true colors shone. It was a mess. He'd left both lights on, and clothes were scattered everywhere, the sweaty ones heaped in a pile as if he'd just dumped them out of his bag and left them. There was an empty water bottle on his nightstand, an empty bag of chips on the floor by the bed, which was unmade, a wet towel heaped in a ball on top. By the looks of the rumpled sheets, he was a restless sleeper, and when she began to imagine him tossing and turning, she'd scampered out. She couldn't afford such dangerous thoughts.

She'd taken Hoover for a walk right after, to clear her head. The one that Terry had suggested barged in every time she closed her mind on it. The cold air chilled her to the bone but did nothing to tamp down the heat that washed over her when she thought of him. She didn't understand the attraction. She'd seen lots of good-looking guys before, worked with some, and she'd never been affected this way. Never felt the need to climb into an entanglement that made no sense. He'd be a complication in a very orderly life. And her life was that.

She was a loner. She'd spent years wishing she were an extrovert, the life of the party, but she'd proven over time that she didn't have it in her. She'd never be like Enrique, who had tons of energy and charm, who could talk to anyone, at any time and in any place. He felt good when he was engaged, thrived in a group. She didn't have the stamina for small talk, nor the patience. She lacked the kind of stimulating conversation people like Rique sought out. She did serve one purpose though. She was the audience they were looking for, but she'd found out along the way it didn't serve her. No matter how well she listened, connected, engaged as soon as she'd start to reply, the person she was with would turn away as if what she had to say wasn't valuable. She'd given up pretending interest because it was never reciprocated. She preferred to give her energy to someone who appreciated it rather than be depleted by the insincere. Rather than force herself to be polite, she'd stopped going to parties, concerts, gatherings of any kind. She was comfortable with nine, maybe ten people tops. More people than that and she'd fade into the woodwork, her energy sapped and drained. She preferred to have deep discussions about important issues, like philosophy and ethics, meaningful interactions that were of benefit, to satisfy her curiosity or improve her life. Better to be alone than with someone like Enrique dos Santos. Even for a night.

The food had been delivered just before she heard a voice in the mudroom. There was no accent attached, so she knew it wasn't Mattie or Rique. When three men emerged into the kitchen, their faces were creased in sadness, their moods somber. The stranger was American through and through, blonde and blue-eyed. All three could have made the angels weep.

He stepped forward, his arm outstretched. "Hi. I'm Seb Layden. Nice to meet you, although I wish it could be under different circumstances. We won't be much fun tonight."

He glanced at the table after meeting her eyes in greeting. It was set with four dishes, the containers of food arranged around them. She glimpsed a wolf's hunger.

She gulped when Rique put his arm around her neck and leaned his head against hers.

"It's been a tough day, Fifi. Meeting death has a way of…making one vulnerable."

"I can imagine it could."

There was a rush of longing. She wanted the gesture to mean something, that he needed her for solace, but she knew better. This was a natural expression of his nature. He was a man who touched without thought.

Seb countered, "I'm just glad he was gone when we got there. It'd be just my luck if he keeled over while sitting across from me discussing the upcoming season. Ugh."

"Not a time to make jokes, my friend."

"I'm not." Seb, gave an involuntary shiver. "It could have happened. I was in his office before we left for the facility this morning."

She felt the arm squeeze her closer, as if Rique had given that some thought. Any one of them could have been witness to it this week. Trying to get her body under control, Rique being much too close for comfort, she relayed what information she had.

"Reid and Izabella are coming back earlier than scheduled. He talked to the owner, but he didn't learn anything new on what direction they're going to go, manager wise. The only thing Larsen said is they have a couple of names at the top of their list."

Rique released her and took a seat at the table.

"Not a great way to be promoted. Come on, let's eat before it gets cold."

Seb pulled out a chair and sat. Matteo waited for Fiona to choose and tucked her chair in when she did. There was a strange look on Rique's face, and he held it until Seb said, "Wonder if Leo's being considered." He'd uncovered one of the containers to find ribs. "Shit this looks great."

Fiona, usually good at masking her thoughts and feelings, spoke with unintended fervor.

"I ordered every sauce they had. Jamaican, mustard, habanero, Greek, BBQ, garlic and parmesan. Got three orders of them, advertised as ten bones of the meatiest ribs you'll find anywhere, coleslaw, and fries."

She took a breath to calm herself and opened her smaller container. Needing another dose of air, she took a moment to inhale the aroma. She glanced up to find Rique half-way out of his seat, asking, "What did you get?"

"A Chicago burger. Everything you'd find on one of their famous hot dogs." She lifted the top of the roll. "Pickles, onions, mustard, relish, and sauerkraut."

She always went for the plain cheeseburger, but she was feeling kind of daring tonight. She'd been doing that a lot since Rique arrived. It wasn't a good omen.

"That won't fill you."

He'd gotten to know her better than she liked.

"I have an order of fries as well."

"What will you pick at tomorrow?"

"There's still some of the munchies you bought the other day. And I can always pick up some myself."

"Oh, I forgot." He reached back and extricated his wallet.

She put her hand up to stop him. "My treat. You can call it a sorry-for-your-loss meal."

She didn't really have the money to waste on feeding three men with man-sized appetites, but she couldn't bring herself to accept payment again. He'd become her own walking ATM.

He murmured an, "Are you sure?" and with her nod, a "thank you."

Seb was holding his ribs by the bone, waiting for their private conversation to be over. When it was, he said almost impatiently, "Back to my question. Think Leo has a shot?"

Rique shook his head. "If anyone currently on the payroll gets it, it'll be the bench coach."

As if needing time to digest this, Seb licked his fingers clean and they could all hear the pucker as he did. In between smacks, he said, "I think they'll go outside to hire."

Fiona couldn't help but notice the difference in eating styles between the two men. Rique had a more refined set of manners and she had to give him credit. There wasn't a speck of sauce anywhere except the napkin he was using. She'd been doing the same but had somehow gotten mustard on her sleeve. As she attempted to hide the evidence, Rique said, "What if they hire from outside the inner circle but inside the system? Like the guy coaching the Triple A team?"

Blue eyes shot up at him, Seb looking totally unhinged.

"Holy fuck. Don't even suggest that. I might as well just run back to Cranston. I'll never get on the roster. He hates me."

Rique's face registered stunned surprise.

"He'd let his animosity rule the field?"

"With me, yes. His women, wife and daughter, are everything to him. Beware any man who hurts either one of them."

Fiona asked, "And you did that?"

"I didn't mean to. It…I… Casey and I were inseparable for the last two years of high school. When I left for college, I…told her I thought it would be better if we dated other people. She had us on the road to marriage and I…needed some single time before I got there."

"She didn't agree?"

"She didn't like that I felt that way."

"Did you ever *get there*?"

His head dipped down. "No. I never did."

When he looked back up, he met her eyes. "It should be ancient history by now, but he holds a grudge longer than most men are alive."

Mattie gave his opinion. "You might be wasting the energy worrying about it. What are the chances they pick the one man who'll have it in for you?"

She barely heard Seb's strangled words. They were said under his breath. "It would be just my luck."

After taking the last bite of her burger, she excused herself, left them to talk baseball. She might have a better understanding of the game than she had this morning, but she couldn't compete with players.

Rique was quick to ask, "Where are you going?"

He'd grasped her hand, holding her in place, waiting for her answer.

The tingles were back, the feel of his skin against hers touching something inside of her. She could feel the callouses at the ridge beneath his fingers, the strength in his grip.

She made the mistake of meeting his eyes and all but fell into his dark gaze.

"I was going to let you play with your friends."

The stutter in her answer made her feel foolish and immature.

As if Seb read something in the interaction that wasn't there, he got up, lifting his empty plate, and said, "We should probably get going."

He looked around for somewhere to throw his refuse and she signaled the draw under the counter, barely able to think coherently with her hand still clasped tightly. Mattie was up and following suit and smiled when Seb said, "I'll take this guy back to my place. He can stay the night."

She fumbled, non-pulsed. She'd be left alone with a man who did too much to her system.

"You don't have to leave on my account."

"I'm not, honest. This was great and I appreciate it, but it's getting late and I have a bottle of scotch at home that's calling to me."

Was that how he dealt with adversity? She glanced back down at Rique and he smiled up at her.

"I told them I was done imbibing for the night. The last thing Leo said to me was *Don't get crazy*. I figure I should stay on his good side just in case he gets a promotion."

He scooted his chair back and released her hand so he could see them out. His words carried over his shoulder as he did. "Don't go anywhere."

She cleaned up while he was saying his goodbyes, her hands less steady than she would have liked. There was something going on between them that she didn't understand. She stilled at the sink. Wasn't there?

She had no experience at this, while he had years of it. He could probably have a meaningful relationship with anyone, just as he suggested. If the woman had what he needed, could provide what he was looking for, he'd be satisfied. Her, not so much. She was much more selective.

So selective she hadn't been on an honest-to-goodness date in over a year. Physicality had never played a big role. It was the mind that interested her...until now. With Rique she felt a rush of desire that was unfamiliar, a throbbing ache every time she just looked at him.

When he came back in, he leaned casually against the door frame, and watched her. She usually felt invisible and had to admit she preferred it to this…intense focus.

"Why did you get up to leave?"

"I thought you'd want to commiserate together."

He was a people person, loved being entertained. Did he expect her to fill that role? He had to know by now she wasn't good at chit chat.

"I'd actually rather be alone with my thoughts. It wasn't a pleasant experience."

He righted himself and walked over to her.

"As soon as I finish up here, I'll leave you to them."

He moved in and she felt confined by his closeness. He leaned down and whispered, "I didn't mean alone, alone. I'd rather talk to you than them."

She bristled, caught off guard by the proposition. She had a deep curiosity as to the why. Another game?

"I thought you were saving all of this…attention for your blushing bride…whoever that might be."

"I'm Brazilian. I think it fair to say we can…attend…to more than one at a time. With no ulterior motive whatsoever. We love people, love connections, are good at juggling emotion."

No ulterior motive.

"Are you saying there's no deception here?"

"How would I deceive you? You know what I'm planning. I just happen to…need your company tonight."

Her expression was one of disbelief.

He almost laughed. At himself. He didn't understand his need to be with her any more than she did. All through dinner he'd kept glancing over to find her listening intently to the conversation, curiosity written all over her face. She was filled with it, with a strong desire to learn, to define, to analyze. She didn't seem to like talking, but when she did, it was meaningful, had substance. He'd always preferred that to useless chatter.

"Let's sit. You can tell me what you did today." He gave her a crooked smile that held some sadness. "I bet it wasn't as…life-altering as mine."

She let him guide her to the family room. He automatically put the TV on, wanting to see if there were any new updates on today's event.

"How about a fire? It's cold enough outside to warrant it and I'd love to feel the heat. Death has a way of chilling you to the bone."

She nodded, took a seat on the couch, and watched as he efficiently set kindling on the grate, a couple of logs on top, and some newspaper beneath to get it going. The match flared when struck, and before long, the flames were dancing skyward.

He dropped down beside her, pleased with his work, and for some reason, pleased by the way she'd followed his every move. With the remote in hand, he pressed the button for a news station. He didn't have to go any further to find what he was looking for.

A montage of the coach's life was being presented. He sat back against the cushion to watch, felt the body next to him, Fifi's proximity alleviating his distress.

Jethro Farina. Husband. Father and grandfather. Played second base for several teams during his ball-playing days. Began his second career as infield coach, was promoted to bench coach and held that position until he took the reins of the Greenliners and pushed them toward the World Series with a relentlessness that the front office admired and encouraged.

The reporters had tracked down several members of the team, Reid among them. In a phone interview, the pitcher had issued all the platitudes one would expect upon someone's death. Anton Bellasario, the center fielder, who'd played for the man his entire career, had offered his biased opinion. Motts, one of their catchers, had provided a story that proved Farina had a heart.

He wondered how the players actually felt. The man was a gruff old geezer who didn't tolerate much. Were they being kind or honest in their assessment? Was there a kinder, gentler man beneath the surface that he hadn't had the time to see?

Next, Larsen appeared onscreen. They were re-televising part of the interview he gave earlier that day after news of the death had been released. When he was asked who was on their short list for replacement, Rique sat up.

The man was impeccably dressed, as he always was, his voice controlled and smooth. He looked the part of distinguished owner and was adept at keeping his opinion close to his vest.

"We're giving ourselves time to grieve our loss. It's too soon to dissect the future."

"Have you been in contact with anyone yet?"

"All I'll say is that we're exploring our options."

"There'll be speculation."

"I'm sure there will be. As we don't know where this search will lead, speculation won't serve any purpose. With nothing further to add, I'll turn it over to the president for questions and answers."

He left the podium, to be replaced by Krasnick. The cameras never left the youthful face, but he was giving nothing away. He pointed to Murphy, one of the sports reporters, who must have had his hand raised.

"As president, will you be looking in a new direction, for someone who can communicate better with your players?"

"Farina got results, last year proof of that. We'll be looking for someone who can command the respect of the team while working with the talents and skills that each individual player brings to the table."

"Will you want a person who's on board with the way of calling a game, a more analytical and statistical bent?"

Farina hadn't liked having to base his opinions on something other than his own gut and experience. He'd resisted the new information age as stubbornly as the bulldog he was.

"Every tool should be utilized, but with common sense."

Krasnick's answers were brief and to the point. Letting everyone know he was done, he said, "Thank you. We'll keep you up to date on the search, once it begins."

He stepped away from the mic.

The screen now featured another one of the reporters who covered the team exclusively during the season.

"The Greenliners front office has been evasive as to who's on their list of replacements. We've taken a look at their philosophy, their talent pool, and have come up with three possibilities. The first is the bench coach, Elijah Garces. Working directly with Farina for the last seven years, he'd be the best one to take them down the path already paved. Second would be Wayne Scherger, the manager still on the market who might be worth a shot. Third, and this is where the real buzz is, would be Mac Calipari. Currently manager of the triple A team in Pittsfield, he's taken the team where no man thought they could go. An icon in left field during his heyday, already indoctrinated in the Greenie culture and history, he'd bring a fresh perspective that might get them over that bump, the one that kept them from a World Series ring last year. This is all speculation to this point, but odds are one of the three will be sitting in Farina's old office before the end of next week. This is Lorenzo Lind, Channel Four News."

He could feel her eyes on him. "I hope Seb isn't watching this. It might ruin his evening."

"He might not want to admit it, but Mac would be a good choice."

"Why?"

He glanced over, her eyes cool and appraising. He knew she'd expect a logical explanation, so he gave her one.

"Managers are trending younger. I think the guy's in his late forties, and from what I've heard he understands the dynamics of younger players. What worked twenty years ago is becoming outdated. He'd bring a fresher perspective, more fluid than Farina's. He's brilliant, well-respected. His number's been retired, and it adorns the wall in left field, even though he never played there. And over the last year, the trend in hiring practices is experience-not-needed."

"What did the reporter mean by adhering to analytics and statistical data?"

"It's become a numbers game. Maybe that's why they can hire the untried, men without managerial experience. The computer spits out the most efficient moves. Take a pitcher out now or leave him in? Check the stats. Want to pull a player who doesn't hit well against a lefty? Which available hitter on the bench has the best odds?"

"I wouldn't think using equations as a basis for winning would be valuable in a field like this. Experience should count for something."

"A lot of teams are hiring what they call information coordinators. Educating players on how they are evaluated, statistically speaking."

"Like on their launch angles?"

He jerked his head to look at her. How the hell did she go from knowing nothing to knowing about launch angles? The computer geeks had come up with another stat that measured the vertical angle at which the ball hit the bat after being struck. The new data had dramatically changed the philosophy of hitting. Ground balls were out; balls hit in the air were in. It had resulted in a higher number of homeruns offset by a higher number of strike-outs. It *was* changing the game. It was reducing the action across the nine innings.

She shrugged at the look on his face.

"I read about them before you guys got back. My uncle said those kind of stats are ruining baseball. Taking away the excitement of the swing, stolen bases, the bunt, said there should be more than one way to hit a baseball. Melinda told me Reid groused about it. He had to drop a couple of his bread-and-butter pitches and go more with the high fastball and well-placed breaker."

He was amazed by the breadth of her knowledge, the amount of information she'd taken in and absorbed.

"And when did you have this discussion?"

"You never did follow up on what I did today."

"You picked up the phone, called your uncle and asked…what?"

"I actually went over for lunch. Melinda knows as much as Jim."

"I can attest to that."

"We watched a couple of games he'd saved. He gave me pointers. I know the difference between an ump and a referee now."

He chuckled. "What else did you learn?"

"That you lost your passion for the game."

His smile faded. He didn't know what to say to that. He'd lost the incentive to keep his enthusiasm high. Was it the same thing?

"Not exactly. I still love the game. What I didn't like was sitting on a bench."

"Were you designated a utility player?"

"I guess, in a way. I was more in-line to inherit the shortstop position, but I began to think it would never happen."

"From what my uncle says, the utility players won it for the Red Sox last year, so they must have immense value."

"They do, but in my mind—"

"You were better than that, too important to be such a mediocre addition to the team."

"That's not exactly true, either. They have to be talented athletes to play every position."

"Interesting how you refer to them as they, as in, other than me."

He squirmed in his seat. She was right and it said something about him that he didn't want to acknowledge. Those who knew their role, played all out to fulfill it, were the true heroes of any winning team. He had felt it was beneath him and had played half-heartedly as a result. His haphazard play had created tension and trust issues, so they'd traded him. The move had dented his ego, but recently he was looking at it as a new start. But he knew his attitude had to change.

How would he cope if a new manager brought in another shortstop? Would he still give it his all or would he carry his irritation onto the field with him?

"I guess I have to work on my mental discipline."

"You either have an affinity for it or not."

He lifted a single eyebrow at her. "Are you saying that I can't affect my attitude?"

She was chewing on her lip, a tentative expression on her face.

"Personality is partially related to your genetic make-up. Psychological differences, say, between you and me, are caused by whatever DNA we inherited. To some extent there are dozens of traits that fall into heritability, and traits that emerge in childhood tend to create patterns in how you think and behave. Your appetite for attention is one of them."

"So, what you're telling me is I was born with an antipathy for mediocrity."

She chuckled. "We all have a dislike for inadequacy. What I'm saying is that you like being at the center of things. It's part of who you are. There's nothing wrong with it. I'm on the other end of the spectrum. I am more of an introvert. I don't like crowds. I don't like superficial which translates to I don't like small talk. I tend to listen, but sometimes I absorb too much and feel drained, whereas you come alive."

"Are you implying that I'll never be able to discipline myself mentally?"

"No, but you'll have to work harder at it than, say me. I come from a long line of disciplined scientists. We're logical, analytical, organized, married to rules and tradition and systematic investigation. It's not something I brag about. There are times I'd give anything to be more gregarious like you."

"But if you were like me, you wouldn't be you."

"I'll concede your point."

Her laugh unbalanced him. It was musical and hit him in the gut.

CHAPTER SIXTEEN

She'd given more of herself away than she'd meant to, or rather he was stealing parts of her, one piece at a time. But this was where she was at her best. One on one, exchanging ideas, on intellectual topics. What had surprised her was he had a facile mind and she knew she could probably talk to him about anything.

"You're not a dog walker by trade, are you?"

She glanced over and smiled. It seemed he was out to get it all.

"Not by trade, no."

"What exactly did you go to school for?"

"Science, just as you thought."

"What branch?"

"It's a field, not a branch."

"I stand corrected. If based on your treatise, I'd say it might be the elements of kissing, but if I had to make a guess, it would be genetics."

She blushed at the memory of her passionate response when she'd rebuffed him for kissing her. It seemed to have made an impression, one she didn't dare dwell on.

Dipping her eyes, she admitted, "Your intuition is working tonight."

"You don't have a job yet?"

"Bingo again."

"You're just doing this for pocket money."

She met his dark eyes, so lethal to her well-being he should carry a permit for them.

Taking a breath, she said, "It's never in my pocket for long." She forced some calm and a smile into her answer. "Although by you being here, I got a boon in the form of a raise and a few paid-for meals."

"My sister gave you more money because I'm here?"

"Yes. She asked that I stay and make sure you didn't destroy her house."

His facial expression was comical.

"How could she think such a thing?"

"I believe you're known for your parties. Then there's the mess you'd leave in the sink. She had visions of coming home to mice nicely fattened by your leavings."

"I have an aversion to mice myself so I would have gotten around to it. And I told her my partying days were over, at least while I'm in training."

"She could believe you?"

His expression read hurt and it was almost cute. "Do I keep my word? Most of the time."

She took a sip of the water she'd brought in with her and shifted her eyes in his direction. "Not only when it suits your purpose?"

He curled his lips in, didn't answer. Was he unwilling to incriminate himself?

When another clip about Farina came on, he raised the volume.

The repetitive clip didn't surprise her. It was Boston, after all, and it was a big sports story, one that would monopolize the news cycle until after the funeral and maybe even beyond. There'd probably be comparisons made between Farina and whomever was chosen as manager, player reactions, editorials on quality and substance.

She was watching him as he was watching the screen, both of them in rapt attention. His profile was compelling, his nose the perfect shape and size, his jaw strong. His full lips were slightly open as if he was still dazed by what had happened.

She let her eyes flutter shut, the coil of hunger tightening with her intimate inspection. She felt so much, about him, for him, lust, she guessed, but who could blame her? He was the prime example of a male specimen, athletic, handsome, and, she was coming to suspect, intelligent.

The thought of satisfying such an unfamiliar need was making headway, through all the qualms and insecurities that plagued her. She'd slept with a few men, the first time more out of curiosity than any sexual feeling evoked. The second with her boyfriend from college, who she'd been with for close to six months. It was uninspiring and something she found she could live without. No one before had caused her heart to stutter or her nerves to sizzle, and it was easy to side step that part of her life because she was so consumed by her work. Since meeting him, it was a whole new ball game.

She was acutely aware of his body, which was only inches from hers, the emanating heat more potent than the fire. Even with the intensity of her emotions, the hunger gnawing at her gut, she felt...not relaxed...not with the kind of tension vibrating through her, but as if she'd found just the right environment to feel cozy and snug. Their discussion had given her an even better understanding of the game and how he played it. Now she'd been given permission to sit without speaking, and in the silence, her mind had shut off, something that rarely happened lately. She was tired and she let herself float away.

She was awakened by the doorbell. And one of Hoover's menacing barks.

She forced her eyes open, trying to avoid the sun streaming in through the window. She was still on the couch, Rique asleep beside her, his head resting against her shoulder, snoring lightly. The loud bong hadn't breached his slumber. Neither had the barking.

After gently moving his head, she crawled up and stretched. A second hit of the doorbell jarred her system, propelling her toward the door. She glanced at the clock on her way, not quite believing she'd slept in so late.

Who the hell was here? Could Seb or Mateo be back? Melinda or Jim come for a visit?

When she peered through the window panel to the left of the door, she gasped.

Her mother and father were standing on the front stoop, her mother's face expressing her impatience. After sliding the bolt, she opened the door and her mother wasted no time entering.

"It's freezing out there, Fiona, and why on God's green earth are you still sleeping? It's after eight."

"Hold that complaint, Mom. I have to let Hoover out."

Her mother had been trying to avoid the wet, welcoming tongue, but her father was giving the animal the hugs she'd been waiting for. Hoover liked nothing better than to feel appreciated.

"Come on, girl. Let's go."

She got caught up in Hoover's legs, who was sidestepping her on the way, and almost tripped.

Rique, who'd finally been woken by all the commotion, caught her and set her back on her feet. She whispered, "My parents are here."

After she unlocked the slider, Hoover scrambled down the steps, just as Rique asked, "Did you expect them?"

She pushed her hair of her face, and croaked, "Gawd, no, or I would have been awake and ready for them."

"Take your time. I'll handle it."

He missed the weak smile she offered in return for his graciousness.

She could hear Rique's voice as he introduced himself to the Barrows and invited them into the kitchen for some coffee. She hoped he'd make it. She sucked at that domestic task like all the others.

The cold air made her gasp as soon as she stepped out onto the deck. She could have just let Hoover out and remained inside, but she needed time to gear up for her parents' unexpected visit. What the hell were they doing here and why hadn't her mother mentioned a visit when she last spoke to her? Edgy, she wanted to get back inside now, afraid her mother was being her assertive, sometimes obnoxious self. She watched impatiently as Hoover raced around the yard before finding a place to squat. Her teeth were chattering when she slipped back inside, the dog running ahead.

Her mother teetered on one of the stools at the counter looking totally out of her element. Her father was having an in-depth conversation about baseball and the Greenies' prospects now that Farina was no longer in the wheelhouse. He knew a lot more about the game than he'd ever let on, and there was some passion there that had been unexplored. The scent of freshly brewing coffee filled the room.

Her mother looked over and gave her a full-body scan.

"I didn't realize you had company, or I would have called before arriving."

"I don't have company. Enrique is Izabella's brother and is staying until he finds his own place."

"Then why are you here instead of looking for a job?"

Fiona crossed her arms against her chest, as if to hold in the anger that was rising.

"I have a job at the moment, and it involves staying put until the Jacksons come home."

It was easy for Clare to look down her nose from her perch. "Fiona, this is so beneath you."

"I know, Mom. You've already told me that, but I made a commitment and I'm keeping it. The job ends Monday, so it will have to wait until then."

"I compiled a list—"

While Rique was pouring coffee into mugs, he cut in. "Fi…Fiona, why don't you go take a shower. Your parents want to take you to breakfast."

Before she could send him a grateful look, her father said to the new shortstop "You're more than welcome to come with us."

He looked up at Fiona, questioning her with his eyes if she wanted him along.

She nodded, grateful there'd be a buffer and someone who could carry the conversation through an hour-long meal.

"Coffee before you go up?"

She nodded vigorously as he handed her a cup dressed just the way she liked it.

She raced up the stairs, not wanting to leave Rique alone too long with the Queen of the Inquisition. Her mother would probe and dig, looking for answers to whatever she was obsessed with-his ethnicity, his gene pool, the scientific probability of earthquakes in Brazil.

She fumbled as she stripped down, clambered into the shower. In and out in record time, she dressed and returned to the bosom of her family, just as her mother announced, "Yes, I understand you're gone all day, but for God's sakes my daughter has her doctorate in genetics. Her brain is going to wither away if she doesn't get back to it as quickly as she can."

Rique's jaw dropped when she entered, his eyes widened as if in stunned surprise before a scowl took over his expression. He was staring intently, and she was becoming unnerved.

"My brain is not going to wither away. I've only had the degree for a couple of months."

Rique rasped out, "That's what's kept you busy." As if he was still trying to wrap his head around what her mother had told him, he asked, "You're a doctor?"

His lips were pursed, and she remembered how they felt on hers. At the moment, she'd trade her degree for another one of his kisses. Flustered, knowing his opinion of her had changed, she stuttered, "No. Yes. But not in the way you think."

His hands were on his hips. "How would a person address you?"

Her mother replied for her. "Dr. Fiona Barrows."

She rolled her eyes, just like she had when she was a child. Her mother had that effect on her.

"*Fiona* would be fine. Your turn to shower. If you still want to join us."

His expression was unreadable. She couldn't tell if he was angry at her or disappointed.

"Yes, I do. I think there's a lot I don't know that would be interesting to learn."

His tone suggested the former. He was angry.

"I'm exactly the same person I was yesterday."

"Yesterday I thought you walked dogs for a living. A little more background would have been helpful."

She sputtered out, "You never asked."

His voice rose in volume.

"I shouldn't have had to."

"You would have looked at me differently."

His eyes gleamed at her, as if that's exactly what had happened.

"We can discuss that later." He began to walk away, his hand knuckle deep in his hair as if he were going to pull it out in frustration. "I'll be as quick as I can."

He left the room, giving her a backward glance as he did. The look was penetrating.

Fiona emitted a long, deep sigh.

"Thanks, Mom. That was smooth."

"Obviously he didn't realize that you're wasting your time here."

Fuming at her interference in her life, yet again, and finally having enough of her heavy-handed opinion, she barked, "Taking time off was important for my mental health. I went straight through. Nine years of academics, writing papers, researching, experimenting, analyzing. My brain needed a break. I took one. It hasn't been a waste of time. Deal with it."

Her father said casually, knowing he was taking a risk, "You took two years off between undergrad and applying for your doctorate. Fiona knows what she's doing. Leave her be, Clare."

"I just don't want her to lose her momentum."

"Sometimes, Mom, when you're climbing a mountain, you need to rest. It doesn't stop you from achieving the summit, it doesn't even slow you down, it gives you the stamina and energy to keep going."

Her mother clicked her tongue against her teeth before she said, "I don't want you to lose hope."

Fiona blew out a breath. There was always an underlying fear to her mother's assertiveness. It was as if bulldozing her way through, no one would notice the doubts that clung to her confidence.

With more patience, she said mildly, "I won't. I love my research, but I'm realistic enough to know I may have to gain some experience before anyone gives me my own lab. You got that before UPenn, I might have to do it now."

Fiona dumped her coffee out and put the cup in the dishwasher before turning and asking, "What are you doing here, anyway?"

"I'm attending a symposium in Worcester later today."

"You never mentioned it before."

"I got the call last night asking me to fill in for someone. We left right after I agreed, stayed over in Connecticut. Being so close, we decided to drop in, check on you. I worry." She licked her lips and met her eyes. "Maybe I shouldn't."

Fiona felt the weight of expectation fall away.

"I hope you're taking advantage of having such a handsome young man at your disposal."

She flashed a look in her mother's direction. Clare was idly inspecting her nails as if the question wasn't a time bomb.

"What?"

"He's very good-looking. Impeccable manners, a sophisticated air about him. Very international."

"And so very much out of my league."

Rique was still standing at the bathroom counter trying to regain his balance.

When Fifi had walked into the room she'd assaulted every one of his senses. So used to seeing her in jeans and a sweater, he wasn't prepared to see her so feminine and...heart stopping. Dressed in a gray turtle-neck dress, with what looked like silver snakes winding around her hips, and short gray ankle boots with tights, she was a picture to behold. Her hair framed her face, which was discreetly made up with some blush and mascara. She'd looked almost...beautiful.

Compounding that new image was the fact that she had her doctorate. Wasn't she too young to be that schooled? How much discipline had that taken? How many late nights, studying, compiling data, foregoing any kind of life?

Dr. Fiona Barrows. He snorted. *Definitely not a Fifi* but yet the name still fit.

He looked up into the mirror. Laughed at himself for possibly the first time ever. He'd jibed about her being a dog walker, of not having ambition, of needing to marry so she could live a life of ease. She'd shown him up on every front but had never countered his attacks on her dignity. Had she ever lived a life of ease? It didn't seem it. Her mother was a task master and he wondered how much pressure she'd put on Fifi to achieve what she had. He had a burning need to know everything about her.

He pulled his cell out and called his sister. He needed a calm voice in the midst of such confusing thoughts.

The first thing Izabella asked was, "How are you doing?"

"I'm a little off-kilter."

"I know it must be a confusing time for you, but whoever they bring in will give you—"

"Not about that. I didn't really know the guy so I can't be taking it as hard as Reid. It's about Fifi."

"Enrique, you have to stop calling her that."

He spun around, massaging his throbbing temple.

"I know. I know. Why didn't you tell me she doesn't walk dogs for a living?"

"I...I didn't think it had any bearing on...anything. She finally tell?"

He ground his teeth in frustration. Why had she kept him in the dark about it?

"No. Her parents were in the area and stopped in, and her mother mentioned it."

Not merely mentioned it, crowed about it.

"You've been living in the same house for close to a week now. You're telling me there wasn't an opportunity to ask her?"

She'd always led the conversation away from herself and back to him and…he'd let her.

"I guess I should have."

"I bet you never veered from you as the subject. Would have been nice to seem interested in a life other than your own."

It would have been. He'd spent the week making her feel inadequate, insisting that she'd put her time and effort into something insubstantial. Maybe it had more to do with her making him feel that way and he was just getting even.

Izabella interrupted his thoughts. "We'll be home Monday. You have just a couple of days left to make it up to her. Ask her about her life, Rique. It's interesting even for someone like you."

He already knew that, even before he knew about her extensive education. It was more about how she walked in the world. She knew who she was, what she wanted, knew her weaknesses and didn't apologize for them. And she was fucking driving him crazy.

He showered and dressed. He'd put on a good pair of trousers, a white shirt and suit coat, but skipped the tie. It looked as if they were going to an upscale place, something he never would have expected. It was his element, but he never would have thought it was hers.

He returned to the kitchen to find the family more relaxed than when he'd left. When Fifi looked up at him, there was a gleam that sparkled. It was another sucker punch to the gut. He wanted things he shouldn't want. Not if he was going to move forward with his plan.

Clare retrieved her coat from the back of the stool and said, "Good. Now we can go. Our reservation was for nine o'clock and if we don't leave now, we'll be grossly late."

"It's just around the corner. Shouldn't take us long to get there."

"Why don't you follow us. We'll have to get on the road soon after if I'm to be in Worcester on time."

"Why don't you follow us, seeing that I know how to get there."

"Fine."

When she stood, Rique realized how much taller than Fifi she was.

His lips twitched when he asked, "The height gene skip a generation?"

"Nope. Just me. My sister's almost as tall as my mother."

He assessed both of her parents and grinned. "The mailman's looking more on target."

She gifted him with a smile back. "You wouldn't say that if you'd seen him."

He escorted her to his car, opened her door, and watched her climb in. She'd left her coat unzipped and she struggled into the confining space, he got a peek at some thigh as her dress inched higher. Not bare-skin thigh but it caused the same kind of damage to his heart rate as if she'd been completely naked.

She regarded him with amusement. "Ever think about buying a car for comfort?"

His eyes crinkled at her in return. "Where's the fun in that?"

She shook her head at him, her curls creating a halo around her face. She almost looked like an angel, the penetrating gray eyes holding him spellbound.

He closed the door and scrambled to the other side. Her parents' car was idling in the drive-way, waiting for him to get moving.

He pulled out with a screech, his adrenaline off the charts, but immediately took his foot off the accelerator in an effort to slow it down. Her mother had already derided his choice of careers, made him sound like a boy who refused to grow up. He'd just given her one more reason to think that. And the car itself spoke to his need to look successful, something else she'd eschewed, suggesting that the less power one had within, the more one tried to compensate. He wasn't compensating for anything. He liked speed, and he liked the way the car handled. It might look expensive, and it was, but it had nothing to do with making up for what he lacked. Did it?

There was little time to talk, her directions coming quickly, one right after a left, then another right and they were pulling into the parking lot. They were on the outer rim of a campus, the old brick building looking historical and stately.

Absentmindedly he asked, "What school is that?"

"Phillips Academy."

He'd heard of it. A couple of presidents had gone there. The ones with money.

"Prestigious."

"One of the best. Very international. You would have fit right in."

"Did you go there?"

"No. When my mother pushed for the second-grade jump, she wanted me close by so she could make sure she hadn't overestimated my skill level."

"You skipped grades?"

"Yes. In second and then in sixth."

"That would have made you…how old when you went to high school?"

"Twelve."

He turned his head slowly to look at her. He was ill equipped to handle his high school years at fourteen, all those hormones, along with peer pressure.

"And you managed it?"

"Survived would be a more accurate description."

Her mother tapped at the window, then wrapped her arms around her middle to offset the cold breeze that was in the air.

"Is there a problem?"

Fiona pulled at the door lever and opened it.

"You've opened up a can of worms that I'm trying to seal back up."

"What do you mean?"

She shook off the question, knowing her mother wouldn't understand the answer anyway.

"Nothing. Let's eat. I'm hungry."

He followed the women, who were strolling arm in arm along the paved walkway.

Pat came up beside him and offered, "They get along better than it looks. Clare will always see her as her baby, which chafes, but Fiona has always gone her own way. It's something Clare respects even if she doesn't always agree with the path."

"Fi...ona's been pushed to achieve what she has, from my vantage point."

"She would have reached the summit no matter how long it took. Fiona's always had intelligence and grit. What she didn't accomplish with one trait, she accomplished with the other."

Grit. Determination. Mental discipline. She had it in spades. What she must think of him? That was easy. Spoiled and pampered. He'd never minded before, but now? He didn't like the way it felt anymore.

Pat hurried forward to open the door for his wife and daughter, who'd waited as if it was expected.

By the time he entered the elegant restaurant, Clare had already given the hostess their name.

"Come this way, please."

CHAPTER SEVENTEEN

Once they were seated, Fiona opposite him at the four-seat table, he looked around. It had the ambience of something out of the past, the dark wood, white linen tablecloths, the crystal water goblets. It was upscale in a town known for its wealth and status, but he couldn't see Reid or Izabella dining here. Too stuffy but maybe just right for an academian, and Clare certainly looked that part. She was supposedly famous for her work and she had the elegance and grace that Fiona… He glanced over to find her eyes on him, the intelligence so clearly written there. No, Fifi lacked nothing.

Her eyes hadn't left his even as the black rectangular menus were handed to each of them, and there was another shift of the ground beneath his feet. He didn't understand it. She was nothing like the woman he had in mind for himself, yet there was something about her that pulled at him. How long would he be able to ignore the heat of the attraction? It was more than carnal; it was mental as well. She intrigued him and that was even before he knew what she did for a living.

After placing their order, he asked, needing to know what her future held, "What exactly was your thesis about?"

Her mother was the one who responded. He was beginning to think that happened a lot.

"It's quite technical. I'm not sure you'd be able to understand the scale or substance of her dissertation."

He stiffened. Did Clare think him a simpleton? He'd done well at university, could have chosen any career given his academic achievements, but because he played baseball…

He struggled to keep his irritation from showing but he failed as his defiance filtered through.

"I know what that involves. My sister has been accepted at the university to further her studies in paleontology. She'll begin her research after the year sabbatical she took to search for bones."

Clare's eyebrows shot up. "Really?"

He smiled at the thought of Felicia and her summers spent digging for dinosaur fossils.

"We lived in Sousa, the only place in the world where visitors can walk along fossilized tracks. It was one of her favorite places and when she was old enough, she went on her first expedition. She'd found her dream and her passion, and she was hooked. Within miles of our home there are vast stretches of unexplored graves. In fact, she was part of the team that just discovered the oldest long-neck dinosaur that they've dated back to the Triassic period." He gave Clare a wry smile as if she wouldn't know what that was. "That dates back to two hundred and twenty-five million years ago."

"I know what the Triassic Era was. I've studied the earth's composition at each of its turning points."

The tone was laced with irritation and sarcasm. He'd gotten under her skin which was what he'd meant to do. She'd gotten under his with her constant harping on Fifi's shortcomings. When he noticed a smile playing at the edge of Fifi's mouth, he studied it. It was a nice mouth, soft lips…

His eyes rolled up at the thought of the pressure, the texture…

He wasn't used to ignoring such attractions. If he wanted a woman, he went after her. But in this case, he couldn't. Fifi knew his agenda and he was convinced she'd never give in to such a shallow interaction.

Getting to know her better might not help his libido, but it would go a long way in making him strengthen the connection. For some reason he needed to.

Directing the question to her, he asked, "What exactly did you research?"

"The alteration of proteins in gene mutation."

His mouth dropped open. "And that is, exactly?"

"Do you remember what proteins are, from that biology class you took?"

"I remember the words amino acids. And I think they come in chains. That about sums it up."

"They are composed of amino acids and they do form chains, very long ones, that are folded into complex shapes, along with some other ingredients. They are actually the worker bees of the body, so if a gene mutates, the protein is what does the dirty work, producing the disorder or disease. You can't really tell from looking at it what's packed inside the chain, so you can't tell what it's doing. If we can figure out how to see inside, and then catalog them, we can treat individual disease more efficiently."

She'd explained it to him in a clear and concise way and he got the gist of it, but there was far too much involved to become conversant in it. It made him even more impressed with her credentials than he'd been before.

Her mother, not to be outdone, added, "It's a new field, one that requires a painstaking number of samples and has a long list of failed experiments. This is what Fiona's dedicated her life to and it's extremely important work."

Clare was right. The world needed her, and he could see her succeeding. Would she need to sacrifice her entire life to scientific discovery, or could she incorporate those other things that made it worthwhile and enjoyable? She needed someone to coax her out of her shell, make her laugh, lighten her very heavy load. He wanted her to end up with someone who could respect her value to science, be willing to compromise, take on some of the domestic responsibilities that came with marriage and not someone like him who wanted a wife at home, in his kitchen and his bed.

The image of her there was like a flash of lightning, the roar of thunder pounding in his head.

It was almost suffocating in its intensity. He took a sip of coffee, choked it down.

"Boring, right?"

His eyes flashed up to meet hers. How could she think she was boring? Her eyes had lit up when she spoke, making her glow. That alone would have kept him listening. Her enthusiasm was catching.

He gave her a knowing grin.

"Not any more so than baseball. There are some people I know who don't want to hear about the intricacies of the game but it's something I could talk about all night."

She returned his grin.

"I know."

Their eyes met with a force that shimmered through his body. When he heard her father clear his throat, he refocused his energy.

"You said you've had a couple of interviews. Where have you applied so far?"

"Harvard and one of the hospitals in Boston."

Impressive places. She was shooting for the stars.

"How'd they go?"

"Disappointing."

The waitress had come over and placed their meals in front of them. He flicked his napkin open and put it on his lap, watched as his three companions did the same. After tasting the omelet, he said, "Reid has a contact at the Dana Farber. Maybe he can ask around, see if anyone's willing to lend you a lab."

She laughed but it came out as more of a scoff.

"Finding someone to *lend* me a lab might be easy. It's the funding part that will get in the way. No one's willing to take a chance on someone so young."

Her mother's ire was up but this time it wasn't directed at him. "Fools, but not surprising. Youth, on top of being female, puts her at a distinct disadvantage."

He had to admit it was still a man's world, but it was changing in increments because of people like the Barrows women.

He asked between bites, "How much would you need?"

"Millions."

His fork stalled and he gulped. "That much?"

"The equipment alone would be prohibitive."

Clare explained, "The university I work at funded me to start, but I had to find other investors to keep my lab open."

Fifi gave her mother a steely glare.

"Writing grants has never been my strong suit."

Her mother returned the look in spades.

"No scientist likes to waste their time and energy doing it." She turned her eyes in his direction and added, "Fiona has yet to come to terms with the fact you must do things you don't want to in order to succeed."

He gave her mother what might have been a scathing look. Was she kidding? Fifi was twenty-five years old and had accomplished more than most at that age. It was also a scathing commentary on his own life. He'd been handed everything and had come up short. He had a feeling that she could have been given more than she had been. Her parents had to be doing well. Well enough to ease her way but they'd only doled out expectation and criticisms, from the look of things.

He looked up at Fifi abashedly, committing himself to being the best he could be, his gene pool be damned.

Pat changed the subject smoothly, as if he'd been doing it most of their lives and directed the next line of questioning to him. He probably felt it was safer territory.

"I get to a Phillies game now and then. I'm going to make it a point to get to one of the Greenies games this year. Your team has a bunch of new players I want to check out."

Fifi sounded more than surprised. "Uncle Jim said as much. When did you start attending baseball games?"

Pat had finished his waffles and pushed the plate aside. It didn't take the waitress a minute before coming over to claim it and refilling their coffee cups.

"Years ago. I never thought to ask you or Siobhan. You weren't interested in anything that had to do with sports."

Fifi huffed out, "I'm beginning to think I missed out on a topic as complex as genetics. Did you ever go to a game with Uncle Jim?"

"A couple over the years. When he was living close by. Not so much anymore. Besides he goes with Melinda now."

Clare said, as if she couldn't believe it, "They go to every single home game. He works around their schedule." She glanced at her watch and rose, placing her napkin on the table. "We've got to go, or I'll be late. It was very nice meeting you, Enrique."

Pat got out his wallet as he waved the waitress over for the bill. After it was taken care of, Clare

shook Rique's hand and leaned over to give Fiona a hug and kiss. "You'll let me know what happens Friday."

"I will."

When they were all bundled up, Pat and Clare walked quickly out through the restaurant, leaving him and Fifi behind.

"Well that went better than I expected. Thank you for coming with us. My mother can sometimes be a little heavy-handed."

"She makes it easy to get that impression."

He helped her on with her coat and guided her toward the exit. As they walked to the car, he took her hand. "It's kind of slippery out here." The truth was he needed to feel it in his.

She seemed deep in thought as they carefully made their way to the parking lot. Finally letting him in on what had taken up head space, she said, "Mom never fully appreciated that we worked around her schedule. I was actually going to toss that grenade but caught myself in time."

"She was gone a lot?"

"Even when she wasn't traveling the globe, she worked late most nights. I get it if you're on the cusp of some new revelation, but every night?"

"You want something different for your life?'

"I hope to fill my life with a variety of things, not be so single-minded. I know dedicated scientists who have it, so I know it's possible." She glanced up at him. "Which reminds me, I dropped by my old lab and my former mentor asked if I could get her tickets to one of your games."

"You told her about me?"

"I explained that you were at the house, and why. Her husband loves baseball and she has a certain fondness for it as well."

"I tell you what, I'll get you some tickets, but you have to go with them."

"She helped me advance my career, so I guess it's the least I can do."

"It must have taken single-minded focus."

He opened the car door and she slid in. When he was behind the wheel and they were inching their way out of the parking lot, she said, "It did. Science has given me everything, but it's also given me nothing. I've been so caught up in my studies, I've ignored the rest of the world."

"I have a feeling lab work suits you."

"Working in isolation suits my personality but it's no way to live life. I don't want to be like my mother, attuned to her machines but not her children." She gave him a deprecating laugh. "I'm nothing like her, actually so I don't know what I'm afraid of. She's a social butterfly. I'm more a spider who's content within her web."

She had a web, all right, and she was casting it around him. He didn't know what he'd do if he found himself completely ensnared in it. If he hadn't mentioned his trip to Brazil for the express purpose of finding a wife, he might have had some leeway, might have...what? Tricked her into bed? Seduced her into thinking she had a shot at a future? She wasn't the type of woman who jumped into bed for the hell of it, so he'd have to have promised something. He'd come to know her more intimately than most women he dated for months. He knew inside her mind, and he was being given glimpses of what was inside her heart. Could he find a woman like her during his search? He glanced over as he pulled into the drive-way. She was in profile. Her hair was clipped off her face making it look longer, thinner. Her nose was pert, and it made a compelling picture. What he missed at this angle were her eyes, the window to her curiosity and expressiveness.

When he put the car in park, she turned to him and asked, "What are your plans for the rest of the afternoon?"

Wanting her meant finding an escape.

"I think I might call that agent my sister told me about, go check out some rentals. I don't want to infringe on her privacy any longer than I have to. You?"

"I might drive to my sister's. Seeing my parents today made me realize I miss her."

"Where does she live?"

"Maine."

"How far up?"

"Far enough that I'll probably spend the night."

He didn't like that thought. He'd gotten used to her company and wasn't sure he'd be able to keep to his new regimen of early nights without her.

"What about Hoover?"

"I'll take her. Siobhan's kids love dogs and she'll get to romp in the snow."

"You can leave her with me. I'll make sure she's attended to."

"I almost believe you but she's my commitment for the next couple of days, so she'll sit shotgun."

"I thought I was, too. One of your commitments. Isn't my sister paying you extra to keep me in line?"

"I have to believe you can behave for one night."

"I don't know. I need stimulation and if the house is empty…"

She'd gotten out of the car and was making her way toward the house. He sprinted out and followed her in, Hoover the kind of welcoming committee a person came to enjoy. The dog didn't jump up on you, she sprung up so she could meet your eyes. She wanted you to know how happy she was you were back. Fifi had her arms around the dog's neck, hugging her, while he studied the interaction. He envied their furry friend.

"What breed will you get?"

She looked up from her squat. Her dress had inched up and he had to force himself to keep his eyes on hers.

"You said when you get a bigger place, you're going to get one. What kind? Big, small, long-haired, short?"

"I don't know. A rescue for sure, so it would depend on what was available when I looked. I gravitate toward big. There's more to love."

He went down on his haunches beside her and began to stroke Hoover's back.

"Me, too. If I wasn't gone for long stretches of time, I'd think about getting one."

"What about this fabulous woman you're going to marry? Won't she be at home?"

He was frowning. She never failed to remind him about his future wife, and her words struck a chord. She probably expected some pithy remark. He had nothing unless he counted the nagging voice telling him here was yet another attribute he had to add to his list. It was growing along different lines lately. What would the advertisement look like today?

Searching for intelligent woman driven by curiosity and a love of learning. Must speak English, listen well, have a sense of humor, be kind, like baseball, love dogs.

He'd left out the hair, eyes, and build. When had looks become secondary to temperament and personality?

He glanced up, took Fifi in.

"I'd like to think she'll travel with me. At least until we start a family."

He heard himself talking but his mind was elsewhere. He'd left out another very important component in his search. What kind of mother did he want for his children? Someone like his, who encouraged her children to forge their own path, affectionate and giving, who embraced those who'd come before. She could have fought his father about bringing Izabella and Jaco into the family, but she was more adamant about it than Paolo. Peaceful and content with what life had handed her. She was a happy woman, satisfied with what she had, never thought she needed more.

Love is all, my Rique, and I am surrounded by it. What more could I want?

Not one of the women he'd had in mind was remotely like her, not in any way. They were wealthy, beautiful, and...self-absorbed. His friends' lifestyle, and their upbringing, were similar to his own. Always searching for better, for more, they were never satisfied with what they had, only who they were. His mother hadn't come from money. She'd worked her way up at the bank, her sweetness attracting his father. Sweetness, like nectar, had more appeal to him now as well.

For the first time ever, he was beginning to realize he might never find what he wanted. Not in the place he'd anticipated.

"Where are you? Rique?"

He came back to the here and now.

There was a furrow across Fifi's brow. "Don't go introspective on me now. It's not like you and I'll start to worry. Then I won't be able to leave."

He took her hand and stood, bringing her with him. A powerful rush of emotion made his chest ache with longing.

"Don't go. Let's light a fire. Talk. You can tell me all about this lab you're dreaming about."

She laughed that magical laugh.

"I've been dressing it up like a doll, whatever that's like, for weeks. I add a piece and then take it out and reassemble."

He took her hand and guided her to where they could sit, where he could probe into her life. He was going to ask her all those questions he should have been asking.

"You never did that as a little girl?"

His sister Leia had. Her whole room was filled with all kinds of them, Barbie, baby, one that even wet. She was such a girly-girl, always in dresses, frills and bows.

"Too mundane, I'm afraid. I preferred frogs to dolls."

Felicia had been more like that. Liked being outdoors, inquisitive about the natural world, both seen and buried underground. She'd still learned to cook, loved being with family, could dance like she was born on the dance floor.

"What did you do?"

She sat back, her hands in her lap. When Hoover circled the area in front of her, she kicked off her boots, pulled her legs up and tucked them under her, giving the dog space to lie down. As soon as she did, Fifi said, "After school some days, I'd go to my mother's lab, watch her assistants, ask a million questions, be told to shush and go do my homework. Other days I'd go home and watch TV, shows on National Geographic, Animal Planet, the Science Channel. It's where I learned to love genetics."

He was standing by the fireplace, relieved there were a few logs left from the other night. He was afraid that if he went to get more out of the garage she'd be gone when he got back. He had it assembled in no time, and when he lit the match, he looked back to find her eyes on him. She seemed content and he relaxed for the first time since they'd returned. He took possession of the other side of the couch and asked, "What show piqued your interest?"

"It was called Genetic Odyssey, or something like that. It traced a couple of tribes back through time to the very beginning. I was intrigued with the premise and stunned by the results. Even today I watch shows like *So Who Do You Think You Are* and *Finding Your Roots.* It's a personal journey that uncovers so much genetic material about the past. You become a more expanded version of yourself when you come to know your ancestors, where they're from, what they did, how they lived."

"How old were you?"

She chewed the inside of her cheek. "Eleven, maybe."

"This is probably a dumb question, but did you ever have your DNA tested?"

The faintest trace of humor lit her face.

"Hello. I'm a geneticist." More seriously, she said, "I tested it myself as part of a course I took."

"And?"

"What? Did I compare it to my parents'? I did. There are a lot of similarities in our double stranded helix."

"Like what?"

She gave him a sly smile and another scientific treatise.

"My primary neurotransmitter is acetylcholine, a physiological characteristic more in line with my father. It's created by thinking and feeling, which means we auto-stimulate through introspection and observation."

He didn't know what the hell that word meant, but he got the gist of the explanation. It made her a good listener and a deep thinker.

"I don't think either of my parents donated that to me."

She went on. "You are more like my mother, one of the social butterflies of the world. You need more active stimulation than I do. Translation: you need to be the center of attention, involve yourself in activities that get your adrenaline going. You tend to get bored when you're alone too long." Her smile was more genuine this time. "Or on the bench too often."

He brightened up. "There's a scientific reason I didn't do well in New York? I like that better than thinking it was a personal failure."

"It's all in how you deal with those traits. I used to force myself out, to parties, to friends' gatherings, forced conversation about things I cared nothing about. What really turned me off, and the reason I stopped going out period? I'd spend five, ten minutes listening to someone's story and when I went to reply they'd turn away like I'd already served my usefulness. It made me angry and not a little resentful."

Did he do that? Talk about himself and then become bored when someone else spoke? He was listening now, interested in what she had to say. It was giving him a deeper understanding of who she was, of who he was.

Had he just circled back to himself, again? Yeah, he did but this time he consciously turned it back around. He didn't like the idea of anyone ignoring this woman or the people who did it.

"I can't blame you. It was rude, plain and simple."

"Then there's a lot of rude out there."

She pushed up the sleeves of her dress as if she were just getting comfortable.

"Tell me about spring training. What is it and why do you do it?"

Should he let her change the subject or probe further into her life? He decided to take a minute to decide. "I saved some coffee. Want some iced?"

"That sounds good."

It took only a few steps before he was back, handed her a glass thick with ice.

He sat closer this time, so that he could feel her body heat. It might be a distraction, but it was a welcome one.

CHAPTER EIGHTEEN

"Now, do you really want to know what spring training's like or are you just changing the topic of our very stimulating conversation?"

"I really want to know. Does everyone on the team go? Are they tryouts of sorts? If I'm going to start watching, I need to know what I'm looking for. Just another tid-bit about me. I'm curious about how things work."

"I would never have guessed."

She let the sarcasm go. Even though it was unsettling that he knew her so well, she gave him more.

"When I was in the lab on Sundays, I'd binge watch a show on the Science Channel. I actually think the name of it was *How Things Work*. No *How Things Are Made.* They'd explain how to make stuff like guitar picks, light microscopes, vacuum cleaners, gummy vitamins. And I forgot to mention I love gummy bears, so that was an especially interesting show."

"I'm sure the one about the microscope was riveting."

"Actually, I stopped what I was doing to watch. Almost lost a whole set of samples."

"You'll have our games to watch next month. They're slow enough that there'll be no risk of losing yourself in it."

"Actually, now that I've studied some of the mechanics, I'll be watching the pitchers and hitters to learn more about velocity and trajectory."

"Probably not during our pre-season. We won't be in it to win it. It is a try-out of sorts, with inexperienced rookies thrown into the mix. The regulars will play only part of the game. The starting pitchers won't have a regular rotation."

"Those aspiring to move out of your farm system?"

"Will be going all out, trying to impress the manager and coaches."

"Regulars won't necessarily make the team?"

"There'll be some old-timers let go or used as utility players."

"How will they feel about that?"

"Depends, I guess, on whether or not they have the right genes for bench warming."

He was smiling, and she could do nothing but return it.

"You play in Sanford, right? Do all the teams fly south?"

"Most of the Eastern Seaboard teams do. The ones on the West Coast train in Arizona."

"I guess you do have to find a warmer temperature. How bad is it to play in the cold?"

"Worse for pitchers than for us. Reid's been bitching about opening day. It's a week earlier than usual but we make a West Coast swing first, so we won't be back until April."

"Is it tough being on the road?"

"Not so much at the beginning. We're pumped, ready to go. I guess it's like a kid who's bored with summer and can't wait to get back to school. It's great at first. You're with your teammates, playing the game, but it grinds after a while."

"You play a lot of games."

"We do."

He hadn't noticed the fire burning down until she got up to stoke it. He jumped up and took the poker out of her hand, gently moved the burning logs until another flame flickered.

"Is this a man's job?"

She glanced up, and he read humor in her eyes.

He let the poker drop against the stone and took a step closer. Without thought, he reached behind her neck and pulled her closer, his lips hovering over hers. Her eyes were glowing, her cheeks flushed, and he couldn't keep himself from kissing her. It was just like he remembered, better than he remembered and when she didn't fight him, he pressed deeper. He felt her hand on his chest, creating tingles of another kind, and the sensation was numbing all good sense.

When he came up for breath, his whole body enflamed by that simple touch of lips on lips, she whispered, "Have you forgotten about your future bride?"

He'd had no thought other than her. There hadn't been room for another woman, every sensation monopolized by her scent, the texture of her lips, the heat in her eyes. Becoming conscious of her stare, he said honestly, "I've forgotten my name at the moment." He brushed his lips against her temple and whispered, "And where the woman doesn't yet exist, I can do as I please."

He felt her stiffen. "You can, but at my expense?"

His eyes closed, knowing she was right, knowing he should walk away, knowing he couldn't. He couldn't remember being this tight with need. Was it the thought of forbidden desire that prompted it? The way she fit against him, or the anticipation of what this primitive force could lead to?

He asked the only question he thought might tempt her to go beyond reason.

"Aren't you curious?"

She was.

She'd never felt like this before, circuits exposed, like live wires ready for an electrical surge. Could she continue to ignore the growing coil of tension? Or her fascination with the man? Terry had suggested she give in to temptation. Even her mother had encouraged her. She'd know going in that he was already taken. The woman he had in mind for a wife might be faceless, but the image was there. The one he thought would suit him. It wouldn't be anyone like her. She'd never be one of the beautiful people, not in looks or temperament. She'd never minded before, but now...

She met his eyes. They were dark with desire. He was offering her something she might never have again. Could she turn down the opportunity to experience the peak of pleasure? She was convinced she'd find it in his arms.

Giving in, knowing this would be a one-time experiment, she murmured, "I am."

With her permission, he resettled his lips on hers, taking the kiss deeper. The provocative pressure of his mouth gave her the measure of wildness that she'd expected. It had ignited something at her core that she'd never known was there and there were the rumblings of a volcano, the hot lava of her blood coming to a boil from the heady sensation. He was making love to her mouth like a man hungry for what she could give him, greedy with need, kissing her as if to devour her very essence. With each turn of his head, each new angle from which he took, she became someone else. Gone was the reticence, the doubt, the fear and in its stead was a boldness she'd never given in to.

Impulsively, she threaded her fingers in his hair and gave back in equal measure, frantic for more.

He moaned, brushed his tongue against her lips before invading her mouth, tongues dancing, twisting, mating. She abandoned all thought, gave in to the tactile sensitivity of his touch, the vibration and pressure stimulating those neurons in the brain that responded to intimacy. They'd been just words until now, empty words without meaning. Now she knew what they meant. Her nerves were on fire, her breathing uneven, spirals of need tightening, coiling. This was something that couldn't be analyzed, defined. It had to be felt to understand it completely.

His hands found her curves and his thumb brushed lightly against her nipple, and the fire banked further. She arched back involuntarily, and his mouth left hers in response. The ached at the absence of his lips was immediate. When he bent his head, gnawed at her protruding nub through her dress, she gasped as an electric current shot through her body. He ran his fingers up her thigh, her dress inching up along with them, until they pressed along the swell of her buttocks.

His voice was ragged when he said, "We have to get you out of these clothes."

In one sweep, she was out of her dress.

The swells of her breasts spilled out and now it was his turn to gasp. She might be a scientist, with a serious exterior, but she compensated by wearing undergarments that were totally feminine. She never thought she'd be stripped down and examined the way he way he was studying her. It made her feel like she could inspire Michelangelo.

His finger was lightly tracing the cleavage, the valley between. "You call this a bra?"

It was sheer with bits of lace that barely covered her nipples.

She tingled at his touch and with a raspy breath said, "That's how it was advertised."

He bent his head and buried his nose in the overflow of skin, breathing her in.

"What other surprises do you have for me?"

His words were soft, buffeting her skin, raising a shiver.

In a voice that was not hers, with a daring she rarely felt, she whispered, "You'll have to find that out for yourself."

His eyes met hers, and she read a predatory hunger there. No one had ever looked at her that way before and it would have frightened her if she wasn't so consumed by the heat of him.

She felt his fingers graze her waist, as he began to peel down the tights, slowly, torturously, as if he had all night to uncover the heart of her. What was left when they were off, was a thong that barely concealed her womanhood.

He groaned at the sight of her bare essentials.

"Fifi…you're beautiful."

And she almost believed him as his calloused hands stroked up her legs and came to a stop at the curve of her ass.

His touch was like streak lightening, creating fissures and quakes that were peaking. Orgasms were a rare commodity for her. Sex was something she'd tried on for size over the years, but she'd never felt this immediate kick. He was stoking something inside that was building too quickly and she wasn't sure how long she could hold up under his ministrations.

With shaking fingers, she began to undo the buttons on his shirt, but she fumbled. As if losing patience, he pushed them aside and stripped himself down until he was standing naked in front of her. He reached for her again, swept her down to the carpet, the fire in the grate still spitting out sparks.

His nose was behind her ear, his kisses molten and deadly. With deft fingers, he unclasped her bra and began to knead and caress. The combination of tender and rough propelled her further toward the edge.

She watched his hands as they worked their magic, the intimacy of his possession stirring a fierce longing for_ she squeezed her eyes closed_ something she couldn't have, not with him. This was a fantasy come to life but that's all it was. She couldn't afford to yearn for more than what this was, a one-night affair that had to stay emotion free.

When his mouth captured her nipple, she was dazed in pleasure, the kisses wet, his tongue lapping, his teeth nipping. The throb between her legs became a bolt of fire.

Her body arched, her thighs opening, almost of their own volition.

"I can't wait much longer."

He grabbed for the packet he'd taken out of his pants pocket, ripped it open with his teeth, hurriedly fingered the condom on and straddled her, a skimpy piece of cloth the only thing between them.

In one deft movement he'd yanked it off, and then he was in her, in one thrust, his hands holding firmly to her buttocks. She spasmed, moist and ready for the onslaught, but he'd stilled on entering her. She squirmed beneath him, clutched at him, begging without words for him to do something, anything to release her from the agonizing torment.

He answered with a slow and torturous in and out motion. Her hips rocked in rhythm with his, with a frantic urgency. She was strung like a bow and quivered with tension until she felt the fissures expanding like pure white heat. There was a shock of pleasure when the climax commenced. She dug her nails into his shoulders as she convulsed, the orgasm washing over her in wave upon unending wave, making her scream out his name.

He issued a guttural expletive when his hard body heaved. Shudders racked him as he detonated, and she shook from the exertion of his release.

She'd totally come undone, never imagining sex could be like this. Explosive, passionate, all-consuming. She'd been left boneless, incapable of movement, her body soaked in sweat. When she felt a slick, wet tongue lap her face, she remembered where she was.

In a weak voice, Rique commanded, "Hoover, go lie down."

She did, right beside where they lay.

"I forgot she was here."

All time had stopped and the only thing she knew for sure was that Rique had just made love to her. She'd expected a quick fuck, but she should have known better. He was a womanizer and knew how to satisfy. What had he said about Brazilians? That they kissed for fun, and endearments were not to be taken seriously. Did they look the same way at coupling? Was it for the sheer pleasure of the moment? She'd known it was just a temporary diversion, that she was a curiosity he wanted unraveled. He'd certainly done that.

He kissed the tip of her nose and rose shakily to his feet so he could walk Hoover into her crate. The dog put her head on her paws, her look one of disappointment.

Fiona began to rise but he was back, compelling her into his arms and denying her an escape.

"Please. Don't. Not yet."

He'd shifted their bodies so they were lounging against the couch and he was cradling her in the crook of his arm.

"Leaving you took every ounce of will-power I had." He kissed her bare shoulder. "I need a reward for my discipline."

His sensual mouth had lifted into a lazy, beguiling smile. His eyes burned into her and she felt the flush of desire ripple through her once more.

"What did you have in mind?"

She almost didn't recognize her voice, it was low and…seductive.

"This. Just to hold you. This is the reward."

Did men delight in the afterglow? None of the ones she'd known had. Was this another of those Brazilian traits that he brought to the bedroom? If so, it was no wonder he was sought after.

She rested her head against his shoulder, letting herself relax. She'd take all the minutes he was willing to give her, knowing she would never find this kind of pleasure again.

They sat there, the quiet welcome after the flurry of feeling, and they watched the embers of the fire burn red and gray. The logs were long gone but she didn't miss the heat, the warmth of his body more than enough to ward off any chill.

He pulled her legs over his so that she could sit in his lap, his arm never leaving her, his fingers gently tickling her skin along her rib cage. When she twitched, he chuckled. "You are ticklish. I love that in a woman. I can make you laugh at will."

As if to prove it, he began to tickle her in earnest without ever changing the type of light touch that skimmed rather than poked. She was finding out her ticklish zone was also an erogenous zone. Instead of making her jumpy, it aroused. When the little ball of need burst to life at the pit of her stomach, she cupped his face, crushed her lips to his, and ground against him. His fingers stilled, and in one fluid motion, his light-hearted play turned amorous. The kiss he reciprocated with was raw and unapologetic.

"I can make you either laugh or love with one touch. It is good to know."

The murmur was seductive, and she felt the flush of her body under his gaze. Their lovemaking was no less potent the second time, but more intimate. He'd kissed every inch of her body, brought her to the edge several times before bringing her back, exerting his power, proving his stamina, until they shattered together, her world exploding into a million pieces. She knew she'd never be the same again.

He lay spent, his arms refusing to budge, needing to feel her under him.

He'd never expected this, hadn't guarded against it. She was his momentary pleasure before seeking monogamy. Would he ever be able to duplicate the sensations that were still coursing through him? Could he be content with anything less than what he'd found with her?

She was not who he was looking for. He wanted domesticity and he knew she'd never be content with being at home. Why should she be? She'd worked hard for what she'd earned, and no one had a right to ask her to give it all up. She couldn't cook, she didn't dress up, she hated small talk. He needed someone who would come to his games, watch him play, socialize with his team and their wives, significant others. And she wasn't classically beautiful. He'd always envisioned a tall, dark woman at his side, one who others would envy, one who caused a stir. One who could set him afire with just a look. Fifi was pretty, her eyes the most compelling things about her. They were truly the window to who she was, her curiosity about the world so vivid, the gray shifting to pewter, to slate to dove with a flick of emotion. And she was smart. Smarter than him, smarter than most. How could she interact with the guys on the team whose sole ambition off the field was to talk baseball? It was a game to her, where it was their life.

You're just overwhelmed by what you're feeling right now. It won't last.

But when Hoover whimpered like she did when she had to go out, and Fifi started to extricate herself from their embrace, he stalled.

"She can wait another minute."

"She hasn't been out since we got back."

He glanced at the window. The sun was going down, and the room was becoming chilled.

He couldn't believe they'd been caught up in each other all afternoon. He hadn't wanted to be alone, and she'd obliged. In ways he could never have expected.

In his moment of contemplation, she scrambled up, grabbed her discarded clothes, and raced for the stairs. All he could do was follow her movement with his eyes until she was out of sight. He got up and got dressed, picked up the thong he'd ripped off, and pocketed it. Wanting a memento was a high school thing, but he felt like a school-boy. His heart still pounded, his blood still rushed, just like it had his first time. He'd been unprepared back then, as well. There'd been no description of the experience that had matched the full effect of entering a woman's body, the arousing scent of her, the spike of heat, the all-consuming sensations that made his balls ache, his dick throb. Fifi had taken him back to that, and he couldn't explain it, refused to admit the significance.

When she returned, she had on her faded jeans, bulky wool socks, and the sweatshirt he'd given her. And the need came barreling back with a vengeance.

She released Hoover from her crate and made her way to the slider. "Think about what you want for dinner. I'll call for delivery as soon as I'm done out here."

He wanted her for dinner. Breakfast and lunch. She was the appetizer, main course, and dessert. His lascivious thoughts stalled when he heard her cell ring and watched her answer it as she closed the door behind her.

Her phone rarely rang or pinged. She carried it with her, but it wasn't her main source of communication. Did she have friends? He had to assume she did, although he'd never asked. She'd already met some of his, had provided supper for them, engaged in conversation. She'd been an exemplary hostess. Curious, listening, asking pertinent questions. She made them feel at ease and not once had she made them feel inferior with her intelligence. Neither Seb nor Mattie could possibly know what she did for a living. They hadn't asked; she hadn't volunteered.

When she slipped back inside, Hoover dancing around her legs, he was partially dressed. Her phone was not in evidence, so she must have wrapped up the call while she was outside. He studied her while she put her coat away, looking for some clue as to who had reached out on a late Saturday afternoon. She gave away nothing. He was going to have to ask if he wanted to know, but it was none of his business.

For some reason that irritated him.

"Did you decide what you want for dinner?"

Her question irked him further.

How could food be her primary concern? Hadn't she felt the connection? The powerful way their bodies had come together? Now that her curiosity had been fed, was she putting it behind her like an experiment that didn't need repetition, the procedure undertaken, having provided all necessary information in her quest for discovery? He was not going to let her push him aside that easily. He would be making a lifetime commitment soon and he was going to enjoy this for as long as he could.

Her cheeks were flushed from the cold, and her teeth were chattering. He took the two steps needed to embrace her, and he rubbed some warmth into her arms before kissing her. When she made a move to evade, he held her in place, kissed her temple.

"I think I will cook again."

Her eyes widened in surprise and the look on her face was priceless. "Why?"

"You may not like to spend time in there, but I am finding it…satisfying. You stimulate my creativity." His buried his chin in her neck. "You stimulate in other ways as well."

She'd stiffened and he didn't like it. He wanted her pliant, like she'd been when she was beneath him, warm instead of this cool aloofness.

"We have two more days before Izabella and Reid get back. Let's pretend the world doesn't exist until then, shall we?"

"And then what, Rique? Then you go to Brazil in search of a wife? Will you be looking for one who can *stimulate*? My impression is I'm not an exception. I'm beginning to think you're right and that any woman will do."

His smile drooped. He couldn't deny he enjoyed the intimacy of deep relationships. But she was wrong about any woman fitting the role. He was beginning to understand that if he couldn't build an attachment that was authentic, he wasn't interested in pursuing it. The one he was creating with her was becoming personal. He'd been caught in the web of friendship that he wasn't willing to extricate himself from. He might have a plan for the future, but he was no longer sure he would find everything he was looking for in one woman. Someone like Fifi hadn't even been on his radar. Being with her was growing his list of necessary traits.

"Every woman is exceptional. I can't help that I enjoy female company."

"Maybe not, but I can choose not to be one of them."

Now it was his turn to stiffen. "Are you going to tell me that you didn't enjoy this afternoon?"

"That would be foolish of me. You were there. You know I enjoyed it."

At least she was willing to admit it out loud, although there was a solemn expression on her face.

Was it longing? For something more? Had he ever asked her what she was looking for? He knew a lab was one of those things, but was that all? She'd told him before that she had no use for a husband, but was that the truth or some jerk reaction to his asshole remark about finding herself one?

"So, what would the harm be if we continued to enjoy each other for the next couple of days?"

"I don't want to be tagged as someone's diversion. And that's all I am to you."

He stroked her cheek, allowing the feel of her skin to soothe the savage beast within.

"You're more than that, Fifi. You're…my friend, and I would never hurt you on purpose."

"I'm not sure about that. You are all about you. What you want is more imperative than what's appropriate or good for you. You know as well as I do that I'm not good for you."

"I'd have to disagree after what we did earlier."

"I'm good for you because I'm here. For today. If I wasn't you'd find something or someone else to entertain you. I'll be a case of out of sight, out of mind come Tuesday."

She might be right, although he wasn't as sure as he'd like to be. He had a feeling it would take longer than a day to wipe away the repercussions of their lovemaking. He was even beginning to feel that it might impede his search. But it didn't stop him from wanting what he wanted. Another exclusive day with her.

How was he going to convince her to go along with it? His hunger hadn't abated. In fact, it only gnawed more relentlessly.

His eyes flashed up at her. "Are you saying I won't be anything more than a memory on Tuesday?"

"That's all you can be. I've got my whole life planned out and it doesn't include you or anyone like you."

Was that sadness in her eyes? The gray had turned to dull pewter.

That spooked him. The look and the sentiment. He wanted to be one of her cherished memories. When she was rocking in her chair on her front porch when she was ninety, he wanted her to look back and remember their afternoon of pleasure with a smile.

"What does it include, Fifi? What do you want, besides your lab?"

She dipped her eyes, shuffled backward and said quietly, "Nothing."

He didn't believe that. She was full of life, and she had a passionate nature. She hid it beneath a wall of isolation, but he'd gotten a peek at what lay beyond it. She had to be lying. Then again, maybe she didn't want more.

"That would be like me saying all I want for the rest of my life is to hit balls and catch grounders. I need to include other things for a rich and satisfying life."

She was staring into the distance, a look of resignation on her face.

"I know. You've told me. A wife, children, family."

"You want none of that?"

"I'm not sure. What if I turn out like my mother? She was…unable to split her focus to include us. I think if you have children, you owe them part of yourself at least while they're young. My father tried to make up for it by being home most nights, giving up a more lucrative job to support his wife. I'm not sure there are many men out there like him. Most are like you and want a helpmate, someone to take care of the inconsequential things while they do the *real* work. Or at least someone who'll share the load."

He didn't think of his mother as inconsequential. She was the glue that held the family together. She did the real work, raising, nurturing, loving each of her children, and they'd grown into responsible citizens of the world. At least the rest of his siblings had.

"You've admitted before that you're nothing like her. And I have to agree. You have a lot of love inside of you. I can't believe you'd choose to remain alone."

"It might not be a question of choice."

"We're born to love, Fifi. It's a driving force that compels us to search for that certain someone. You're telling me that you won't look for it, or at the very least keep the door open?"

"The door will always be open, but I might be too preoccupied to notice anyone standing outside."

"Then I hope they barge right in and sweep you off your feet."

And in one fluid motion, he picked her up and swung her around and around.

He was making himself dizzy, but he couldn't stop. She was clinging to his shoulders, and her unexpected laugh was shimmering through him.

CHAPTER NINETEEN

When he finally put her down, Fiona was breathless. He constantly surprised her, in the way he touched her both physically and emotionally. She couldn't imagine anyone else spinning her around like that, so playful, so full of himself. She didn't mind his bouts of selfish delight when she was the object of his attention. He wanted another day together and she knew she'd be unable to deny him. Or herself. And why should she? Just a look alone could cause funny little jumping jacks to spring in her stomach. And it wasn't only sexual. She admired his way with people and his warmth, his emotional expressiveness. He was like an open book. She'd uncovered who he was within ten minutes of meeting him. It didn't take a genius for that. He had a mocking disregard for others that was not very appealing, but it was offset by his charm and boyishness. There'd been an immediate connection in the form of a thunderbolt. Maybe he was right, and humans were driven to find love, one that could withstand the test of time. Maybe sex wasn't the primal urge to mate, a biological design, serving an evolutionary purpose. Had she become so clinical that she only measured it in scientific terms? The exclusive study of DNA had given her a microscopic view of genes along with the endless possibilities that came from mixing two separate helixes. Since meeting him, she'd been shown the other side of it, the emotions that also prompted it. Her heart had become involved, and it was whispering its intent to fall in love with him. It was her brain screaming he couldn't possibly be the one. How had she fallen so deeply?

Did it have to do with timing? She was going through a transition, a shift from student to scientist, with unemployment hanging over her. It was producing stress, and with the upheaval of emotions, she'd become susceptible to passion. That the man in question was gorgeous, athletic, and had a hidden sensitive nature didn't help quench it. The circuits in her brain had gone haywire, pushing her down a path that was a dead end. It was a frustrating attraction, but the wanting wasn't going away. Especially now that she'd tasted what he had to offer.

She watched him as he made her dinner, a dish towel tucked in the waistband of his pants. His forehead was furrowed in concentration as he peeled the garlic, smashed it with a knife, and flaked away the outer skin. After sprinkling it with salt and pepper, he put it in a black skillet with some butter. His movements were sure, his body tempting. It was an aphrodisiac in itself.

He glanced over at her and explained, "This is one of my mother's recipes that only takes fifteen minutes to make, and seeing that you said you were hungry…as am I, if you must know, I thought it would be perfect. And I found some pão de queijo in the freezer when I took out the skirt steak. Izabella makes it almost as good as my mother does so you're in for a treat."

"What is pão de…pão…that." She was pointing to the sealed pouch on the counter.

He grinned at her. "Cheese bread. I wouldn't dare serve you goats' intestine or calf brains."

"You eat that?" It was more a croak than a question.

"On occasion."

He'd opened the pouch and put the bread on a cookie sheet, placed it on the first rack of the oven before turning his attention to the steak. She was fascinated with the way he worked, precise and methodical. It was how she conducted an experiment and she wondered if cooking might not be outside her comfort zone after all. Not if she thought about it that way. All she'd need was a set of directions, some measuring tools, and the right utensils. Just like in the lab. She smiled to herself and decided she'd give it a try one day. Outside his purview.

"It's almost ready."

He transferred the steak to a cutting board. "I have to let this sit for a few minutes, or it will bleed out. Why don't you grab something to drink while we wait?"

She pushed herself away from her ring-side seat at the island and did as he asked. "Beer?"

"One shouldn't hurt."

She twisted the cap off the water and beer and brought them back to the counter. She was sniffing the air, her hunger pangs suddenly boisterous. "Is it ready yet?"

There was a repressed chuckle. "It's coming. I didn't realize that food was so high up on your priority list."

"It is when I'm thinking about it."

"And when you're not?"

"I have to be in the lab for that to happen. It's easy to skip meals when you're—"

"On the brink of some new discovery?"

"Yes. As a matter of fact." She took a sip of her water and then asked, "Have you heard anything about Farina?"

He was slicing the steak and plating it before topping it off with the butter garlic sauce. She thought the chopped green stuff he was adding might be parsley.

"Yeah. I checked my messages when you went upstairs to get dressed. The wake is Wednesday, the funeral Thursday."

"They're just waking him one day?"

"Yeah. Hours are noon to eight with an hour supper break at five."

"With all the people attending, it doesn't give them much time to get here."

"His wife was thinking about just a graveside service, but her children talked her out of it due to the numbers of condolence calls coming in. With so many mourners who'll want to pay their respects, she reluctantly agreed but just for a day. From what I hear she's not taking his death well."

"It was unexpected."

As he carried the plates over to the island bar, where she was sitting, he must have noticed what she was drinking.

"Just water?"

She reclipped the tangled curls behind her ear. Passion had a way of making them even more unruly than usual. What did he think when he looked at her? Did he think her pretty at all? She certainly wasn't a classic beauty and men were more attracted by visual processing than women and sought proportion and symmetry. With her thoughts incessant about her hair, she said, absently, "I don't drink much."

He reached out to grasp her fingers and pulled to gain her attention. When she looked up, his eyes had a certain gleam. "What's your preference when you do?"

She unconsciously began to stroke the edge of his hand with her thumb.

"Don't really have one. If push comes to shove and I have to order something, I'll have a glass of something bubbly, like a wine spritzer. Champagne's my favorite but they don't sell that by the glass."

He lifted her hand and kissed her palm.

"Good to know."

She studied him for a minute, not understanding why it was good to know that about her and extricated her hand from his.

"You keep saying that. After Tuesday we'll probably never see each other again."

He gave her a first-rate scowl. "I won't accept that I'll never see you again."

She didn't like that thought, either, but she was a realist and knew once they went their separate ways, the chances of being in his company were nil. He'd go back to Brazil, find a wife, live his life, probably never giving her another thought. That she'd remember him vividly was her problem.

She cut a piece of her steak and brought it up to her mouth, let the fork hover there, and said, "I hope you don't expect me to attend your wedding."

She needed to remind herself that he was already taken. That the woman in question hadn't been selected didn't mean it wasn't going to happen. He could get anyone he wanted with a crook of his finger. Needing something other than his presence to occupy her senses she tasted the beef and closed her eyes. It was delicious. She could so get used to someone cooking for her.

Only when she felt the stare did she glance over. He could have burned a hole in her forehead, it was so laser focused.

"What? You don't, do you? I draw the line at being present at my ex-lover's nuptials."

He began to chew his lip, and she noticed he hadn't even taken a bite of the dinner.

"I thought you were going to go to a game. Once the season starts. With your friends."

"As long as you don't sit me near your wife, maybe."

His forehead creased, his lips pursed. "You could sit with Izabella."

"Who will more than likely be sitting with her new sister-in-law."

His expression shifted and tension stiffened his features. He obviously hadn't thought this through, hadn't come to terms with the fact that he'd soon be married, or at least engaged. He was leaving on Thursday for Brazil, taking the weekend to scout out his options. Word had come down that the practices had been suspended for the foreseeable future. Until they hired a new manager, everything was up in the air, so he was leaving earlier than expected for his exploratory trip.

Wanting to abandon all talk about his other women, she went where her current thought process had taken her. "Isn't there a meeting today to discuss new leadership?"

"Yes, it was this morning. I still haven't heard anything."

"Will they group text you like they did about Farina?"

It didn't seem the polite way to go about announcing a major change, but group texts made it easier to get the word out to all rather than do it one call at a time.

"Probably."

He seemed distant, far away, and she wondered where he'd gone.

"Are you worried?"

"Huh? About the new manager? Not really. Nothing to worry about until I hear who's accepted the position."

"Then why aren't you eating? You've created a masterpiece and you're letting it get cold."

She took the last bite of her cheese bread. She'd have to tell Izabella how much she enjoyed it. Maybe get the recipe… *Seriously?* She'd need to take baby steps, like tea and toast, first.

"You have become a friend, Fifi. I don't want to lose you because I'm getting married."

She felt her eyes go wide. She hadn't expected to continue their…whatever it was they had together. Lovers? Friends? Had they really crossed from acquaintance to friend? Was she truly friendship material or was the relationship superficial, based on proximity and need? Curiosity? He'd be off-limits once he said those vows. No way would she sleep with a married man. Could they sustain another type of dynamic once they went their separate ways?

"I'm not sure that's wise. Your life will change soon and there won't be room for female friends. Wives don't take kindly to their husbands palling around with women they've slept with."

There was a vehement shake of his head. "She would never have to know that."

She let her fork drop onto her empty plate and turned to look at him. Meeting his eyes, forcing herself not to fall into them, she said bluntly, "You're going to begin this new life of yours with secrets and lies? I'm disappointed but not surprised."

He was not thinking clearly. He couldn't be. But then again Rique, saw the big picture, didn't bother with the details. And he had missed a big one.

"She has to be able to trust you, don't you think?"

"I will be faithful, but I won't be stifled. I am not willing to cut you out of my life. Not for anyone." He reached out and took her hand in his. "You know how to settle me. I have had no desire to go out, drink, or party with you here."

Her eyes fluttered closed. She couldn't lose control, not of her heart or her head. She not only had to go slow here, she had to s-t-o-p thinking that she could take what he'd said and go with it.

With a tight voice, she told him simply, "I can't be your live-in settler. You'll just have to find someone who has the same effect."

He knew that. What he didn't know was how he was going to go about that. What he'd found here with her was a true connection, a meeting of minds and bodies, something he'd never expected. He was looking at her differently than he had that first morning, her hair dripping wet, her face covered with grit. He'd been mocking and arrogant, but she'd turned the tables on him, putting him in his place and making him feel the inferior one. She'd never wasted his time with unemotional or irrelevant small talk. Her comments were on target or filled with intelligent anecdotes. The one about kissing had broadened his perspective. In fact, every time he kissed her, there was a heightened awareness of touch and texture. They'd had heart-to-heart talks that had awakened his curiosity, and he'd found, once her sexual appetite was whetted, it equaled his own. She'd taken him on a journey into her psyche and he'd found parts of himself along the way. In the time he'd spent with her, he was whittling away what were the unnecessary attributes on his mental list and discovering what were the important traits he'd need in a mate. She was helping him define his ideal, the one with whom he could create a meaningful and inspiring union. In order to keep his eyes on the prize, he'd need to keep Fifi with him.

"Actually, that's what you have been for close to a week."

There was mischief in his eyes, and a slight smirk on his mouth.

She said breezily, "As they say, all good things must come to an end."

She slid off the stool and was about to take the empty plates to the sink, but the movement alone caused his body to stir. He snaked his arm around her waist and nestled her between his legs.

When his lips settled on hers, he felt the sparks he thought might fade, in all their vibrant colors.

"Not yet. Please, not yet."

She acquiesced more easily than he'd thought she would, slid her arms around his neck. Before he could edit the thought, he asked, "Who called you earlier?"

She dipped her eyes and said softly, "No one you'd know."

He tightened his hold on her. "You don't have a boyfriend, do you?"

Her eyes shot up and met his. "I wouldn't be here, like this, if I did."

"Good to know."

"You can't keep—"

He silenced her with a hard kiss. He liked knowing she would devote herself to one man at a time. He was going to make sure that man was him as long as he could.

It was his cell that signaled an incoming this time, not a call but a text. "This might be it."

His voice was tight, apprehension now coursing through him.

"What?"

"It's the Greenliners front office." He'd read the partial message before swiping and reading the full text out loud.

We have just reached an agreement with Mac Calipari and he has been hired as the new manager of the Greenliners. He will be assuming Jethro Farina's duties immediately and will be handling all administrative concerns. He will be contacting all players and staff to discuss their futures with the team. He has a lot of ground to cover with spring training just weeks away, and I expect full cooperation from everyone involved.

"Looks like speculation was right on target." It wasn't a surprise. He had the managerial experience to take this on, even if it wasn't at this level. Was it his history with the team that had sealed the deal? Or his standing in the minors?

Fifi had an expression of concern on her face but not for the reason he'd thought.

"Poor Seb. Do you think he'll be traded?"

He shook his head, not willing to believe the new manager could be so vindictive.

"Calipari is supposed to be a genius. I can't see him letting a kid breaking up with his daughter five or six years ago have any bearing on what's good for the team."

"But Seb hasn't played for the team yet. He doesn't have a history or any stats that would support any kind of move."

"Seb's been generating talk for the last couple of years. He's been touted as one of their up-and- coming stars, had been called up often enough they know what he can do out there. He's the future of the team. Why would Mac throw that kind of talent away?"

She met his eyes with hers. Hadn't management done it to him? He had the same kind of status in the minors, had been promoted to the big league with the same kind of promise.

"Seb gives it everything he has. That's the difference. It's Leo and the other coaches that might be at risk."

"Calipari will bring his own people with him?"

"They usually do."

He grabbed her hand and pulled her toward the family room.

"Come on, let's put on the MLB station. The story should break soon, and I want to see what they have to say about it."

She resisted. "I should take Hoover for her walk. I haven't gotten to it yet today."

"Just let her out. She doesn't really need a walk, does she?"

"Part of my job, and unfortunately, I'm the responsible kind."

"Are you trying to tell me, in not so many words, that you're not as anxious to hear about my new manager as I am?"

"Actually, I do want to hear about him. I'm a fan, you know. I have the hat and sweatshirt to prove it."

"Tell you what. We'll watch the interviews together and then we'll both take Hoover for her walk."

And that's what they did. She was surprised that he kept his word, but as soon as they'd listened to every scrap of information in the ether about the new Greenliner coach, they walked Hoover to her heart's content, all within the limits of street lighting, debating all the while the pros and cons of the upcoming season.

When they got back, he went beyond surprise to stunning the life out of her.

CHAPTER TWENTY

"Let's go dancing."

"What? It's almost nine o'clock."

"Most places don't even open until ten."

Trying her best not to let the panic show, she stuttered out, "I thought you weren't going to party?"

"I won't be partying. I'll be with you."

She wasn't sure how to take that, but she had other more important things to worry about.

"I don't have anything appropriate to wear. Besides, I don't dance."

Visions of him at Izabella's wedding came back with vivid details of his smooth moves across the floor. She could never keep up with him.

"Everybody dances. Whether they do it well or not is the only thing debatable."

"I don't."

"I'll be the judge of that."

"That doesn't solve the problem of my inadequate wardrobe."

"You can borrow something of Izabella's."

Feeling a slow burn of embarrassment creep up her neck, she blurted out, "No, I can't. That would be an invasion of her privacy."

He pulled his cell out of his pocket and next thing she knew he had the cell up to her ear as Izabella confirmed it would be fine if she borrowed something from her closet.

Once the phone was back where it came from, he rubbed his hands as if taking pleasure in this.

"Okay? You have permission."

"Are you brain-dead as well as an idiot? Haven't you noticed there's a little bit of a difference in our height and weight? Nothing of hers would fit me."

He examined her as if studying something of great import. When he was done, he met her eyes.

"A blouse would. You must have a pair of pants that you can accentuate with something silk."

He took her hand and dragged her up to her room, went to the closet, and began moving hangars around.

In apparent frustration, he spun toward her and asked, "Don't you go out? Ever?"

"Only when I have to."

"Where's the dress you wore to brunch?"

"In a ball ready for the dry cleaners."

Along with the suit she'd worn to her first interview. The one now covered in grit and probably still wet from the soaking it'd taken.

He huffed and went back to his inspection of the closet and finally, with no other alternative, removed a pair of black knit pants.

"These will have to do. You get ready, put these on, and I'll find something you can wear with them." He was on his way out, when he glanced back and said, "You can wear those ankle boots you have."

She stood there, tongue-tied. She hadn't even agreed to go out and here she was being dressed by a man she'd known for just over a week. And she was letting him.

He came rushing back in, a top more jersey than blouse, in his hand. It was a sequined, ruffled number in tomato red. She knew it would have looked fabulous on Izabella but on her? She wasn't taking odds.

"Here. Get moving. I'll throw something on, and we'll head out."

"Do you even know where we're going?"

"Not yet. But I'll find somewhere. You just concentrate on getting ready and I'll take care of the rest. It'll be fun, Fifi."

He looked psyched and it fueled her own curiosity about a night out with him. It would be the only one, so she might as well give in and take advantage. It wasn't as if her dancing skills were going to make or break the relationship. There wasn't one.

She did as he'd suggested and spent an extra fifteen minutes in the bathroom with make-up and hair gel. When she looked at the finished product in her mirror, the red of the blouse giving her some contrasting color, she thought, *Not half-bad.*

"At least I shouldn't embarrass him."

"I should say you won't."

He'd come into what should have been private space. He was a picture to behold, dressed in a suit, minus the tie, his fitted shirt half unbuttoned, giving her a peek at his chest hair, and she swallowed the lump that had caught in her throat.

He buried his chin in her neck, his hands braced on her hips, and she almost swooned.

"Mm. Something to look forward to. There's nothing as seductive as dancing with someone. It can lead to a very satisfying night."

He turned her to face him, kissed her lightly on the lips, and led her out into he night.

She was fidgety in the silence. She clasped her hands together and held them fast in her lap. As soon as they were on the highway headed for Boston, Rique asked,

"When was the last time you were at a club?"

She licked her lips and admitted, "Never."

She could feel his eyes on her, and the consuming heat it always provided.

"Never? Not even in college?"

"I was sixteen, remember? Too young to even think about sneaking in."

She'd watched with envy as her dorm mates would get ready on a Saturday evening, laughing, conspiring, girl talk filling the hall as they made their way out. She'd never felt so lonely.

"I get that, but later?"

"By then I had my routine. And I never did catch up age wise."

He was scowling. "You missed out on a lot because of your mother's aggressive push."

"Like throwing up all night from binge drinking or waking up with a killer hangover?"

There'd been nights she'd tended to the sick and supposedly dying. It was not something she wanted to experience for herself.

"Those things can be avoided."

"Says you, Mr. Suave."

"Mr. Suave. Yes, it fits."

She looked out the window, rolling her eyes as she did.

"I'm glad I'll be the first one taking you. I promise to monitor your intake. I have other plans for tonight and they don't include keeping you company as you hug the toilet bowl."

If she was going to hug something all night, she was going to make sure it was this man. Her time with him was running out.

When they entered the darkened room of the dance club, the music was blaring, the floor was filled with bodies moving to the beat. He found them a bar table at the back of the room, removed her coat, and hung it on the back of the stool. As he looked around, he said, "I guess it does pay to come early."

A waitress was at his elbow before he finished the task and took his order; a tequila mimosa for her, a sparkling water for him.

"I thought you were going to monitor my intake, not get me drunk?"

"You said you liked champagne, and this is it with a twist."

"Tequila isn't a twist, it's an arm wrench."

He kissed her on the forehead.

"It'll loosen you up."

"I don't need…"

The waitress was already back and placed the sparkling orange mixed drink on a small square napkin. What was she wearing Speedo-shoes?

Rique took a sip of his water and asked the brown-bobbed-haired female, "Can you start a tab for us, please?"

She nodded and ran off to deliver the rest of the drinks that had been on her tray.

Fiona lifted the flute like glass and took a sip. It was cold, tangy, and the bubbles tickled the back of her throat. The tequila gave it a punch that she probably didn't need. Just looking at Rique gave her the same kind of rib-crushing hit.

"Good?"

"It is."

She continued to satisfy her thirst as they listened to the music in silence, Rique's foot tapping under the table. Nervous, she was slurping at the bottom of her glass with her straw like a vacuum cleaner sucking up cookie crumbs. Loudly and with growing frustration.

Rique flagged the waitress over to order her another. It arrived just as a new song came on, and before she could take her first sip, Rique had her hand in his, pulling her to the edge of the dance floor.

She resisted until the music began to thrum through her. She hadn't been honest. She did like to dance but did it in the privacy of her condo. She could get a bit crazy when immersed in a good song. And this was a good song.

She felt her hips begin to move of their own volition, sashaying to the beat. Her eyes slid closed, and she raised her hands to the sides of her head as it kept the same tempo. When she felt Rique take her loosely in his arms, she gave in, draped herself within the embrace, and became one with the motion. He pressed her close, molded her to his body, then twirled her under his arm before reeling her back in. His hands were everywhere. Each touch was an electric shock. Each drum beat pounded in competition with her heart.

He whispered, his breath hot and steamy against her ear, "I thought you said you didn't dance."

"Not like you."

His fingers trailed down her arm, clasped her hand in his, pulling her back against his rock-solid form.

"Where did you see me dance?"

"Reid and Izabella's wedding video. Your date was able to keep up quite well."

Her voice was breathy, almost seductive. It wasn't like her but when she was with him, he did such funny things to her metabolism, she became someone else.

"I don't remember who I brought."

Her eyes flew up to meet his. "You certainly seemed pretty cozy."

Desire lit up his dark brown eyes. "I love to dance."

He proved it over the course of several more songs, most upbeat, until they finally played something slow and sensual.

"Come here."

His arms were tight around her middle as he guided her in a what might have been something international, the movements precise. It wasn't the box step, which she'd learned in dance class when she was in elementary school. He was graceful, powerful, and she could do nothing but melt against him.

His chin was in her neck, and he began to trail light kisses along her jawbone. The heat he was generating was of the delicious carnal variety, his knee probing between her legs, as he pressed her around the floor. She could feel the bulge beneath his zipper when he arched her in, pelvis to pelvis. His moan created a yearning so abrupt it felt like a stab of pain.

"We need to go home. Otherwise, I'll be tempted to ravish you right here and now."

"This isn't ravishment?"

It seemed like even his eyes possessed her.

When he crushed his lips to hers, she lost all sense of time and place. It was as if he was making love to her mouth, letting her know how he would make love to her body.

When the music floated into nothingness, he whispered into her ear, "Why don't you finish your drink and then we'll go."

"We haven't even been here an hour." Now that she had a slight buzz going, she wanted to stay. Dancing with him was another mind-altering experience that she didn't want to end.

"It served its purpose."

"And what was that?"

"Foreplay."

With a hint of tightly controlled restraint, he kissed her again before leading her back to their table. He helped her into her coat as she finished the last couple of mouthfuls of the tasty concoction. Even without it, she would have been light-headed. She was more intoxicated by Rique than by the tequila. The combination might prove to be lethal.

He guided her out to the car, his adrenaline running so thick in his system that he felt like a horny teenager. He would not take her here, not that there'd be room. He wasn't sixteen anymore, but he couldn't believe how hormonally challenged she was making him. He wanted her as desperately as he'd ever wanted a woman. She'd been putty in his hands on the dance floor, molding herself to his body, following his lead as if they were one. Dancing always made him amorous. The sweat, the closeness, the intimacy, but dancing with Fifi had… It had driven him to leave the venue early. He'd always been able to stall the emotions, relish the anticipation, but not with her.

He wanted to feel her beneath him, to fill her with all he was. He couldn't remember being this tight with need.

As he tucked her into the seat, he pleaded, "Don't fall asleep on me."

When her glazed eyes met his, she said, "Not until much later, I promise."

He slammed the door, raced to get behind the wheel.

In order to keep her awake, not quite trusting her to do it herself, he asked, "Do you know the story of Reid and Izabella?"

"Bit and pieces. I know they got married years after Melina was born but that she's his. That when he got traded, they bumped into each other, and when Leeni got sick, he was there for them."

"He was not known for his ability to commit. He'd loved my sister since they were kids but refused to acknowledge it. They spent a lot of wasted time apart from each other. Even the day of the wedding some of us weren't sure he'd show up. It was only when we found out he'd taken dancing lessons so he could tango with Iz at the reception that we knew he'd been

sucker-punched into submission."

"He looked like he knew what he was doing."

"He was a little stiff, but he didn't do a bad job. It's a very sensual dance if you do it right. Do you know who he took lessons from?"

She shook her head before saying, "No."

"Izabella's old flame, or rather his wife. They owned a dance studio, where Izabella used to go once a week. It was her one night out to relax and recharge. Everyone needs one of those, don't you think?"

"I'm beginning to."

He wanted to be the one to escort her out. If Carlos could remain friends with Izabella, why couldn't he remain friends with Fifi?

"Maybe we could do this again someday?"

She turned her head and he could see a sad smile appear on her face.

"That would be courting danger, don't you think?"

"Dancing doesn't have to lead to…sex."

He said that as they arrived back at the house.

Fifi put her hand on the door release. "Then I guess I'll go right up to bed."

He cupped her neck with his hand, preventing her from escaping. "All right. It would be courting danger. Dancing does have to lead to sex…with you."

The kiss that he'd been anticipating all the way home ignited a fire that he wasn't sure even orgasm would put out. When he lifted his mouth from hers, those gray eyes singed him further.

He fumbled with the door, went around to extricate her from her seat and in a frenzy of feeling, he spread hot, liquid kisses all over her face, his hand finding her curves, his body screaming for release. His mouth never left hers until they stumbled into the mudroom, where Hoover did her best to break them apart.

He groaned out, "Not now, girl."

Fifi pushed at his chest. "Let me take care of her."

"I'll come with you."

He needed to be touching her in some way, even if it was just holding her hand. As they stood on the deck, Hoover running around, chasing the wind, he slipped his arm around her waist and trailed kisses along her neck.

As soon as the dog was run ragged, Rique carried Fifi to his room, stripped them both of their clothes, and spent the night making love to her.

CHAPTER TWENTY-ONE

Rique was nestled against Fifi, perfectly content with the night's passion. She was uninhibited in bed, and she'd driven him to the brink of insanity and back several times before the morning came. He wasn't inclined to move, but the jarring ring of his cell, forced him to turn away and answer.

He sat up with a jolt, took a breath and swiped.

"Hello, Mr. Calipari."

"You don't have to be so formal. It's Mac, Enrique. Mr. Calipari is my father."

"Okay…Mac."

"Sorry to call so early but I'm hoping you can come out to my house this morning. I'm setting up meetings with some of the key players. I'd rather not use Farina's office until it's been cleared of his personal belongings, but I want to get started as quickly as I can. I also don't want it to look like I'm swooping in before the dust settled but time is of the essence, as they say. Can you be here by eleven?"

The voice was deep, the tone brusque. He was all business. Was it a good or bad sign? And what did it mean that he was a key player?

"Yes, sir."

Mac gave him the address, and before hanging up, said, "See you then."

Fifi had rolled over, the sheet covering her body, her eyes half-lidded. If the call hadn't shaken him, that look might have beckoned him back to her side.

Groggily, she murmured, "You've been summoned?"

He nodded. "He doesn't seem to be wasting any time. I didn't think he'd get to it quite this swiftly."

He thumbed a text and then put the phone down

She didn't ask but she had a question in her eyes.

"Seb. I want to see if he's got a meeting today."

They'd been texting back and forth since yesterday morning, recapping the news reports, worrying together over the future. He knew Seb would be more concerned about it now than he was. He'd hate to lose the two friends he'd made. They'd formed a tight triumvirate and he knew the chemistry would be out on the field with them.

At the ping, Rique picked the phone back up and read the one word typed. *Yes.*

The second ping with the words *shit, fuck* typed might have been humorous if he didn't know what lay behind the sentiment.

Fifi shifted to a sitting position, pulled the pillows up and rested against them. "What did he say? You look nervous."

"He got a call, which doesn't bode well for me. Is Mac going to get rid of the both of us?"

"Don't worry just yet. Hear what he has to say. He might be bringing you guys in because you're the more recent acquisitions. Neither of you has worked under Farina, so he's got a blank slate to start with."

That was a possibility. Or maybe he was calling in the players whom he thought might be expendable. All cockiness had evaporated with that one swipe, and he wished he could go back, redo last year, save games, play his position the way it was supposed to be played. About to tell her his regrets, he glanced over, and stopped. If that had happened, he wouldn't have been traded, and he wouldn't be here, with her. A strange calm came over him and he sat down on the bed, took her hand, and said, "Come with me."

Her jaw dropped open. "Are you crazy? You can't drag me along to that meeting."

He knew that but it didn't erase the need to have her there with him.

"Yes. Sorry. I'm not thinking clearly."

Without meaning to, he increased the pressure on her hand. Her wince relaxed his grip.

"The meeting's at his house. Do you know how far Lexington is?"

"Half an hour, forty-five minutes. Being Sunday, you won't hit much traffic."

He got up off the bed and went directly into the bathroom to relieve himself. When he returned, Fifi was just getting up. He had come to know every inch of her body, but it still amazed him that she was so lush and soft. It also aroused him. His morning erection had gone down with the call, followed by the pee, but it had come back with a vengeance. He needed to lay with her, fill her, empty himself of the nervous agitation that had ignited since he'd spoken to Mac.

She was sitting on the edge of the bed, reaching for her pants, but before she could get them back on, he was there, fingering her naked shoulders, tickling the skin with featherlike strokes. She dropped her head back and moaned.

"We can't, Rique."

"Why not?"

He sounded like a pouty kid who wasn't going to get his way.

"Hoover needs to go out and you've got to get ready."

"It's not even eight o'clock. I have hours until I have to leave."

She maneuvered around him and this time was able to snag her pants and get them on before he stopped her. After pulling the shirt over her head, and hiding her assets, she said, "Why don't you text Mattie. See if he's one of those key players."

He watched as she scooted out of the room, heard Hoover greet her, and Fifi's soft voice as she muttered words of love back.

He dropped to the edge of the bed, his head in his hands. He'd almost whispered similar words to her last night that would have proved problematic in the light of day. They were words better suited for a mate, than a friend. He had to admit she'd become more than that, but he didn't know what to do with it.

Maybe if she were more like her mother, cold and detached it would have been easier to separate lust from…caring. But she wasn't. She'd been willing to make room in her life for his passion. Last night, while they were walking Hoover, something he rarely did, the cold had invigorated, the conversation had stimulated. She was a great listener and he was able to talk to her about everything. She offered valuable insights, not only about the game, but into who he was and what he could do if he put his mind to it.

He scrubbed his face. His feelings about her were becoming complicated, something he didn't need right now. He'd come up with a plan and he meant to see it through but… He looked up at the empty doorway. He didn't like knowing what they had together would change once those plans were in play.

He picked up his phone and texted Mattie like she'd suggested. It made him feel a sliver better when he heard his meeting was for eleven thirty. No way would they be trading the new third baseman. Maybe Fifi was right and Mac wanted to talk to the newest members of the team before he reached out to the others. He wouldn't know until he got there, so he'd put the worry aside.

He showered and changed into a suit, wanting to impress his new boss. When he got down to the kitchen, Fifi was freshly dressed in her standard jeans and sweater, and there was a steaming cup of coffee ready and waiting.

She smiled and all the lingering nervous tension evaporated.

"Don't you look nice. Do you think it's necessary?'

"It can't hurt."

He blew on the hot liquid and carefully took a sip. And winced. "For someone who measures things for a living, I'd think you'd have this down."

"You'd think. I guess I just don't care enough. I'm not all that fond of the taste anyway. I drink it for the caffeine."

He leaned back against the counter and asked. "Now what do I do for the next two hours?"

"Pace?"

"Not my style. How about we go for breakfast?"

"Are you sure? There was a big article in the *Globe* this morning about the team, the new manager and some of the players, you being one of them. It might get you noticed."

He saw the paper lying on the table, sectioned off, and the sports page was front and center. Had she developed a fondness for the game? The team? Or was it plain old curiosity?

"Thought you went for news that impacted your life."

"Today, this meets the criteria."

He had one arm across his chest, the other clutching the mug.

"What did the article say?"

She shrugged. "There are question marks, who'll stay, who'll go. Most of it had to do with Mac's credentials but some had to do with team chemistry, the fresh faces, youth and a new energy. The prognosis is good for a winning season."

"I like the sound of that. I also like the sound of breakfast. I'm hungry."

His appetite had never been better. He was especially ravenous after a night tangled in the sheets with her. "Izabella says the townies leave you alone. It's one of the reasons I want to relocate here."

"Then sure. Where do you want to go?"

"There's a place in Shawsheen that I've been to with Reid before. The food's greasy but good."

"Let me get my coat."

He was able to pass the unwanted free time in animated conversation and as soon as he dropped her off, he headed south.

The nervousness came back as soon as he pulled up to the gated house. He pushed the button to announce his arrival and waited for the iron-rod gates to open. When they had swung wide enough for him to drive through, he proceeded down a narrow, winding lane until he came to the secluded sprawling cape. There was another car there, and he pulled up beside it, shut off the engine, and sat, trying to calm his nerves. He straightened his tie before climbing out and approaching the double front door. The bong of the bell echoed both inside and out and it took less than a minute for a woman to open it. She was young, with shoulder-length brown hair and glasses. Almost as tall as he was, she was dressed in professional attire. He didn't have to wonder long if this was Mac's daughter.

"Hi, Enrique. I'm Casey Calipari. Dad's just finishing up with his earlier appointment. Please come in. You can have a seat in the family room while you wait."

He rubbed his palms along the legs of his pants and followed her to a comfortable room just beyond the foyer.

She gave him a watered-down smile and said, "You seem nervous. Don't be. He doesn't spout fire. You'll leave in the same condition as when you arrived."

That might be the case, but would he still be the shortstop for the Greenies when he did?

He stuffed his hands in his pants and stood waiting for further instructions. She must have noticed his restlessness. "Why don't you have a seat."

She'd pointed to one of the comfortable-looking couches and he surveyed the area before choosing one. She sat opposite. Was she the welcoming committee or the cheering section? She was definitely easy on the eyes but there was a lack of warmth there. They sat in silence for a moment, and to break it he said, "I've heard very good things about him. His stats in Pittsfield were impressive."

With obvious pride, she remarked, "He turned that team around in one year. He's hoping he can take this team all the way."

He was curious now about this woman, the one who Seb had dated in high school. He liked getting to know people and she was no exception.

"Do you work for him?"

He hoped for Seb's sake she didn't.

"In a way. I manage the sports facility he owns."

"That's not the one—"

She nodded. "We rent it out to the Greenies and Red Sox when they need it, so yes, it is the one you used this week."

"Were you there?"

"In my office. I don't usually make it a habit to watch the practices. I'd never get any work done."

He wondered if she'd made an exception with Seb there. Was she still enamored? When she tucked her hair behind her ear, he glimpsed the glint of a ring on her finger. He had his answer.

He nodded at it and asked, "Have you set a date yet?"

She glanced down, fingered it, and said somewhat carefully, "Not yet. Greg just proposed on my birthday."

He didn't know when that was, so he didn't know how recently it had taken place. Maybe with the engagement, Mac wouldn't be as ornery toward Seb. He studied her expression and wasn't sure there was as much pleasure in the rock of ring as one would think.

Before he could ask any more personal questions, Mac came down the hall, Verducci walking alongside. The new manager was a large man, or maybe he just had a large presence. At six foot four, he carried his girth well. He was tanned and relaxed, and he took up all the space in the room.

Rique rose as he approached and extended his hand. Mac took it with a firm grip. "It's good to meet you, sir."

"Rique this is one of our catchers, Rafe Verducci. Rafe our shortstop, Enrique dos Santos."

With that pronouncement, Rique felt the tension in his shoulders loosen. Being introduced that way was a good omen, implied that he was staying. It seemed Rafe was, too, but teams didn't usually carry three catchers throughout the season. One would have to go. Would it be Motts or Dorfman? If he was pressed to guess, he'd bet it would be Dorfman. Motts had been catching Reid since he'd gotten there, and the front office would probably want to keep their ace happy.

Mac had walked Verdi to the door, turned back, and said, "You're up next. Follow me."

Before doing as told, he glanced at Casey. "It was nice to meet you. Maybe I'll see you again someday."

Mac slapped him on the back. "You'll be seeing lots of Casey from here on in. She's coming with us to Sanford. She's my right hand."

Casey had dipped her head, becoming consumed with the carpet. It didn't seem she was happy about that. Would she have to leave her fiancé behind? She glanced up, met his eyes, sadness shining there if he read her right, before she walked off in another direction. It appeared her work here was done.

Now that some of the agitation was gone, Rique took the time to absorb his surroundings. The house was well-decorated, grand yet homey.

"You have a beautiful home, sir."

"I told you it was Mac, and my wife is an interior decorator. I'll pass along your compliment."

He guided him into an office, the desk an old one that must have been refurbished. It gleamed in the sunlight streaming through the three-panel window. The seats opposite were black leather, and when he sat, he felt it mold to his body. There were framed pictures of his wife and daughter scattered around the room. An oil painting of the two of them hung on the wall.

"You have a beautiful family."

You've said the word beautiful twice now. Have you no other descriptive words in your vocabulary?

He felt like an imbecile.

Looking at the man who was standing close by, Rique couldn't quite describe the smile as warm. More menacing… maybe intimidating.

"My family's the most important part of my life."

He'd heard that from Seb, but he wasn't giving away anything his new friend had told him.

"I agree. I'm very close to mine."

"Jackson's brother-in-law, right?"

"Yes. He's married to my sister Izabella."

"I've met her. Lovely woman."

He was surprised when Mac sat beside him instead of using the desk as a barrier between them. He didn't need it. He'd crossed his arms over his broad chest. It had the same effect. In a steady, low-pitched voice he asked, "So, how you settling in?"

Clearing his throat, Rique said in response, "Very well. I'm staying with Reid and Izabella. Although they're still on vacation, they gave me full use of their home." He added in more somber tones, "They're coming back early due to Farina's death."

Mac's expression turned somber. "For the wake and funeral. Most of the veteran players have had to cut their family time short due to the circumstance. It's a great loss to the organization and to the world of baseball."

Was that the company line or did Mac really believe that? Farina wasn't known for his mild-mannered temperament. Didn't matter to him, so he went along.

"It is."

Mac leaned back and studied him before admitting, "Reid is one of the people DeLorenzo spoke to before making the trade for you. He's on your side in this, although Farina was on the fence. I'm not sure where I stand, but when I spoke to Leo about your practice sessions, he told me you've been busting your ass."

Thanks, Leo, wherever you are.

In a steady, low-pitched voice, he said, "I want this…Mac. I'll do whatever I have to to make it work."

Mac cleared his throat, thumbed his ear, before making eye contact.

"We need someone strong at shortstop if we're going to go all the way. Most of the men I've played with at that position were leaders. They have to be. They're the backbone of the team. Do you have that in you?"

Enrique thought carefully before replying, "I have to earn their respect first. I can't ask anyone else to give it up for the team if I'm not willing to. I hope to prove myself not only to you but to them as well."

Mac leaned back, his fingers steepled under his chin.

"I like that answer. What happened to you last year?"

He could articulate that logically because of the conversations he'd had with Fifi. He knew now what they problem had been and accepted it as such. He wasn't going to give excuses.

"I got bored. I'm not good on the bench, but I should have played my role as a utility player with as much grit and determination as if I was the main attraction. I regret my…apathy."

Mac was taking him in, stroking his closely shaved chin.

"I used to get bored, too. I hated days off, didn't like being side-lined. As a manager, I look at it differently. I know what a season can do to you. It's long and you can burn out if you're not careful. You'll be getting days off. I don't care if you're in the middle of a hitting streak, I'll be benching all starters, every ten to twelve days. I expect you to get as fired up as if you're out on the field. A leader cheerleads from wherever he is."

Rique didn't like it, but he understood it. He also appreciated that the man was looking out for his players.

"I can do that."

Thumbing his ear again, Mac looked up at him and smiled for the first time since sitting down.

"You wouldn't have been traded if you were living up to your potential. If you turn yourself around, your…apathy…could turn out to be our good fortune."

"I'm ready to settle down. I'm mentally prepared to do the job, and I have the skills to get it done."

"No more of your infamous parties."

It seemed his reputation preceded him. He wasn't going to get into the why behind it, but said simply, "Won't have a need for them."

"I treat my players like grown men who know their roles. I don't play babysitter or nursemaid. I'm depending on you to monitor yourself. Understood?"

"Understood."

"Now that I have what I needed about you and your mind-set, let me tell you a little about me, what my expectations will be, and something about my style."

Rique nodded and sat forward, wanting to hear every word that came out of the man's mouth.

He'd become a better listener over the last week.

"I expect to win the World Series and I have the team who can do it. I expect everyone in the clubhouse to step up, get better. I want aggression in the batter's box, and I want every hitter to hunt for the right pitch to hit. I will be using analytics but will be filtering out what I don't need from what I can use to win the game. I want to have a good relationship with the players. I won't be your best friend, but I will be there to listen. I can only get the best out of you if there is a connection between us. And as I already mentioned, you're grown men, who know the game.

I'll be treating you like professionals, not kids. Any questions so far?"

"You won't be looking for home runs?"

"Every manager loves home runs, but I want you to work the count, go after pitches that might not look great but will get the man home if you drop it in the right place. I want everyone working toward the goal, as a team. From what Leo's told me, you, Mattie, and Sebastian have already become friends. There's chemistry there and it will work in our favor."

"Mattie said he'd work with me on hitting."

"I'd love to see you be our lead-off man, but you'll need patience, especially your first time at bat. You'll give the guys a sense of how the pitcher's working that day. You might have to sacrifice yourself at times, but if and when you get on, your speed will create some momentum."

"With Mattie and Ovitz as the three-four punch, I'll make sure I get to first so they can hit me home."

He felt his enthusiasm and passion for the game amping up.

He liked Mac. He could only hope he'd earn the man's respect through hard work and mental discipline.

Mac checked his watch when the doorbell rang and stood. "Looks like your time in the barrel is over. I want you ready for spring training like you've never been ready before."

Rique nodded. "With another couple of weeks before the trucks leave, I was wondering if I could use the sports facility again, the one we used for drills with Leo. From what I understand it's yours."

"This tells me you're not bullshitting me. Talk to Casey and arrange some time. Maybe I'll have her block out some time every day for you and whoever wants to join you. When will you want to start? Thursday?"

"I've made arrangements to visit my family in Brazil one last time before the season starts. My ticket is for late afternoon the day of the funeral, my return will get me here for Monday."

"Monday it is. That will give her time to move some things around if she needs to."

"Thanks. I'm looking forward to working under you."

"*With* me. I can't do anything without the players."

They walked down the hall toward the front door. Mattie was waiting in the same chair as he had and rose to his feet as soon as they approached. Alicia was there as well. She must have driven him over. Mattie didn't yet have a license.

Mac addressed both players. "I've heard you're the one-two punch our infield needed. I can't wait to see it for myself. Oh, and by the way, Leo's agreed to stay. He's one of the best and he'll bring continuity, something we need to a certain extent. There'll be plenty of new bodies around to shake the box."

Rique smiled at Mattie and said, "Good to know."

"I'll see you at the funeral, if not at the wake. I expect you'll be wearing a suit to that, but you don't have to dress up every time I talk to you. Suits have there place, on the road when traveling, but not for quick meetings with me. It's one of the perks of managing. I don't like to be strangled by a tie unless I have to." He laughed outright, "It's the main reason I turned down their offer as Greenliner President."

Rique's eyes widened. He didn't know Mac had been asked to fill the president's role. He was glad he'd turned it down.

"Thanks, Mac."

"Nothing to thank me for yet. I expect a lot from you. Don't let me down."

"I won't."

And he meant it.

When he left, he sat in his car, rethinking the decision of a small one. He would have loved room for his legs, especially now. While he waited for Mattie, he put a sports radio station on to listen for updates, hear what the callers had to say about Mac. He thought it would have been great if Seb was available, but he wasn't meeting with Mac until mid-afternoon. The outfielder was sure he was saving him for last. Just because.

CHAPTER TWENTY-TWO

Fiona rushed into the eatery in Stoneham, her phone pinging from the inside of her purse. Whoever it was would have to wait until she found Bohdan. She couldn't wait to see her friend and lab partner. She'd called him as soon as Rique had left for his meeting with Mac to let him know she'd heard from the head of the science department at the university in Boston last night. Their most common lunch dates were in the courtyard outside the school, where he'd all but force feed her, making sure she had the sustenance needed to keep her brain cells from shriveling into nothingness. He was an undergrad, she a doctoral student but they'd formed a partnership that he'd kept going after graduation. He got a job working days and dropped by the lab afterwards to work with her until the wee hours of the morning. They never socialized, so meeting outside the school, was a new experience.

She stood at the periphery of the room and scanned the interior until she saw him, seated at a table in the corner. He had a smile on his face, but then he always did. Life for him was one big adventure, and he brought life into a lab that could have been sterile and impersonal. He'd made the tests measurable and the outcomes bearable, helped her run her standards, one failure at a time until they'd conquered them, and they were able to claim victory. They'd always talked about working together again, when one of them got their own lab, although he still had a ways to go before he was finished with his dissertation. He hadn't even started the application for his doctorate.

She eased through the room and he was on his feet by the time she got there, reaching out to give her a bear hug. Laughing, she sat down opposite him and said, "It's been way too long."

In reality it had been only a few short months, but when you work with someone every day for weeks on end, even a couple days seemed like years. And when that person made you feel less alone, it was more an eternity. It's how it would feel when Rique was out of her life. Giving her no time to dwell on that, his words rushed out. "I'm glad you called. I was worried when I hadn't heard from you. You could have texted, you know."

She shifted in her seat. "There was nothing to tell. This is the first real possibility and I'm terrified it's too good to be true."

She needed him to convince her it wasn't, that it was the natural progression for her in reaching her goal of advancing science. He knew what she did and how she did it, knew what was possible. He'd kept her running on positive and she needed the high-octane fuel of his conviction.

"Tell me the facts. You skipped all important facets of the upcoming interview."

She settled in, her hands clasped, and she could hear the excitement in her voice.

"They've just recently freed up one of their laboratories and they're looking for a new tenant. That would be me. Us. It's partially equipped which will cut down on the amount of money they'd have to donate to our cause, although it would still be up to me to find a grant to keep it open."

"From what you said, they reached out to you?"

This was the key. She hadn't gone searching.

"Yes. He, that would be Dr. Kurtis Michaels, heard about my upcoming interview in Amherst, talked to Terry, and decided he wouldn't allow me to go to his in-house competitor."

The University of Massachusetts had several satellite campuses, the home seat established in the western part of the state, where her next interview was scheduled. She might be able to cancel it, stay in the area. She still couldn't believe her good luck. The call had come just as she was about to take Hoover outside and had caught her completely off guard.

After he'd given her his name and the reason for the call, she'd been tongue-tied. She'd wanted to ask him to repeat everything he'd said, so she could savor the invitation to interview, but was able to control herself. Her maturity or lack of it was the one major hindrance in finding a sponsor and she wasn't going to let him rethink his proposition. She'd agreed to a Wednesday appointment to discuss the offer and swiped off, reeling from the conversation.

She'd told no one about it, not even Rique when he'd finally asked who'd called. She'd needed to process it in her own mind before sharing it with anyone else. When her eyes fluttered open this morning, a secret smile on her lips, she'd decided to share it. But then the call had come from Mac Calipari, and she decided to postpone telling him. He'd been nervous and edgy about his own meeting, feelings she could relate to, so she had spent the precious few hours between the call and his departure, allowing him lead in conversational topics.

It was only after he left, his good-bye kiss one for the history books, that she'd called the man she was meeting. She was chomping at the bit now to tell someone, to scream and holler her good fortune. Not only would Bohdan be happy to hear the news, he'd understand that the offer was a treasure trove of all she'd wanted, hoped, and dreamed about. Working together in Terry's lab, she'd found he complemented her strengths and weaknesses. Originally from Ukraine, he'd come to the States as a boy and had polished his interest in science any way he could. He'd gotten her through the transition point that came in graduate school where you have to turn the corner and be willing to explore unchartered territory.

Spending years being told what to do, it was sometimes hard to become your own teacher. When she'd come up with her hypothesis, embroidered it with complexity and improbability, he'd worked with her to bring it into the realm of possibility. When she'd finished, he'd been as much responsible for her success as she was. She'd promised she'd take him with her wherever she went. It was a way to thank him for all he'd done. Today she was keeping that promise.

He asked again, "Come on, spill. Tell me about it."

She moved her purse off to the side and rested her arms on the table, leaning toward him.

"It'll be small, but that's okay, because it's an on-campus site, in the heart of the city. Michaels heard about the new discoveries being made in the field at a recent conference and read more about it in an article written by Argosy that was published in *Science America*."

Bohdan would know who that was. They'd been in constant contact with the man during her writing phase of the dissertation. He was a key player in the field and any article, brief or long, would be consumed by scientists.

"When Michaels heard I was looking to further my research and one of the UMass satellites was in the running, he picked up the phone and called Terry. She gave him bullets of my thesis and told me she'd sold it. I'm meeting with him on Wednesday to discuss the particulars, but it sounds like a solid offer."

"He knows your age?"

Bohdan knew this would always be the sticking point. She'd discussed it with him ad nauseam.

"He does. When Terry called just before I got here, she confirmed that he'd been impressed by all that I'd accomplished. Her glowing recommendation didn't hurt." She looked up and smiled. "Or so she said."

He gave a quiet whoop. "We're on our way."

She made eye contact with him. There was five years of shared experience in their history. He was as brilliant as any scientist she'd met.

"We are, but you need to get moving on your application. You can work with me, do your own thing on the side."

"I like working as your side kick. I don't need the doctor thing added to my name."

She chewed her lip. "I didn't either."

"Yes, you did. One of us had to. Better you than me."

Bohdan didn't like regulations, didn't like the political taste of the doctorate process. There were protocols to follow and stringent parameters set, and he was a free spirit who wanted to work at his own pace, on his own passions.

Her phone pinged again. She looked up and apologized with her eyes as she scrambled the cell out of her purse and thumbed the message icon.

There were two texts from Rique. He must have been the one who'd reached out as she was coming into the restaurant.

The first message read:

Meeting went well. I'm waiting for Mattie to finish with his and am going out for coffee or lunch to compare thoughts. Later.

The second had the tone of annoyance.

Where are you? You didn't get back to me. I'm with Mattie now. Will be home later to tell you all about it.

Home? He made it sound like they lived together, was irritated that he couldn't connect with her. Had she missed the memo that said he was part of her life? Could he possibly want her in his life? For real?

She glanced up to see Bohdan peering at her.

"I know that look. You wear it when you don't understand something."

He did know her, better than most. He was her translator to the rest of the world when she was overwhelmed and under-energized. Did she tell him all? She was sure he'd nag until she had, so she admitted, "I…I've found myself in a conundrum."

"What are you confused about?"

"It's more a who than a what."

He plopped back against his chair. "Really? You? You actually might have a life?"

Bohdan was married, the father of a young daughter, and his wife was as much a part of the scientific community as he was. Ardita worked in the emergency room of a local hospital, her hours as fierce as theirs were. Bohdan's mother lived with them, took care of their daughter Priyanka, so they were able to fulfill their lives doing the work they loved, without sacrificing family.

She'd often envied him.

"I didn't go looking for this kind of complication."

"Does anyone? It usually rushes at you from out of the blue."

The waitress came over for the third time and they allowed themselves a moment to scan the menu and give her their order. When she'd hurried away, he said, "Tell me about him."

And she did, leaving nothing out.

"What the fuck, Fiona? Do you do this to yourself on purpose?"

He'd startled her with his outburst.

"What do you mean?"

"Nothing can come from it. You'll never have to make a commitment to him or the relationship. Which is why, I think, you went along."

That stung, yet she had to consider the veracity of the statement. Was that why she'd given in to the attraction? Rique was safe, and she wouldn't need to choose family over career.

She shook her head. It wasn't as simple as Bohdan was suggesting. It was more layered and complex than that. It might have been part of the reason she'd been inclined to say yes. Now she wanted more… not only time with him, more of the intimacy they'd shared, but also the space to explore it, see if it went anywhere. He didn't. That stung, too.

The ache in her heart told her she'd gone farther downstream than she'd anticipated.

Needing to defend herself, she said with more conviction than she felt, "I went along because he's handsome, athletic, and had the potential of getting an A in bed."

"Something tells me he made the grade."

She might have blushed, but this was Bohdan and he knew a lot of her secret longings.

"He did."

Their meals arrived, and as soon as the waitress left them alone, he picked up a fry. "And now?"

She slid down in the seat. "Now, I'm fucked because I care about him."

He whistled.

"You've finally succumbed to love, and you've…been stranded on first base."

She wasn't sure she'd go that far. Love was a scary proposition. Yet she couldn't entirely rule it out. The fact remained she was all alone in it.

She was playing with the napkin that was curled around the utensils.

"That's a cute baseball metaphor but I'm not even in the ballpark."

He leaned in, caught and held her eyes.

"I wouldn't say that. He's texted you twice."

"He met with the new manager. He wants to tell me all about it."

"Then you can share. You've got some pretty impressive news of your own."

"He wouldn't understand the significance."

That wasn't fair. Most wouldn't. They wouldn't know what it had taken to get here, or where she wanted to go.

"Doesn't mean he wouldn't be interested in hearing all about it."

"Rique is interested in very little beyond himself."

Even as she said it, she knew it wasn't exactly true. He'd been asking questions, sifting through information as if he wanted to understand.

"And you love this guy? What are you, a masochist?"

She was about to deny the remark about love but didn't. She might be able to fool Bohdan that love had nothing to do with it, but she had a feeling it was herself she'd be trying to fool.

Instead, she agreed with his assessment. "Apparently so."

She'd have to be okay with that. Rique had given her the most exquisite night of her life.

Bohdan was holding an onion ring, waving it in the air, punctuating his words.

"Which takes us back to my original hypothesis."

She slumped back and admitted, "Which might be on target, but I also thought it would be fun, an adventure, lust being satisfied." She didn't realize it would be the most intimate thing she'd ever done. She'd never let herself be swept away before.

"For shits and giggles, let's say he decided he wanted you. What would you say?"

She bit her lip, taking the time to think about that.

"I don't know. Not only because I'm driven, but because I'm not sure we'd work…outside the bedroom."

"There must be something about him that makes you overlook his ego. What is the one trait that attracts you over all others?"

She didn't have to think long or hard. "He pulls me out of myself. Makes me laugh."

"Shits and giggles aside, I think you're a goner. Anyone who can do that deserves a prize."

As they ate, they relegated the topic of Rique to the back burner and focused on that what they'd do once they had their lab, how they'd dress it, what they wanted to accomplish. It was a more comfortable topic for her, involving less heart, more brain. When they parted, Bohdan kissed her cheek before saying goodbye.

"Call me after you talk to Michaels. I'll be sitting on pins until I hear from you."

"You'll be my first one. Wish me luck."

"You won't need it."

She wished he was right, but luck was going to be a big part of this, and she might already have received her full portion. As she drove toward Izabella's house, all her thoughts were on the interview on Wednesday, preparing a mental checklist of all the questions that might be posed. She'd spend the next few days coming up with logical answers that might tilt the decision her way.

Rique was waiting for her when she arrived, standing at the door that separated the house from the garage.

"Where've you been?"

He sounded anxious, as if he hadn't been sure she'd ever return.

With little room to maneuver, she opened her car door and squeezed by the screens that were leaned against the cement wall, waiting to be hung in the new windows come spring.

As breezily as she could, she said, "Having lunch with a friend."

He stopped her by placing his hand on her wrist. "What friend?"

Shrugging, she said, "Someone I worked in the lab with."

He seemed satisfied. With no further questions, he followed her into the kitchen where Hoover was waiting for her. She scuffed the gray head as a strange feeling floated through her. She wondered if this was what it would be like to be with this man, come home to him, a dog…a family. She suddenly wanted all that it entailed.

With a flutter of excitement, wanting to share her news, she put down her purse on the counter and turned to him, but before she could say anything, he began a soliloquy on his meeting. She might have been deflated but his enthusiasm was catching. She loved watching his expressions, hearing his passion, learning new things, so she sat absorbed, and listened. Until he said, "He was even cool about my trip to Brazil. Said Monday would be fine to begin training again."

Reality smacked her right between the eyes. Izabella and Reid would be back tomorrow to reclaim their house, their dog, their life. This, what she had today, was not something she could build on. That's when her bubble popped, and deflation whooshed her happiness away.

As if she hadn't made a seismic shift in attention, he continued. "I haven't heard from Seb. I'm not sure that's a good sign." He checked his watch. "Never mind. He hasn't even met with Mac yet. I won't hear from him for an hour or so."

Distracted now by her despair, she forced herself to be part of the conversation, tried to inject some humor where there was none.

"It doesn't sound like he'll be going back to the farm."

He passed right over her remark, as if she was merely a sounding board. Any woman with good manners would do.

"I liked the guy but if he lets history decide the roster, I'll be deeply disappointed." He glanced up. "Oh, by the way, I met Casey. She was the welcoming committee."

She nodded at him, not wanting to take the risk her voice might give away her raw emotion.

"Aren't you going to ask what she's like?"

She didn't really care one way or another. "That's more a guy thing, I think."

He was up, his hands on his hips. "Maybe. Anyway, she's tall, wears glasses, looks pleasant."

She looked up, took him in, and then dipped her eyes. The sight was too painful.

"Is that like saying she has a good personality because her looks are suspect?"

"No. She's pretty enough. Cool as a cucumber, though."

"Maybe she doesn't like ball players."

It made sense in her book.

"Her father's one of the best Greenliners who's ever played."

"Not the same thing. A father's rarely anything other than a father in a daughter's eyes."

He threw his hands up in the air, as if she were missing something important. "She grew up with the sport."

He was exasperated. Was it because she wasn't showing interest in Casey or she was giving him minimal feedback?

She could feel his eyes on her, as if waiting for some scientific explanation. She looked up and met his gaze, swallowed the lump. "Are you asking if there should be a predilection for wanting an athlete for a mate? The answer would depend on a lot of other variables."

Like was she hurt by one when she was younger.

"She manages the sports facility he owns, so she has a toe in."

"I like sitting at the edge of a pool with my legs submerged but I don't like going all in. Maybe she doesn't, either. Besides, I'd say that has more to do with financials and admin work than how fast she can run or how well she can hit."

"Well, Seb doesn't have to worry. She's engaged if the rock she was wearing says anything."

This piqued her curiosity. "She's over him, then."

She wondered what it took. How long before the longing went away?

"I'd like to think so if she's marrying someone else."

She gave him a slight sigh. That pretty much said it all. One couldn't be hung up about a person and marry another.

Hoover had been lying peacefully on the carpet, her head on her paws, so she suspected Rique had taken her out at some point since getting back, but she probably still needed a walk. She could use one, too. She needed to clear her head, put away the desire for something she'd only recently begun to want. Being the kind of person who needed to think her problems through rather than talk about them, or talk period, she had to grab some alone time so she could solve a dilemma that was becoming more complicated by the minute. She got up and went to get the leash.

"Want me to come with you?"

"Thanks, but no."

"Why?"

He looked almost hurt, as if she were rejecting him in some way. It would never occur to him he'd done that to her already.

"I need some head space. With you talking non-stop, I won't get it."

And with that, she slipped the leash on and slid out of the door.

CHAPTER TWENTY-THREE

Enrique watched her go, uneasy at being left behind. Why did she need head space? Had he drained her with all that talk about baseball, the team, the new coach? He hadn't given her an opportunity to interact. He'd just gone on and on. But that's the way she usually liked it. Unless they were involved in some deep discussion, when they traded opinions, philosophies, attitudes. It was one of the reasons he thought they got along well together. They exchanged qualities each lacked. He was a grand thinker; she attended to detail. She was more comfortable in small groups; he thrived in large crowds. He liked to talk; she liked to listen. She supplied resources he lacked, grounded him, and he was gaining a more well-rounded approach to life. He wanted to believe he was providing her something similar. Yet he knew they couldn't fulfill the deeper needs that came with a lifetime commitment. She wanted a career and deserved a rewarding one for all the hard work she'd put into getting her doctorate. He wanted someone who would cook him meals, make a home, give him children, provide him a place to hang his hat when he came off the road. It was a hard life and it took a lot out of a player. He didn't want to come home to an empty house, devoid of human companionship. He wanted a woman, his woman, waiting for him. Fifi just didn't fit his ideal.

And he didn't fit hers.

He couldn't play the role she needed, someone patient with her hours in the lab, someone who matched her in curiosity and intellect, someone who'd take on some of those wifely duties she'd abdicate. Where would she meet the man who would? If she isolated herself, she'd be cutting herself off from the possibility of a relationship, and she'd miss out on the most important part of life.

Maybe she already knew him. He still hadn't asked her a lot of personal questions. Who had she had lunch with? He'd been more than mildly curious but hadn't followed up. He wasn't sure he wanted to know. If she'd met some guy, he would have... what?

He gravitated to the family room, turned the TV on for some background noise and dropped onto the couch. There was a slow rumble of emotion that hit him, but he couldn't define it. He'd wanted her to find someone, someone who would make her feel cared for. Loved.

He just didn't want her to find it while they were still here and he still needed her.

He jumped up, restless, and began to pace. They only had one more day together and then she'd be going home. He'd find a place of his own and their lives would branch off. They'd go their own ways. Him to Brazil then Sanford for spring training, her to…where? Would she have to leave the area to find a lab? Could she end up in California, like her mother suggested? He could see her when the team was out West, to play the Dodgers or Padres. They could hang out, talk…but it would have to end there. He'd be married by then, and no matter how well they fit together or how intimate they'd been, he couldn't make love to her.

That thought hit him hard in the gut.

Don't be ridiculous. You'll have found another lover. One who you'll have promised to love and cherish. Her bed will be the one that calls to you.

But he couldn't imagine it. The only face he saw there was one with soft dove-gray eyes and framed by curls.

He felt itchy, his nerves rubbing his skin raw, his body as tight as a bow. As he got ready to bolt, to go for a drive to clear his mind, his cell rang.

He grabbed it up, needing another voice to break through the silence and his chaotic thoughts.

"Seb? What happened?"

"I'm still with the team, if that's what you're asking."

He smiled, not only because his friend was still a Greenie but because the statement had made him think of Fifi. "I knew he wouldn't send you back to the farm."

"If there's probation, I'm on it. He made it very clear I'm to stay away from Casey, who happened to be there I might add. It should be easy enough. She's fucking engaged."

"Is that annoyance I'm hearing in your voice?"

"No. I couldn't care less."

"Could you try a little harder to mean it?"

There was a pause, then a gulp.

"She looked good. Like the Casey I knew. But I'm still not ready for what she wanted. She's found it with someone else and I'm happy for her."

"Sure, you are."

"Mac spent at least ten minutes extolling the virtues of her fiancé. He's a graduate of Wharton, like that's some big deal, and has a job at a Fortune 500 company. Good husband material and would never break her heart. Blah, blah, blah. You want to grab a drink?"

Rique wavered. He did but he also couldn't afford to miss his last night with Fifi.

"Can't. Maybe tomorrow. The Jacksons will be home, and I might need a reprieve from Reid's harping."

He'd also need to be out with friends so as not to miss a woman who'd come to mean too much to him.

"Fine. I'll call Mattie. Later."

Rique clutched the phone in his hand. Maybe he should have gone, gotten out of here. Another night with Fifi wouldn't be enough. Should he put off his trip to Brazil? Take all the time he needed to extinguish the feelings she evoked in him? But what if that didn't happen? Would he put off a family for a relationship that couldn't go anywhere? No. He'd made a commitment to himself and he meant to keep it. Discipline. All he'd need was some discipline.

But when she walked in the door after a half hour of panther-like pacing, he gave her time to release the leash and take off her coat before he scooped her up in his arms, savoring the feel of her, her scent, the tickling sensation of her hair against his skin.

It took an eternal minute for her to wrap her arms around his neck and her legs around his middle. The kiss was deep, wet, and satisfying. The night in her arms was bliss. She spoke to him through her touch, and it was more information than he could handle.

He was almost glad he was alone when morning came. The sheets a tangled mess, the only reminder of how they'd consumed each other.

He dragged himself up, pulled on his pants, and went looking for her, tripping over Hoover who was lying outside his door. Knowing the dog would be hanging with Fifi if she was here, he said,

"Hey, girl. Did she go out for breakfast?"

The dog picked herself up, nudged his side, and he rubbed behind her ears as they descended the stairs. Only silence welcomed him. No one was in the kitchen. The coffee carafe was sitting on the sideboard. Fifi's coat was no longer hanging on the back of the stool. Where was she? He looked around for some sign. What he found was a note lying on the island. The writing was small but neat, and the message was clear.

Izabella,

Reid, and family should be home by mid-morning. I fed Hoover and took her for a short walk so she should be fine until they get here. Good luck with the season. You better give it all you've got. I'll be watching you.

Thanks for the memories.
Fiona

P.S. I hope you find who you're looking for.

P.P.S. I saw this shirt on-line and thought it would be perfect for you. It was on the doorstep when I left this morning. Wear it in good health.

As he read the last sentence, he felt an emptiness like he'd never felt before consume him.

He opened the yellow mailer and pulled out a deep green tee shirt. He unfolded it and smiled at the message written in white letters. *In my defense I was left unsupervised.*

He was still sitting on the couch three hours later, still clutching the tee and the ragged slip of paper she'd written on, when he heard Hoover barking at the garage door. He hadn't showered, was still wearing the same pair of pants he'd put on upon awakening. He couldn't find the energy to meet his sister and her family at the door. Couldn't seem to move for the life of him.

It was Reid's voice he heard first. He was standing just outside the room, had yet to venture in.

"We're back."

Without inflection, he said, "I heard."

"What the hell's wrong? Did Mac slice you up?"

"No, Mac was fair in his assessment. We've come to an agreement. I'll work hard and he'll let me play."

"So why are you moping around?" Reid finally came in and stood facing him, his hands on his hips. "You're not hung-over, are you?

Rique dropped his head against the back of the couch.

"No. I haven't had more than a beer a night since I got here."

"It can't be grief. You didn't know Farina well enough."

It was grief, in all its dark colors and muted shadows. It would just take him a few days to work through it. By Thursday he'd be in Brazil, surrounded by family, and he'd find someone else to fill his mind. And heart.

The kids had come running in, jumped on him, and he let their hugs and kisses soothe him. He cradled Leeni who was sitting on his lap. Alex's arm was around his neck, Hoover's snout resting on his knee. He wanted this, wanted to live with something bigger than himself.

His sister leaned down and kissed his cheek.

"Are you sick?"

He shook his head.

"The place looks just like we left it. I have Fiona to thank for that, don't I? It surprised me when texted this morning saying she'd be gone by the time we got back. You didn't drive her away, did you?"

He hugged Leeni closer. "She kept me in line, just like you asked her to."

Izabella had come around and taken a seat next to him.

"She told you?"

"She did."

"Why are you…just sitting here? It's not like you and you've got me worried."

It wasn't like him. He was usually the life of the party. He didn't want the role right now.

"I'm fine, Iz. Just thinking, is all."

Wide eyes were staring at him. He wasn't known for his contemplative nature. He felt her hand rest against his forehead.

"No fever but you look pale. Are you sure you're all right? Are you mad at me because I asked her to stay?"

He closed his eyes. He should be. If Fifi had gone home, he wouldn't be feeling the effects of her absence. He had to come up with something to satisfy their curiosity. A misrepresentation of the facts would have to suffice.

"I just didn't sleep well last night, woke up groggy."

"Why don't you go up and take a shower. I'll set up some appointments, show you some rentals."

He gave her a weak smile. "Want to get rid of me already?"

"Not at all. I just figured you don't have much time before spring training starts, and if you're still planning to go to Brazil for a few days, you might want that task behind you."

"Are you sure you want to go right out. You don't want to unpack first?"

"I'll have plenty of time to do that later."

"Then sure."

It might be good to have a place to call his own. And maybe the activity would take his mind off an absent house sitter.

He kissed Leeni's temple, put his arm around Alex to hug him from behind and forced himself up. He didn't miss the look of concern on Izabella's face when she glanced over to her husband.

"I'm fine, Iz. There's been a lot of changes, and I'm ready to go home for a few days."

"From what you told me, you're setting yourself up for one of the biggest changes in your life."

He was, but no matter how stridently he tried to hold on to that thought, another slipped into his consciousness. Fifi was gone.

Izabella had changed while he showered, looked the part of Andover agent. Not that she didn't always look presentable, but she always traveled in more casual attire.

They were standing in the kitchen, the kids off with Reid from what he could hear coming from the other room. They were playing video games if the hoots and hollers meant anything. He wanted to go in and play with them, but he couldn't change his mind now. Izabella was holding her iPad.

"I never asked you what you were looking for, so I guessed. I'm thinking condo."

"Yes. I won't have time for the upkeep."

"Small? Large?"

If he was planning on sharing the space, he wanted big. That way they'd have the room for alone time. Never having lived with the person before, not even knowing who it would be, he wanted the extra square footage, just in case. It might take them time to mesh.

"Large."

"There's two that fit that parameter. One of them is in the same area where Melinda and Jim live. It's close to four thousand square feet of living space and it's furnished which I think will suit your time frame. You can afford the rent and you can move right in."

"You are trying to get rid of me."

"Am not. But I know you. You'll want your own space so you can do as you please and not what Reid suggests."

He leaned his arms across the counter and looked up at her.

"Seems we're on the same page there. I want to see the one near Jim and Melinda." As an afterthought, he asked, "Is it pet friendly?"

She raised her eyebrow at him before checking her iPad. "No. Sorry. You can't have a pet anyway. Who'll take care of it while you're on the road?"

His heart rate picked up. Maybe Fifi would be willing...

What the hell are you thinking?

He clicked that off and said, "You know I'm looking to get married. Maybe my wife will like pets. What if she already has one?"

A laugh sputtered out. "Right. I can't see any of the women you usually date wanting a dog. Wait, maybe she would. The small kind that will fit in her purse and she'll take everywhere."

He groused at her in-depth knowledge of his dating patterns.

She shook her head, her long black hair moving with it and she narrowed her brown eyes at him. "You don't really believe you can just make a list of traits you're looking for and find a woman who has them all, over a weekend, do you?"

"All it will take is some discipline."

He'd keep his eye on the prize and not get bogged down by looks or stature.

"And very good luck. Actually, a miracle. You are not easy to manage, Rique."

"What do you mean? I'm a piece of cake compared to some of the men I know."

"You're spoiled and the women you run with are spoiled, as well. Who will keep the center, mediate when it's needed, encourage you to focus?"

He studied her, and there was an aha moment. She offered all of that to Reid. His brother-in-law respected his wife, listened to her advice and was a better ball player because of her encouragement and support. He needed someone who could do the same. Letting Izabella know he'd prioritized, he said, "I've crossed all of them off my list. I have a better idea who I need now."

"And how did you come by this awakening?"

He couldn't tell her the truth. If his sister knew he'd been sleeping with the house sitter, she wouldn't be pleased.

"I've started paying attention. To you and Reid, Mama and Papi. You have the kind of marriages that work."

"But we are totally different. Everyone has a different…love map. I am not Livia. Couldn't be. I can't be an appendage to Reid. I need my own work, my own life. He's away too often for me to while away the minutes waiting for him to get back. He appreciates that I have somewhere to put my energies when he's gone."

"I like Mama's steadfastness. She's created a home."

Her hands went to her hips. "And I haven't?"

He straightened, lifted his hands to stop the spit and fire he knew was in her.

"Yes, you have. I didn't mean it like that. Her life is about him and it suits Papi. I think it would suit me."

She was shaking her finger at him now. "You need to be careful Enrique. I wouldn't trust some of the women you know to stay faithful with those long, lonely nights they'll endure when you're on the road. Keeping the home fires burning only works if you're home to enjoy them."

She'd packed up her briefcase and led him out to her car. All business now, she talked rents, amenities, and fees on the way over.

It didn't take long to get there or for him to make a decision. The condo she showed him was perfect. Gleaming hardwood floors, lots of sunlight, three bedrooms, a garage and furnished in a comfortable style. He filled out the application, put down a deposit and they put down a move-in date that coincided with his departure for Florida. He'd have a place to bring a wife. Now all he had to do was find one.

CHAPTER TWENTY-FOUR

After wiping some foam off her upper lip, Siobhan said, "Tell me about the guy."

Fiona was sitting in a brewery for some lunch and beer on tap with her sister. They'd spent an hour walking around Old Port and had worked up an appetite. Siobhan's husband, Derek, had offered to take the kids sledding at the local park, giving them time together. There was always more snow here than at home and the residents took advantage of it in the form of winter sports. Derek had lived here all his life and it had been an easy decision to settle here when they'd married. Siobhan wanted to leave Pennsylvania behind as much as Fiona had. Not so much the state but the parents who lived there. Not much of a doting grandmother, Clare hadn't minded. Not like some mothers who might not want to miss the benchmarks and growing years of their children's children. Patrick made a solo trip now and again and, from what her sister had just told her, had taken the kids to the local baseball park to see some minor league games.

It was their father who'd told her about Rique and brunch.

"It's Izabella's brother. Not much of a story."

"Dad said you two looked pretty chummy. From what he gathered, you'd both been asleep on the couch."

"I feel asleep while he was talking. He likes to. A lot."

"You're not usually known for giving a man the time to do that."

She was right. The men she interacted with usually reached ten out of ten on the boring meter quickly and she'd learned to be rude. In a nice way, of course.

"He's...different. And even if his topic of conversation begins to wear, he's nice to look at."

"I've never heard you say that, either. You can take them or leave them, something I've never understood. For that reason, I'm asking again. Tell me about the guy."

Fiona's shoulders slumped. Needing to fortify herself, she took a gulp of her beer and met her sister's eyes.

"I think, given the right circumstances, I could fall in love with him. He's funny, smarter than your average Joe, loves his family, has talent and passion." She smiled at the memory. "He's very passionate about some things."

"You've slept with him."

It wasn't a question, so she didn't bother answering it.

Her sister asked, "I take it the circumstances aren't right?"

Fiona emitted a long, deep sigh. "He's off to Brazil to find a wife."

Her sister sputtered out, "And you slept with him?"

"Curiosity, proximity, foolishness. I'm beginning to think the cat's run out of lives."

Siobhan took her hand. "I'm sorry.

"Don't be. It was the most daring thing I've done and worth it."

She'd spent years cooped up in her lab, not wanting to test those dating waters because of past disappointments. She'd gone out on a limb for Rique and even though she was stranded in the damn tree, it had been worth the risk.

"There'll be someone else, someone who will appreciate you and all you bring to a relationship. Who'd want a baseball player anyway?"

Fiona gulped. She did but her attributes didn't meet his needs. If she looked at it honestly, his didn't meet hers, either. No way would she be able to mix and mingle with the team as a whole. And cooking him a home-cooked meal? Laughable. He'd want her to spend time at his games, which meant time away from the lab.

"Right. Who'd want a baseball player? I'll be too busy soon to dwell on it."

After they'd eaten, they returned to the house to find the kids and Derek munching cookies and drinking hot chocolate. They spent a languid afternoon in front of the fire watching movies. For as much as she'd traveled miles to get away from thoughts of the shortstop, he'd texted her several times since leaving. It had been non-sensical statements, much ado about nothing.

Guess who got dog-walking duty with you gone? Not fair, Fifi.

Does Hoover always circle around before she poos? I froze my balls off waiting for her to find just the right spot to squat.

At my suggestion, Izabella ordered in tonight from that Mediterranean place. Everyone enjoyed it. She's got it on speed dial now. I think you started something.

I'm grabbing a couple of beers tonight with Seb. I'll fill you in on the gossip next time I see you.

Right before she climbed into bed, she got another.

One response would be nice, Fifi. If I didn't know any better, I'd say you've already put me in the past. I'm not going to let you keep me there.

That's what he thought. She was done putting herself at his disposal. And try as she might to prevent it, images of him came on like a tidal wave. Unable to get him out of her mind, she tossed and turned for hours, the memories of the night before bittersweet. She'd known then it would be the last time she'd feel his lips on her, his hands on her body, be brought to the brink of pleasure and plummeted down the other side. She'd made the decision to leave before he woke up before they'd even begun their love-making marathon. But she pulsed with need, wanted him to fill her. Knowing that would never happen, she finally gave in to the tears that burned for release, accepting it was over.

She spent the next day, while Siobhan was at school, in a daze, sleep-deprived but not in a good way. She'd gone many a night during the last year with minimal rest, but she'd awoken energized by what she'd accomplished, not depleted. She'd been wasting her time missing him, dissecting every minute of their time together, looking for something that didn't exist. Why hadn't she moved on already? She was ordinarily so decisive, never allowed herself to look back, never bothered to look at a problem from every angle, always skipped over ancillary data when searching for a solution, but this infatuation had her head spinning in all directions. Her life had been a singular pursuit of knowledge before Rique, and she'd successfully achieved her goal. Now, her focus had splintered. She was letting her emotions hold sway and the forecast was impending doom. No matter how badly she wanted to spend her life with him, it wouldn't be possible. They just didn't meet each other's needs. She thought she'd be content with his body but instead she'd fallen in love. Getting over this, him, was going to be difficult. The pang wasn't easing no matter how much she willed it to, even though she was miles away from temptation. Living with someone for as short as a week could do some major damage to your routine. She'd need to learn how to manage the pain, needed to find her way back to before. When she was content to be alone, satisfied with her career consuming her life. With her dream about to become a reality, she'd need to devote all her time to it.

She stopped in at the Starbucks in town, grabbed a seat at an empty table by the window as soon as her drink was served. She was thinking to watch the passers-by, zone out for a minute, and let her mind rest from the swirling turmoil, but her attention was caught by remnant sections of the *Boston Globe* lying there. Before she knew what she was doing, she picked up the sports page and scanned the headlines. Most of the news was about the upcoming Super Bowl event due to take place this weekend. There were two articles that interested her, the first "Who Is Mac Calipari?" It was a rundown on the man and myth. It gave his history as a Greenliner and more personal bits about his family. There was a photograph of him, his wife and his daughter. Suddenly interested in what Casey looked like, she brought the paper closer. Here was another woman who'd been left behind by a ballplayer. Could they have commiserated together? Rique had implied she lacked warmth, using the words cool as cucumber, but the smile she wore in the picture countered his assessment. She was lovely and you could tell from the photo that the three were close. Their arms were around each other, their bodies leaning in, a seamless unit. Their faces were engaged, signifying they were happy at being together. Casey was a feminine version of Mac from what she could see in the blurred, grainy picture and she wondered at the color of her eyes, the size of her feet. Letting the curiosity about her DNA go, she went on to the next article entitled "Out with the Old, In with the New." The reporter had presented a detailed outline on the differences in style and technique between Farina and Calipari. They were numerous and stark. She got the distinct impression that the reporter was in favor of Calipari's methods. She thought it might have been more sympathetic to Farina's family if he'd waited a day or two to print it.

She got up to leave, taking her half-finished latte with her, never once checking the front page to see what was going on in the world.

That night she packed up all her fantasies about Rique and put them away. Once she regained control of her mind, she was able to get hold of her heart. She was ready to absorb herself in her research again. When she left for Boston on Wednesday morning, her heart and mind were on the upcoming interview. Work would be the only thing that could save her from the agony of her unrequited love.

CHAPTER TWENTY-FIVE

Rique was straightening his tie, his thoughts automatically drifting to Fifi. The last time he wore this jacket was the night they'd gone dancing. Her scent still clung to it, and if he closed his eyes, he could feel her here with him. He hadn't been the same since she'd left. He'd lost his appetite, not only for food, but for his upcoming trip. The night before he'd met Seb and Mattie for dinner, muddled through the meal, and left as soon as Seb mentioned clubbing. He had no desire to fake conversation, plaster on a smile, and he certainly had no intention of dancing with anyone else. Not when the memory of her was still so fresh in his mind. It should have left him restless and bored, but it hadn't. It seemed Fifi's absence was as grounding as her presence had been.

Melina and Alex had gone right back to school on Monday and Izabella had gone back to work. It was supposed to be for a couple of hours of floor time, but then she got caught up in a relocation family and a couple of listing appointments. She'd been out of the house more than she'd been in it, but she made sure to call and check in with him. At first, he thought it was to make sure he and Reid hadn't come to blows. He'd been left in Reid's clutches, but his brother-in-law had been almost conciliatory, suggesting they meet Jaco for lunch. He hadn't seen his brother since he'd arrived, and it had been wrong of him. At least Jaco didn't disappoint and gave him shit about it, which he took. Jaco gave him shit about that, too. He wasn't acting himself and it was apparent to everyone.

A voice called out, "Are you coming with us?"

Izabella had to be standing at the bottom of the stairs, yelling up.

"I am. I'll be right there."

"We'll be in the car."

He was sure that meant to pressure him into moving more quickly than he was, but it had little impact. Neither did the horn Reid began leaning on.

He slipped out the side door, after coding in the alarm and walked over to the car that was idling in the drive-way.

Once inside, he turned to Izabella and asked, "Where are the kids and Hoover?"

"Reid took them to Melinda's while you were showering."

Reid almost growled, "I could have dropped them in New York and been back before you got out. What the hell is your problem?"

"Nothing." As Reid glided down the drive toward the street, he asked his sister as nonchalantly as he could, "Have you heard from Fifi?"

"This morning. Why?"

"I was just wondering if she still had that interview on Friday."

"Why wouldn't she? And if you want to know, why don't you ask her?"

She hadn't returned any of the texts he'd sent since she left. He'd gotten the message.

When he didn't answer immediately, Reid glanced over and asked, "Something going on there?"

"I like her."

"Is that why you're acting strange?"

"Strange how?"

"I haven't had to lecture you once. You seem more than content to hang out with the kids, me, or Izabella. You're even taking Hoover for walks."

"Fifi's fault. She spoiled your dog. She sits and stares at me until I can't stand it anymore and give in."

"You're blaming Fifi?"

Izabella leaned forward and smacked her husband on the shoulder. "Her name is Fiona."

Reid had jerked forward, surprised by the move, before amending, "You're blaming Fiona for your lack of assertiveness with Hoover?"

He was blaming Fifi for everything wrong in his life right now. His lack of assertiveness was just the tip of the iceberg.

Izabella offered, "I think the old girl misses her."

Hoover wasn't the only one. Maybe that's why he relented and braved the frigid air. It took his mind off the loneliness. He just had to make it through one more day. He'd be home tomorrow, and things would get back to normal. He was counting on it.

Izabella's phone had rung and as soon as she ended the call, she said, "The keys are yours whenever you want them."

His application had been accepted and he'd already dropped the check off for the first and last month's rent plus security deposit. When he had, Izabella had given him a warning. Melinda had given him a glowing recommendation and she didn't want it to come back and bite her. Like he even had the energy to call people, never mind host a party. He just wasn't feeling it.

"When do you want to swing by and sign the lease?"

"I can do everything before I leave for the airport."

"What flight you taking out?"

"United 537 out of Logan. It arrives in Rio at ten-fifteen tomorrow morning."

"How many stops?"

"One. Texas."

"I still can't believe you're going down for less than two days. You'll be spending more time on the plane than at Papi's."

"The plan was to go for longer, but I've made the commitment to be here now. I want to keep up the regimen Leo started."

Reid glanced over at him again and just shook his head. He didn't have to say anything. He knew what his brother-in-law was thinking. It was one of two things. *At last* or *where have you hidden my brother-in-law?*

The church where the funeral was being held was packed with managers from other teams or some representative who'd been handed the task, every member of the current Greenliners, many retired players who'd come to pay their respects. It was long and boring, and he couldn't keep his mind on the litany, the hymns, or the speakers. It kept drifting….

"Rique. Move."

His sister was prodding him to get up and move out of the pew. They were at a mid-way point in the church and he hadn't even noticed the mourners had gotten up to file out. He rose and walked slowly toward the exit.

As he waited in the lobby of the restaurant where the mercy meal was being held, he fingered inside the tight collar, readjusted the tie. The posh eatery in Brighton was filling up quickly. For as much as he'd had enough of the dead and dying over the last two days, attendance was mandatory, and he knew Seb and Mattie would be here soon. They'd sat in the same pew with him, and he could have left with them if he'd wanted, but he was on automatic pilot and mindlessly stayed with the family he came with. Now, he wished he had been more awake. He preferred being with them. They wouldn't ask questions or give him worried looks.

He'd seen Seb's car in the mirror on his visor, which he'd pulled down to mute the gaze of the morning sun. Reid had kept the speed limits and his friends weren't far behind. He stepped out to the parking lot, on the lookout for the dark blue BMW. Nothing. A lot of the players had arrived and passed him by, most of them as couples. It was a stark reminder that he was alone. He'd never thought to ask Fifi to stick around, come with him. Not that she'd given him the chance. He still couldn't believe she'd just up and left, without even a goodbye. He'd wanted a more personal one, a kiss maybe. Or another round of lovemaking. His heart thundered, thoughts of her like a hammer on nails in his chest. He didn't know he could miss someone this much. Never had before. Sure, his family. He missed his mother, father, his sisters but not to the point it made him nauseous. He had to keep looking ahead, not behind, to the woman out there waiting for him to claim her. He'd once been able to see her so clearly. Now she was a blur, out of focus.

So wrapped in his thoughts, he didn't notice Reid had come out looking for him.

"What are you doing out here?"

Rique shoved his hands in his pockets. "Waiting for the others."

"Your sister's worried. Come in and join us."

Rique looked around one more time and gave up rubber necking for his friends, still fixated on their arrival. There were people inside he could talk to. He knew everyone by now, the whole team, staff, coaches. He'd played against most when he'd worn the Mets uniform. They were all a bit more jocular now that he was on their side.

The entrance was choked by mourners, the bottle neck creating a funnel as they filed into the restaurant and he elbowed his way through, keeping Reid in his line of sight. The conversation was less somber than it had been, but the tones were still hushed in reverence. The entire first floor of the funeral home had been used as a viewing area, so it never seemed crammed. There, he'd been with Mattie and Seb and they milled and chatted, with no lack of air. Here, even though the number of attendees was the same, the space seemed inadequate to accommodate everyone. The tables and chairs were close together, leaving little room to navigate. When Mac walked in, with his wife, Galen, all heads had turned, and he was no exception. He'd gotten his first glimpse of the blonde woman when they'd arrived at the funeral home. Casey and, whom he assumed was her fiancé, was with them. She looked uneasy, as though she didn't like being in the spotlight. Rique had begun to dissect her traits and features to see who she most resembled. She got her height from her dad, and most of her features, but her eyes were definitely inherited from her maternal side. So were her grace and sense of style. He was looking at them through Fifi's eyes, and he had the urge to call… But he wouldn't. He knew where he stood. She'd run off to Maine, hadn't answered any of his texts and he had to face the fact that she was done with him. Not that he could blame her. But she'd left something of herself behind. She'd helped him see the world in a different way than he had before. And he never wanted to go back to the days when he was the sole attraction in his mind.

When Seb and Mattie finally got there, he signaled to them and they wove themselves through the crowd until they reached him.

"Where the hell have you been?"

Mattie said, "He got cold feet."

He'd whispered it loudly. Rique didn't understand the reticence.

"About the meal?"

Mattie nodded in the Caliparis' direction. "About seeing Casey again."

When Seb vehemently denied it, he surmised the truth.

"I couldn't care less if she's here or not."

Mattie gave a smirk as if to contradict the statement. "He doesn't seem to like the guy she's marrying either. Said he looked like a true millennial. Whatever that means."

It wasn't a compliment.

Rique gave him an insight into the meaning of the word. "They've been described as egotistical, lazy and spoiled."

His jaw dropped open. He'd just described himself, or rather how others saw him anyway. But he wasn't lazy. Not anymore. And he'd dropped the egotistical aspect over the past week. He might still be categorized as spoiled, but he'd refer all questions back to one and two.

Seb said through clenched teeth, "Look at the suit the guy has on. I bet it costs a thousand bucks. Thinks of himself much? What will he have left to give Case?"

Rique glanced over at Mattie, then they both stared at Seb. It seemed he hadn't gotten over the girl from his past, or maybe he was looking at her now as the woman she'd become.

Seb began to move toward the last table against the wall. "Let's sit back there."

"Better vantage point?"

"No, I don't want to be eyeballed by her father."

Rique patted him on the back. "He hasn't even glanced in our direction."

"Or so you think. The man has eyes where his ears are, and another pair hiding under his hair."

Mattie asked, "Are you always this paranoid?"

Reid interrupted before Seb could issue a not guilty plea.

"Mind if we sit with you?"

Reid and Isabella were standing with Jason Motts and his wife Nancy.

Mattie said, "Please. It would be good."

When they took their seats, the threesome finally sat as well.

Rique looked at Reid. "I would have thought you'd want to sit with your friends."

"Maybe I wanted to make new ones."

Rique's eyes narrowed, believing it was for another reason entirely. "I'm not going to drink."

Reid leaned in and poured water from the pitcher into everyone's glass.

"I'm beginning to believe you."

Reid and Jason started talking about spring training, giving the new players some insight into what would happen and what they'd need to do to get a permanent spot on the roster. Both pitcher and catcher would be leaving before the others, having to report on an earlier date than the rest of the team.

Motts admitted, "Verducci's going to be my main competitor."

Reid took a sip of his water. "He's good, but so are you."

"Mac told me that he wasn't assigning a catcher to any one pitcher. I think our days of playing catch might be over."

"He pretty much told me the same thing. I didn't think it was worth arguing over but if it comes to that, I will."

"What's the buzz about Buzzley?"

Rique glanced over to see where he was sitting but noticed he wasn't. He was all alone at the bar. He rose and asked, "Would you mind if I bring him over to sit with us?"

There was a vacant chair and he didn't want anyone to feel left out.

Reid glanced in the direction of Rique's nod. "No. Good catch."

A month ago, he wouldn't have noticed.

When Rique approached the pitcher, who most likely would be their closer if things worked out, he introduced himself.

Buzz extended his hand in what appeared to be gratitude.

"There's an empty seat. Want it?"

"Yeah. Appreciate it. Standing at a bar is probably not my best option."

After the introductions were made at the table, Rique lifted his water glass and tapped it against Buzz's. "It'll be nice having someone to not drink with."

"You a member of Bill?"

Rique pondered what that implied. Reid came to his aid. "It's AA."

Buzz explained further, "Alcoholics Anonymous."

"No. I've got partying down to a science and I'm abstaining for the foreseeable future."

As soon as he mentioned the word *science,* Fifi came back in dazzling display. He still had the thong he'd stolen from her and he was keeping it as a…not trophy, even though bedding her had been a prize he hadn't expected, but as a reminder of how much the time with her had meant to him. He quieted during the meal, as conversation buzzed around him. Izabella, who was sitting on his left, leaned in and asked, "You okay?"

"Yes."

"What's going on in that head of yours?"

He peered at her, her expression one of concern. He couldn't tell her the truth.

"Just thinking about getting home."

CHAPTER TWENTY-SIX

Looking at her reflection in her bedroom mirror, Fiona turned from one side to the other, taking in the new ginger-colored cashmere suit she'd picked up in Portland. She'd walked around the business district the day before and was drawn into a boutique while window-shopping. She wasn't a clothes horse by any means and the business clothes she had were outdated and dull. She wanted something new, something that gave her confidence, made her look the part of successful scientist. This had done it and she smiled at her newfound daring. She'd clipped her hair back so it wouldn't be a nuisance, had on a pair of gold hoop earrings her parents had gotten her one Christmas that she rarely wore, and a new pair of ankle boots. She almost didn't recognize herself. In the lab it was jeans and leggings, comfort clothes, with a white lab coat worn over them. But to get there, she had to look the part.

The drive to Boston seemed short in comparison to her earlier drive home from Portland. It hadn't given her the time she needed to relax, and her nerves were buzzing. She needed this job, needed an outlet for her misplaced passion for Rique.

This is not the time to be thinking about him.

She straightened her suitcoat and slung her purse and briefcase over her shoulder. She made her way across the parking lot to the building that housed the vacant lab and the office of Dr. Michaels, the man she was meeting with. When she got to the door, she took a deep breath and knocked. A female voice echoed out to the hallway, telling her to come in. A woman stood at her desk to greet her.

"You must be Dr. Barrows. Please have a seat. The president is just finishing up a phone call. He'll be with you in a moment."

She did as directed, looking around the space. Papers were everywhere, file folders stacked in a neat pile in the tray, and she wondered if her file was among them.

Without giving her time to think more about it, Kurtis Michaels came out to greet her. He was mid-forties, tall and lean, with a closely cropped beard and moustache. His smile was warm as he welcomed her in.

"I've been looking forward to meeting you. So young, yet so accomplished."

She forced a casual stride into the room, instead of scooting past him like a scared juvenile.

"I hope you don't hold the young part against me."

"I wouldn't dare. Some votes went against me when I was up for this position, for just that reason. I say we have more energy to give to the job, and more enthusiasm. We haven't been jaded yet by repetition and failure."

"I hate to admit it, but the field I'm in you can expect a lot of that."

"But if successful, the benefits will have been well worth it."

"I agree."

He nodded to the seat opposite the desk and she sat as directed. She crossed her ankles, kept her hands in her lap, waiting to hear what he had to say. Her nerves weren't so easily controlled.

"I've skimmed through your dissertation and would very much like to offer you the vacant lab to see if you can pick up where you left off. There are a lot of different ways you can go with it and I'm interested to hear the direction you've chosen."

Her heart began to race. Had he just offered her the position?

Calm down. Breathe.

She gave him the detailed outline that she'd worked on in Maine. It was concise, articulate, and she was pleased that she'd remembered it point by point. Michaels nodded as she went, asked questions when he needed clarification. When she was finished, he had a grin on his face.

"Exactly what I'd hoped. Now for the last part of the agreement. You'll be teaching a minimum of two classes in genetics each semester. You'd be expected to begin this summer. It might give you time to get your feet wet as a professor."

Her breath froze in fear. She'd never considered this, although she should have. The university was willing to invest a lot of money, time, and effort into her research. This was payback. Her mother taught at the school where her lab was based. It was a matter of course. Could she do it? She'd be drained, certainly but most classes lasted an hour or hour and a half tops. She could hold up for that long. As long as she had some free time to get a breath of fresh air, find a place to recharge she should be fine. A professorship at twenty-five. A flicker of pride puffed her chest.

"What types of courses did you have in mind?"

"Upper-class biology. Structure and function of genes, genetic methods, analysis of protein function, gene regulation, and inherited diseases. We've recently lost one of our science professors to retirement and your resume dovetails nicely with what we need. It will also give you a plethora to choose from as far as assistants go. You might even consider mentoring a doctoral candidate. We'd love to increase our presence with post-graduate work among the college community. You'll be the linchpin."

"Could you provide me with the syllabi for what's gone before?"

"Absolutely. I'll have Jenny put them together for you before you leave. Are you willing to sign a contract with us?"

"Is this a formal offer?"

"It is."

He went over what the school was willing to spend on the initial start-up and it was more than generous. There wasn't a need for negotiation, although a lawyer might have disagreed with her.

"Then I accept."

"Would you like to see your lab?"

"More than I want to take my next breath."

Dr. Michaels talked all the way to the basement, informing her about the other occupants in the building, who they were and what they taught. It was obviously the science building, with professors from all over the world teaching chemistry, physics, geology, and astronomy. When they got to the end of the last hallway, they came to a locked door. She was trembling with anticipation. As soon as he opened it, he handed her the key, which she gripped as if it were a sacred icon. And when she walked across the threshold, she entered her place of worship, the hum of the machines her choir, the scientific ritual her High Mass. Her fingers skimmed the surfaces of desk, tables, deep freezer, and auto clave with reverence. This would be her escape hatch, where she'd find refuge when things were overwhelming, when her energy was sapped by the students she'd teach. She'd have the best of both worlds. Connection and introspection.

"I take it you're satisfied with the space."

She nodded and met his question with one of her own. "When can I move in?"

"How does next Monday sound? It will give us time to get the contract in order and for our janitor to clean it up."

In five days, she'd be able to take possession. She could hardly believe it had been that easy.

Right. Easy-peasy. All it took was five years of hard work. A regular walk in the park.

Michaels turned to go. "I've got to get back. I have another appointment scheduled. Can you lock it up for me?"

Before she knew, what she was doing, she asked, "Can I sit here for a little while, take it all in, mentally dress it, jot down what I'll need?"

He gave her a wide smile. "For as long as you like. You can drop the key off when you're done and pick up the syllabi you asked for."

The ebullience almost carried her away before she remembered.

"Oh, and I have an assistant in mind. Can I offer him a position?"

The smile dimmed when he said, "The university is unwilling to hire anyone else to work here. However, if you can find a way to fund his or her salary, you can do anything you want."

She smiled to herself and said, "Good to know."

"Jenny will give you a call when the contract is ready for your signature."

"Thank you, Dr. Michaels. You'll never know how much I appreciate your trust."

"It's an honor to have you on staff, Fiona. And the name is Kurt."

With that pronouncement, he left her alone.

Her eyes sought out every inch of the room, which was larger than she'd expected. This would be her haven, where she'd regroup, regenerate, repair her emotional armor. She was sure there'd be dents in it at the end of every day. Terror swamped her but she'd never felt so invigorated. She sat down on the stool and pulled out her phone. She wanted to share her news, but with whom? There was one person she would have loved to tell, if only to hear his voice, but she knew Enrique wouldn't be interested and probably far too busy to listen. His incoming texts had stopped, and she was sure he'd already moved on. Izabella had called this morning, before the funeral, asked her to drop by for the money owed her for the two-week stay. She mentioned that Enrique was leaving for Brazil right after the mercy meal. Nothing had changed. Well, maybe one thing had. Her heart was a bit more tattered than it had been.

She opted for the one person who would share her news with the same kind of exuberance. As the cell rang, she tried to modulate her excitement.

When Bohdan answered, she asked, "Can you start Monday, or do you need more time?"

She didn't know how she was going to pay him, but she was willing to share her salary with him until she figured it all out.

There was no mistaking the tremor in his voice. "You got it? You got it."

She looked around, the tingles making this seem more like a dream than reality.

"I did. I'm sitting in our lab right now. It feels…it feels…" She took a breath and admitted, "There's no word in the English language that describes it adequately."

One of the reasons they got along so well was they approached life the same way, in a direct and concise manner. He got right to the crux.

"The guy knows where you're going?"

"I laid it out for him, bullet by bullet. I was afraid he'd shoot them down. But he didn't."

Michaels knew every tee she meant to cross in her quest for answers. She began to chew on her thumb nail. "There is a down-side."

She heard the hesitation before he asked, "Oh, and what's that?"

"I have to teach."

He chuckled in the face of her trepidation.

"I thought you knew that. It comes with the territory."

"I forgot."

She'd been so focused on the lab, all else had fallen away.

"You'll be great. You're engaged and technically skilled. You're also passionate about the material and you're newly minted. You'll understand their pain."

She was young enough to be one of them.

"Kurt, that's Dr. Michaels, said that he wanted to enlist some doctoral students. You could be the first."

"Or the last. I'm not ready, Fiona. You know what it feels like to be pushed. Please, don't do it to me."

He'd been along on many of her mother's bulldozer rides and had helped her find her way out from under it. She didn't like the reference to Clare or the truth behind it.

"You're right. I won't mention it again."

"Good. Then I can accept the position you've offered me."

A feeling of relief rushed through her. She wasn't sure she could do this without him.

"I'll call as soon as I know the details."

"Congratulations. You deserve this."

She swiped off and put the phone away. There were several people she'd have to call later, her mother for one, but the woman would talk her to death. She wanted to hold her victory close and celebrate on her own for a while longer.

She took off her coat and sat at the desk, opening the file that Jenny had given her. It was an old handbook, and it listed the descriptions of all courses offered. She found the two she'd be taking on and read the short blurb. She'd have to get right to the vitae. Dr. Michaels said he'd need it before the end of the month. They were putting together the on-line application for the summer classes and they'd need the information before it was added to the curriculum guide. She'd seen enough of them to know how to compose the brief description, but she'd never had to plan out a five-week course load. She mentally highlighted the areas she'd want to cover, leaving out the extraneous pieces that the students would have learned in their most basic biology classes. As a student, she resented repetition of her earlier studies. She always thought the professors should be more inventive and offer fresh, new material in her third and fourth year. She glanced at her watch when she felt a chill. She'd gotten lost, like she always did within these walls, but it was time to go home. The sun was going down and without it, the room had darkened and cooled. As she slid the folder into her briefcase, she thought about her small condo and the future. She was going to talk to Izabella about finding a new place, maybe a house to buy, once her signature was on the contract. She'd have the money for a bigger place, and maybe she could find something with a yard. If she wanted companionship, a dog might be the way to go. It would give her a warm body to sleep with at night and wet kisses.

They wouldn't be passionate ones, but they'd have to do.

When she got home, she called to order something for dinner, sat down, and made the call she'd been dreading all day. Her mother answered on the second ring, which meant she wasn't in the lab. If she had been, the call would have gone to voice mail and it would be hours before Clare would find it.

"This was unexpected. Something come up?"

She was relieved Siobhan hadn't said anything. She twirled an unruly curl away from her face and wove it under the clip, snorting to herself. Like her mother would have called her sister just to say hello.

"Actually, I was offered a job this morning."

"And you're just getting around to letting me know?"

Thanks, Mom, for the congratulations. I'm happy and relieved about it, too.

She refused to apologize for the need to savor.

"I spent a couple of hours in my new lab. I needed to breathe it in, make it mine."

"Tell me everything."

She did, between stops and starts, her mother intruding the flow with questions and snide statements in an unrelenting drone.

"I start Monday. Bohdan is coming with me."

"Why in the name of God's green earth would you hire him?"

"Because he's good."

"He isn't qualified at this level."

"He has more knowledge about genetics and proteomics in his little finger than anyone else I could bring in. He worked with me on my thesis for cripes-sakes. He knows as well as I do where we'll go next."

And he'd get her there one small step at a time.

Her mother's smugness gave her the right to offer her opinion, at least in her own mind.

"I don't think—"

"That's okay, Mom I do, and it's my lab. I can do what I want. I've got to go. Just wanted you to hear the good news before I went to bed."

Her mother stuttered out a good-bye and Fiona swiped off, inhaling a deep breath to get her calm back. She hoped one day she could have a conversation with Clare that didn't drain her or leave her worn out. The woman was like a vacuum cleaner, sucking the life right out of her.

She let it go and smiled. She had her lab and she wasn't going to let anyone poo in her field of possibilities

CHAPTER TWENTY-SEVEN

The mercy meal lasted longer than anticipated. As soon as it was over, and people began to file out, offering the last of the condolences to the family on their way. Rique left Seb talking to Buzz and Mattie talking to Alicia, telling them both he'd be in touch on his return to the city. On the way home, Reid stopped by the real estate office Izabella worked at, as planned. Once the lease was signed, they returned to the house. Rique only had time to grab his carry-on and head back out. He had the key to his new life. Now he just had to find someone to share it with.

He hugged his sister. "Thanks. I appreciated you letting me stay."

"Give everyone a kiss for me. Tell them I'm looking forward to seeing them again."

"I will."

Reid shook his hand. "You're doing well, Rique. I hope you can stay the course."

"I will. That's a promise. One I will keep."

"Good. See you when you get back."

He climbed into his car, and as he drove away, he glanced at them in his rearview mirror. Izabella had her head on his shoulder and Reid's arm was around her waist. There was love there. A deep, abiding love. It was what he was looking for. He had to believe there was a woman for him out there, but as he flew thousands of miles away from Boston, he couldn't leave the picture of Fifi behind.

When he landed in Rio, he walked toward the exit, his carry-on wheels clicking on the concourse floor. He was home and it felt… He glanced around the wide halls trying to decide. Security personnel were visible as they monitored all passengers' movements. A wheelchair was being pushed along at a fast clip toward the gate area. An airport worker, a mop in hand, was swabbing at a spill on the floor. He could smell the disinfectant, burning coffee, and a whiff of perfume as a woman walked close enough to touch. She'd met his eyes, signaled what she wanted and whispered an endearment in Portuguese, but he wasn't in the mood for temptations. Though the language was familiar, it wasn't his anymore. Was this place no longer home? He thought for sure he'd feel a rush of nostalgia when he stepped off the plane but there was nothing…

He put his head down and kept moving, his thoughts a review of the last two weeks and how Fifi had left him before she'd needed to.

Do you blame her?

He'd offered her nothing but a few nights in bed. He inwardly moaned at the memory. There was no inhibition in her. She gave fully, and he could do nothing but give the same in return. Sex had always been enjoyable, but with Fifi it was mind-altering. Beneath that serious exterior was a wild cat who was capable of reaching intimacy in a way he'd never experienced before.

He scanned the area, hoping to see his father, hoping to get his mind off the woman who intrigued him. He was here to find a wife and having another woman on his mind would not help his cause. The problem was, he missed her and couldn't seem to shake the emptiness that had come with her absence.

He heard a voice call out his name, then saw the welcoming smile that greeted him. His father was a good man, who held family above all else. It's where Rique had learned the value of love, devotion, and duty.

Paolo grabbed him in a bear hug, kissed both his cheeks.

"We hear you are doing well."

That would be Reid's assessment and he felt a flicker of pride in his new work ethic.

"I'm working my ass off, Papi. It's long overdue."

"This is good to know. I am proud of you for turning it around so quickly. Come. Your mama is waiting to see you. Leia and Felicia are with her. They both flew in so we could spend time together. They've missed their brother."

"I've missed them, as well."

They began to walk toward the exit. There was no need for baggage claim. Rique wouldn't be here for more than a couple of days and he had everything he needed in the small case. At the moment it didn't seem long enough.

"When will you and Mama go to New York?"

"We are leaving earlier than usual. With Leia there now and you in Boston, we are thinking about another home, perhaps in Connecticut. According to Izabella, it is a half-way point so we would only be an hour away from both of you. Oh, and Felicia has been accepted at the University of New Mexico. She has sent in her form and will be attending come fall."

That came as a surprise. His sister had cut her teeth dinosaur hunting in this country.

"Why there and not here?"

"They have an excellent paleontology department, with many excavation sites. She tells me that it was the home of the T-Rex before the meteor hit and she wants to investigate a new environment. We can visit her when we travel west to see you play."

His father had groused when Rique chose baseball over soccer, but now that he'd become knowledgeable about the sport, he was a dedicated fan and followed his team all over the country. Rique loved seeing him and his mother in the stands of the various ballparks, each one unique. The well-worn faces made each one feel like home. He'd let this man down over the last year with his sub-par performances and he promised himself he would never do it again.

"All your kids are in America now. Does that sadden you?"

"Why should it? You are all doing what makes you happy."

"But this is your home, Papi."

"Home is where my family is. Where Livia is." Paolo tapped a loose fist against his chest. "Where my heart beats strongest."

Rique wetted his lips. Was that why he felt the foreigner here? Did his heart beat stronger somewhere else now? It was a question he'd need to answer before he made a mistake concerning his future.

Once they reached the car, Enrique put his suitcase in the trunk and took a seat on the passenger side, putting his window down, the temperature a balmy seventy-nine degrees. This was something he missed.

"I want to know about the team. Your chances to win it all are good, are they not?"

"They are. I met with the new manager this past weekend. He seems like he knows what he's doing and we're all hopeful he can pick up where Farina left off."

"Reid says he will be better." He winked at him, said conspiratorially, "But that is between us."

When his father's attention was back on the road, Rique began to study the profile. It would be his profile when he reached his sixties and it jarred him that they looked so much alike. Would his own son inherit the same looks, or would his wife contribute more to his features than he would? Did it matter? What he wanted was the kind of relationship he had with his father. It was easy, open, and affectionate.

He jested back, "I won't tell anyone, besides he said pretty much the same to me the night they got back."

He appreciated the in-depth analysis about the upcoming season. He'd been having them, every other night with Fifi. It was one of the things he'd miss. Did miss.

He shook thoughts of her out of his head, but they boomeranged back. He looked back at this father and asked, "What drew you to Mama?"

"I believe I've already told you. It was her sweet nature."

The warmth of the smile told him everything. Paolo was still in love with his wife. He wanted to be able to say that about himself thirty years down the road.

"That was important to you?"

"It was. Julianna had a more acerbic nature and we fought a lot. I wanted something different and I found it all in Livia. You, my son, need someone different."

"What? Why?"

His father paused, as if considering his words.

"You are...spoiled. My fault and I will apologize to whomever you marry. Someone sweet could not stand up to you. You need more assertiveness in your wife." His father took his eyes off the road and met his. "Have you found someone?"

He narrowed his eyes. His father's tone suggested he knew…what? Had Izabella said something about Fifi? Did she think there was more there than there was?

"No. I'm here to do that. I want to settle down, Papi. Find a woman so I can have what you have."

"And what do you think that is?"

A small smile played at the corners of Paolo's mouth. He'd found humor in Rique's line of questioning. Did his father think he didn't know what held value?

"A good partnership, a woman who makes me smile when she enters a room, a companion who I can discuss things with, someone who keeps me grounded."

When he heard his own words, he blinked. He hadn't mentioned one thing that had once been important: a woman to cook for him, keep his bed warm, be pliant and willing. Instead, he'd described what he'd found with Fifi. With a lot of bonus points to add to it: a fine mind, interesting conversation, a passion all her own.

Reluctantly, as if giving something away, he asked, "Would you have married her if she wanted to work?"

His father's eyes grew wide. "What would that have changed?"

"Let's be honest, Papi. She devoted her life to you."

There was that endearing smile again. It appeared whenever Livia was mentioned. Then it was gone as he considered the question.

"You think so? I think she did the work that most fulfilled her. That was raising a family and catering to my needs. It made me a lucky man, but if she had come to it without passion, what good would it have done any of us?"

Rique thought about that and had to agree. His mother found joy in the simple everyday tasks that consumed her life.

His father added, "She's been faithful to herself, Enrique, which makes her a pleasure to be with."

Faithful to herself.

Livia did what made her happy and in doing so, brought happiness to everyone else. Was that the key?

He didn't have time to answer his own question. They'd pulled into the driveway of his parents' home. It wasn't the one he'd grown up in. They'd moved a couple of times over the years, to better and safer neighborhoods. As soon as Felicia had graduated high school, they sold the house in Sousa and were now living outside of Rio. It's where the action was but it had been too late for him to take advantage of what it offered. He was already living in the States by then. When he noticed his mother and sisters waiting for him by the door, it was as if he belonged here. He embraced them all, glad to be where he was loved.

Even as the sun was going down, the weather was still warm, the windows open letting the fresh air float through the house. Nothing like the weather he'd left, but there was something to a cold night, snow coming down, and a fire burning in the grate. Romance could burn as brightly and with as much heat.

Stop thinking about Fifi.

He was beginning to get aggravated that everything led back to her. Even his dreams during the short nap he'd taken earlier had been filled with her.

What was she doing? How long had she stayed with her sister? He knew she had one, that her name was Siobhan and that she was a math teacher, but that was the extent of it. No, he knew she had kids. Fifi had mentioned bringing Hoover to visit because they liked dogs. Which led him to assume she was married. Were the sisters close? Did they look alike? His curiosity was growing. He wanted to know more.

He cleared his mind of the fog and remembered Fifi had an interview tomorrow. Would she get the job? Would she think to call him and let him know? Maybe he should check in with her one more time, let her know he was here.

And remind her again of why you've come?

He closed his eyes and let the voices of his family penetrate his consciousness.

He took a sip of the wine his mother had poured for him, let the fruity taste satisfy the growing hunger. They asked him about the team, and he answered all questions but then he turned it around so they could catch him up on all their news. Leia and fiancé were in the process of opening a bed and breakfast on Long Island, just miles outside the five boroughs. She'd be cook and Tom Marano would be bottle washer. He'd been working as a home inspector when Leia had met him, but he wanted more, wanted to create a family business where they could live, work and raise a family. Tom had found them a rambling old Victorian built in the 1850's with ten bedrooms and eight baths on over two acres of land. They were renovating it and bringing it into the twenty-first century one room at a time with an end goal of holding weddings on the sculptured grounds they expected their brother Jaco to design. Felicia was excited about her new adventure in New Mexico. She'd grown bored with the dinosaur fossils discovered in Brazil and was looking for a new experience in another fertile area where the big boys had lived and breathed millions of years ago.

They were all happy, living their passions and he hoped he could raise a family that produced the same results.

He rose from the chair and announced, "I think I will cook for us tonight, Mama. Is that all right?"

"When did my son discover the joys of cooking?"

"I have cooked for myself before, when in need, but only recently have I found enjoyment in it. I made your stroganoff and it came out very well, I must say. It made me feel proud."

That Fifi had liked it made it that much better.

He swore under his breath. There she was again, claiming territory in his head. He had to find a way to ban her from his thoughts. He had too much riding on this trip to be anchored by a woman who didn't want to be part of his life. She'd proven that by ignoring him.

His mother had followed him into the kitchen.

"I have fish, calamari and prawns out for *moqueca baina.* Are you up for that? I can be your assistant."

His taste buds woke up. His mother's fish stew was one of his favorites, with a coconut base for broth.

Leia laughed. "I have to watch this. I didn't know you could boil water. Maybe if your baseball career doesn't work out, I can hire you to cook for the Marano

Inn."

"I'm making sure my career is solid but thanks for the offer."

Felicia grabbed a front-row seat at the kitchen table. "We'll provide commentary as you go."

Leia asked, "I don't get it. Why all of a sudden? You fall in love with a woman who can't cook?"

He stilled before shrugging the comment off. She was way off base. He hadn't fallen in love yet. He was waiting until he met his wife to do that. He was getting out the pots he'd need at his mother's direction and in answer to Leia's question, forced out a chuckle. "Like that would happen."

Livia said in a quiet voice, "That wouldn't be the end of the world. She might have other talents, more important things to create."

Felicia added, "There are two skills Rique is looking for. One is performed in the kitchen, one in the—"

Livia's tone was firm, "None of that talk. Your brother will choose wisely, I'm sure of it."

Felicia's eyes widened. "And what, may I ask, do you base that opinion on?"

She ruffled his hair. "He is a good boy and we've taught him what's important."

He met his mother's soft brown eyes. Was she looking for confirmation that she was right? He wanted to give it to her, but he was confused and couldn't admit it.

She turned away to put an apron on and instructed, "Take the fish out and coat it with garlic and lime juice, then refrigerate it."

When he'd completed that step, he began sautéing the onion, bell pepper, tomatoes, and scallions he'd chopped up, seasoning them as he went with salt, paprika, and red pepper flakes.

His sisters laughed at his efforts, jabbed him when he didn't know how to complete his mother's directions, made fun of him after he'd put an apron around his waist, discussed who'd best serve as wife material.

Leia informed him, "When Mama and I were at the market this morning, we bumped into Giovanna and she asked about you. She said she'd been waiting anxiously for you to get home. Thinks you might be here to offer her a ring. I sure as hell hope you don't."

He layered the vegetables, fish, calamari and prawns in the pan and added the coconut milk.

More out of curiosity than anything, knowing he wouldn't be doing any such thing, he asked, "Why not?"

"Let's just say she doesn't pine. If you're not around, she'd make it a point to find someone who was."

Felicia was munching on a carrot from a tray her mother had filled with crudités. "And where you're on the road as much as you're home, that might cause the end of any marriage. You are going into it for life, aren't you?"

"Of course I am."

His mother was the one to ask, "Then why are you in such a hurry? I think you should take your time with something this important."

"I'm not in a hurry. I've been thinking about this for a long time."

Leia chortled, "Haven't exactly acted like it."

He knew what she meant. He'd been attracted to women the way bees were attracted to honey and enjoyed their sweet nectar when the mood struck.

He leaned against the counter as the broth and ingredients bubbled in the pan, the wooden spoon in his hand. "I am ready to be serious about life. No more frittering away my time on useless activities. I need my head in the game and a wife will help me settle down."

Livia flashed her eyes at him. It was rare that anyone saw her fiery temper, but it was spitting in his direction. "Is that what this is about? Izabella said something to that effect, but I didn't believe her. Is that what you think a wife is for?"

He didn't expect her anger or his role as the target. In his defense, he asserted, "Look at Reid. He needed Izabella to tame him."

"He needed Izabella because he loved her." She cupped his face in her hands and repeated it, face-to-face, eye-to-eye. "He needed her because he loved her." Dropping her hands to her sides, she shook her head, her disappointment in him obvious. "It was only when Reid admitted he did, allowed your sister to love him in return, that he was able to meet life head on, and do the things he needed to do, to win. You are the only one who can tame your appetites."

Leia said snidely, "I bet you think all women are the same. That one will suffice as well as another." She gave their mother a twisted smile. "What were you saying about trusting him with this?" Turning back to address him, she added, "I think, if that's the case, you might as well let Mama arrange a marriage for you. She'll know what to look for in your perfect mate."

He bristled even though recently he'd thought exactly that.

Felicia asked, "Mama, what kind of woman do you think would be right for Rique?"

Livia wiped her hands on her apron, having just finished washing one of the pots her son had used.

He didn't face her but listened in rapt attention. "She would need to be humble. And unpretentious." He could hear the smile in her voice when she said, "Your brother has ego and flash covered."

Leia giggled. "So far so good. What else?"

"She would need to be kind, smart, and have a life of her own. If she was too needy, she wouldn't like the life he leads. Izabella's work keeps her occupied while Reid is traveling, and it works for them. She would also need to be independent. For the same reason. If children come, she will raise them alone for nine months out of the year. She needs to be willing to sacrifice parts of her life for his, which means she can't be selfish."

Felicia laughed, took another bite of the carrot. "That pretty much leaves everyone you know here in Brazil out of the running."

His sister was right. It did. So, what the hell was he doing here? He looked around and knew it had more to do with what was in this room than who he'd find outside of it.

It didn't stop him from hitting the clubs, and his old haunts, after dinner.

CHAPTER TWENTY-EIGHT

Enrique went right to the front of the line, some groans among those waiting, accompanying him. He spoke softly to the bouncer and exchanged some money and was given immediate access to the glittery night club. He'd lived close to the city while attending his first two years of college and he'd spent many an evening here flirting, dancing, and seducing, many a beautiful woman. Most of the friends he was meeting here tonight were from his college days. It was funny how there was an outcry about a college admissions scandal in America right now. Here, it was the way of doing business and most of his peers had been accepted based on how much their parents could afford in bribes. There were a couple who'd taken advantage of the arrangement and were doing quite well. Others preferred partying the night away or gaming and had dropped out, flunked out, or been asked to leave on principle.

The lights pulsed overhead, the music challenging the woofers to sweat. It wasn't a conducive atmosphere to talk but they weren't usually here to sit and shoot the shit. Tonight had been the exception. He'd come for one specific purpose. He'd have to table it for now. He noticed a hand waving high above the crowd, heard his name, and slithered through the crowd toward the table.

The air was stuffy and the scents of sweat and pot, did little to improve it.

"You made it. I wasn't sure you were going to. You're usually the first one to arrive."

His friend Alfonso was standing and reached out to shake his hand. They'd been in touch over the last month, making arrangements for the night of his return.

"It's good to have our leader back."

That remark made him cringe.

"I was here just here for the holidays."

He'd gotten caught up in the revelry of downtime, after a season of burnout and disappointment, and had spent very little time with his parents, more time here and other dance clubs. He was seeing it all with new eyes tonight.

Johanna, another of the women he'd dated once had come over to kiss his cheeks, placing the third on his lips. It tasted like lipstick, and he found no sweetness there. It didn't set off any kinds of bells and whistles that should come with all those exploding neurons. He noticed for the first time that she looked old, or maybe there was just a lack of life sparkling in her eyes.

"Are you going to dance, *amável?*"

She didn't hear him say no. He had to yell to be heard, and he all but screamed in her ear, "Thanks but I'm not in the mood."

He noticed everyone's head swivel to stare at him like he had three heads. He was always in the mood for dancing. But not tonight. He didn't want any body molded to his, not when erotic thoughts of Fifi pressed close were still frittering away at the back of his mind. He could have danced the night away with her, almost wished they had. His mood darkened. He'd never get the opportunity to hold her again.

Johanna was glowering at him. It shouldn't have come as a shock that she could turn it off and on at will. Her mood shifts were erratic, and he'd do well to stay out of her path.

He claimed a vacant seat, next to Eduarda. She had classic features, long light brown hair, and dark eyes that could captivate a thousand ships. Her mouth was a pout of generous lips, and if he were looking for beauty alone, she would have qualified. He knew it was only the tip of a very cold iceberg. He'd been in a couple of classes with her freshman year and she sat filing her nails the whole time the lecturer was speaking. She had no use for academics, no original thought in her head, either. She was rich, or at least her parents were, and was well taken care of. She didn't need to exert any more energy than was necessary to live. And she didn't. She'd need someone by her side to screw in a light bulb. He'd definitely be able to afford a live-in maid, but he wanted someone feisty, who'd insist on doing things for herself. Pedrina was the only one left of his college friends whom he'd originally considered, until he remembered she loved extreme sports. Needed her adrenaline rush like most needed breath. He didn't want to live with someone so restless with life.

He got up from the table to peruse the room, the inane chatter all about fashion and unflattering gossip annoying. One of the skimpily clad waitresses rubbed against him on her way to deliver drinks, flashed eyes at him that spoke to hunger and desire. He passed and headed for the bar. From there he observed the comings and goings of the patrons, waited for someone to catch his eye. That had been easy once. He'd been looking for a night, a brief and shallow exchange of bodies, and there were endless candidates. Tonight, he was looking for a woman who could hold his interest for a lifetime. Would he find her by looks alone? He was sure he could not. With each woman who walked by, he measured her for beauty, grace, stature, facial expressions, smiles, stride and bearing. They were all beautiful in their way. Long hair, short, bobbed, updo's, make-up flawless, dresses flowing, clinging, to the knee, to the thigh, bodies dressed for show. There were so many to choose from but who would be the perfect fit?

Thoughts of his mother came in a rush. Nights when he'd sat in her room with her as she perused her closet for something to wear to some dinner engagement, charity event, or bank function.

I need something perfect, Enrique. To make your father proud.

She'd push hangar after hangar to the side, inspecting each dress for suitability, pulling one out, perhaps a cocktail dress in mauve, to return it to its place, before moving on to a gown with a golden hue. Shaking her head, she'd put it back and begin again. That's what this exercise felt like. He was going through the closet, looking for the perfect choice. His mother always found it. No matter what she wore, she looked beautiful. It wasn't in the clothes or the looks or the stature. It was in the heart, something he'd never uncover from this stool.

He clinked the ice in his glass, all that was left of his first drink of the night. He threw his glass back and took some of the crushed shards into his mouth, needing to moisten his parched throat. Sweat was trickling down his back from the body heat that had taken over the room. A woman sitting at the curve of the bar was adjusting her cleavage, communicating it was his for the taking. He glanced away, tossed back the last of his ice, and stood. This wasn't him anymore. This is not where he wanted to be, and it was certainly not the place he'd find a wife.

Not even bothering to say good-bye to his friends, he paid his tab and went out into the sultry night. There were thousands of stars overhead and he took a moment to appreciate them. It gave Johana just enough time to come running after him.

"Where are you going, *meu amor*?"

"Home."

She twined her arms around him, brought her face close enough that all he'd have to do was move a muscle and their lips would touch.

"But what about us?" she whispered low against his mouth.

This was his fault. He'd insinuated he'd be down to find a wife, hinted that it might be one of the women from his past.

He unwound her arms from his and took a step away.

"There is no us. I'm sorry if I led you to believe that might be possible. It isn't."

Her eyes narrowed. "I thought you would bring me to America with you."

"This is where you belong, Johanna. The Americans will just have to make do without you."

"You couldn't have found another more perfect for you than I."

"You're not. Perfect for me. It just took longer to realize it than it should have. *Tchau*, Johanna."

And good riddance.

His mother was still up when he got home, her feet resting on the top of a chair. Her glass of wine was half-empty.

"Where's Papi?"

"In his study. We have our separate nightly rituals. You know this."

He did. It had been this way since he'd been a boy. His father would retreat to his study for a brandy, a cigar, and a good book. The bookcases filled with all kinds of reading material that lined the walls spoke to his voracious curiosity about the world. His mother would sit here in her domain with the scent of her herbs and a glass of wine to unwind from her day. They were two distinct personalities that came together as a perfect whole.

"May I sit with you or do you want to be alone?"

"Please sit. I wasn't expecting you back until much later."

He dropped down into a chair, toed off his Louis Vuitton leather loafers. It felt good to wiggle his toes. He'd gotten used to wearing sneakers and cleats over the last week and the shoes he wore tonight had pinched the blood flow. Next, he loosened his tie, shrugged out of his jacket and draped it behind him. He slumped down, his legs out straight, and admitted, "I wasn't in the mood to drink."

Or anything else he could have found there. For the first time, he'd felt out of his element. Had he changed that much in just a couple of weeks? He'd been here just a short month ago, but it seemed like a lifetime. He hadn't been traded yet. That was in the works even though he'd had no idea…

He glanced up to find his mother scrutinizing him as she sipped her wine. "I think this is a good thing. You are serious about your game."

His mother was easy to talk to. Things he couldn't admit to his father rolled off his tongue when in her presence. She could always see into the heart of him, knew before he did what he was looking for.

"I've become more serious about a lot of things."

"There is a woman you left behind it, isn't there?"

"Not really. I set the intention to settle down when I was traded. I don't want another repeat of last year." He peered at her and smiled. "Mental discipline is the order of the day."

"What does *not really* mean? It was a yes or a no question."

When Livia wanted to get to the bottom of something, she probed like a scientist. It appeared she was not going to let him evade her question. He might as well give in, talk to her about his confusion.

"You know I spent the week at Izabella's, and the dog walker she'd hired was there, as well."

She took another slow sip of wine before acknowledging, "I do know this."

He leaned back, got comfortable.

"She isn't really a dog walker. She was that week, but it's not what she does."

"I know that as well. She's a scientist."

He let his eyes flutter closed. There wasn't much this family didn't share.

"What else did my sister tell you?"

She arched her brow. "That she was able to keep you in line."

He smiled at that and said sardonically, "Without even trying. She made me feel like a loser most of the week."

"And you didn't want her to see you as a loser."

His eyes dipped to his hands, which were clasped in his lap. He swallowed hard over the lump of sadness in his throat.

"No. I didn't."

"And now?"

He flashed his eyes at her, his emotions raw and sore.

"She's all wrong for me Mama. She's consumed by her career. Or will be when she gets a job. She doesn't cook. She doesn't like parties, crowds, small talk. She's logical, direct, and doesn't take any shit. She has curly hair, is short, dresses in jeans…I could go on."

"She doesn't meet your ideal?"

He shook his head in resignation.

"She's nothing like the woman I thought I'd marry."

"Yet there is something about her that attracts you. You did not stay at the club long enough to find what you were looking for. Is that because you've already found her?"

He shoved his hands through his hair.

"I don't know. The only thing I do know is that I miss her."

Her smart mouth, those luscious lips, her laugh.

"She has the most beautiful gray eyes, brimming with curiosity. She reminds me of Papi with her thirst for answers. She listens when I talk and can delve into any subject with laser focus."

"Those are important qualities. Maybe more important than the superficial you've been chasing."

"Even if I…decided she was the one, I'm not sure I would be hers. I tried texting her, but she ignored me."

"Did she know you were coming here and the why behind it?"

Guiltily, he admitted, "Yes."

"Then you can't be surprised. I wouldn't have responded, either. You made her feel like a loser, too. She knew she was a diversion, and that you didn't think she was good enough for you."

He had not made her feel like a loser. He'd made love to her…

"When I met your father, he was with Julianna. I knew he had children with her and refused his advances. The attraction was strong, and I finally gave in to it. I had dinner with him, went to the theater, and we'd talk for hours. When he mentioned her or his children, it hurt. Over the months, he gave no indication that he would leave her, even though all they did, according to him, was fight. I became a convenient distraction from the hostility at home, and I was allowing him to toy with my affection. I broke it off. Told him I wanted a man who could make a commitment to me and me alone. To put it mildly, he didn't take it well. He would show up in my boss's office to see me, asked, begged, pleaded with me to reconsider. I began avoiding him and that's when he started calling me."

She gave him a smile. "We didn't have texting back then. And if we had and that was how he was communicating with me, I would have been even angrier. Hearing the vibration of the voice is as important as the words being spoken. He came to my office one day, professed his love, and told me he'd made the break. I didn't know whether to be excited or sad. I was sorry the children would lose their father. I was very glad I was able to make it up to them when they became part of our lives. The bottom line, Rique? Why would she respond to you knowing that you'd rejected her?"

"I never did that."

He'd welcomed her into his bed, with more passion than he thought he had in him.

"But you did, as soon as you told her you were boarding that plane and the reason why."

She drained the rest of the wine and set the glass down on the table.

"From my perspective, Fiona is the perfect woman for you. She has a life of her own, she's independent, intelligent and passionate. And as for your differences? They are like pieces to a puzzle, interlocking, making a whole. You love crowds, so you can help her navigate them. She's direct where you tend to finesse. She's logical, you're more insightful. You don't really want someone like you, do you? It would get boring very quickly."

He'd already come to that conclusion.

He gave her a lopsided smile. "You only think so because she keeps me in line."

"I think, rather, she makes you want to stay in line. Didn't you say she did it without even trying?"

The truth of that statement almost blindsided him. He'd been wrong. It wasn't marriage, it was the woman, just like Fifi had told him. He wanted to be a better person because of who she was. He'd come to respect her. Fuck, he'd come to love her.

It had taken only a second to see that Fifi was different than any other woman he'd met. If he closed his eyes, he could see her standing there in the mudroom, her hair dripping wet, covered in the grit from the puddle, yet she had radiated a shimmering energy that washed over him. There'd been an authentic connection, and he was almost sure it could lead to a deep and satisfying union.

"Can you fall in love this quickly?"

"Are you asking is there such a thing as love at first sight? I think yes. There can be an immediate kinship, a curiosity that compels you to learn more. Timing plays a key role. You're ready for commitment, and this woman comes along who complements you, who you like being with and who, hopefully, excites you. It also has to do with what you need from the other when the time is right. If I'd met your father before Julianna did, I'm not sure we would have lasted this long. He needed sweet after such bitterness."

He bounced out of his seat and began to pace. He was fidgety now, nervous about the future.

"I always wanted my wife to stay home with our children, like you did."

"If I'd had something valuable to offer the world, I would have given my time to it. Your father loved me enough that he would have supported and encouraged me."

"Fifi wants to succeed. She's ambitious. I'm not sure I like it."

Her face expressed horror. "You do not call her that, do you?"

He could feel a bubble of remorse burst.

"I did. Do. I'm not sure I can call her anything else now."

It was term of endearment, and in that one word he'd found it all. He just wasn't sure they could inhabit space as a family.

He knew there was only one way to find out.

"I'm going to go…home earlier than I planned. You'll understand, won't you?"

She got up and embraced him like she had when he was five. "I do. I think I will like her."

"She's not as outwardly affectionate as we are."

"She was raised differently, that's all. You have seen the love in her?"

He nodded.

"Then you will show her how to express it with words, gestures, and actions."

He would. If she'd let him.

He kissed his mother's cheek just as his father came in to collect her for bed. "See you both in the morning."

On his way to his room, he knocked lightly on Felicia's door.

"Come in."

Rique peeked his head in to find her reading. She was the most like their father in that regards. "Can you run an errand with me tomorrow?"

"Sure. What kind?"

"I'll explain it when we're in the car."

"Okay. Sleep well."

"You, too."

And for the first night since Fifi had left his sister's, he fell into a deep and untroubled sleep.

CHAPTER TWENTY-NINE

Fiona was up early on Saturday morning, dressed and ready to go. Ripped jeans, a long sleeve shirt, her Greenliner sweatshirt and boots. She had a job that others would envy. Well, some others, anyway. She couldn't see Izabella stepping out into the business world in these kinds of clothes. But then again, Izabella mixed with people. She didn't, and she liked it that way.

Yesterday, Keith had reviewed both contracts provided by the university, and they'd been signed, sealed and delivered that same afternoon. The employee contract was a single-page notification to which she'd agreed to provide up to twenty hours a week of instruction, including lecture and labs, during the upcoming summer, fall and spring terms. The courses were entitled Proteins: Alignment, Analysis, and Structure, Genetic Sequencing, and Genetic Data Analysis. Payment of services would include the prompt correction of all papers and exams. The lab document was more cumbersome. It was six pages of tiny print that set out all parameters for the research to be done, including financial compensation and set-up fund along with a list of equipment that was currently housed there. She'd all but danced out of the building after dropping them off and been given the key she'd reluctantly returned Wednesday. She was the proud lessee of a lab in the Sullivan Science Complex on the college campus. Michaels had given her permission to get a head start. She wasn't going to have to wait until Monday.

She'd been in constant touch with Bohdan since. She'd picked his brain for ideas about course material and lecture topics and she'd labored far into the night, organizing, and synthesizing, and finally completing the curricula vitae. The course descriptions had been emailed to Kurt's secretary soon after. Up at dawn, she went right back to her desk and had a completed a syllabus for the for ten-week course on Proteins. She had fleshed out an outline for both genetics courses, pulling out all her old study notes to make sure she didn't miss anything of importance.

Keeping busy had been her salvation. It had kept her mind from drifting to Rique. Or at least had kept her from dwelling on him twenty-four seven. She'd gotten next to no sleep over the last two nights, imagining him on his search, scouring the clubs for his life partner. Had he gone dancing?

Did he hold the woman the way he'd held her? Had he left early to complete the seduction and take her to bed? She hated the way that thought made her feel. Him in bed with someone else was an image blurred with shadow and darkness.

Was he drinking? Staying out of trouble? Had he found himself a wife yet? What did she look like? Every question she'd asked soured her stomach.

Frustration spilled out in a fiery sigh. There was a fantasy that played out when she least expected it, about him not finding anyone and coming back, telling her he couldn't live without her and asking her to marry him.

Not that she'd agree to it.

They'd never work as a couple. She should know. She'd spent hours listing all the reasons he couldn't love her, repeating the mantra as she lay in bed, restless and alone. The problem was she missed him, wanted to feel his lips on hers as much as she'd wanted her own lab.

That pretty much told her everything about what she felt.

Gawd. She had to stop doing this to herself. He was gone. She was here. She'd have to start dealing with it and stop thinking about him.

She shrugged into her coat. She was meeting Bohdan at the lab at eight. They had a lot of work to do. They had to take an inventory of what they had and what they'd need to purchase from the money the college had put at her disposal. As she was hefting the briefcase over her shoulder her buzzer sounded. She looked over at it, as if it would tell her who was at the outer door. Slowly, she walked across the kitchen and pressed the intercom.

"Yes?"

"Fifi, it's me."

The blood drained from her face and her legs began to shake. What the hell? Had he come to tell her all about his…upcoming marriage? Inviting her to be a witness? How dare he…

"I'm busy. Go away."

"I need to talk to you."

If he was looking for advice or needed her to settle him about something, he was out of luck. Those days were over, even as the memories lingered too vividly for her own good.

"I'm sure Izabella would be more than willing to listen."

"I need to talk to *you*."

Gawd. Every time she thought she'd outdistanced him, he showed up. How the hell was she supposed to put him in her past if he continued to be in her present? The pull to see him again was strong but she fought it with every ounce of discipline in her.

"I was just leaving. I don't have time."

"Come on, Fifi. Give me five minutes. I'm not going away until you do."

Five minutes. It wasn't nearly enough time. Not if she wanted to drink him in, hear his voice, listen to one of his stories. But five minutes was more than she'd thought she'd get again. And if he wasn't leaving until she talked to him, then she couldn't leave for the lab. There were two voices drowning out all thought. One said, see him, the other told her she'd be crazy to give in.

Crazy won. It seemed her only choice, so she might as well get it over with.

She released the lever, picked up her purse, briefcase, and keys. After locking the door, she took a deep breath and walked down the two flights of stairs to get to the front lobby. She could see the back of him through the glass, his hands in his coat pockets but when he heard the creak of the inner door he turned, and her breath held. He looked just like she remembered, maybe even better if that was possible. Her heart skidded across her chest as she pushed through the door. And passed right by him. She couldn't do this to herself.

He ran down the brick stairs after her, took hold of her arm, stopping her forward motion.

She avoided his eyes, couldn't take the chance of falling into them.

"What?"

She braced herself for some kind of monologue on his upcoming wedding.

"I…I found who I wanted to be with."

The words hit her like body blows and her voice was nothing more than a whisper.

"Great. Mission accomplished."

"She wasn't anything like I'd envisioned, but I fell hard and fast."

I guess you did. Even faster than I fell for you. That took a couple of days. Bullshit. It took minutes.

There was such surety in his voice, she thought maybe he had. Like his father and mother, love at first sight.

She struggled to get out, "Congratulations. Now I have to get going."

"Don't you want to know who it is?"

As she pried his fingers from her arm, she said, "Not particularly. I can truthfully say my life will be complete without it."

He shoved his hand into his pocket and pulled out a box. What? Was he kidding? He was going to show her the ring he'd bought for the mystery woman?

Her eyes flashed up to meet his. As soon as her stomach fell to her feet, she knew it was a mistake. Those eyes could do serious damage to her heart.

"I am not doing this. Can't you just leave me alone now? I can't keep being your handler."

There was a stupid grin on his face as if he found this amusing.

"I want you to be my handler for life, Fifi. I've decided you're the one."

In a flash, the need to get away was replaced with the stirrings of anger. Maybe she'd heard him wrong.

"What?"

He said cavalierly, "I couldn't find what I was looking for there, and the more I thought about it, the more I thought you'd be the one best suited to me."

Flashes of irritation stung like a swarm of bees.

"You did, did you?"

The smile dimmed.

"Yes."

"I thought you wanted a woman to stay home and devote her life to you. That's not me."

"I know, but—"

"I'm not going to be the one you settle for, for lack of someone better. And I'm certainly not going to accept a ring you bought for some other woman."

She was sure he'd carried it down to Brazil and back. Had it ready for that momentous occasion when he popped the question. Didn't matter the woman, didn't matter the ring.

"I didn't—"

She all but ran to her car, keeping the tears from falling until she was driving out of the parking lot. She'd woken this morning seeing this as one of the best days of her life. Why did he have to ruin it for her? Now it would be forever linked with his half-assed proposal.

He'd proposed to her. Just like that. No flowers, no music or violins, no words of love. She'd always thought romantic love was artificial, that sweet words were a waste of time, but with him, she wanted that, wanted it all. The affection, the attention, the promise. Instead? He wanted her to be his handler. His handler. Like that would be enough to bind them together for life. She didn't want the type of relationship her parents had; she wanted something more. What he'd offered was devoid of emotion, more clinical than intimate. Hah. He hadn't offered anything. He asked for it. He'd needed something from her so why the hell not. Any woman would do. For some reason, he'd rained down his luck on her.

After starting the engine, which strained from the deep freeze that had gripped the night, she backed up and pulled out, skirting around him as he tired to flag her down. It would have been justice if there'd been a puddle, but all water had turned to ice. Just like her heart. For good measure she flipped him the bird on her way by.

Rique jumped out of her path and watched her go, his heart bleeding out. He'd struggled with this decision, lost sleep over it, had finally found himself willing to accept that he loved her, and how had she reacted? By giving him the finger. He'd told himself she might not accept it, but he'd thought maybe he could convince her…

Did you even try?

This wasn't the way it was supposed to go. When he finally got around to proposing to someone, he'd had a different picture in mind. He'd get down on one knee, find the right words to tell her what was in his heart, ask her to spend her life with him. She'd smile and say yes, tell him how much she loved him. It was romantic and memorable.

He shoved his hands through his hair. He was exhausted. He'd taken the first flight he could, thought endlessly about how he'd approach her all the way back, gone right to her condo, unable to wait to see her again. Then she was there and every one of his cells had come alive, but his mind was so muddled he'd made a mess of it. What kind of a half-assed proposal had he offered? He hadn't asked her to be his wife, he'd asked her to be his handler, like it was some job he was asking her to take on. She thought he was settling for something less than his ideal because he hadn't found it. But he had. It was her. Didn't she know he didn't want to be with anyone else?

How could she. You never told her. Never once mentioned the word love.

He scrambled into his car and took off, heading in the same direction she had. Where was she going? Couldn't be an interview, not with the way she was dressed. He scanned the road before him, as he sat at a set of lights, not sure which way she'd gone. Then he saw a flash of blue to the left, making the turn toward the highway. He gunned the engine, passed a couple of cars on his right before cutting around and veering onto the secondary road. He was three cars behind, and he knew if she was paying attention, she'd see him trailing her. He hung back a bit more, trying to get lost from view while keeping her in his sights. When she turned south on Route 93, he followed. When they passed through the city, he began to worry. When was she going to get off? Where the hell was she going?

And then her blinker was on and she slid into the exit lane. He was still behind her, one car separating them. They wove up one street and down another, then along the harbor until they came to a campus. She drove by a gray building, concave in shape, and around back to where rows of orange brick buildings led one into another, walkways connecting them. Was she going back to school? Unable to find a job in her field, she'd decided to…That couldn't be it. She'd gone as far as she could with her education. So why here? She parked in one of the lots, locked up her car, and began walking to the building in front of her, her briefcase banging against her leg. She was on her phone, so she was mentally occupied. It gave him the opportunity to pull his car in besides hers.

He entered the building, peeked around a corner to see her descend some stairs, waited, only to hurry forward so he didn't lose her. They were in a basement, the cool interior unable to hold much heat. She'd freeze down here if she wasn't careful.

She opened the door at the end of the hall and disappeared. The welcoming voice made him quicken his steps.

He stood at the opening to see her giving a man a hug. A tight bear hug and it sounded as if she were crying.

"Hey, what's wrong? I thought you'd be in seventh heaven when you got here."

"I was. I am. I'm just…"

Then the man looked up and saw him. He asked, "Can I help you?"

Fifi broke free and turned. "Gawd. You followed me?"

Her expression told him it pained her physically to see him.

"Is this why you wouldn't accept my proposal?"

"What? The lab?"

"Him. Is he the reason?"

She swiped her arm against her nose and then pierced him with her eyes. "I didn't accept because I don't want to be anyone's life-long handler. I want a man, not a child. But mostly I said no because I want to be first choice, not an afterthought."

He was stuck on the man and there wasn't a word she'd said that had registered.

"Who is he?"

She just stared at him and he felt a tight band clamp around his middle.

It was the man who answered the question. "I'm her assistant. Bohdan. I'm here to help her set the lab up."

A thrill shot through him. Not only because the man wasn't any competition but because she'd gotten a lab, here, in the city. Not far from where he'd be working nights when in town.

"You got your lab?" He couldn't help but grin. "Why didn't you tell me?"

She sniffed, pulled a tissue from her coat pocket and wiped her nose.

"I figured you were busy. You know, looking for a wife."

She sounded sad, the tone tinged with irritation.

"It was a wasted trip. The woman I was looking for was here."

He stepped closer to where she was. He needed to feel his arms around her, tell her…

He needed to tell her first. Then maybe, if he was lucky and she was a forgiving sort of woman, he'd get to the embrace part.

He glanced up at Bohdan and took a step closer. The man had the grace to step back, giving him some room.

He touched her cheek with his thumb. It felt…like he'd come home.

In a low voice, he said, "Fifi…Fiona. I have missed you *meu amor*. These last few days have been a nightmare and I realized that I can't live a happy life without you by my side. I left to go home only to find it is not my home anymore. That this is my home because you're here. Where my heart beats the strongest. I love you, Fifi and I wish with all my heart that you will marry me."

Her eyes were wide and searching his for the truth.

"I just got my lab."

He was hoping for something else after his heartfelt message. What if she didn't return the feeling? What if the lab *was* the most important thing in her life? What if she was telling him that she finally had what she'd worked so hard for and she wasn't giving it up?

"I see that. I'm proud of what you've done and would never ask you to quit now."

He stepped closer still, until she was a hairsbreadth away. He took her chin in his fingers and leaned down to kiss her lips. When she didn't fight him, he thought he might still have a chance for a redo. One that held a different answer than the one she'd given him less than an hour ago.

"I took my sister Felicia shopping with me yesterday. As you know, she is a scientist as well, and although she works in the soil, I thought she would know what kind of ring would suit you. I don't want you to have to take it off if you accept to wear it. In other words, this ring was chosen and purchased for you, no other."

He went down on his knee and pried open the box. Taking her hand, he looked up, his heart racing. There was love there, in her eyes, and it was shining on him.

"You are my heart, and my home and I want no other. Will you marry me?"

He stopped breathing as he waited for her answer.

"I want to."

"Say yes, then."

A myriad of emotions crossed her face and he was afraid she was going to turn him down. She was trembling when she finally said, "Yes. Yes, I'll marry you."

"Thank God, *meu amor*. I don't know what I would have done if you'd said no."

He slid the ring on her finger, straightened, pulled her into his arms, and began to spin them around. Before he could kiss the life out of her, she said, "There are a lot of things we need to resolve, Rique."

"There are none that we can't figure out if we want to be together badly enough. I am willing if you are."

"I don't cook."

"Ah, but I do. And if I'm tired, you can order us something on speed dial."

"I won't be able to travel with you."

"I'm sad about that because I want you with me always, but I understand. Maybe you can let your assistant here work some weekends for you and you can come to some of my games?"

She was threading her fingers through his hair. The intimacy of that small touch made his heart swell.

"I promise I will. And when I can't, I'll have the game on here in the lab, so I know how you've done."

"This is very close to Harborside. I can come visit after my games if you're not on the edge of some important discovery."

He couldn't believe how excited he was for her, hopeful that she could achieve all she wanted to, all she was capable of. He was marrying a woman smarter than him, and it should be scaring him senseless. But it wasn't. He saw it as a challenge, one which could make him a better man. He'd certainly never get bored.

When she said, "I'm nothing like who you wanted," there was vulnerability in her eyes.

He kissed it away as best he could and replied truthfully, "You are everything I ever wanted, I just didn't know it. I didn't know you were out there."

They heard Bohdan's voice as he welcomed someone in. "Hi, hon. New discovery. Fiona's in love and getting married."

Rique glanced back at a petite woman holding a baby. She was inspecting him critically before saying, "It's about time."

He put Fifi down but held her in the crook of his arm as she introduced them. "Rique, this is Ardita, Bohdan's wife, and their daughter, Priyanka."

Ardita went over to give her husband a kiss. "I came by to see the place. It's perfect."

Fiona glanced around as if taking it in for the first time. "It is, isn't it? Now I just have to figure out how to keep it running once the money from the college runs out."

Rique's eyes had followed hers around the space, taking in every square inch. This was where he could help. He might not have the kind of brain matter to bring a dramatic shift in science, but he could contribute another way.

"I think we could spare some money to keep you working. My job, which you call a game, pays pretty well. And I have some friends with deep pockets."

"I told you, it will take—"

"Yeah, millions. I can't think of a better way to spend it, can you?"

She'd sucked in a breath, those gray eyes wide with surprise.

"I can't ask you to do that."

He kissed the tip of her nose as if it were no big deal.

"You won't have to. Once we're married, it's yours, as well. This'll be my way of taking care of you, supporting you in a sense. It will definitely help my ego."

There were tears shimmering in her eyes. "I promise, I'll take care of you as well as I can but I'm new at this."

"We both are. We'll figure it out together."

Bohdan had taken his daughter in his arms, and the little girl held on tightly.

"What do you say we put in a few hours and then call it a day, start up on Monday like we planned. Dita has the day off, which is a rare commodity and I think you need to do some celebrating outside the lab for once. If there was a day for it, I'd say this is it."

Rique shrugged out of his suit coat and hung it on the back of a chair. "Can I stay and watch, maybe help?"

Bohdan nodded. "We could use some brawn. We might have to move things around. Fine by me."

Ardita took Priyanka back and said, "I've got some errands I can run and then I'll swing back, pick you up for lunch."

"Does that work for you, boss?"

She tilted her head up to Rique's for a kiss, a sparkle in her eyes.

"It does."

CHAPTER THIRTY

Fiona kept looking down at her finger, still not sure this wasn't a dream. The ring was perfect, flat but chock full of diamond chips, surrounding what had to be a couple-of-karat nugget, expensive she was sure, but modest in setting. She could work with it on and swore she'd never take it off. It was an expression of love. Not the ring itself, but the care and consideration Rique had taken selecting it. He knew who she was, and it seemed he'd accepted it. When she wasn't examining the ring, she was examining her future husband. He was wearing the tee shirt she'd found for him, and he'd told her he hadn't worn much else since she'd left it for him.

He was going to be her husband. How she'd managed to attract someone like him was still a mystery. Or maybe not. He was as far from her ideal as she was his, but they seemed to work well together. She grounded him; he drew her out of herself. They'd lived together for over a week and it had seemed so easy. When she didn't want to throttle him.

"Fifi." She finally heard her name the second time he called out, "Fifi. Is this where you want this thing?"

She lifted her head and couldn't help but smile. She'd never thought she'd see him again, and here he was helping Bohdan move heavy machinery around. Anticipation about tonight and how he would love her thickened the air in her lungs.

"Yeah. It's perfect."

And so was he.

Not perfect in the real sense of the word, but perfect for her.

Just before noon they finished up. Ardita and Priyanka were back and as they gathered their coats to leave, Rique said, "I've got to get back to the practice field on Monday, but I can stop by afterward, help again if you need me to."

"Um, you're not exactly in the best of conditions when you're done for the day."

He put his arm around her, kissed her head. "I don't want to go home to an empty house just yet. Maybe after we're living together and I can feel your presence, but…not yet."

His gaze was startlingly possessive and she felt that coil tighten. She placed her hand on his chest, needing to touch him, and felt his heart beating against it.

"You're not still staying with Izabella?"

There was excitement in his voice when he said, "No. I rented a place after you left. It's close to Melinda and Jim. I think you'll like it."

Those condos were expensive. Beautifully detailed, and exquisitely landscaped. She could never have afforded to look there.

"You rented there?"

"Yeah. Why?"

"They're out of my price range."

He bent down and kissed her nose.

"I've got it covered."

What did a baseball player make? If he was willing to contribute a million dollars to her research and live in a palatial home, it had to be a lot. She wasn't going to ask him here, in front of the others, but her curiosity would sooner or later get the better of her.

They walked out to the parking lot, Bohdan now carrying his daughter, holding his wife's hand.

Rique clasped her fingers in his and nodded to the threesome just ahead. "Seems some scientists make it work. The marriage thing."

She rested her head against his shoulder. It felt so solid and safe and her heart skipped a beat.

"Some do."

She thought of Terry and promised herself she'd make the effort to spend time with her man. The way she felt now, she'd have to force herself to leave him.

After walking her to her car, Rique kissed her again, but she didn't allow for a light one. She twined her arms around his neck and went for one that was wet and deep. His moan told her what she needed to know.

"I have missed you, Fi. I can't wait until we're living together, and I can wake up to you every morning. Last Monday was one of the worst days of my life."

It had been one of hers, too. She'd wanted to stay in the cocoon of his body but knew if she didn't leave before he woke up, she'd do something she'd regret. Like tell him she loved him.

"Have I agreed to that?"

"You're not going to make me live alone, are you?"

He kissed her again until her head was spinning. She couldn't come up with her name, never mind a reason not to.

"We'll go to your place first, pick up some essentials and then christen the new bedroom."

He opened her door, tucked her inside, and said, "Follow me."

"Try to keep it close to the speed limit. My car doesn't have wings like yours does."

His arm was on the frame, his body bent as he looked in at her. "You want a new one?"

"No. I like my Bug."

"Okay, but if you do, say the word."

"You're spending your money like it's water. We'll need to save something for our old age."

She knew ball players didn't get the thirty-year retirement watch. They had only so many good years before they had to quit.

"We'll have plenty in our old age. My future wife is going to kill it."

She laughed at that one. Even if she made some kind of incredible breakthrough, it didn't necessarily mean she'd make it rich.

"I wouldn't count on that."

"Well if you don't achiever fame and fortune, you'll still have me."

Still not believing this was real, she asked, "Why?"

"Because I love you, *meu amor*. It is that simple."

"I thought you'd pick from the big leagues."

Just before he closed her door he said, "*Meu amor*. You're in a league all your own."

When she let him into her small condo, he stood and glanced around, taking it in.

Almost apologetically, she said, "It's kind of cramped."

Scrambling over to the table, she began to tidy up the mess of papers she had out to write the syllabus. Her clothes were fresh out of the laundry, folded but not put away yet.

"You'll have room in our place for an office. It's kind of ironic. I put the deposit down thinking I wanted lots of space in case…"

She stopped what she was doing, a pile of notes in her hand, and looked over.

"In case?"

"I was going in blind, not knowing who I'd be living with. What if we didn't get along as well as I'd hoped? I wanted room to escape if I needed to." He added, "I could live here with you, and be perfectly content."

She wasn't sure. He liked what his money gave him, a fast car, a big house, expensive clothes but it was nice to hear.

"I still have several months on my lease. I'm not sure they'll let me out of it."

With a wave of his hand, he said, "We'll pay it off."

"How much money do we have?"

"In savings or in yearly income?"

"Yearly income."

"I have one year left on my current contract at a little over five million, annually. I'll be re-writing it next year, and if I can live up to my potential this season, I'm guaranteed more."

"For playing a game?"

"I told you it's not just a game. And just so you know, I've saved most of it over the last three years. Seems I've inherited my father's financial genius."

She knew her mouth was open, but she couldn't seem to close it.

The smile her gave her was almost evil. "Just think. Our kids can't lose. They have a fifty-fifty chance of inheriting your DNA, a fifty-fifty chance of inheriting mine, with bit contributions from all who came before."

She'd thought of having kids in an abstract way but never considered the details. She knew one thing for sure.

"I'm not pushing them. They go at their own pace."

"I agree, but we do want them to be challenged. They could get my propensity for boredom. And then what?"

"We'll make sure they're well supervised."

He began to laugh then stopped. She watched as he walked over to the instrument sitting on its stand and picked it up. "You play this?"

The violin was a Fiddlerman master, not the most expensive brand, but it was hand crafted and had great sound and depth. If she ever traded up, she'd get another.

"In my down time."

She wouldn't have much of that now that she had her lab, and a new husband, not that she'd had a lot while working toward her doctorate. But she knew there'd still be times she'd be stymied by some problem and she'd pick it up. In the middle of playing, she'd somehow come up with a solution.

"How long have you been playing?"

"Since I was ten. I can play a couple of other instruments, but this was the most portable."

He put the violin back where it came from.

"Did I mention our kids can't lose?"

"You're wrong. It's not easy being smart."

"I know. Felicia had some trouble along the way. Kids can be cruel but ours will have us. Love can heal anything."

"And if one of them has my hair, and one of them has yours? Sibling rivalry aside, I can see a lot of resentment growing."

"I will be partial to the ones who have your hair. It will make them as unique as their mother, whom I've come to adore."

He'd come over to hold her. "Let's get your things and go home. I can't wait much longer to prove just how much."

She gathered up some clothes, threw them in a duffel, along with a toothbrush and hair accessories. "I should clean out the refrigerator before we go."

"Knowing you, there's not much in there. We can come back tomorrow and do it. Will you have the time to pack up everything and move or should we get a moving company to do it?"

"I…"

She'd planned on finding a bigger place, closer to Boston, but hadn't thought about the actual move or how she'd manage it.

"Moving company?"

"We'll have to rent a storage unit. The condo is furnished."

That should have bothered her, but domesticity wasn't her strong suit. She could live just about anywhere, the background not of any import. There was one thing that was.

"Can we get a dog?"

He frowned. "I'm sorry, no pets. It might be a good thing. We have a lot on our plates right now. This time next year, we should be married and have a home of our own. Then we can think about adding to our family."

Next year she'd be married. To this man. It still had a way of putting her on edge.

"You're probably right but a dog would be good company while you're gone."

He came over and put his arm around her. "Maybe I can convince the owner to rethink it."

Her head was resting against his shoulder, but he must have felt her stiffen.

"Is there something else?"

"I'm not sure we should get married until the season is over. Make sure this is what you want."

He tilted her chin up. "Do you think this was an impulsive proposal?"

"You…you might be… This might just be a way to have what you thought you wanted."

He chuckled. "You think I still believe every woman is the same, interchangeable, and that any woman will do. You're wrong, *meu amor*. No other woman will do for me, only you. I knew before I left for Brazil, and only confirmed it when I got there. I sat in the club the first night in, and I was looking for you. You were the one I wanted to talk to, dance with, make love to. So, the next day, I spent time with my family, took Felicia shopping with me, and took a late flight out to come home. This is my home now. You are my heart. I will never be bored with you in my life."

"And when you're on the road?"

"I will be thinking of you always. I told you I would be faithful to the woman I married. I can promise you I will. Knowing you will be, as well, will make it easier to leave you."

They didn't wait until they got to their new place. They couldn't.

Only when they were completely satiated with each other did they stop for some dinner and bring it home.

EPILOGUE

Fiona was standing with Izabella, at the gate waiting to board. She was nervous and fidgety.

"Are you sure this is a good idea?"

"Of course, it is. What are you afraid of?"

Spring training had started a couple of weeks ago and Izabella had convinced her to accompany her to Florida. She was surprising Reid with a quick weekend visit and thought Rique would be disappointed if she showed up alone.

"I don't know. We haven't known each other all that long. What if he's figured out this is a mistake…?"

"Has he given you any reason to feel this way?"

He hadn't. In fact, it was the reverse. The time they'd spent together before he left for Sanford had been easy, filled with conversation, laughter and passion. He never once complained about her hours, joined her many a night after his training or hung out with his friends, always home by the time she got there. Since leaving, he'd sent flowers, they'd Skyped, discussed the games for hours when he'd call, and he was proving he had the potential to be one of the great shortstops in the league. And he'd told her numerous times it was because of her.

"No."

Izabella placed a hand on her arm and looked right into her eyes.

"My brother has been looking for someone to love for a very long time. He comes from a loving family and I knew once he made up his mind, that would be it. You have to trust it is good."

That was the sticking point. She did know it was good. At least she had earlier this morning. when she'd dropped Dylan, her rescued black and white terrier mix, off at Melinda and Jim's. Somehow Rique had convinced the owner of the condo they were leasing that a small dog wouldn't hurt anything, and he'd gotten permission to house one. She'd bet her right arm he'd paid big-time in order to give her what she wanted. Love had washed over her as she squeezed her buddy goodbye. Rique was doing thoughtful things all the time, even from the road, and she didn't know why she was so nervous about surprising him. They'd talked about her attending some of his games and she promised that once she got the lab up and running, she'd be there, at least for a weekend. But she hadn't told him this was the weekend. She'd left Bohdan in charge, with a couple of assistants, students who'd volunteered to be part of the research. She was putting them on stipends, at least until she worked out the budget she'd been working on. This was new to her, but she was learning how to manipulate the numbers with some help from Rique, who offered his father's expertise as soon as the man was in town. She'd yet to meet his family. That was another month away. They'd be coming to Boston for opening day and Rique had planned a whole weekend around it. She wasn't sure how she'd fare with such a loving family, but she wasn't going to worry about it until she had to.

She walked down the tunnel and stepped onto the plane, rethinking the first-class ticket. The price had been exorbitant, and she wasn't used to squandering money, but if she was going to sit with Izabella, she'd had no choice.

"I don't know why I let you talk me into this."

"Trust me. You can afford it."

"I can't even afford my daily coffee yet."

"That's only because you're being obstinate about spending his money."

"That's the operative word. Until we're married, it's his."

"The only reason you're not yet is because you want to wait until the end of the season. If it had been up to Rique, you would be. What are you planning? A big, fat Brazilian bash?"

They'd talked about it and decided to forego the destination wedding and hold it in their hometown. She hadn't spent her life dreaming about the day she'd say I do, like others did, and had no idea how she'd go about it. Rique had offered his mother's services to help with the details. She was definitely going to take him up on that. It would be better than conferring with her own. She'd be no help what-so-ever. Clare *didn't* return calls more often than she did.

"We're going for smaller, more intimate."

"Not sure how you'll manage that. We have a very big family and then there's the ball players who'll be invited, the manager, the coaches, his friends, your friends."

"Stop. I'm not good in crowds and he knows it."

"You'll be fine. You don't really remember anything about the day anyway. Too caught up in the sentimentality and emotion of it all. Have I ever told you how glad I am we'll be sisters?"

"A couple of times."

"And how grateful I am he chose so wisely. I trust you with my brother and his heart."

Izabella knew she'd take good care of it.

They chatted most of the flight down, about how her lab was coming along, Izabella's work, about their families, about the weather. It was only when she felt the wheels grind down that the butterflies in her stomach began a flutter fall. By the time the cab dropped them in front of the hotel, their wings had gotten tangled into a tight knot.

What if the time away had diminished his feelings? How would she react when she saw him? Would he be surprised and happy she was there, or surprised and dismayed?

What the fuck is wrong with you? How many ways does he have to prove he loves you?

While she was standing at the registration desk, a group of ballplayers came off the elevator. When she caught a glimpse of Rique, her heart stuttered. He was wearing the mandatory suit and tie. Looking so damn good should be illegal. She took in her fill, from the rugged looks, to the athletically toned body. And then he looked up, as if he could feel her eyes on him. His eyes widened and his face glowed in pleasure. He said something to Mattie and Seb and rushed over to grab her up off the ground.

"How did you know I wanted you here? I texted you before I came down, but you didn't answer. God, I've missed you."

When her feet were back on the tiled floor, he kissed her and every nervous thought she'd had evaporated.

"I wasn't sure—"

"Why didn't you tell me? Anticipation would have made it sweeter."

Izabella had come over and handed her a key card. "It was a last-minute change of heart. She said she couldn't afford it. I told her she could. Could you please get her a credit card? I want company when I come down."

She must have texted Reid because he came racing out of the elevator and toward them, gave his wife the same kind of warm welcome.

"Today. I'll get one today." He looked into Fiona's eyes and said, "Use it. Please. Daily if you want to commute to the lab from here."

He was an affectionate man, with such a loving nature, and it was helping lower her inhibitions about telling someone how she felt.

She kissed him lightly on the lips. "I've missed you so much."

He returned the sentiment just as Reid said, "We have to get going."

"I wish—"

"I know. Me, too. The anticipation should make it sweeter."

His finger had found a stray curl and it clung as he stroked her cheek.

"You still love me?"

There was concern in his expression that she didn't understand. Considering who they were, how they looked, that should have been her line. Might have been if she'd been open and honest.

"How could I not, dark and handsome?"

"I need you to love me for more than my looks."

She fiddled with his hair, the sincerity in his eyes making her dizzy.

"I've loved you from the minute you appeared in Izabella's doorway toweling your hair dry."

"Same for me."

She laughed then. "I was a bedraggled mess. You can't mean it."

"You were glowering at me and it kind of turned me on."

"You're crazy."

"About you. I'm sorry it took me so long to figure it out."

"You'll have the rest of our lives to make it up to me."

"And I promise, I won't waste one second."

They fell into each other's eyes, and she could read the love there. She'd spend the rest of her life making him feel hers.

"I think you have a bus waiting for you."

He kissed her once more and didn't let go of her hand until he had no choice.

As she sat in the stands, she followed the play with a keen eye and growing fascination. She'd been watching the Grapefruit League games since they started, read the sports page first thing every morning. She was getting used to seeing Rique's name in print more often than not, at times for his skill, at others for his leadership on the field. Today he was proving again why he might out-shortstop every other player. Even though he only played four innings, he'd won the game with his five-foot leap and catch and a homerun his last time at the plate.

As she looked around the section of wives and girlfriends, the smiles and excitement making her feel a part of something she'd never experienced before it felt surreal. She was succeeding in her chosen field, but willingly taking time away from it, forming friendships, expanding the meaning of family, opening up to affection and feeling whole for the first time in her life. All because of the man who loved her.

Now if he'd just stop calling her Fifi in the lab…

To My Readers

When I was writing Thrown for a Curve, I decided I needed to tell Enrique dos Santos' story and although it took some time, I finally got to it. I'm not sure it had to do with who he was, or what sport he played. More than likely it was a combination of the two. He was spoiled and pampered, and I needed to take him down a notch.

So, I began to imagine what kind of woman would be capable of that, and Fiona Barrows began to come into focus. She needed to be smarter than he was, and she just so happened to have a doctoral degree in genetics. She was on the opposite end of the spectrum of what Rique was looking for in a wife. He wanted a beautiful Brazilian wife, with long, flowing dark hair, who would dote on him, cook him elaborate meals and attend to his every need.

It was a lot of fun seeing him fall for a curly-haired blonde, with no culinary skills whatsoever, who was not the doting type. In fact, she was able to put him in his place with ease.

League of Her Own became book two of a new series, all about the Greenliners, and a few of the players on the other baseball team that plays in Boston.

I hope you enjoy.

Faith

Books by Faith O'Shea

The Greenliner Series
Thrown for a Curve
League of Her Own
Clutch Hit

The Scalera Family Series
Cold Sweat
Edge of Forever
Thin Blue Line
Coming Home to You
Finding Joy

Fire and Ice Series
Consumed by Fire
Skoli on Ice
Heart on Fire
Heart of Ice
Tendril of Ice
Rekindling the Fire

Clutch Hit

Alicia Nilsson, the Vice President in charge of Player Development for the Boston Greenliners, would do just about anything to see her team win the World Series. And she'd proven it. She had also proven, quite possibly, that she was crazy. But when she bumped into a Cuban player at a bar in Cancun, what else could she do? He was the third baseman she'd been looking for and he came with a strong bat to boot.

Mateo Alvarez couldn't believe his luck, or how far a woman would go to provide for her team's future. He chalked it up to some pretty strong existential winds, the kind you don't mess with.

At least he wasn't willing to.

Could he convince Alicia that his glove and bat might be clutch, but they weren't the only things she needed?

Excerpt from Clutch Hit

Alicia Nilsson approached the Campari Sports Complex, the knot in her stomach tightening with every step. It was the first time in the two years she'd held the job as Senior Vice President of Major and Minor League Operations for the Boston Greenliners that she felt this kind of dread. She usually relished the interaction she had with the men she'd drafted, traded for or farmed in their minor league system. When she'd taken the job, a rise up the front-office ladder, and only the fourth woman who'd risen that high in the ranks of Major League Baseball, she couldn't wait to put her well-defined plan into action. Dan DeLorenzo, her boss and President in charge of Baseball Operations had given her the green light to create a manual that spelled out exactly what it meant to be a Greenliner. From clubhouse behavior to how to wear the uniform, to rules about facial hair, she'd defined what administration expected from their team members.

The expectations, no longer ambiguous were clearly stated and she hadn't stopped there. She culled the scouts until she had the best, and she gave them quantitative measures for what she wanted from them- specifics on strengths, weaknesses, stats, family, attitude, any and all information they could gather about the person in question. And she insisted each player be treated as if he were a precious investment.

Because he was.

She'd done her part, objectively evaluating each of their prospects, discussing their skills and talents and what she thought they'd bring to the team with the managers. She'd had individual sit-downs with each of them, wanting to get to know who they were, and how they approached life. She challenged the professionals in the big leagues to be better, and she outlined ways they could achieve those goals. What had surprised most of her critics, is that they had all listened. What the naysayers had missed in the gender equation was that she was good at her job.

She'd been talking baseball since she'd been a toddler at her father's knee, interned with the team in high school, and when she'd graduated from college with a degree Sports Management, she was hired as Dan's assistant. From that moment on, she'd made a point of learning every player's name, from every league, minor to major, every stat, where the men came from came, how they got where they were and what it would take for them to move up. Every detail was at her fingertips, and she could answer any question Dan put to her. All of her hard work paid off for as soon as her predecessor had retired, she'd been promoted. Even the owners had given their blessing. Dan knew she'd do anything to help her team win, whether it be working twelve-or-thirteen-hour days, traveling across the country to meet their rookies, mediating between the front office and her guys, which is what she called the players, or putting organizational goals ahead of anything personal. They had a mission statement in the two-word motto, "Bring It". They wanted to win and insisted everyone commit to the kind of team spirit that would accomplish that goal.

Last year they'd almost done it, but almost didn't cut it. She'd spent most of her time since the loss in October helping to fill in the missing pieces in their quest for a ring, but she'd gone over and above in one instance. It was what was causing the dread.

With clammy hands, she opened the glass door of the facility and stepped inside. She could hear voices, the crack of the bat, all the signs that a practice was in session. At her request, Leo Quijano, the infield coach, had brought three of their potential stars in two weeks early for a mini-training camp. She wanted to see if her instincts had been right, see if they'd *bring it.* It looked good from what she'd heard but she needed to give it a more personal touch, strengthen the connections, show up. The players needed to know she was paying attention, that they were valued. They were the biggest investment the team would make and in order to earn dividends she needed to monitor their progress daily.

When she moved to the edge of the field, the dread came with her, increasing in weight and mass. The Cuban she'd rescued from Mexico was standing at the plate, totally focused and she watched, spellbound. He looked so good standing there, and there was an unexpected ripple of pride. His swing was near perfection, and he met the balls that came flying at him with the kind of power she knew would win ball games. It was what his body did to hers that caused the concern. His muscles rippled with each stroke of the bat, and her breath held as he lifted one ball after the other into the nets over four hundred feet away.

He was hers. Her find, her…

Her mind drifted back to the day she'd met him, sitting at a bar in Cancun. She'd needed a break after the World Series loss, needed to regenerate for the hard work that was ahead, so she'd moved forward with her plans, going solo when her usual traveling companion had been unable to accompany her. She'd walked the beach, gotten some sun, slept in late, all those things she'd come for, but by the third day she'd gotten restless. Scenes from the last game of the World Series began streaming again. It was top of the ninth inning, fucking Rick Watters, the Greenliner closer, one strike away from a win when, crack, the batter sent the ball flying out over the Green Monster, taking back the lead and the Series win. That one ball, placed smack dab over the plate, had ended the team's run for their first championship in over eighty years and a coveted duck ride through the streets of Boston. The rival team had been touted around the city holding the trophy high in the air, while she was laying by a pool, drowning her sorrows in tequila concoctions. Her team's victory had been dashed by a single clutch hit. She'd needed to find a new closer, a third baseman, and a shortstop. They would be the pillars on which they could build a winning team and she'd been chomping at the bit to find them.

After a morning strolling the open markets, trying to decide if she should head home and get back to work, she'd found a cantina where she decided to grab some lunch. It was an open-aired eatery, the rotating fans overhead creating just enough of a breeze to spell relief from the hazy, hot sunshine. After glancing around for an empty seat, she claimed one next to a good-looking man at the end of the bar. While sipping a margarita, light-headed from the heat, the potent tequila and lack of sleep, she threw caution to the wind, and began to flirt with him. He was dark, gorgeous actually, and she felt a burst of heat that knocked her off her stride. She'd been ready to end her dating drought, here, far away from those who knew her, and all that was familiar, and he seemed to fit the bill. In a big way.

His lips were full, his eyes bits of obsidian, his shoulder length dark hair brushed back, a widow's peak framing a heart shaped face. And he carried himself like an athlete, all muscle and sinew.

She leaned over, was a breath away when she asked, "Are you alone?"

He met her eyes and she felt another surge of fire streak through her.

"I am. Yes."

His voice was heavily accented, but his articulation was precise. She was more than intrigued. She swiveled toward him, crossed her legs, allowing her sundress to shift up. It gave him a glimpse of some thigh.

"Where are you from?"

He searched her eyes. She felt his hesitation, thought maybe he wasn't as attracted to her as she was to him, attracted at all. His scrutiny was unnerving, and it caused another flush of heat.

When he said, "Cuba," all she could do was gape.

She knew some Cubans who had defected to play ball. She'd heard some of the horror stories about their attempts to get to America, the ransom, the threats, and a death. It wasn't an easy country to escape.

There was concern in her voice, when she asked, "How did you get here?"

She sensed his body stiffening, as if she were a threat to his well-being.

"A fishing boat."

His eyes kept wandering to the doorway as if he were expecting someone, or maybe he'd been planning his exit strategy. She still wasn't sure which.

"When? Recently?"

His eyes had narrowed at her inquisition.

"This morning."

He slid off his stool and took some rumpled bills from his pocket to place on the bar.

"I must go."

She put a hand on his arm. The sizzle that came was mind numbing.

"Where? Where are you staying?"

She hadn't seen the duffel he had with him until he picked it up and shouldered it.

"I do not know yet."

No wanting to let him go, she asked, "What are you doing here?"

"I am a ball player and I must find a way to get to America."

All she'd heard was ball player. She'd whisked him away to her hotel room, all thoughts about physical satisfaction receding into the mist.

She'd sat him right down, pulled his whole history out through a series of questions.

When he'd told her he played third base, she'd felt the hairs on her neck rise in attention.

He'd played for the Camaguey Alfareros, one of the provincial teams, and he'd seen some action on the national team, had travelled to Rotterdam and Canada with it.

She'd known only the best were given that prerogative.

When she'd asked why he left, he'd told her he was tired of playing for no more than blood, sweat and the glory of the state.

Expecting the worst, she held her breath after she asked if there were any repercussions that came out of the exodus. She let it out when he'd told her he'd landed safely, without any problems. Only later did she find out he'd come with little money and no real strategy on how to get to America.

During the many conversations that followed she'd asked what he would have done if she hadn't come along. He had no answer other than, he'd waited for a mystical solution. He'd quoted something written by Rumi, about his soul needing to be somewhere else and he intended to end up there.

She'd been stunned by his reply. The man read Rumi. She didn't know much about him other than he was poet, centuries back. She'd shaken her head at his faith in the impossible, thought the sentiment might have been wishful thinking, *if it hadn't worked.*

It made her wonder if her presence had been fated? She'd almost chosen Cozumel as her starting point. Almost hadn't gone, once Casey had told her she was needed in Boston.

Unwilling to dwell on it, putting it down to coincidence, she went right to work.

It had taken days to do her vetting, and when she was finally convinced that he might be the third baseman she'd been looking for, she'd called an agent she knew and got the official ball rolling. It was Keith Zamoutto who'd ultimately helped Mateo apply for a visa and began negotiating a contract with a major league team. Her major league team.

It had taken months to get him here, along with a few sacrifices. She'd put the organization before her own personal integrity.

Now she had to live with it.